I0590085

THE SCARLET QUILL SERIES

DECK
of
SCARLETS

INTERNATIONAL BESTSELLING AUTHOR
AMANDA SINATRA

DECK OF SCARLETS

Copyright © 2025 by Amanda Sinatra

All rights reserved. Printed in the United States of America. No part of this book may be used or reproduced in any manner whatsoever without written permission except in the case of brief quotations embodied in critical articles or reviews.

This book is a work of fiction. Names, characters, businesses, organizations, places, events, and incidents either are the product of the author's imagination or are used fictitiously. Any resemblance to actual persons, living or dead, events, or locales is entirely coincidental.

This book is not to be shared, copied, distributed in any form or fed into Chat GPT or any other version of Gen. A.I. For information contact:

Amanda Sinatra

authoramandasinatra@gmail.com

Cover design by Everaftercoverdesign

Edits by Marni MacRae

Copy & Line Edits by Karen Sanders

Interior Chapter Design by: MayFlower Studio

ISBN: 979-8-9931318-0-1

Second Edition Paperback: September 2025

10 9 8 7 6 5 4 3 2 2

 Formatted with Vellum

AUTHOR NOTE

I always want readers to be aware of sensitive content in my body of work no matter how mild that could be. This book contains content such as anxiety, alcohol consumption that is use for coping mechanisms, gore, graphic description of dead bodies, and spice-on-page love scenes.

PRONUNCIATION GUIDE

Magidoz – *Mag-ah-dahz*
Olemak – *Oh-lah-mack*
Drarkoth – *Drah-koth*
Azroneg – *As-roe-nehg*
Ulrodak – *Ul-row-dahk*

"Come now, and let us reason together, saith the Lord: though your sins be as scarlet, they shall be as white as snow; though they be red as crimson, they shall be as wool."

For the ones last in the dark, may you find your way back to the light.

PROLOGUE

S he kept the scarlet wool cape her mother made draped securely around her small frame. The fabric was soft under her touch, a reminder of home as she began to trek up the most prominent hill in the village. Her reddish curls hung loose around her shoulders, some strands catching in her open mouth from breathing heavily up the trail. Frigid nights were not letting up anytime soon; the farther she traveled, the colder it got.

She passed by crowded villages, where some sold an abundance of fresh fruits and vegetables. Her father had given her enough coins to purchase such fine eatery, and she ended up leaving with a small parcel of the crispest apples and a bundle of carrots. Thanking the little boy at the market stand, she continued on her way, apple in hand. Days passed, and the voyage to the convent was nearing its end. Finally, the tallest point of the building peeked over the hill, signaling the conclusion of a very long journey. She would be welcomed with open arms and start her new life there. A life that none of her sisters wanted, but she felt the calling deep within her soul. The Lord was ready for her to ascend to the holiest place, where prayer and blessings were abundant. All she wanted was to help and give to her village.

The trail began to broaden as she reached her destination. A two-story building of gray stone, built strategically, with wide wooden doors faced her. Lit sconces illuminated a small portion of the frosted ground. Bare trees and dead bushes graced the foundation with old acorns from the previous season, just like the dried leaves crunching under her shoes. Bricks on the church were worn from relentless years in the sunlight. Crusted sap coated parts of the stone steps as she ascended, the clicking of her shoes echoing in the silent night, marking her arrival.

She approached the wooden doors, her hand inches from the metal handle, when a male voice halted her in place.

"You made it." A male with a voice smoother than honey dripping lazily in summer heat halted her in place.

"I wasn't expecting to be greeted at this hour," she mused, her hand remaining still.

"Your arrival was expected. However, the timing is a bit late."

She flexed her fingers, ready to retort a remark, but it died on her dry lips, as an enormous shadow cast over the door, claws as long as the dead branches swaying in the night joining the now distorted figure. That was when she screamed.

CHAPTER 1

I awoke in a cold sweat just as my alarm went off. The late afternoon sun had barely set over the city's skyline, and my chest rose and fell in shallow breaths as I tried to regain any sense of awareness. Sweat stained my shirt and pillow, my hair plastered to my forehead. This was the second week in a row I'd had that dream. The same sequence of events right down to the precise detail of her clothing. A red-headed female wandering through crowded villages in the snow, always stopping in front of giant wooden doors, never quite making it inside because of *him*. He made his presence known every time. Unfortunately, when she's about to turn around, I wake as if my mind has decided of its own accord not to reveal her or him. I couldn't understand why it had been happening, but it never failed to return and haunt me, even when I napped.

However, this was the first time I saw the claws and heard her scream.

The shrill sound of her voice left my heart pounding, the

vibrations of her vocal cords pulsating my eardrums as if the scream was loud and clear in my room.

Whatever or *whoever* made her scream left me shaken and unsure of my mental stability, but the most unsettling feeling was not knowing if she survived.

But it was a dream. None of it was real, right?

Right?

I rose from my bed with shaky hands and retrieved the small silver flask from my bedside table. The aroma of cinnamon whiskey rose from the opening as I took a couple long sips. A burning sensation coated my throat, suddenly easing my shaky hands and a pounding heart. With a heavy sigh escaping my lips, the tension in my shoulders loosened.

The sudden urge to pee had me leaving the comfort of my bed to trek quietly down the carpeted hallway. My toes sank into the soft material as I reached the bathroom, quietly entering to relieve myself. Once I was done, I unintentionally found myself standing before my grams' old room. Unwanted familiar smells of bleached sheets and sanitized medical equipment had me spiraling as my hand hovered above the doorknob.

I hadn't entered the room since her death, and yet I couldn't bring myself to even turn the knob. An internal battle since I let go of her weakened hand four months to the day, when my mother ushered me out. Her sunken eyes never left mine as the door closed behind me.

Her funeral was only four days later.

I shook the haunting memory and made my way back to my room, downing the rest of the warm liquor from my flask, letting it soak in and relieve me from the terrors of my soul-stirring thoughts. Every taciturn sip I took was one step closer to an early grave, yet the comfort of warmth it brought to ease the anxiety coursing through my veins was enough to continue.

Just enough to quiet the noise and let me breathe deeply for the first time in months.

Hiding it back in the drawer, I walked over to the long, ornate windows in my bedroom, gazing down at the busy streets. I was greeted by the New York City lights of the Upper East Side, unaware of me watching from above, or so I thought.

My eyes scanned the shops as per usual, mesmerized by customers coming and going, couples holding hands, people walking their dogs, even a small girl on her father's shoulders in the summer heat. Everything was so mundane, and yet there was an odd factor that stood out from the rest.

I noticed a man tucked in the shadows of an alleyway in between the frozen yogurt shop and Katina's Boutique. His attire was black as midnight, with jet-black, shoulder-length hair. How he was not sweating in the blistering heat, I couldn't fathom, but he seemed so out of place in a city like this. He stood with just enough coverage that others were oblivious, and yet through the hustle and bustle of such a busy city, he noticed *me*. The way his eyes flashed left me a bit breathless, and I leaned closer, almost pressed against the glass, on the edge, waiting for him to move.

Was he waiting for someone? He leaned carelessly against the building, one foot crossed over the other, a perfect statue, as if someone carved him from marble.

Locked in an unbreakable stare, he unsheathed some type of dagger from his hip and placed the blade on his wicked lips.

A warning to keep quiet.

Then, with a wink, he faded backward into the alley,

shadows swallowing him whole. I remained frozen, my hand clenching the windowsill, waiting for him to return, but he never reappeared.

Disappointed by his departure, I didn't realize how hard my forehead was pressed against the glass until I stepped back, my skin sounding like Velcro pulling from the pane.

Rubbing my forehead, I thought of his strange appearance once more, taking one last peek out the window, down the busy streets and sidewalks.

But his absence remained a mystery, just like my dreams.

CHAPTER 2

The muggy, sticky air clung to my club clothes, pools of sweat sticking to the back of my neck. The smell of stale rain stained the asphalt and left no promise to cool the summer air. It had been a treacherous pattern since June. So much so that my black, skin-tight dress started to soak in sweat no matter how short of a time I stayed outside.

New York City was buzzing with activity, more so than any other night. Crowds of young teens flooded the streets to get in line for the final concert of the SummerFest season, myself included. My friends, Jeremy and Nickie, stood by me, basking in the same energy, excited to end the summer on a high note.

It was the last summer before we headed in different directions come fall. Nickie had decided to take a year off, and Jeremy chose New York University. His parents weren't thrilled with the idea of him skipping out on an Ivy League school, but Jeremy never stuck with the status quo. Granted, we'd continue in the city for school, but in distant parts. As for seeing each other, my mother had made it clear that Nickie was not welcome.

"Earth to Rem?" called Jeremy, waving a hand in front of my face.

I began to refocus. "Sorry, just thinking about how much sweat is ruining my clothes."

"I can feel my balls sticking together as we speak," he confessed.

I pretended to gag. "Ugh, gross!"

"I think we can begin the drinking now," said Nickie, diving deep into her bra to retrieve the small silver flask.

She was just about to take a sip when Jeremy snatched it from her grasp, his face twisted in disgust. "Eww, it's warm from your tits." He wiped his hands down my exposed arm, and I almost swung at his head.

"Seriously?" I snapped.

"Boob sweat makes me gag," he said.

"But your balls sticking to you didn't make me?"

Twisting the cap off the silver flask, Jeremy took a deep sip of whatever mixed drink Nickie had created before handing it back to her. "I need something stronger; I can't feel the burn anymore."

Jeremy's slanted eyes were already smudged with eyeliner, sweat dripping down his forehead. Even in his black fishnets and sleeveless tank, he was suffering just like the rest of us.

"Maybe you should stop drinking every night," snickered Nickie, taking a swig more than Jeremy. Nothing screamed sex appeal like Nickie's low-cut black top and mini skirt, with tattoos covering most of her arms. One of her many features attracted the rock band members' eyes every time we attended these events. And it was one of the many things my mother hated about Nickie. Nickie knew she disliked her and made it a point to piss off my mom any way she could—especially with her cross tattoos. My mother's disdain for anything related to church or God ran deeper than the Hudson River but remained a mystery, and, honestly, I didn't care why.

"Maybe you should stop drinking every night," he mimicked in a botched version of her voice.

She flipped him off while shoving the flask in my direction. . "Here, Remi, drown your sorrows like the rest of us."

"Don't have to tell me twice," I said before joining them in their alcoholic stupor. I swallowed it willingly, burning into my empty stomach. It was sweet, with a sour aftertaste, making it more addictive. I greedily took another long sip, getting a couple of angry comments from my friends to save some.

I'm going to regret this later.

The stench of cigarettes and something rotting made my stomach turn, the alcohol fighting to come back up.

I needed to remind myself to eat before parties like this. Then again, it was best if I had an empty stomach.

"What's taking so long?" complained Nickie as she fanned her face.

"Last night of the season, so it's expected," Jeremy reminded her.

"Yeah, well. I'm hot, and my tits are pooling with sweat."

"Do you honestly think it would be any better inside? It's packed tonight."

Nickie shrugged and said, "At least there's AC."

After a few mishaps, we finally inched our way to the front, excited to start the night.

Booking anything from underground rock bands to B-list mainstream pop, Electric Haze in downtown Manhattan was the place to be, especially during SummerFest. This year's lineup was dedicated to all new and upcoming artists, and as long as I kept drinking from the flask, I was guaranteed a good time.

From our view, we could see flashing lights just beyond the entrance, the bass thumping hard. My excitement escalated, and I couldn't wait to get on the dance floor.

Nickie hid the flask back in her bra, adjusting it until her boobs were almost hanging out. A playful wink from her as we approached the front doors paid our entry fee, the bouncer stamped our hands for being under twenty-one, and we slithered inside, moving with the crowd ahead of us. Nickie slipped the flask back out, taking her second sip of the night.

"Hey, save some for the rest of us, you heathen," said Jeremy, ripping the flask from her hands.

She adjusted herself by loosening up a couple more buttons on her tight shirt. "Chill, drama queen. There's plenty of liquid gold to go around." She gave a little shake of her boobs and quickly ran her fingers through her hair.

Nickie handed me the flask again, and I took a greedy sip. "Whatever you did this time, the taste is incredible."

She gave me a wink. "I got connections."

Whatever that meant, I linked my arm with hers and Jeremy's, strutting inside to the sound of some techno beat.

The club's atmosphere always gave me the biggest rush. The music's vibrations from the speakers pulsated my eardrums as the alcohol entered my bloodstream. People all around me, dressed in similar attire, some more scandalous than others, moved with the music as a prism of colors flashed in and out of tiny lights above the empty stage while the crowd waited for the next act. Hot stage lights and sweaty bodies collided as Jeremy, Nickie, and I approached the front. Hypnotic sounds matched the tempo to some of the strobe lights stationed around the dance floor, beckoning us forward.

But not before I went to pee.

"Girl, you have the bladder of a squirrel, I swear," commented Jeremy.

Nickie secured our spots at the front and gave anyone who tried to invade our space a dirty look.

"Hurry, princess. These girls tonight are fucking catty," she said.

I gave them both a shut-up-I-know look before joining the wave of people until I ended up next to a small line of other females waiting their turn to use the toilet.

Tapping my foot to the beat, I observed each group that mingled, laughed, and flirted with others. I would miss these nights, especially ones where you knew someone would go home wasted and regret everything. Those were always the best stories to tell.

Every couple of minutes, the line would inch closer, and I noticed my vision seemed skewed. The colors from various strobe lights displayed throughout the room started to pulsate, and some even began to float away in little balls. I suddenly wanted to reach out and catch one, to know what it felt like.

The more I saw the floating colored balls, the faster they moved. Up, down, left, right, swirling and twirling. I stepped out of my place in line, trying to capture the pretty objects, when a male's voice rang loudly in my ear.

Oh, fuck, I'm tripping out.

11

"Come on. The crowd is getting impatient." The next thing I knew, someone barreled right into my side, knocking me off balance, the floating balls dropping to the floor just as I did.

"Oh, crap! Sorry!"

My mind and body were surfing on a white puffy cloud, completely unbothered by what had just happened. The balls began to float again; this time, they circled my head and someone else. A man. A beautiful man.

His brown, curly hair, a messy mop on top, and blue eyes that sparkled under the fluorescent lights delivered an apologetic smile as the intense strobe light colors surrounded his head, giving him an angelic silhouette.

Those baby blue eyes were captivating, and all I could do was stare with my mouth slightly agape. I could jump his bones right now and nobody would give a shit.

"I'm so sorry," he said again. His words came out all warped, making me laugh. I noticed something shiny on his earlobe, possibly a little earring, but all it did was sparkle in a weird shape.

"Josh, come on! We're on next!" somebody shouted from behind us. The one named Josh loosened his hold on my arm, a torn look on his face as if he were debating whether to leave or stay. That touch sent waves of electricity throughout my body, making me squirm. Or maybe it was the drugs causing the weird feelings. The balls around his head started to change their form. Swirls and exotic patterns zigzagged and wiggled on the walls behind him.

"I'm fine. Go ahead," I said. My voice was two octaves too high, as if the colors of the rainbow were spewing from my mouth.

Can he tell I'm tripping balls right now?

He nodded once and stalked off to the stage, disrupting the strange pattern on the wall, but not without looking back once more to double-check my well-being.

And I still had to pee. *Shit. How am I going to do this?*

By now, the line was gone—an easy shot to the bathroom was unheard of in a club this late in the city.

Inside, the bathroom smelt of cheap soap and marijuana. Graffiti all over the walls started to jump out at me, and even the toilet warped.

I swayed a bit, trying to steady myself. "Shit."

The struggle to slide my underwear down to my ankles from underneath my tight dress and sit on the toilet took longer than expected, or maybe shorter; my concept of time was fully lacking. Judging by the bitching outside the bathroom, my guess would be longer.

I tried to judge which way the toilet moved until my ass hit the porcelain seat hard, shaking the backing loose. The relief of peeing had me sighing loudly, and I cleaned myself up for what seemed like an eternity, smothering my hands in the cheap soap.

Finally, I was back with my friends near the front of the stage before the first act.

"Did you fall in?" joked Nickie. The room spun slowly, making my mind go a little hazy.

I nudged her shoulder playfully. "Shut up and give me that flask!" Nickie held the shiny object out of reach.

"What gives?" I shouted, trying but failing to steal it.

"Trust me, you've had enough," she warned with a lazy smile, her eyes half closed.

"You think she knows?" Jeremy called Nickie over my head.

"Oh, she definitely does."

Their vague conversation held no interest for me, as all the lights went down, and the background music stopped.

A microphone screeched on, and a female's voice filled the quiet room. "Ladies and gentlemen, welcome back to another year of Summerfest!"

The room erupted with whistles and screams of excitement.

"Now, we have a few new bands tonight, and some returning favorites. So, without further ado, please welcome to the stage for the first time, Gods Sacrifice!"

Multi-colored lights danced feverishly across the stage, changing in hue and intensity until finally shedding an intense white light on each of the five black-clad men standing center stage. They had red paint splattered on their band's logo on the backdrop behind the drummer. The lead singer's dark and seductive voice sang the lyrics to an unfamiliar song, pointing at a fan in the crowd as she screamed, "I love you!"

The exact lead singer I collided with by the entrance of the bathrooms.

Josh.

My eyes laser-focused on him; I watched the vibrant colors switch to deep blues and purples, changing the club's vibe.

"My God, he's so hot!" screamed Nickie in my right ear.

I kept my mouth shut, mesmerized by how he moved along the small stage, using every inch to sing the lyrics. Even with my trip down the psychedelic drug lane, I knew his features were temptations.

"You can say that again!" agreed Jeremy.

Nickie shook her head. "I call dibs!" She punched his

arm playfully before snagging the flask out of his hands and taking a big sip.

"Let me dream, bitch!" he said as he bumped her hip.

Nickie tossed him back the flask and rolled her eyes. "Ha, sure."

The band began to change their tempo, a slower sound than the chaotic one we heard when we first arrived. Jeremy put his arm around me, lifting a lighter in the air. Nickie leaned closer to the stage, exposing her lady parts to all. Josh would look at them occasionally, eyeing her up and down, utterly aware of her goodies out on display.

With his brown hair pushed back from the sweat on his forehead, Josh knelt right in front of Nickie, putting his finger under her chin, singing to only her. Her eyes sparkled as if she saw the stars for the first time.

"Looks like she's taking another home," I told Jeremy. My voice was laced with jealousy.

"Are we surprised?" He snorted, completely missing the venom in my words.

No, I wasn't. And I didn't know why that bothered me so much.

Maybe he realized my drug trip and didn't want to take advantage of me. Or he thought I was a total mess and refused to get caught up in my scandalous ass, which was probably for the best. But I couldn't help but admire him through my drugged out haze.

Josh grabbed Nickie by the hand to help her on stage. The crowd began to cheer uncontrollably, and Nickie adjusted as she stood, smoothing out her short, black skirt, taking one step forward to the mic, waiting to sing. Suddenly, a familiar tune began to play, their voices filling the room as they sang, the crowd losing their minds.

It wouldn't be a SummerFest if Nickie didn't end up on stage. And it also wouldn't be Nickie if she didn't go home with the lead singer. Jeremy and I began to cheer, calling her name, whistling like crazy. Lost in a haze of colors and odd shapes in the air, I let the music take control, basking in the company of my best friends.

As they continued their duet, I scanned the rest of the band members, shifting through the bright, zigzagged patterns until my eyes landed on the bass player. Wet, copper hair and fair skin flushed from the stage lights as his fingers moved effortlessly over the chords.

He made wearing all black look hotter than ever, and I swore my stare was hypnotic when he finally looked directly at me. My heart jolted in the best way. The waves of colors flowed like the ocean between us. Maybe finding another distraction would help take my mind off of Josh.

He understood the hormones I projected, and a heavenly smirk displayed on those lips I knew I would kiss right after the show.

Yeah, this could be fun.

"Another bass player?" Jeremy snickered.

I nudged him playfully. Indeed another, and they were always so mysterious; I could never get enough. No harm no foul in finding someone else to suck face with. Besides, I had every right to have fun with no strings attached.

The show continued, different bands switching in and out, the music getting louder and darker. The 'drugs' hadn't worn off yet, and I thought I would be in a never-ending loop of tripping out. The flask was finally empty by midnight, a clear sign for us to start heading back before our parents found us plastered on the side of the road. But I wasn't ready to leave just yet; I had someone I needed to meet first.

After Gods Sacrifice's set, I'd followed the hunky bass player all night, watching him mingle with other people and drink a few beers. He moved his body effortlessly and was carefree when friends approached him to talk, as if he were too cool to be there. But I wanted to be right next to him. To hang onto every word that left those lips that seemed to be in a constant pout. How he gripped his bottle of beer, played with the cap on the bar table, and laughed when someone said something funny. I became feral just watching him.

These drugs were making me unbearable.

Our eyes eventually met, and heat ignited my body, almost setting me on fire. His stare was just as hot and heavy as my need for him to touch me. Catching on, he jerked his head toward the exit, signaling for me to follow.

He moved confidently; the whole room wanted his attention, including me. Hugging a few girls goodbye and giving his bandmates high fives, he slipped out the back door, my cue to sneak right by as the rest of the band was distracted by their groupies, one of them being Nickie, drooling over Josh as he slipped his arm over her shoulder.

I shimmied my way past some of the girls, only for Josh to stare me down, whose eyes never left the back of my head once I reached the exit.

I was welcomed with a blast of muggy air, somewhat unbalanced as I checked my surroundings, trying to find the man I'd been plotting to make out with all night.

CHAPTER 3

The alleyway was dark and deserted, and the smell of decaying mice and week-old garbage made the setting *super* romantic. The sky above churned a pale purple from the city lights, hiding the constellations from view. A few people lingered, standing in a circle, sharing a cigarette. Cars rushed by, heedless of what was occurring in the dark.

I had just passed the rusted dumpster when two strong hands grabbed me by the shoulders, pinning me against the brick building, the jagged edges stabbing my skin. The sensation trickled throughout my body, the high of the drug feeding into the pleasure of being handled with such force.

I smirked, enjoying his proximity to my body. "It's not every day a girl gets handled by a strong man."

He chuckled, the sound giving me goosebumps. "It's not every day a pretty girl stalks that strong man."

I bit my lip, letting the high of the drugs take control of my motor skills, and gripped the back of his neck, kissing him greedily. My hands flew to his hair, wanting to feel the texture between my fingers, still drenched in sweat. I pulled him deeper into the kiss as he set my skin ablaze with his touch. Hands traveled to my waist, thrusting his body to mine. A soft moan escaped, teeth catching my bottom lip. Bliss ebbed as his fingers slipped underneath my shirt . cupping my right breast, until his fingers slipped inside my black bra, the palm of his hand grazing over my nipple. The sensation had me grinding my hips against him.

"Get a room!" someone shouted. We ignored the comments directed at us, caring more about where our hands were traveling.

The more we kissed, the more intense our actions became. Gripping, squeezing, pulling, our movements mirroring each other's. He eventually grabbed both my legs and hoisted me up, wrapping them securely around his waist, my back against the jagged brick wall, my dress riding up to my ass, ultimately evaporating thoughts of Josh and Nickie being together.

I tugged at his jacket, desperate for it to come off, when suddenly, an alarm sounded inside his pants, vibrating on my thigh. He leaned his clammy forehead against mine, our breathing mixed together, lips grazing just to savor the taste.

He eventually untangled himself from our embrace and placed me down gently before retrieving a phone from his front pocket.

"Damn it," he murmured. His voice, breathless and hoarse, had no right sounding that hot. I gazed down, the bulge in his pants frantic to escape. My insides tingled with pleasure at the sight.

"Does Cinderella have to go?" I teased, breathing heavily, trying unsuccessfully to avert my eyes away from his constricted erection.

He laughed. "Unfortunately."

"That blows."

He tucked his phone away, fixed his hair from my assault, and readjusted his jacket. "Sorry this was cut short."

"No worries," I said, also readjusting myself, smoothing my hair and dress.

"Um..."

"Remi. My name is Remi," I introduced myself.

"Right, Remi. Well, I'll see you around."

I sighed. "And the pattern continues." I leaned against the wall, crossing my arms.

"Huh?"

"Every time I make out with a guy, he 'forgets' to give me his name."

"You make out a lot?"

A sly smirk formed on my lips. "Wouldn't you like to know?"

His hazel eyes twinkled under the streetlight. "Maybe."

My cheeks flushed. He stepped in front of me again, taking a strand of my blonde hair and twirling it with his pointer finger. "Kal. That's my name."

Chills formed on my arms. *Kal.* "Kal, huh?"

He smiled, a dimple forming on his cheek. "Yes."

Another ring from his jeans pocket went off, his expression turning dark. "I'll see you around."

"The city is too big to collide again."

He snorted. "You're optimistic."

"I'm realistic."

Kal kissed me long and arduously one last time before collecting his belongings and heading toward the street, getting picked up by a black SUV with tinted windows. The car skidded hard around a corner, leaving smoke and a sense of sadness behind.

My palm lay flat on the brick wall for support, the psychedelic trip ebbing away at a snail's pace. Colors were less vibrant, and objects remained in place, but the feelings lingered in my bones, and the heat of Kal's lips stained me forever.

Or I'm so high I can't tell the difference.

Completely unaware of what time it was—for all I knew, minutes could've passed though it felt more like hours—I gazed around, noticing the earlier crowd of smokers had dispersed. My lips felt swollen, my skin flushed from the way he touched my body, my nips tender and throbbing to be assaulted once more. Leaning my head back to gaze up at the sky where the city lights washed out the stars, I basked in the euphoria that invaded my senses. No strings attached, yet I wanted to see him again. The way he made me feel in just a short amount of time was a ride I didn't want to get off; not yet.

A dark shadow whizzed past my line of sight, and stumbling along the alleyway, I caught a whiff of rotting flesh. The scent of death traveled through the streets, wafting up my nose and causing me to gag uncontrollably. Swallowing a hard, nervous lump, I craned my neck to get a better view, afraid to move too fast and disrupt whatever lurked in the shadows. Everything was the same; no trashcan or pile of cardboard boxes were out of sorts. The previous crowd of strangers were all inside or had gone home for the night. So, why couldn't I shake the feeling of being watched? My vision was slightly obstructed, and I tried to squint in the distance when a strange figure emerged from the shadows on the opposite side of the street, hidden in another alleyway directly across from where I stood.

Its long fingers curled around the brick wall, dripping with an unknown black substance, staining the asphalt. With another step forward, part of its body began to show, wet with a foreign liquid. Black shoulders bulged just as the head poked around, its angular face smiling with rotten teeth. Three distinct points were rooted to the center of its forehead, and black goo dripped from the tips as an eerie hiss escaped its horrifying mouth, exposing its complete form. Tall, with skinny, crooked limbs, it started walking forward rather than crawling. I stumbled, taken off guard by its presence, one of my heels catching on something. I tumbled backward against the brick wall, scraping my arm down to my elbow.

The pain from the blow increased with each step I retreated. "I'm just hallucinating. This isn't real." The once vibrant colors turned to shades of gray and black, as if my mind could sense the creature's reality as it began to morph and distort my happy trip.

Its head, long and pointed at the chin, twisted and turned, a clicking noise echoing with each step toward the crowded street. But nobody seemed to notice. My current state of mind tricked me into seeing such a disturbing creature. *There's no way in fucking hell this shit exists.*

I was about to run for it when something red caught my eye from behind the gruesome creature. A piece of crimson fabric darted out, grabbing the attention of whatever lurked in the shadows, and attacked it with something shiny. The sound of it screaming with pain had me stumbling back as I quickly found my way inside, searching for the safety of my friends, when I collided with something hard.

"Whoa there," he said, steadying my balance.

I looked up into the eyes of a familiar face. *Josh. Why do I keep running into him tonight?*

"I'm s-o-sorry," I stammered, looking around frantically to ensure nothing followed me inside. My arm began to throb, the feeling of warm liquid cascading down my skin.

"You look like you've seen a ghost. Are you okay?" he asked, touching me lightly where the brick wall made a deep gash and pulling his hand back to find blood on his palm. "You're bleeding. What happened?" His eyes were intense as if he were searching for something.

"I saw... something," I managed to say. As I tried to focus, the room seemed to spin with hazy waves and odd objects.

Josh's eyes pierced through mine with such intensity that I barely had time to register him stepping closer to me, his nose inches from mine. "What did you see?" He then pulled out a black handkerchief from his breast pocket and tied it around my wound, creating a bandage to stop the bleeding.

"I—" Everything from the lights to the sounds made weird waves as I tried to focus on what he said.

Laughter erupted from somewhere around us, snapping Josh out of his hard gaze, and he stepped back to give me space again.

Would he believe me if I told him the truth? Would anyone believe a girl tripping on drugs at one of the most popular underground nightclubs?

"Yeah, just, uh, not feeling too hot right now. The liquor isn't settling right."

His eyes squinted as if he didn't believe me. "Just wanted to make sure you're okay."

I could hear Nickie's obnoxious laugh from somewhere behind him and shook off his hand, creating enough distance between us. "I am, thank you."

"Remi! Over here!" called Jeremy.

I was surprised to find him and Nickie lounging casually against the bar, laughing and mingling with a new set of people, clinking glasses together like they were old friends.

I waved and started to head over when Josh brushed his hand along my arm.

"I thought they were kidding about your name." He chuckled, trying to change the subject.

"Wouldn't be the first time someone referenced me to the rat," I added with a laugh, thankful he dropped our earlier conversation, even though it left a dark cloud above my head.

Nickie met us with a drink filled to the brim and thrust it into my hand. Some of it splashed on the floor, including on my shoes. "Drink, bitch!" She then grabbed Josh's face and planted a sloppy kiss on his lips. The small group at the bar cheered like they were at some sporting event, making it even more awkward standing there with a full glass of God knows what.

She finally let go, and he had the goofiest grin. "God, you're so fucking hot!' she shouted, squeezing his ass.

He squeezed her waist and said, "I have to go now. I'll call you later." Josh leaned in for one more kiss, gave me one last look of uncertainty, and left us watching him go.

Nickie sighed in a swoon and then grabbed me by the arm to drag my ass to the bar, where Jeremy sat flirting with some guy. He had his hand on Jeremy's thigh, stroking it romantically.

I still had the stupid drink in my hands.

Nickie could sense my distaste for it. "Girl, you better drink that. It wasn't cheap."

"I'll pass," I snapped. My stomach swirled with uneasiness as I gripped the glass, ready to pawn it off on someone else. As much as the alcohol would ease my emotions, the idea of Nickie spiking it again with psychedelic drugs didn't sit right with me.

"You're leaving me for some stupid elite college. I want one night where we completely let loose before our teen years get washed away," she whined.

"Why do you always do that?"

"Do what?"

"Whoa, ladies, let's have a good night," interjected Jeremy.

I ignored him by stepping closer to Nickie. "You always throw the college thing in my face. I didn't ask for it."

"I know you didn't ask for it, but I just wanted one last night to enjoy our crazy shenanigans before you're sucked into the corporate lifestyle from hell!"

"Who says that's going to happen?"

Jeremy tried to get in between our heated argument, but neither of us was having it.

"Oh, I don't know, your parents? Especially your mother," sneered Nickie.

"You know how she is. Besides, it was stated in Grams' will," I reminded her.

"And I asked for proof."

"You're ridiculous. I'm telling the truth!"

"Then drink," she ordered.

"What?"

"You heard me. If you're telling the truth, then drink."

Jeremy went to reach for the glass, but I sidestepped him. "How the hell does that prove anything?"

"You know exactly what it proves."

I gripped the glass tighter, trying not to scream. What did she want from me? I tried my best to please both my parents and her, but lately, that had been a losing battle. If I didn't please my mother, I disappointed Nickie, and vice versa. All summer, we did everything we could to make unforgettable memories, and somehow, that wasn't enough for Nickie. I hated the way we acted toward one another under the influence.

She tapped her foot impatiently. "Well? Are you gonna let that monster you call Mother win?"

I froze, images of the creature coming back tenfold. My hands began to shake from the fear of it waiting for me outside, or worse, coming in here and killing all of us. The liquid inside the glass swished from my shakes, trying but failing to calm my erratic breathing. The others behind Nickie started to chant, begging me to chug whatever she'd ordered.

The quicker the alcohol was consumed, the faster these memories would fade.

My favorite coping mechanism.

Fuck it.

I chugged the whole glass, slamming it down on the bar table nearby. Nickie grinned like she had won the lottery and wrapped one of her arms around my shoulders. "Let the real fun begin!"

CHAPTER 4

I stumbled into bed at three-thirty in the morning, my feet on fire from standing all night in heels. I didn't know when the high of the drugs wore off, but at some point, Nickie held my hair while I vomited in the club's dirty toilet. Nickie had convinced us to order late night burritos, going balls to the wall with the works, consuming it in under thirty minutes.

She had to wash my hair in the sink, as chunks of that same burrito had gotten caught in the strands when I'd missed the toilet the first time.

Not my finest moment.

Standing just under the threshold of my room, I tossed my heels on the carpeted floor, the warmth of the rug seeping between my sore toes. Leaning against the door-frame, I thought of Nickie, and our earlier argument faded like graffiti on the concrete in the city, washed away until something new replaced the mess.

We never resolved anything between us, we just

continued to dance around our issues. A friendship that had lasted for years yet hung by the thinnest thread. If it wasn't for Jeremy buffering most of our squabble, I didn't know who would live to see another day.

But I continued to stay, because ten-plus years of friend-ship seemed harder to throw away, especially when they'd seen you at your lowest low compared to the highest high.

Pushing myself off the doorframe, I hit my knee hard on one of my bedside tables as the sound of my insulated water bottle crashing to the floor made me jump. Cursing loudly over the pain, I tried to undress, struggling to remove arti-cles of clothing, but I couldn't reach the stupid, tiny zipper down my back, which irritated me more.

Eventually, I gave up and left my dress half unzipped and rolled on my bed.

Incredibly thankful for my blackout curtains, I passed out right away, only to wake an hour later to nightmares of ugly creatures lurking in the shadows in the alleyways of New York City. The clicking sound repeatedly replayed in my head as I struggled in my dream, trying to escape it from coming after me. Its long claws scraped across the brick walls as the gooey substance drifted along, creating a path where it once walked. But it always ended the same, with something or *someone* dressed in that red fabric destroying the gruesome thing.

Reaching for the silver flask under my pillow, I took steady sips, waiting for the waves to stop rocking the boat and fall back to sleep.

A few hours later, my mother hovered above me as if she were at a funeral service, praying over the dead.

"Ah! Can you not do that?" I said, wiping the drool from my cheek.

"I wouldn't have to if you just came home at a reasonable time," she said.

"You said it was okay for me to go," I reminded her.

"Yes, I also said..." She paused, her eyes bulging from their sockets. "Remi, what happened to your arm?"

She reached for the wound, and a hiss escaped my mouth from her touch. "I tripped, that's all." Leaning away, I felt the sting again.

"That looks too bruised for a trip." She tried to get another closer look, but I blocked her with a pillow.

"Linda," said my father sternly. He leaned casually against the entrance of my bedroom, his reading glasses on the bridge of his nose.

"Robert, have you seen her bruise? It's huge."

He looked at me over his reading glasses. "Jesus, Remi. What happened?"

"I told you, I tripped. It's fine," I huffed.

"On what? Where did you land?" Mom questioned.

"You never gave Aiden this much flack for going out." I rubbed away the exhaustion from my eyes.

"Aiden got over it once we picked him up from the hospital after his stomach was pumped," Dad reminded me.

"Robert," muttered Linda.

I remembered that night all too well. I thought my brother was dead for the first twenty-four hours until my parents wheeled him out of the elevator. The bruises covering his arms and the deep gash across his left eyebrow, almost touching his eyeball, scarred me for life.

My fingers found the flask hidden underneath my pillow, guilt rising in my throat. "I'm a little bit more responsible than him."

Dad pushed off the doorframe. "Yes, Remi, you seem to

surpass the hospital visits. Now, clean yourself up and join your mother and me for breakfast."

My parents retreated to the dining room while I was left cleaning up last night's mess.

Finding the water bottle I knocked over just before bed with the lid still screwed on tight was a bonus. My heels were flung across the room, and I had no recollection of tossing them in that direction. Excessive makeup wipes were scattered across the little rug near my bed. Black eyeliner smudged in bold swipes and bent fake eyelashes stuck to one wipe like glue. Red lipstick was smeared down my arm; I wasn't surprised I didn't use the makeup wipe to get it off. My mini Gucci cross-body purse was wide open, with its contents dumped on one side of the bed. Either I searched for my stupid phone again, or I got the urge to shop online drunk and couldn't find my platinum card. It wouldn't be the first time I did that.

It occurred to me that my parents cared very little about the mess when visiting me. *They must be in a perfect mood today.* Which could only mean one thing; they scored a massive sale in their company.

Having both parents work in real estate and owning their own company meant less time seeing them at home, but it also meant double the losses if something fell through the cracks.

And I would hear their silent anger throughout the whole penthouse.

I found the strength to get my stiff body out of bed and head to the bathroom. I was pretty damn lucky to have my parents, especially for them giving me a free pass this summer to do what I wanted before the first semester of college started. You're talking to the incoming freshman of Columbia University, class of blah blah blah; this was my Grams' idea. Her will stated I would attend, everything paid for with her money, including room and board. Aiden received her convertible; I got a free ride to fucking college.

I won't lie, the satisfaction of watching my mother hear the will read to her when she was banking on her daughter attending Yale or Harvard was priceless, but that didn't ease my frustration with my deceased grams.

It explained her sudden interest in having me apply to all those colleges. I loved her, but she did me dirty.

I never understood why she bothered with the other Ivy league schools, maybe to throw my mother off her tail— either way, I got accepted, paid in full.

With the last makeup wipe tossed in the wastebasket, I ditched my clothing, which required a copious amount of effort to unzip, including the black handkerchief around my arm, and took a shower, getting last night's sweat and club smell off my body. I began to wash my hair, wincing when I lifted my arm to find the tender wound in shades of purple and red.

"Shit," I hissed.

Trying to avoid the water hitting it, I cleaned myself, getting lost in my head again. I could enjoy college, join a club, or become part of a sorority. The possibilities were endless. But the more I thought about it, the angrier I got. Because the very last thing I wanted to do was join the mundane life society had to offer.

I stepped out of the shower, dripping from head to toe, grabbed a towel, windshield wiped the mirror, and saw my reflection. My summer tan was glowing; you would never know I turned into Casper during the winter. Bloodshot eyes and a swollen bottom lip reminded me of last night's events.

Kal. God, he was so handsome and mysterious, and who the hell was texting him, interrupting our make-out session? Regardless, his last words left me a little disappointed. *I'll see you around.* Yeah, right; the chances of me seeing that pretty face again were slim to none, especially in New York City. All I had left to remind me were sore lips and faded memories.

Replacing the welcome thoughts of Kal pressed against me in the alley, horrifying images of the terrifying creature lurking in the shadows left me chilled and wondering what the flask had been spiked with. Then my dream suddenly flashed in snippets, like a broken memory, and I had to use the sink for support to get my wits about me. There was no scientific explanation, no concrete proof that what I saw last night existed. I got caught up in the high of the drugs and the feral emotions of Kal. *There's no way in hell what I saw was real.*

I dashed from the bathroom, retrieved the flask from under my pillow, and took a sip. The whiskey took everything bad away, and I refused to let whatever lurked in the shadows haunt me forever. Breathing evenly through my nose, counting backward from ten, I took one more sip. Eventually, my unsettled nerves calmed, and I was able to put the flask away in exchange for a hairbrush.

I untangled the blonde mess I called hair, dried off, and put on some sweats and an old T-shirt. I went commando because I tended to forget to wash my undies and our housekeeper was on vacation for the week.

I trekked down the stairs and slid into my usual seat across from my brother, Aiden. He was on his way to the

University of Maine, or as I liked to call it, Hicksville, USA. He chose a school far from my parents and society so he could be part of a pyramid scheme selling marijuana out of his dorm room.

At least he stopped drinking.

"You look rough," he pointed out.

"It's the glow after a hangover," I said, grabbing a piece of toast.

"Is that what you're telling yourself these days?" he teased.

I chucked a piece of crust at his forehead. "Shut up."

"Guys, not at breakfast," warned Dad over his cup of coffee.

Aiden brushed the crumbs off his shirt and gave our dog, Tito, the crust. I could hear his little Corgi mouth chomp on the burnt piece underneath the table.

My mother walked in carrying a platter of waffles and fruit. "I forgot how much I love to cook."

"Should we fire Rose?" my dad suggested, looking over his newspaper.

She took her seat and gave him a warning look from the other end of the table. "No. Her help is much appreciated. But maybe some nights, I could let her go home early."

He hid behind the paper again with a smirk. "Good call."

"I wanted us to enjoy one last breakfast together before *all* my children went to college," said Mom.

"You sound like we're moving across the world." Aiden laughed, helping himself to some waffles and fruit.

"Maine is far," she stated.

"I wish I went far for college," I mumbled, piling up my plate. I wished I never went at all, but *if* I had a choice...

Mom pursed her lips in a tight line. I could tell she was holding back her distaste for my *chosen* school.

Dad folded his paper and began to pile his plate with waffles. "Columbia University is a wonderful school to get into."

"Please, Remi is literally down the street. It's more of a vacation for her," interrupted Aiden.

"You don't think I can handle being on my own?" I asked. I loved being in the city, but college... not so much.

"Nope. Not a chance," admitted Aiden.

"You're an asshole—"

"Robert!" my mom called.

Dad sighed deeply into his hands. "Can we please just have a nice time together? Just once?"

I looked down at my food, trying to keep my cool.

It was no surprise to my family that New York would be my home until the day I died, another reason why Grams' will almost made my mom break her favorite coffee table.

"Besides," Aiden said in between bites of waffles, "Remi couldn't go two seconds without her posse."

That sent me over the edge. "You couldn't go two seconds without getting arrested, but here we are."

My mother had, at this point, walked away from the table, and my father was inhaling his food, ignoring our childish banter.

I got up, which left Aiden hanging on his rebuttal, but I wasn't going to give him a chance and headed to the kitchen, where my mother sat on the stool at the island, looking over the mail. She looked so small on the chair, her blonde, curly hair tied back in a ponytail. There was a time in her life when she was young and wild and had done some of the same reckless things her children had, and if I wasn't mistaken, she fought with her siblings as well. Sometimes she forgot the apple didn't fall far from the tree.

"I'm sorry," I apologized, watching her shoulders slump with a deep sigh. Even though saying sorry was at the bottom of my list of favorite words, she was still my mother, and at times I took things a little too far.

"Would it kill you two to just be nice to each other?" asked Mom, the hurt in her voice clear as the morning sky.

Was she right? Of course. Would I admit it? No. My silence was an obvious sign of my stubbornness, which led her to toss a pile of mail aside. "Columbia sent you more mail."

I stared at the pile. "Thanks."

"Aiden leaves tomorrow morning. We have dinner reservations tonight. Please behave." Without another word, she left the room, the mail scattered all over the counter.

Not hungry anymore, I picked up what was mine and went upstairs.

Taking the carpeted staircase two at a time, I retreated safely inside my room, crawling back into bed. Family gatherings were overwhelming; I was part of the problem, but so was Aiden.

Dropping the mail on my bed, I looked over to the picture frame of Grams and clutched it in my hands, admiring one of the most influential people in my world. Features that any model would kill for, her smile was wide with freedom, her light hair blowing in the breeze on a field in northern Vermont. Her death took a toll on me; I stayed underwater in despair for a while, afraid to resurface to let the pain in again. It was sudden and left me hollow until recently. Until a small silver flask became my companion.

It'll be a year this December, and I never got to say my final goodbye.

If she were here, I knew things would be different.

I kissed the picture and put it back, letting the emotions in for a moment before shoving them back down.

I sifted through the mail, consisting of pre-qualified credit card crap, a copayment bill for a hospital visit when I sliced my hand open on a can lid two weeks back, and then a thick white envelope from Columbia. Tossing the junk aside, I tore open the welcome package, another painful reminder of my future. It amounted to a multitude of pamphlets offering all types of services, info on tutors, library access, and lists of sports I could join. A pile of junk I would be sure to set on fire at Peter's place later tonight.

I reached inside to see if anything was left, discovering an average-sized envelope at the bottom. Strangely, it seemed heavier than the welcome package. With nothing written on the front, I proceeded to open it, finding a scarlet card with a large letter S on the front. The card was thick and had vines of an engraved rose intertwining with the S.

"What the hell is this?" Flipping it over, the back showed words written in an elegant scribble addressed to me.

To Miss Remi Marie Watson,

We are pleased to have chosen you to be inducted into the Order of the Scarlet Quill. It is the highest honor to be selected, and you are the perfect fit to complete our last spot in this exclusive society.

Below is the date, time, and location for your induction. We hope you can come and accept our invitation.

Date & Time: September 23rd at 7 pm.

Location: Cathedral of St. John the Divine.

Attire: All black.

I sat back against my bulk of pillows and gawked at the card, distinctly remembering I'd ripped, burned, and flushed anything regarding clubs or sororities down the fucking toilet, and they still sent me this shit. I chucked the fancy piece of rubbish at my trash bin, hitting the rim, and it landed underneath my desk. Rose would dispose of it later.

"No, thank you," I muttered.

No, thank you, indeed.

CHAPTER 5

Curled under a homemade quilt on Jeremy's leather sofa, Nickie began dumping the contents of our favorite local Chinese food into various bowls, while Jeremy set up the mini projector in his living room. His parents, big-time lawyers, had their law firm here in New York, so they typically worked late hours. That gave the three of us alone time while raiding their expensive cheese collection.

After several profanities from Jeremy, he finally got it set up, dimmed the lights, and popped in our all-time favorite movie.

"I told my parents to just mount it on the wall, but nooo," Jeremy complained, stealing some of the blankets. "So, where did you run off to the night of SummerFest? You were missing for quite some time."

I rolled my eyes at his shitty question. "You know where."

Jeremy flicked my nose and said, "Bitch, tell me!"

Taking one of the many pillows on his couch, I hit him square in the face. "Stop doing that!"

Jeremy grabbed his pillow and turned it into an actual pillow fight. After several minutes of assaulting one another, he slung his arm around my shoulder and said, "So, did you fuck?"

I pushed him off. "No! God, we just made out." Although, from a distance, it would've looked like we were about to or in the middle of it.

I loved Jeremy, but sometimes he wanted too much detail about my sex life.

"So, are you going to see him again?" he asked.

"Nah, I think that was a one-time thing. His whole 'see you around' was another indicator of that. Never got a chance to even ask for his number either." I sighed.

"Ugh, men. This is why I'm making out with chicks most of the time." He laughed.

I gave him a sly look and said, "Most of the time?"

"Men are confusing. At least you ladies are upfront about what you want."

We laughed some more when Nickie came in with a silver tray of Chinese food. "What did I say about having fun without me?" She placed the tray down on the coffee table and handed us each a pair of chopsticks as she picked up one of the bowls overflowing with Lo Mein.

"Sorry, Jeremy asked me about the mysterious man I made out with at the club," I said.

"Oh, so that's where you went."

I rolled my eyes. "Yeah. Surprised you realized I was gone."

"Sorry, the singer held my attention." She swooned.

Since that night, Josh had become Nickie's official unofficial boyfriend for four days. The lead singer was known for open relationships but seemed to take a liking to my best friend, and this had become his first monogamous one.

I took another container piled with Lo Mein. "Either way, I made a promise not to get all committed. I don't have the energy for the mind games."

"So, he turned you down?" Nickie's tone dripped with pity.

Jeremy slammed down the remote and ran from the living room. "Fuck! The wine!"

I stabbed the lo mein with my chopsticks. "No."

She shrugged her shoulders and took a mouthful of food.

I bit my lip, trying my best to let it go, when I remembered the laced flask from that night. "By the way, what did you do to the drink that night?"

Nickie swallowed. "Mitch Lester gave me some of his good shit."

"So, you have no idea what was in it?"

She shook her head, taking another big bite.

"And you trusted him?" Getting fun party drugs was one thing, but getting it from Mitch Lester was asking for a hospital visit or an early trip to your grave. The fact that Nickie would be so stupid as to trust that piece of shit had me livid.

Nickie rolled her eyes and put her food down on the tray. "Mitch's stuff isn't laced with anything heavy."

I slammed my container down, the chopsticks flopping over and hitting the floor, staining the luxurious carpet. "Doesn't matter. It could've been!" She had more trust in the city's notorious drug dealer than her best friend since elementary school.

Jeremy rushed back with three glasses of wine. "I got the goods la—okay, which one of you bitches stained my mom's favorite carpet?"

Nickie stood, her eyes turning into dangerous slits. "Jeez, Rem. Didn't think it would be a fucking problem."

My hands began to tremble, and the image of the creature crept around the edges of my mind. "It is a problem, Nickie! Mitch is known to lace his shit with the heavy stuff."

She crossed her arms. "Since when? And why do you fucking care all of a sudden? Is mommy's perfect little angel suddenly done with the party life?"

Jeremy stood inches from our heated bubble, watching our interaction escalate.

Clenching my fists, I gathered my belongings and made my way to the front door, completely over this conversation.

Nickie, on the other hand, wasn't done and was the CEO of the last word. "Just because you're going to an Ivy League school doesn't mean you get to treat the rest of us like shit."

"I'm trying! I'm trying to be there for you and Jeremy, but you make it really fucking difficult," I snapped.

She took a step toward me, Jeremy inched with her, watching her hands in case she decided to swing. "Me? I'm sorry I don't want to be left behind."

"Who the hell says that's going to happen? What world are you living in lately, cause honestly, I can't figure it out."

"Not yours, apparently. Since it's the only world that seems to matter around here."

Jeremy stepped in. "Woah, I'm actually going to stop you there."

She gave Jeremy a dirty look. "Please, you were thinking the same thing."

"I was not!"

I'd zoned out, my thoughts twisting and turning inside my head. They had no idea what dark and sinister thoughts crept into my mind, how my only escape was the flask of whiskey underneath my pillow, which kept me afloat. They had no idea how every night I sipped it, enjoying the burn that slid down my goddamn throat.

It hadn't been malicious when I'd chosen to close off that part of my life from them, but I was at my wits end with Nickie because if I tried to explain myself, she would twist it to her advantage.

I tried to sneak past them, but that didn't go over well with Nickie.

"Where the fuck are you going?" she demanded, trying to move around a very pissed off Jeremy.

"Home for some peace and fucking quiet."

I slammed the door shut and leaned against it, breathing heavily. A rush of panic went through my whole body, making my legs shake..

Through the door, I could make out Jeremy's angry words. "Nickie, can you not be a raging bitch for five seconds?"

"She started it!"

On wobbly legs, I removed myself from the area, finding comfort in the quiet elevator. Leaning on the cool, metal walls for support, the chill tamed the heat radiating from my body but not enough to stifle the irritation settling in my nervous system.

I tried to reason with myself, insisting that maybe it was all in my head. Maybe what I saw that night was the effects of Mitch's party favors, a mere illusion of objects in an alleyway morphing into one of the most hideous nightmares from a horror movie.

Because we didn't live in a world full of *Goosebumps* stories.

And I was too terrified to find out.

CHAPTER 6

At seven in the morning, my alarm clock buzzed like an annoying bee in my ear, yelling at me to get my ass up. It was time, the dreadful move-in day to hell. I'd packed, unpacked, and repacked my remaining crap in my suitcase all weekend. I tried to avoid the inevitability of going to college all summer, but the days crept up faster than the imaginary monster under my bed.

Jeremy texted me good luck, but not a peep came from Nickie, and, honestly, it was for the best. I would deal with our argument another time when I had a clearer head.

My mother had a car sent to the apartment around seven-thirty. The rest of my belongings were already in the dorm room I would be sharing with Heather Price. I had no idea what she looked like, her interests or hobbies, nor did I care. A roommate was the last thing I wanted to deal with, but a single suite was hard to come by, especially as an incoming freshman.

Kissing my dog Tito goodbye on his head, I made my way to the outside world; the smell of fresh-baked bread and outdoor flower shops made me feel all warm inside on this miserable day. In the backseat of the black SUV, my mother and father had me sit in between them as the driver finished loading my belongings in the back. The anxiety of just sitting with them made me feel like I was drowning. Sometimes, family wasn't always good to be around. Not that they didn't love me enough, but the overbearing feeling of it all made me want to wither away to nothing just to get out of there.

The urge to reach into the trunk for my flask to calm my nerves resulted in picking at the leather on the seat with my fingernails just to relax.

Traffic in New York City, no matter what time of day, was always a fun time. Green could mean go, but if you had to take that right turn and the crosswalk was lit up for pedestrians to cross, then you better brace yourself for a lot of honking at your rear and hoping you could cut through the crowd without killing anyone.

Why would anyone want a car or license while living here baffled me. I learned about the subway system at twelve and never looked back.

The driver effortlessly weaved his way in and out of traffic as if he were playing a round of Mario Kart. A strong indicator that he was a native of the city.

My mother patted my knee, a failed attempt to make me more comfortable about this new transition in life. "I hope you enjoy yourself, Remi." The undertone of disgust about my Grams' secretive ploy was not lost on me.

"I'm still in the city, Mom," I mumbled.

"Yes, and could you at least make *new* friends? Preferably *normal* ones," she sniped.

"Jeremy *is* normal."

"You know what I mean."

I knew *who* she meant.

She began to text on her phone. "Maybe a sorority?"

"That sounds like torture," I commented.

"Just promise us you'll try to stay a few weekends?" requested Dad. Fixing the buttons on his freshly tailored suit, he extended his arm to uncover an expensive, silver watch, gifted from my mother last Christmas.

Checking the time, he gave me a quick smile. "I know you'll do great."

For once, my returning smile was genuine.

"Although this would not have been my first choice for you, at least make use of your time," Mom muttered.

I knew the dig she made wasn't directed at me, rather, it was toward my deceased Grams, who couldn't defend herself because she was buried six feet underground. It took every ounce of strength not to tell her to fuck off.

Biting the inside of my cheek, I remained silent for the rest of the way there. I didn't have enough energy to argue with my parents, and it would end up nowhere regardless of how hard I pressed them to leave me alone about certain things. Thankfully, the traffic getting into the school was a mess, and I convinced my parents to let the driver drop me off at 113th Street inside the campus compound. The view ahead was of a beautiful, old stone church, like a cookie cutout of a fairy tale story and dropped by a helicopter at Columbia University.

After a few hugs and kisses goodbye, I dragged my luggage down Amsterdam Avenue to the college walkway. The streets were flooded with incoming and returning students for the fall semester. I pulled out my campus map from the back pocket of my jean shorts and followed the path that led to my dorm building. Hopefully, I could avoid human interaction until then. Note to self, never fill out an about me card again, or be subject to the roommate's annoyance. The late summer heat trickled into September and appeared on my neck, and I was grateful I stuck with a white tank top and jean shorts so I wouldn't arrive with sweat-stained patches all over my body. As I made my way through the crowd, trying not to step on anyone's feet even though there were a couple of moments I wanted to elbow a few girls in the head who wouldn't move out of my way, I made it through a joyous crowd of teenagers.. At one point, a group of guys—just by the look of their clothes and cocky attitude —whistled at me, but my quick hand gesture shut them up before any of them opened their obnoxious mouths.

"Come to our open house tonight!" A tall blonde shoved a vibrant pink flier in my face. I declined, shooing her away like an annoying housefly, and continued on my merry way.

"You'll regret it!" she shouted back at me.

I gave a dirty look over my shoulder. "Fuck off." The sound of her gasp had me snickering. *Good. Leave me the hell alone.*

Entering 116th Street, I realized with complete horror that I stood directly in sight of a group of girls sitting at a table for their sorority Kappa Alpha Theta. I almost gagged when they called me over. They waved me down like fans at a boy band concert, and I never wanted to run the other way so badly in my life.

"Hi! Here's a flier for our mixer! We would love for you to come by this weekend and check it out and see if the Kappa Alpha Theta sisters are a good fit for you!"

"Thanks," I muttered. I was retreating before they

harassed me any longer. Completely out of view from their table, I found the nearest dumpster, crumbled up the flier, and tossed it.

This was a total nightmare.

Finally, after some unnecessary detours, I made it to the famous college path, with my dorm building just a few feet up ahead.

Carman Hall. It had a charming feel to it, and I almost—*almost*—saw myself enjoying living there.

In front of my dorm building were two young girls with dark hair. One was shorter than the other, but they smiled at me as if I were their favorite person.

"Hi, I'm Georgia! Can I have your name to sign in?" she asked pleasantly.

I was relieved she didn't coax me into joining an all-girl cult group.

"Remi Watson."

Georgia skimmed through a box of folders and pulled out one that matched the schools' colors. "Here, we have your brochures of all the local restaurants and shops, the key to your dorm room, campus map, and I.D. to scan in and out of the buildings on campus. Your class schedule for this semester and the menu for September for our dining hall are in there too. After that, the menu will be online on the campus website. We're your RAs. I'm Sam, and this is Georgia. We're both located on the second floor of Carman Hall. I'm in room 204, and Georgia is in room 230. If you have any questions—"

"Oh! Your dorm number and floor are on the back of your I.D.," interrupted Georgia.

"Girl, I was getting to that." Sam laughed.

"Sorry," she apologized sheepishly.

"Thanks," I said with a forced smile. At least they didn't offer to escort me to my room.

"Enjoy your first day!" they said in unison. Their cheeriness made me cringe as I walked to Carman Hall.

I.D in hand, I dug aggressively inside the folder, trying to find the stupid key, only to discover it at the bottom. My heel slipped off the step, tripping backward, but hands grabbed me before I took the fall.

"Oh, shit! Are you all right?" he asked.

Stars clouded my vision as I tried to get my balance in order. Solid hands gripped my waist, pulling me back.

"Yeah, I think."

"Wait, Remi?"

He let me sit down as the spots started to vanish, and there, right before my face, was Josh, the lead singer of Gods Sacrifice and Nickie's beau.

"Josh?" This was so fucking annoying bumping into him all the time.

"Yeah! Hey, I forgot she told me you were coming here! Welcome!" He laughed. Josh took it upon himself to retrieve my runaway suitcase and placed it right by my side, then grabbed a water bottle from one of the side pouches on his backpack and handed it to me. "Sorry again."

His curly brown hair was tousled in a way male models only wished to achieve. Clinging to his skin was a white T-shirt above khaki shorts. Josh stood with confidence, all six feet of him or more.

That was when I spotted the little hoop earring in his left ear. It screamed rock and roll for his aesthetic when he played with his band.

And it was kind of hot.

Jesus fucking Christ.

"No, it's okay. I wasn't paying attention." Taking a seat on one of the stone steps, I sipped the water he offered me; at least he was friendly.

"You do that a lot?" he asked.

"What, exactly?"

"Not pay attention."

I snorted a hearty laugh as Josh joined me. "I guess lately I've been distracted."

"If you ever need a place to unwind, there's a little nook on the library's third floor you can chill in," Josh offered.

I nodded, giving him a solid thumbs up. "Thanks."

"I'm guessing this is your dorm hall?" Josh pointed to the building behind us.

"You guessed right." My head was pounding. Thank God I had a big bottle of pain relievers in my bag.

His smile was bright and inviting as he joined me on the steps. "What's your major?"

"Uh... Business Management."

His knee brushed mine. "Oh, nice. Mine is Music."

I snickered. "I should've known."

Josh bumped his shoulder against mine. "I know, I'm that predictable."

"No, I think it's great that you're applying it to your studies." And I was impressed.

"Glad to see you recovered," he commented, ignoring my compliment. His blue eyes traveled down to the large bruise on my arm. Josh gave the impression he cared more about my injuries than the small talk.

My instant reaction was to touch the bruise, but I refrained, the grotesque creature lurking at the back of my mind. "Yes. I'm surprised you remembered."

"Hard to forget when you came in white as a ghost."

I swallowed. "I looked that bad?"

"What scared you, Rem?"

My heart skipped a bit at my nickname. Nobody called me that but my closest friends. I wondered if Nickie had used it in front of him.

Josh waited for my response, his hands placed on his knees, a perturbed expression contorting his angelic face. Even in daylight, he was a breathless sight to see.

I need to stop analyzing everything about him. For fuck's sake, he's with my best friend.

Sitting there patiently, Josh's gaze lingered almost unnervingly, as if he saw the same black, shadowy monster haunting my dreams.

"I'm the last person to judge," he added.

But would he believe me? Hard to tell, especially with him; a mere acquaintance no matter the status he held with my best friend.

Shrugging, I conjured up a party girl response, because not even a pretty boy like him could get me to admit the wild imagination my mind seemed to run with. "I got too drunk and felt too high from making out with your bandmate."

Josh slung his backpack over his shoulder, shaking his head with laughter. "Ah, yes, the infamous Kal."

"How did you—" *Nickie.*

Josh registered rather quickly that I figured out who spilled the tea. "I didn't mean..."

I waved his attempted apology away. "No, it's fine. I should probably get myself settled." Josh helped me to my feet. His hand supported under my arm, and his calloused fingers brushed against my too-hot skin. I wanted to melt in a puddle where I stood.

What the hell is wrong with me?

"I'll see you around campus. I gotta help some freshmen out."

"Yeah, uh, thanks again." I shook the water bottle at him.

"No worries. Sorry I almost killed you," Josh joked before waving goodbye. I watched him walk across campus to the other dorms, staring at his back, trying to understand his weird behavior toward my well-being.

Nickie never mentioned Josh attended the same school. I mean, she could have, but that night we were too busy screaming at one another to even get that far about him, or anything for that matter.

I let the dizziness subside before I got back on track to my dorm room. At least nobody had to call 911 for an ambulance on my first day. That would've been embarrassing, but it wasn't the first time. During my freshman year of high school, I tripped, fell down two flights of stairs, and broke my right leg because some kids wanted to be first in line for lunch.

Karma took care of them eventually—rather, I helped it move along.

The doors to Carman Hall were a little tough to open, or I just lacked upper-body strength, but after another good tug, I finally managed to make my way inside. Blue carpeted floors greeted me, with a big, round, red table surrounded by matching chairs to the left side of the room. A live ivy plant scaling the wall between the staircase had me thinking what a peculiar idea to have a plant growing inside. I'd been so used to concrete walls and the smell of gasoline outside my window that a plant would be the last thing I would expect in a place like this.

At the front desk inside the hall, a guy with curly dark hair, big square glasses, and stubble on his chin held up a scanner to students' IDs to access the building. Each one thanked him before they ascended the staircase to the second floor. I followed suit and let him scan mine, offering the same monotone thank you in return, then joined the train ride of students until I broke free to find my room.

The hallways were semi-narrow, and nothing pissed me off more than a crowd of girls trying to walk side by side, forcing me to push up against the wall to pass them while they laughed and flipped their overly sprayed hair.

My biggest fear was not finding my room, but lo and behold, in gold, elegant font, number 201 was nailed to the door, which stood ajar. Inside, Heather Price and some older lady were fixing a flowery bedspread on a twin-size mattress. Her long, curly red hair hung down her back like a curtain, with her slender figure all of five feet. Any shorter, and I'd have been convinced she was an elf.

She noticed me under the threshold and jumped for joy like a kid in a candy store. "Remi! You're finally here!"

I forced a half-smile. "Surprise."

The older woman peeked around Heather's frame. "Hello, Remi. I'm Heather's mom, Cindy."

I should've known since she boasted a striking resemblance to her daughter, with the same vibrant red hair, diminutive height, and arresting green eyes.

"Hi."

Our room was set up exactly like the pictures from the website—a crappy twin mattress on either side with a matching light brown closet and desk. At least our things covered most of the underwhelming furniture with matching colors and patterns, but it didn't soften the dread of being there.

I placed my suitcase on my bed, grateful for once for my mother having someone set up my room already and unzipped it to reveal my neatly folded clothes.

Heather's side of the room looked like a four-year-old threw up candy and sparkles, with a dash of country bumpkin on the side. Posters of country singers and mediocre art on canvases that probably came from a local decor shop adorned the walls, with splashes of blues and purples on her comforter and matching pillows and curtains that she was in the process of putting up. My side of the room was so modern-looking that I never wanted to set something on fire so fast. Of course, this was indeed my fault; since joking with my mother about wanting goth-style decor, she had a fit and took it upon herself to pick my color scheme. I guessed my sarcasm fell flat on that one.

I watched the interaction between Heather and her mother trying to set up the curtains, and it made me a bit envious of their relationship compared to the stiff one I shared with my mother. There had been a brief time in my childhood when she was warm and gentle, but as I got older, she became busier with our family business, becoming one of the most well-known real estate agencies in the city.

"Remi, are you going to the freshman mixer tonight?" Heather asked, pulling me out of my thoughts.

I would rather stab my eyes with a cafeteria fork than expose myself to that cliche shit. "Uh, I don't know."

"You gotta! It's supposed to be fun!" she bragged. Heather made her way over to her closet and began to organize her winter jackets. I peeked at her shoes and gave her a mental thumbs-up for having an impressive collection.

"I think it would be good for you girls," added Cindy while she condensed the rest of the brown moving boxes.

Poor Cindy had no idea how much I hated stuff like mixers and lame social parties, and all she wanted was for her daughter to attend one with her new roommate like we were old friends.

I sighed. "What time is it?"

Heather smiled. "It's at seven. "

"I'll give it an hour, but if it starts to suck, I'm out."

She held up her hands. "Fair enough."

Cindy ended up saying goodbye early; she had dinner reservations with her aunt in the city and wanted to explore more of Manhattan before her flight back to Florida.

"The mixer said casual, but my mother kind of overdid herself by buying fancy clothes for my wardrobe," she said.

"How about your birthday suit?" I joked.

Heather laughed as if I'd told the funniest joke in the world. "I mean... would that be too much?"

"Too much? Or not enough?"

"Oh, you're right. I'll show the world all my goodies."

"Just the freshmen of Columbia."

CHAPTER 7

After a good few hours of exploring the campus with Heather, minus the odd detours we took—how we ended up in the men's bathroom was beyond me—we found ourselves back in our room getting ready for the mixer.

She went to the bathroom as I pulled up my jeans over my butt. Paired with black Converse and a matching black shirt, I threw my hair back in a low ponytail. I was good to go with a little bit of blush, concealer, and mascara. I had to hold back on my entire face of club makeup; the heat would melt it right off.

She offered her vast collection of high-end perfumes, and I couldn't pass up an opportunity to check them out. Some smelt of lilac and vanilla, and others reminded me of hot summer days in mid-July, eating watermelon or standing in line at one of the many ice cream shops New York City provided. Citrus perfumes were my go-to; she might've had the best one I'd ever come across. A little spritz on my body and neck would be perfect, but not before my clumsy hands dropped the cap to the bottle underneath her bed. The sound of it rolling to the back made me get on all fours and mumble profanities, reaching blindly, hoping to catch it before it was too far gone. My fingers touched not the round cap I expected but grazed against something smooth and flat. I dragged it out from underneath, surprised to see Heather's name on the front in black ink.

Why would she have this under the bed?

I opened it to the familiar scarlet card, trailing my fingers along the pattern along the edges, remembering mine and how it felt, and I wondered if the message was the same. Sure enough, written out in that beautiful scrawl was Heather's invitation to the secret society known as the Order of the Scarlet Quill.

So, why did she hide it under her bed?

And if it was so secretive, then why the fuck did I have one?

Did she know I had one? But her invitation was a secret to me as well. Maybe she had no idea about my status with the Order and we just happened to win the luck of the draw, both receiving one. But what were the odds of us being placed together in the dorms?

"Hey, you ready?" Heather called from outside our room.

Panicked that she might have caught me red-handed with her stuff, I placed everything back the way I found it and hid it under her bed as the door opened behind me.

"What are you doing on the floor?" she questioned.

"I uh... dropped the cap to the perfume," I admitted, trying to come off nonchalantly.

"Forget it. We'll find it later." The nervous tenor in her voice was a red flag that I couldn't ignore. She didn't want me to look under her bed, and if she didn't know about me...

Her eyes flicked back and forth from my face to her bed. "Seriously, Remi. It's fine. Leave it."

I got up off the floor, not wanting to push her. "Okay, that's fine." I could have told her right then. Told her everything about my invitation, but her nervous demeanor was enough to keep the secret. Enough to find out exactly how important The Order of the Scarlet Quill was.

CHAPTER 8

The walk to the University Hall had become awkward. I contemplated as we crossed the college path whether to finally come clean and tell Heather or let it die on the tip of my tongue. The more I thought about it, the more things started to piece together.

There was a good chance they placed the ones invited in the same room so nothing was exposed. Apparently, it was a tight-lipped society that now had my curiosity piqued, and as much as I would rather stick to avoiding the abundance of clubs begging for recruits, there was no harm in finding out.

Fucking fantastic.

Call it a hunch, but I instantly knew who to ask. I just hoped he was here tonight.

We entered the building under a decorative balloon arch of the school colors; blue and white. The school mascot, Roar-eee the lion, was leaning casually against the wall, talking to one of the many photographers of tonight's event.

A hearty welcome sign hung just above, blowing softly in the summer breeze.

Crowds of freshmen covered the event room from wall to wall. At the back were six tables adorned with fancy tablecloths, which displayed silver trays overflowing with fancy school food. Long blue and white drapes hung from the ceiling, and soon, Roar-eee was dancing in the middle of the dance floor.

Some weird techno music thumped for background noise, while others around us chatted and gushed over who had the best summer. The further we traveled inside, the more chaotic it got. A group of young men started a beer pong game, screaming and high fiving one another whenever one of them scored. A few girls set up a karaoke machine, and others were left mingling in small groups, while the RAs and upper-class students ensured we had drinks and something to eat.

A random guy came over, I assumed one of the RAs, and handed Heather and me a red solo cup with weird red liquid.

"Uh, thanks," I said. It had a bubbly look to it. Most likely, they gave us some carbonated beverage.

Before he could disappear, Heather grabbed him by the arm and pulled him back with such force he almost knocked the drink out of her hand. "Um, is there alcohol in this?"

He smiled and shook his head. "Unfortunately, no. Some of the teaching staff are present, so we couldn't spike the punch." He left us staring at our cups in the middle of the room.

"Don't like alcohol?" I teased, taking a sip of mine. The flavor tasted of cherry with a sour kick; it was rather enjoyable and reminded me of one of the many birthday parties I attended as a kid, which ended with me crashing on the couch from the sugar rush.

"I just can't have alcohol while on anxiety medication," she stated. Heather's mouth hesitated on the lip of her cup, afraid to believe the RA.

"There's none. You're fine," I assured her.

The panic on her face began to subside slightly. "You sure?"

"Yes. I do know what alcohol tastes like." I laughed.

"Well, good. I'm glad you're here to let me know." Heather then went ahead and drank from her cup, looking relieved when she finished.

Just then, a woman with dark hair and wearing a purple skirt and white blouse held a mic to her mouth, trying to get the crowd's attention. "Hello! I'm Jordan Reiner, and welcome to this year's freshman mixer!"

Everyone cheered around us as I drank more from my cup, completely over this night already. Jeremy and Nickie would be spiking the punch and trying to play strip poker somewhere exclusive.

"Tonight is all about mingling with each other, getting to know the faculty, and understanding the importance of being a Lion!"

More cheering and whistling erupted in the room, with some frat guys behind us hollering like animals.

"Please, enjoy the food, drinks, and party games! At the end of the night, each of you will get a bag of goodies to help you survive your first semester here at Columbia University! Thank you again for listening, and have fun!" she finished.

Everyone gave her one more cheer until she stepped out of view.

"Well, let's get to talking," Heather said, bumping her shoulder into mine.

I crushed the empty solo cup with my bare hand. "Fantastic."

Observing the rest of the room, I was getting more bored by the second. I promised Heather I'd mingle and try my best to be here, but my social meter was running low. Too many people, and the idea of trying to smile and converse with others felt mentally draining. I just wanted to go to bed.

That was until Josh came into view.

When we first arrived, there was no chance of me coming across him again, and by the grace of God himself, he somehow ended up on my path a second time just at the right moment.

Fingers crossed he knew the deal around campus. Columbia was a big school, and I might not get a chance like this again.

Leaning against a marble pillar, he held a red solo cup, drinking casually and talking to a few of his peers. In a black T-shirt and jeans, his tousled brown curls never failed to send my pulse racing a bit.

"I'll be right back," I promised Heather.

She raised her cup in response before I made my way over to him. He immediately noticed my presence, and we met in the middle.

"Hey, freshy," he said, reaching for a fist pump.

Our fists hit, and I smiled. "Hey." He had a different demeanor than earlier.

"How's your head?"

"A little sore but better." A couple of Tylenol later and I was good to go, thank God.

"I'm sorry about that," he apologized for the second time.

"Could've been worse. You could've killed me," I joked.

"Nickie would never speak to me again."

That made two of us.

"Enjoying your freshman mixer?" he asked in a teasing tone.

"Yeah... it's... interesting." It was a complete drag. I would have more fun in the cemetery with the dead than here with the living. I never went to these types of events at my old high school; everything was a cringe-fest.

"I hated mine. I'm only here because I got nominated to be a team leader. The downfall of being a junior," he explained in horror.

I tried to stifle a laugh, but just by the look on his face of whatever horrifying flashback he went to, I couldn't help myself. "Oh, yeah, I bet it was horrific." Good, a casual conversation. That way, I could ease into asking him.

Josh chuckled along with me and finished the rest of his drink before tossing the cup in a nearby trash can, which seemed to be piling up by the second. "The redhead over there? Is she your roommate?"

I turned around to find her standing awkwardly near a fountain of fruit punch, trying to converse with three model-like blondes, and by the looks of them standing away from her, her attempt was unsuccessful. *I better finish up here fast to save her from embarrassment.* Because although Heather herself was way too perky for my liking, I had some weird motherly instinct toward her.

"Yes, that's Heather Price. But I had a reason to come over here and talk to you. I have a question."

Josh gave me a puzzled look, trying to figure out where I was going with this.

Where the heck did I even begin? Did I just come right out and say it? Would he have any idea what I was talking about? He'd probably think I'd lost my goddamn mind.

"Is the university..." *How the heck do I even ask?* "...are they known for their... clubs?"

Josh cocked his head to the side. "I assume so? You know, the website can direct you to all the clubs available on campus."

Here goes. "Even the secret ones?"

"Josh!" some girl yelled from across the room, interrupting me and my train of thought.

He held up his finger to signal the person yelling at him to give us a minute. "Sorry about that. Anyway, what were you trying to say?"

Fuck this. "The Order of the Scarlet Quill?"

Josh froze; his eyes darting around before he stepped toward me, leaning in so nobody else could hear.

Jackpot.

"Remi, whatever you think you know—"

"I don't know anything, so I'm asking you." My tone came out a little harsher than expected, but I wasn't going to get anywhere by beating around the bush.

His baby blues flashed an emotion I couldn't pinpoint. "I don't have the answer you're looking for."

"Never said you did." Judging by the hostile tone he carried, he knew exactly what I was talking about. But did he know about my invitation? Heather's? Was he even a part of it to begin with? Was he trying to warn me because there was a danger in knowing?

Josh clenched his jaw, his eyes scanning my face as if he

were trying to decide whether to tell me the truth. "Remi, you need to forget we ever had this conversation. It's not safe—"

"Josh!" she called again, only this time she got the attention of others.

I could see the frustrated look in his eyes when the girl who screamed his name came right over but not by herself. She was followed by a small group, and within that small group was Kal. His blond hair hung over his eyes, and his posture stiffened when he took notice of my appearance. My heart stopped, then picked back up as if a defibrillator restarted it.

This could not be happening right now.

If Kal was involved too...

"Josh, we have to go," she said sternly. She looked over at me like a piece of trash on the side of the road. Her long dark hair came down in waves over her shoulders, and just by her stance and strong presence, I knew she had to be the leader of their little pack. Kal hung in the back, but his eyes never left my face.

"Yeah, Anna, I'm coming," Josh responded coolly.

He gave me an apologetic look before joining them. "I'll see you around, Remi." There was a warning in his tone to forget what we just discussed.

But I couldn't hear him, not over the loudness of Kal's stare. He hesitated, his mouth opened slightly as if he were about to say something to me, but no sound came out, and just like that, he was gone with the rest of them.

They knew something. All of them did.

Heather appeared beside me like an obedient dog. "Hey, are you okay?

"Yeah..." I trailed off, watching them leave out the door.

"Who was that?" she asked, watching me glare at the front entrance.

"A fucking headache."

I think she could sense my anger because the following words out of her mouth surprised me. "You want to get out of here?"

We left the mixer, goody bags in one hand and a crappy mood in the other.

WANTING A BREAK FROM SOCIAL INTERACTION, I left Heather alone in our dorm as I made the trip to the showers. Finding solitude under scalding water, I avoided thinking about the last several events, but eventually, I needed to revisit them. Why did I care so much when I made it pretty fucking clear I wanted nothing to do with social clubs, let alone college.

Was I losing my goddamn mind?

I turned off the water and wrapped myself securely in a soft, expensive, white towel, courtesy of my mother.

Maybe finding out would give me something to do to pass the time. Then again, I berated myself once more, *why the fuck* did I care?

Gripping one of the many porcelain sinks, I leaned forward, seeing my tired hazel eyes in the mirror, surprised to find a woman with long blonde hair and a frown staring back.

A flashback of my mother forcing me in a white ball gown to attend my first cotillion made me shudder. I wiped under my eyes, removing the last bit of smudged mascara. and tried to untangle the knots in my hair with my fingers. It would be the first club without my mothers involvement too. I huffed a sigh and dried myself off, throwing on a fresh pair of sweats and a loose T-shirt. It somewhat scared me, that maybe it wouldn't be so bad if I tried to attend. I squeezed whatever water lingered in my hair and threw the towel over my shoulder, slipping on a fresh pair of socks and slippers.

Stopping to readjust my shower bag strap, I trekked out of the bathroom, surprised to find the hall empty. It wasn't so late that the RAs called curfew, but then again, the rest of the freshmen were probably still at the mixer.

I was just used to compacted clubs with sweaty bodies at this hour.

Approaching my room, I hesitated just outside the door. Part of me wanted to question Heather about the invitation. The other part... well, I hadn't figured out if I wanted to ignore it.

Strange how both men who were a part of the same rock band were somehow linked here...

It wasn't a coincidence, right?

Once again, why the fuck did I care?

Goosebumps coated my arms, and the feeling of being watched trickled an uneasy sensation down my back. I turned to find Kal a few feet from where I stood, an unsure look on his face as if he were contemplating whether he should approach me.

I made it easy for him. "Yes?" I fully turned to give him my undivided attention.

"Uh... um... hi."

I snorted back a laugh. "What do you need, *Kal*?"

Adjusting himself, he took a cautious step forward. "I'm sorry about earlier."

"Why? You didn't do anything wrong." And it was true. No strings attached, no nothing. I couldn't fault him for anything. So why did it look like he was going to shit himself?

"I wasn't expecting to see you again, let alone here of all places. I'm sorry I didn't say anything sooner." He tilted his head, a boyish, sad smile touching his lips.

At least he was sincere.

I smiled. "You're forgiven." Reaching behind me, I gripped the doorknob, ready to move on, when I saw Kal take another step forward from the corner of my eye.

"Remi?" His sheepish smile told me there was more than just an apology tonight.

Letting go of the doorknob once again, I crossed my arms, ready to hear his next line. "Kal?"

"The other night..." Kal took another step forward. "... I haven't stopped thinking about it." He took the final step toward me until very little space separated us.

His proximity started to overwhelm me, and it took every ounce of my self-control not to lean back and offend him. Granted, what we did that night had been pretty fucking hot, but nothing was exchanged besides names and a possible see you around. If he wanted to hook up again, then yeah, why not? But anything beyond that was something I couldn't commit to.

Especially in this godforsaken place.

So why couldn't I take that final step and close the distance?

Why couldn't I just dive right in and enjoy myself?

Why couldn't I?

My hesitation was enough for Kal to step back, a look of dejection on his face. "I just wanted to apologize for how I acted. I would love nothing more than to take you out to dinner to make it up to you."

His offer took me by surprise. "Dinner?"

Kal nodded, waiting for my response to his invitation. A free dinner from a hottie like him wasn't a totally bad idea, and he wasn't forcing my hand, either. Just because I wasn't ready to commit, didn't mean a friendship couldn't blossom from this. Why not?

So, why was I hesitating? Why couldn't I say yes? My nerves sank, hitting the pit of my stomach, and my smile faltered. There was nothing wrong in accepting our date, but for some reason, I couldn't shake my unease the longer we stared at one another.

But he didn't catch on when I said, "Sure."

His mood changed as soon as he heard my yes. "Carmen Hall right?"

I agreed and retreated into my room, finally able to breathe a bit better, instantly regretting my decision once my door clicked shut.

CHAPTER 9

Hot summer air fanned my face as we descended the stairs from the University Hall the next afternoon. Groups of young adults scattered across the campus lawn, laughing and hollering at one another, probably on their way to dorm parties, where they hid all the booze from authorities.

We had another lame assembly about our expectations as freshmen, and if we were struggling in our first semester, there were resources available to us in the Common Study building. Guidance counselors were also in the same building if we needed a safe place to talk to someone.

All through the assembly, I tried to come up with different ways to approach Heather about the invitation, and in the end, I decided against every single one. Why did I care so much about some stupid society I had no intention of joining? Maybe because my constant need to find the truth took over my logical thinking and I acted on impulse. At the end of the day, I didn't want to be there, so why bother with the other shit in between?

I worked up a sweat from being in my head too much, and it must've shown on my face because Heather barely looked my way the rest of the assembly.

I just wanted an easy time here so I could get in and get out without forming friendships or memories.

Heather kept quiet as we walked side by side, giving me the space to cool down, but the summer heat made it that much harder to climb back down that ladder.

I needed to try and act normal until I could figure out what was going on, then approach Heather and get this all out in the open.

I found her lying sprawled out over her bed, reading a book, twirling a strand of her hair. Already dressed in her pjs, makeup off, she gave me a quick thumbs-up, acknowledging my presence.

After my mini self-care routine and a quick trip to the bathroom, dressed in a matching shorts and shirt pj set, I crawled into my squeaky twin-sized bed. Lying there, staring aimlessly at the ceiling while my roommate barely spoke to me all day while she sat a few mere feet from them in the same room was enough to build the unnecessary tension.

"Hitting the hay early?" asked Heather.

Her voice made me jump a bit. She caught my reaction and half frowned.

"Honestly? I'm too wired," I confessed.

She pulled out a deck of cards from her desk drawer. "How about a little game?"

I smirked in amusement. "What kind of game?"

Heather hopped off her bed, sat cross-legged on the rug, and began to shuffle. "My favorite is poker," she reached under her bed and pulled out a drawstring bag, dumping a mound of different colored poker chips on the floor. "I never lose."

I slid off my bed to join her on the floor. "Interesting. You never mentioned it on your index card."

She laughed. "I don't tell a lot of people."

Heather dealt our cards with fast precision.

"I can see why."

We divided the chips evenly, stacking them by color. I checked my hand, surprised to find a two of a kind for kings.

"I can be dealer if you like?" she offered.

Giving my cards another scan, I nodded in acceptance. "Sure. That way, I can concentrate better."

Heather threw down some yellow chips in the middle, a smirk on her face. "I always start out small for my bids."

I tossed a couple of my own yellow chips on the pile. "Before you pummel your opponent?"

"Exactly."

I never thought of myself as a good poker player, even the times with Jeremy and Nickie when I ended up winning most of the rounds, even though we were drunk, but Heather was killing me.

Her poker face was another story. Every hand she threw down trumped mine. If I showed my straight, she would up me with a flush. And if I came at her in the next round with a full house, somehow, she would eliminate me with a four-of-a-kind.

By this point in the night, I had a few poker chips left to my name and a pounding headache.

Heather tapped her fingers on her knee, looking over her hand as she said, "What's your class schedule like this semester?"

I realized that as roommates, the one thing we had never

discussed was our semester schedule. Shifting the cards around in my hands, I reorganized the order, trying to judge from the half-decent hand if anything was worth salvaging. "A lot of intro classes. I'm dreading the math portion."

Heather tossed a couple more yellow chips in the center. "Did you score low on the placement exam?"

I matched her chips in the middle. "I scored well enough to get into a normal math class. That's the problem." Jeremy was the sole reason I passed any math classes in high school. Now who was I going to cheat off of?

Heather flipped over the second card. An ace of spades. "Math isn't all that bad."

I knew my hand was shit from the beginning. "Easier for you to say. That's your major."

She laughed and then shoved all her remaining chips in the middle. "I'm feeling risky tonight."

I followed suit because the probability of me actually winning any games tonight was nonexistent, so I truly had *nothing* to lose.

The card lineup was a king of spades and an ace of spades. If she flipped another over of the same suit, I was royally fucked, because knowing Heather, she had an unbeatable hand.

Heather massaged the card on top of the deck, prolonging the inevitable, because I knew deep in my bones this bitch was going to win.

She flipped, revealing a fucking jack of spades.

"Holy shit! A royal flush! My first one!" She revealed her hand, the other two spades, a ten, and a queen.

What the actual fuck. I knew the probability of someone getting a royal flush in a poker game was a slight chance, but of course she got it as we played for fun. "You're impossible to beat," I sighed, throwing my cards on top of the mound of chips.

"I'm not *that* good," she commented.

I shook my head in disbelief. "Girl, you're freakishly good at this game. Either you can read my mind, or you have a horseshoe up your ass."

Heather grinned as she began to collect the poker chips in the drawstring bag. "My dad taught me when I was seven. That's how I was able to swindle the crap out of my two older brothers." She then gathered the cards, only she flipped the ace of spades in her hand. "I always seem to get this card, no matter who deals. I call that a sign of good luck."

Aces were known to be the highest-ranking cards in a standard deck, a sign of strength and authority. I'd barely had any in the hands she'd dealt me.

"Anyways, that was fun. Let me know if you want to play again sometime." Kicking the boxed deck and bag back under her bed, Heather got herself comfortable under the giant flower quilt.

Crawling back under my own covers, I tried to stifle a loud yawn and failed miserably.

"Sorry, I didn't mean to keep you up so late," Heather expressed with regret.

"It's okay. Today was a lot to process."

She started to pick at the details in her quilt, biting her lip as if she were debating her next words.

"What is it?" I asked.

Heather's striking green eyes flashed an uneasy look. "Are we okay?"

Ah, shit. A clear path was laid out in front of me to ask, yet I couldn't form the words on my tongue. Did I want to go there with Heather? Would she react the same as Josh did when I asked about the Order of the Scarlet Quill? Now I was having second thoughts. Our poker night had solidified a possible friendship, and it was the first time an honest one came from nothing but sharing a single room.

I chose the latter. "Yeah, I'm fine. The adjustment is a little tough."

Her reply was simply turning off the light, and for once, I appreciated the silent goodnight.

I waited until her soft breathing filled the silence and slipped my hand under my pillow, feeling the cool metal flask in my hands. The first sip gave me relief, the second gave me peace, and the third threatened a path I wasn't sure I could come back from.

But the numbness that followed helped me sleep a little easier that night.

CHAPTER 10

My bed, stiff as a board even with the mattress pad, made me shift uncomfortably for quite some time until my body crunched down in the fetal position, where I awoke shortly after to a loud alarm on the opposite side of the room.

Heather's alarm, to be exact, screeched like a bird, and she was lucky my body had no intention of rising from the bed to smash it to the floor.

My classes didn't start until Monday, so unless she was getting up early to practice running for a marathon, there was no need to have the alarm blaring at this hour. I tried to cover my ears with a pillow to soften the sound but was too annoyed to go back to sleep. I groaned, grabbed the box of tissues on the side table, and chucked them at her head.

"Ouch!" she yelped in the dark.

"Turn it off!" I demanded.

"What?"

"Your alarm!"

"Ah! Okay!" Silence returned, and I sighed in relief.

"Why was your alarm set?"

"I used to get up and run around this time."

Go fucking figure.

I glanced over at my clock and choked. "At five-thirty in the morning? Are you even human?"

"Damn, you figured me out," she joked.

I rolled over to face her in the dark. "I came close to smashing it."

"Wouldn't be the first time," admitted Heather.

"Really?"

"I shared a room with my sister back home. She smashed about four of them."

That gave me a good belly laugh. "Damn, girl."

"I know. Hey, there's a freshmen breakfast later at nine-thirty. Do you want to come with me?"

Did I? After what happened last night, a part of me never wanted to attend the bogus events this school created again, but Heather had become someone I didn't mind spending time with. Yeah, I missed the crap out of Nickie and Jeremy, even though the two of us were not on speaking terms—mostly Nickie, Jeremy texted me briefly last night before bed—but it had been nice to have someone else out of that friend group who did ordinary things, even though some of those everyday things made me want to gag. Then there was the not-so-secret society Heather had been invited to, and I had no clue how to bring it up without her thinking I snooped around through her stuff. Trying my best to be a good roommate but also wanting to confront her gave me a headache. I could attend the stupid thing, but that would mean I had to dress up and be a part of something I'd refused to associate with from the beginning.

Heather bit her lip. "So...?"

"Yeah, sure. Maybe they'll have mimosas there," I dreamed.

"Is that..." Heather paused.

She had zero knowledge of the alcohol world. "Yes, it's an alcoholic drink."

"What's your favorite drink?"

Surprised by her question and interest in my taste in mixed drinks, I decided on my top three. "Hmm, I like rum and Coke, sometimes a chocolate martini, and I'm obsessed with any drink mixed with watermelon vodka." Saying it out loud totally pinned me as an alcoholic.

"I wish I could drink."

"May I ask..." Should I? Was it rude? I'd never met someone who took anxiety medication; then again, how many people came right out and told you what demons they fought?

The flask underneath my pillow burned with regret and lies.

Heather could sense my awkwardness about asking and immediately shifted, her bed creaking in protest. "Nobody has asked me straight out before."

"Oh, I'm sorry—"

"No! It's okay!" she interjected. "It makes sense since we're roommates to talk about personal stuff, eventually."

Yeah, except not this early in the semester, or day, for that matter, but she was here and ready to be vulnerable with her personal life with me. Minus the little secret society part.

Heather took a deep breath, the sound somewhat shaky, and unleashed her first demon. "Junior year of high school, I dated my first boyfriend, Dan. I was sickly in love with him, to the point I would blow off friends and family to be with him. One night after a basement party with his football buddies, Dan wanted to drive home after a few drinks. I told him no and to let me drive. He wouldn't have it, and neither did his friends, who were just as smashed. Instead of giving me the keys, his friends carried me to the car, laughing, until one of them hit my head on the door, shoving me into the back seat. I screamed in pain and fear, begging Dan to make them stop and to pull over, when he turned around and told me to shut up and how I always told him what to do and he was sick of it. I had never felt so low in my life. Eventually, the car did stop, only it hit a guardrail, flipping over a few times before landing us in a ditch. I woke up in the hospital, thankful to be alive. Dan and the others didn't make it. And since my accident, I often wake to my screams from nightmares of what happened." Heather finished her story with a heavy sigh.

I, on the other hand, was speechless. We sat in silence for I don't know how long. The air felt tight with emotion. I wasn't used to vulnerable people, so I felt honored that she would trust me with that personal detail of her life.

When I didn't respond, Heather continued. "People blamed me for the accident. Some said I should've died instead. The football season was ruined, but nobody cared how I felt."

The lump in my throat grew, making it difficult to speak. "I'm sorry," I managed to say. Was that even the right thing to say? Her heavy secret made the room thick with sorrow, choking the air from my lungs. How could someone carry the burden of something out of their control? The idea left me feeling as if I were drowning under constant waves, never fully reaching above water for air. I could only imagine how Heather felt under the constant scrutiny back home.

I looked over at her through the darkness, barely making out her body. "And now?"

"I survive with the medication and video therapy," Heather said.

"Do you take medication every day?"

"Yes. Every morning when I wake up, I take this little orange pill."

"Ah."

What could I contribute to this conversation now that she had laid herself bare?

I thought of my grams and how she would want me to be honest, but to share what I kept for so long in the dark was not a step I wanted to take.

Instead, I chose a less calamitous secret. "I'm only here because of my grams."

"Did she encourage you?" queried Heather.

"To apply? Yes. Her will stated that if I was accepted, my schooling would be paid for in full and I must attend." But I took it anyway, cause nothing satisfied me more than watching my mother lose her shit. Now she puts on a fake smile, completely on board with my decision, most likely internally cussing out Grams for having a one up from beyond the grave.

A memory flitted through my mind of us sitting outside on the balcony, my grams tossing a stack of college applications on the wrought iron table. My hand ached after a few hours, because she wanted me to hand write each one out, stating computers were unreliable and faulty. She was alive to see me receive every acceptance letter but Columbia. It came in the mail three days after her death.

A reminder of her once being alive.

Little did I know, her will was set in stone. A full deposit was already made before I even received the letter. Conniving woman.

"She truly believed in you," commented Heather.

"No, she truly despised my mother's wishes and planned this little charade behind her back. I never wanted to go to college, but the satisfaction of watching my mother listening to my grams' will never get old."

"Oh my God!"

"Yeah, Grams knew what she was doing."

"Clearly. Maybe in a month I can ask you how you feel about being here."

"Sure, but I don't think my answer will change."

Heather chuckled. "A lot can change in a month."

She had too much hope for me to change my mind.

"So, are we still cool for breakfast in the morning?" Heather asked again.

"Just let me try to catch some extra sleep. And keep that alarm off!"

She laughed and tossed back the box of tissues, which hit the wall and fell on the floor with a soft thud. "You got it!"

THE DARKNESS of the alleyway contorted into monstrous shapes, sounds of unnatural growls echoing through the emptiness of where I stood, braced against the brick wall. My feet were glued to the concrete as fear laced through my pounding heart and the air constricted in my lungs. Fear of what stalked the midnight shadows—fear of the darkness creeping forward. The stench of death coated my nostril as its dark, menacing form grew.... One reached forward. Long talons circled around my throat, black sludge dripping off its distorted form. Teeth as sharp as needles hissed in my face, saliva spraying in every direction. It sniffed my hair, my clothes, its black tongue glazing over my cheek. Any attempt to cry for help was lost in the grip of its claws. All the blood rushed to my head, my hands limp by my sides, refusing to touch its skin to break free. Its eyes, an endless black pit, with a head covered in horns of all different sizes, was nothing short of demonic.

Every passing second was another waste of trying to escape the clutches of the ghastly beast. My vision started to blur, the hissing turned into snapping, and I braced myself for the impact of teeth. My life flashed before my fucking eyes, every minuscule memory on a film reel, rapidly show-casing what I was about to leave behind. From my friends to family, places, and emotions rooted deep in my psyche.

As if time stopped altogether, I let my final thoughts be of my grams. Her sweet face and strong demeanor never faltered in distress. The last of her words to me came on a wind, of promises to never let my mother control who I was. To never back down and embrace all of me.

Which would cease to exist in a matter of seconds.

All at once, its claws disappeared from around my neck, a rush of air passing through my lungs, sputtering a cough to regain some consciousness of my surroundings. Falling to my knees, the concrete ground dug into my flesh, a stran-gled whimper escaping my lips from impact. My head hung low, gulping in air. Every inch of my skin seemed to be covered in the sludge it produced from its grotesque body.

I was startled by cool fingers grasping my chin, the action rough and demanding, lifting my head, only for my stained hair to cover my eyes. Too weak to fight, I submitted to whoever held me in place, my body drained and defenseless.

Four simple words chilled me to the bone.

"I will find you."

I jolted awake, my body shaking with alarm. Looking around my room, night still covered us, Heather softly breathing in the silent space we shared. Racing with anxiety, I quickly grabbed the silver flask, taking a hearty sip, trying to stay silent while recovering from the nightmare that plagued my thoughts.

I took another sip, then twisted the cap shut, shaking the flask only to find barely a shot was left. I would have to head home and refill it as soon as possible.

Unable to fall back to sleep and refusing to revisit whatever sinister nightmare invaded my REM sleep, I shuffled on my slippers, snagged my key card off my desk, and snuck out of the room, into the deserted hallway.

Alcohol rushed through my veins as I descended the stairs and tiptoed right out the front door. I needed to be somewhere else besides that dorm room; the walls felt like they were closing in, and not even the alcohol could snuff out the anxious thoughts.

I sat by myself in the dark on the front steps of Carman Hall, thankful to only hear the normalcy of sirens in the distance. Putting my head between my legs, I focused on trying to steady my heart, still racing at an abnormal pace. I couldn't let my mind wander back, not yet, and maybe not ever, to what lurked in the shadows of my dreams.

It was the male voice, dominant and threatening, issuing a promise to find me that shook me to my core. Who was he? Why did it seem so real?

Dreams of the mysterious red-headed female hadn't resurfaced since my arrival, and part of me wished for something so dependable to return. At least it comforted my mind knowing what I already expected from the dream.

Who was the man with the baritone voice, and how had he slithered into my unconscious mind? Surely, I couldn't conjure up something so otherworldly if I even tried.

When my heart slowed down its erratic beating, I lifted my head to the night sky. Stars were never seen in the big apple; rather, the city lights created a soft pink, hiding the little beauties from sight. How I wished sometimes the whole city would shut off the lights just for a few seconds, just to get a glimpse of the world above.

A warm summer breeze lifted a few strands of my hair, my clothes still damp from night sweats. With a shaky breath, I stood, stretching out my limbs and rotating my stiff neck. The alcohol did exactly what it needed to do—tame the phantom that lingered in my soul.

I should go back inside and try to sleep, but how could I when my gaze was drawn to a shadow draped in scarlet.

I didn't hesitate as I rushed off the stone steps, straight through the dewy grass, almost slipping as I ran toward the cloaked figure. If this had any connection to what was going on, now was my chance to unmask them.

They must've spotted me because they began to run, the scarlet cape trailing behind them. I kicked my legs faster, thankful for the years of chasing my older brother at the country club house, and just made it to the other side when a strong tug pulled me back.

"No!" I shouted as I watched the figure disappear in the night.

I spun around to find Josh holding tightly to my arm. "Let me go, you asshole!" Trying to wrangle myself free was like trying to uncuff my own hands—fucking impossible. "What is wrong with you?"

Josh released me rather quickly and retreated a step back. "Go to bed, Remi."

"Excuse me? Who are you to tell me what to do?" I snapped, rubbing my arm.

Josh was tall enough to lean down without moving, inches from my face. He wore black pants and a black zip-up hoodie, covering his head with the hood, a scowl forming on his lips. "You're lucky it was me who found you."

It didn't go unnoticed when his eyes flicked up to peer over my head before giving me his full attention once more. I glanced behind me to see where his eyes had traveled, only to find an empty campus. Whoever that mystery person was with the scarlet cape, they were long gone by now.

Turning back to his stupid, gorgeous face, I crossed my arms in irritation. "Lucky? Right now, you're lucky I haven't kicked you in the balls. What are you, the campus police?"

The sneer he showcased on those plush lips was enough for me to reach forward and try unsuccessfully to smack him across the face. Josh's giant hand closed over mine, pulling me up against his chest. "Trust me, they're around. Like I said, you're *lucky* I found you first." He looked over my head again. I was about to follow his line of sight once more when he pulled me even closer.

I struggled against him, only to realize my breasts were

pushed against his chest. That was enough to cause my nipples to peak. "I just needed some fresh air."

Josh almost closed the distance, just enough space to speak without our lips touching. My toes curled guiltily. "Don't ever come out here again this late."

When he finally released me, I stumbled back on the wet grass, only to take my slipper and give it a good throw at his head. "I can't believe Nickie is with you."

He dodged it at the last second, shaking his head. "Really? You're ridiculous."

I assessed him up and down. "Says the one dressed in all black."

Josh smirked at my wandering eyes. "You're quite fixated on my attire."

"Stop trying to change the subject."

Those dangerous lips curled into a Cheshire Cat grin. Fuck, I hated how it made my stomach flutter. "Go inside."

"Make me, asshole."

Josh smiled at the challenge and came forward. Trying my best to sneak past those large hands, I was too slow and got tossed over his shoulder, then he carried me back the way I ran, leaving my other slipper completely drenched in the grass.

"Put me down!" I whacked at his chest, only to find hard muscles under the layer of clothing. My hands throbbed.

"Keep your voice down," he commanded in a tone so deadly that I remembered my common sense and kept my mouth shut.

Not a single complaint came out of his mouth carrying me back up the steps, only to drop me right in front of the Carman Hall entrance.

I stood facing the doors, lacking a slipper, waiting for him to leave.

"Get your key out. I'll make sure you get safely inside," Josh quipped.

Rolling my eyes, I pulled the lanyard attached to my key card out of my pajama shorts pocket and waved it over the censor, hearing the click indicating it was unlocked.

Without looking back, I entered, only to turn around to find him holding the door open. I threw my arms out, exasperated. "What do you want now?"

Josh's baby blues traveled from my bare legs up and over my arms, where he took notice of the little arrow tattoo on my inner right arm. His unexpected touch against my skin where the tattoo was embedded sent goosebumps all over, revealing my forbidden desires.

His lips parted as if touching me was an intimate moment we shouldn't have shared. Leaving my skin sizzling from his soft fingertips, Josh removed himself from my personal bubble and let the door slowly shut on its own, but not before he had the last word. "Sweet dreams."

Snapping out of the lustful stupor, I flipped him off through the glass and said loudly, "Good fucking night, asshole."

He smirked and gave a little sarcastic salute of farewell and disappeared, leaving me with a guilty conscience, heated in forbidden areas of my body, and one shoe.

CHAPTER 11

Sneaking back into our room without a sound, I huffed a soft sigh in frustration. *Who the fuck does he think he is telling me what to do? What makes him the goddamn boss?* I needed to relax and keep my cool before I disturbed Heather. She slept as if nothing could wake her.

Lucky.

Eventually, I found myself dozing off after I took the last sip from my flask, trying to simmer the rising irritation.

Morning came faster than expected, with Heather awake at her desk, curling her red hair. She carefully parted each piece and twisted it until steam sizzled, reminding her to release that piece before it disintegrated on the metal plates.

"What time is it?" I asked, my voice sounding hoarse.

"Eight-forty-five," she replied, twirling another piece around the curling wand. "You okay?"

"Yeah, I'm gonna shower."

"Okay."

Grabbing my bag of toiletries, I left our room and

trekked down the hall to the female bathrooms. A few girls were already in some of the showers; one had their music blasting, while another stall smelled of vanilla and lavender, filling the room along with the excessive amount of steam. I chose the shower second to last and slipped in, discarding my clothes and turning on the tap. Cold water shot out from the shower head, making me yelp with surprise. I quickly adjusted the temperature before sticking my head back underneath the waterfall of grimy city water.

I missed my filtered water back home.

I lathered, rinsed, and repeated the shampoo in my hair, letting the water soak my entire scalp. It felt good to just let the water touch my face, if only to hush the loudness of my thoughts for a few minutes. Finishing the shower in roughly ten minutes, I then wrapped the floor-length towel around my torso, only to remember I lost my other slipper and returned to my room. Rounding the corner, I was unprepared for the stiff body standing just outside my room, colliding right into them headfirst.

"Ouch!" I yelped.

"Oh, crap, sorry! Remi?"

It all happened so fast that my head spun from the hit. "Uh... yeah, that's... me."

"Where's your room?"

Man, that male voice sounded familiar. "Uh..."

My eyesight blurred from the pain; I couldn't comprehend where I was standing.

"I just need to..."

"Whoa! Your towel!"

But I continued to rub my eyes, trying to subside the unwanted specks in my vision, until, eventually, they diminished from my line of sight. That was when I realized Kal's hands were holding the towel around my body.

"Oh!" I tugged the towel away from his grasp and stepped back, wrapping it securely around me.

"Hi," he said with a smile.

"Hi."

"I wasn't—"

"I know," I interjected as my cheeks burned.

"Right. I'm sorry I almost knocked you out," Kal apologized.

I started to laugh. "It wouldn't be the first time... or second." Josh's stupid face came to mind. The prick.

He also joined in with the laughter, his smile contagious and bright.

Then I remembered I was standing there wholly naked underneath a towel, wet hair dripping on the floor.

"Well, I'd better get back to my room and change," I announced as if it wasn't obvious.

Kal pushed back his blond hair from his eyes. "Yes, that would be a good idea."

When did the air between us get so awkward? Maybe because I subconsciously rejected him the other day but agreed to his apology dinner that wasn't an actual date.

I thought I made it known I wasn't interested on a deeper level... was agreeing to the date sending that message? Shit.

"Right, well, see ya around, I guess."

"Right. See ya."

"Kal?"

I jerked away from him, trying to create as much space between us as possible.

"Fuck off, Chloe." His eyes bored into mine, and I swallowed nervously.

Chloe was a dark-haired short stack with a sourpuss on her face as she glared at me like a nasty pile of dog shit. "Nah, I don't think I will. Stop screwing with freshmen; we're needed downstairs," she said, leaving Kal and I too close for comfort.

Kal sighed. "She's such a buzzkill."

"Right."

He tucked a wet, loose strand of hair behind my ear. "Is it wrong to say I don't want to leave?"

But I did. "I think you're needed downstairs." Phantom fingers lingered from his touch, and I shiver.

I was ready to escape, when Kal gently tugged me back, his expression somber. "Are you okay?"

"Yeah, why wouldn't I be?"

"I was wondering if we could finish what we started." He tugged me closer as other students started to flood the hall.

I stopped him with a hand on his chest. "Maybe another time?"

The hall was getting too crowded, and I just wanted to change into something comfortable.

"Didn't see you as the type of girl to deny a little fun."

"I'm not denying the fun, but I think it's our cue to move on for now."

Kal's lips brushed against my ear. "I'm not the one who started it. Looks like you have to finish it."

I recoiled, untangling myself from him. "I may have started it, but it doesn't mean I want to finish it. Excuse me, but I need to change." I stormed off down the hall.

Entering my room, damp and mad, I tossed my dirty

garments on my bed and started searching through my dresser drawers, opening and slamming them shut to find a clean pair of underwear and a bra.

Heather sat on her bed, watching me stomp around like a two-year-old throwing a fit. "Remi?"

"What?" I snapped, putting on my clothes and throwing the towel aside.

"Girl, what happened?"

"Men." Now was not the time to ask questions.

"Anyone in particular?"

"Kal."

"Wait, Kal? The hottie at the mixer?"

I wished she would stop the interrogation. "Yes. That very one."

"Do you want to talk about it?"

"Not right now." Afraid I might blow up in her face, I gave her a warning look before turning back around and facing the wall.

"Okay, well, I'll meet you downstairs."

"Great, thanks."

To be honest, I had been too dramatic about what happened and needed to cool down before I showed up at the freshmen breakfast. Without a second thought, I hit the call button on Nickie's contact page, aware our last fight wasn't resolved, and waited through three rings until she picked up.

"Girl! What's up?"

"I ran into Kal," I huffed, picking at the fuzz balls on my bedspread.

"And?" she prompted.

"I don't know, he's kind of giving me the creeps now."

"But you made out with him?"

"So? I can change my mind if I want to."

"Then why waste his time?"

She had to be kidding me. Leave it to her to twist it so I was the problem. My guess was she was dating his bandmate, so she was getting defensive on his behalf. I highly doubted Josh had a goddamn clue. *How fucking typical of her.*

"Are you serious right now?" My voice boomed through the speaker on her end.

She rolled her eyes. "Well, you wouldn't want it to happen to you, right?"

Suddenly, Jeremy popped up behind Nickie. "Hey, Rem!"

"Jeremy, tell Remi to take a chill pill," ordered Nickie.

I slid down to the floor, hugging my knees. For once, I wanted my two best friends to act responsibly and give me decent advice.

"I thought we sold all your mom's Xanax last summer?" questioned Jeremy.

"Oh, yeah, we did," Nickie remembered.

I leaned my head back against the door. "You're both insufferable right now."

"Hold up, chica. What's going on? I'm parched for tea. Spill it, Lipton," demanded Jeremy.

"Oh, Remi thinks Kal is creepy after leading him on," explained Nickie.

"Did he do something to her, though?" Jeremy inquired.

"No!" I exclaimed. *Now they're getting on my fucking nerves.*

"Then why are you freaking out?" Jeremy asked.

"Because he expected us to continue after I turned him down!" I snapped.

"Who the fuck cares? You said it yourself you wanted no strings attached," reminded Nickie.

Jeremy gave me a funny look. "Are you catching feelings?"

I rolled my eyes. "Abso-fucking-lutely not."

Nickie propped her phone up so it showed her and Jeremy at his kitchen table. "Is there someone else?"

Why would she think... Josh's infuriating smile and big hands came to mind. The way he looked upon my body as if the act alone was forbidden... the gentle touch of his fingers on my tattoo. No, no. He was with Nickie, and an arrogant ass.

They took my silence as defeat, and both began to laugh. "Honey, come home Friday night and take a break," suggested Jeremy.

I bit my lip. "Maybe. I'll see."

"You better! It's ladies' night at Electric Haze!" gushed Nickie.

I rolled my eyes. "Okay, well, great. I'll text you if I decide to go. Bye." I hung up before any unnecessary chatter leaked through.

It was time for that dreadful freshmen breakfast.

CHAPTER 12

If I'd ever wanted to dig my own grave, today would be the fucking day. The dining hall looked like someone projectile vomited the school colors all over the walls and tables. Soft, classical music drifted in one ear and out the other, and each table had flowers as the centerpieces and fancy silverware with matching plates displayed at each seat. Over to the far right, a table seemed to be stocked with fresh fruit and veggies, and just beyond that, a conga line of colorful drinks in clear kegs with shiny stouts awaited. The windows were long, casting an abundance of light inside the building, which made the room much hotter than outside. Every seat seemed to be filled by the time I arrived, but luckily Heather had saved us a place at a table dead center; how joyous.

She waved me down like a survivor on a deserted island, signaling me to join. I gave her a thumbs up to get her to relax and maneuvered my way to our table, trying to avoid pointy elbows and obnoxious laughter. The only type of crowds I could tolerate were clubs and concerts, and I was about three seconds away from hightailing it out of there. But just the simple smile on Heather's face made me refrain. Once you spill your struggles with someone, you tend to ease up on their cringe behavior.

Chloe, who caught me with Kal stepped into my view. Her sour expression had returned, or never left, and she held up her well-manicured hand to signal me to stop.

"Freeze," she commanded.

What could she possibly want from me?

"You're the same chick whose throat Kal almost stuck his tongue down, right?"

But judging by her half smirk, she knew I was that same chick.

"Almost? Try never happened." Well, once, but she didn't need to know that.

"Did he say anything to you?"

I raised an eyebrow. "About?"

She paused, searching my face, then shook her head. "Keep away from him; more importantly, away from anyone associated with him."

"So, you too?" Alright, she was fucking weird. "Cause if he's a part of some underground drug deal, then I'm all set." To hell I get dragged into some messy shit like that.

"Just stay away from *us* " She stalked off then, leaving me more confused than before.

I concluded that everyone in this fucking school had lost their goddamn mind, and I couldn't wait to hurry up and graduate from this loony bin.. I decided it wasn't worth the hassle trying to decipher her cryptic riddle and tossed Kal out the window.

Heather scooted a food tray piled high aside to give me

some room on our long table. At least she wouldn't try to bite my head off.

"Feeling better?" Heather asked. Just by the tone in her voice, I could tell she was testing the waters with me, making sure I wouldn't snap like a rubber band.

"Yeah, much better. Just took out some nasty garbage," I joked.

She gave me a big smile and pushed the tray in between us again. Heather had piled some mini chocolate muffins, fruit, bacon strips, little sausages, and scrambled eggs. I gave her a warm smile and popped a mini muffin in my mouth.

"I wasn't sure what you liked, so I grabbed a variety," she said.

"Good choice on the mini muffins," I said between bites. "And thanks for grabbing me breakfast."

Just then, a loud gong silenced the cafeteria as the same woman from last night stood in the middle of the room, grabbing everyone's attention. Jordan, if I remembered correctly, held a black microphone in hand and smiled, waving at a few other students before unfolding a piece of paper.

"Good morning, freshman class! Today, we're going to have so much fun! Icebreakers and games galore!" she gushed.

If I wasn't holding in my vomit so hard, I would have projectile my breakfast all over the table by now. *I need to stop agreeing to come to these useless events.*

"I won't lie. What she said was kind of lame," whispered Heather.

Her comment caught me off guard, which turned into a burst of laughter I couldn't entirely control when prissy pants front and center gave me a warning look to keep my mouth shut. Heather thought that was funny and giggled into her hands, trying to stay quiet as well.

"Now, before we begin, I have a few rules to review with everyone," she said.

The crowd groaned, and then someone shouted behind us. "C'mon, Jordan!"

"All right! Settle down!" she demanded, then flipped the paper over. "These are the rules. First, please do not cheat. I know this rule is stupid, but you would be surprised to know that some have cheated in the past. Second, please clean up the area you participated in. The quicker we do this, the quicker we return to our dorms. Lastly, and I cannot stress this enough—"

Some guy came around Jordan and snagged the mic from her grasp. "We get it, Queen of Rules. Now, who's ready to play?" The crowd erupted in cheers of agreement and began to slam on the tables, creating a loud drum sound from their palms.

I watched as Jordan tried to steal the mic back, but he kept turning just out of her reach. It also didn't help that he was more than a foot taller than her.

"Let's do this!" he shouted, dropping the mic dramatically. The sound penetrated my eardrums.

"What the heck just happened?" asked Heather over the loud crowd. Most students were standing, cheering each other and high fiving like maniacs.

"Who the fuck knows," I replied.

I wonder if it's too late to drop out.

Heather chuckled and took a sip of her orange juice. I smiled in return, about to take a sip, when the hairs on my arms stood, an unsettling feeling of being watched crawling along my skin. Using my peripherals, I caught Josh and the others clustered around one of the marble pillars, regarding me with a stony expression. Josh must've told them I knew about the Order; it was the only explanation I got for how hostile they presented themselves. It seems I peered into the eyes of the hidden members, exposed, but only I knew. Josh crossed his arms as I lifted my glass of orange juice to my lips, giving them the same cold look, trying to keep my composure.

"Heather," I said, never taking my eyes off the little posse.

"Hmm?" she mused in between bites of bacon.

If anyone knew, it would be Heather. "Does Columbia have a curfew?"

She slurped down the rest of her orange juice, wiping her mouth with the back of her hand. "Apparently so. I guess to avoid high crime rates or something. Didn't you read the handbook fact sheet?"

I snorted a hearty laugh. "Does it look like I read handbooks?"

The crowd continued to cheer, Heather reaching for another piece of bacon. "I don't know. You're mostly a closed book."

Chloe leaned into Josh, whispering. His eyes flashed with rage, nostrils flaring. What the hell could she have possibly told him? When I gave nothing but the truth away, Kal didn't tell me anything.

Josh's gaze flicked to me, darkening his expression. I refused to back down from the heat of his gaze searing into me.

Refusing to squirm or give into their cat and mouse

chase, I winked. This was for truth, and I was going to win, and it would be oh so sweet.

My reaction must've ruffled his feathers because he stalked off, leaving the rest of his posse to watch my every move.

At that moment, I realized the Order was dangerous, and I might have stirred the beast.

CHAPTER 13

After Sunday's escapade of useless games and unnecessary icebreakers—I reminded Heather never to drag me to that kind of shit again—we managed to survive our first week of college classes. It was interesting, considering I took—more like was forced—Business Management as a major, so some were dry introduction courses, others were prerequisites, but overall, I managed to navigate each one without drawing too much attention to myself. Taking five was average; in reality, I wish I had taken two and called it a day, but the way my family's connections ran deep in New York, they would find I half-assed the experience and scold me like a child.

Sometimes I wished my parents' intense involvement in my life would end. And by intense, I meant less throwing lavish parties and products at me and actually giving a fuck about mundane stuff.

Once again, thank you, Grams, for this *marvelous* experience.

I liked a few of my professors, some not so much, but at

least some were bearable and didn't call on me when I wasn't paying attention. It wasn't at all like the movies I watched growing up or the scare tactics my previous high school teachers threatened us with. I called that a solid win in my book.

I hadn't seen Kal since our uncomfortable encounter. Josh had been MIA since his little tantrum that day during freshmen breakfast. Whatever Chloe told him was enough for him to give me a dirty look before storming off.

What a fucking pansy.

I'd seemed to avoid them all week, and although that would've been amazing, it made me worry, especially for Heather. The mere thought of her getting involved with such a violent group of people set me on edge every time she left our room. Granted, I had no proof they were evil, but I couldn't help but shake the uneasy feeling their hidden agenda was dangerous.

But that night... after that frightful nightmare, sitting on those stone steps, that scarlet cape, then Josh just showing up randomly? I happened to find my stupid handbook in that acceptance folder and read through it. Sure enough, there was a curfew in the facts sheet.

What gave him the right to boss me around when he was clearly breaking the rules himself? Had he seen what appeared on campus? That striking scarlet cape? Was he trying to look out for me? But what if... shit, what if he was involved instead? Could he be protecting *them*?

If so, then Nickie had to get far away from Josh as soon as possible. But I knew she wouldn't listen, she never had since our friendship began. And besides, dangerous men were her favorite to screw around with and chase.

The lack of presence from Jeremy and Nickie made me

realize one thing; I never thought for myself. All my actions reflected theirs and how they presented themselves. No, they weren't bad people, but it would seem I'd been hiding behind a mask made by two people unsure of their own selves.

A mask I wasn't expecting to take off.

But I did anyway because I gave them the okay to meet them tonight.

I sat in front of my LED vanity mirror propped on my desk, slapping on my makeup, trying to hide my designer eye bags that I didn't buy purposefully.

Never again would I take an eight a.m.

Heather had left for the night. She'd made some friends in her accounting class, and they wanted to go out for pizza. The invitation was extended, but Electric Haze called my name, along with Jeremy and Nickie, several times. I guess they missed me despite the fact there was a lack of communication, but it went both ways, and I was equally to blame for not reaching out.

I would be lying if I said I didn't miss them too.

A soft knock came on my door. Unless my parents decided to stop by for a surprise visit or Heather forgot something of hers, I wasn't expecting anyone to come by at this hour.

So, when I opened the door, my double surprise followed soon after, as the hallway remained empty. Confused, I stepped out, giving it a thorough check, waiting for someone to pop out and yell surprise, but all I heard were the girls down the hall laughing obnoxiously through the thin walls.

Annoyed and slightly embarrassed with myself for opening it in the first place, I began to retreat inside, when I noticed a scarlet envelope taped to my door. Strange how I didn't see it before, but then again, when did I ever really pay attention to what was on my door these days? I peeled the tape off the wood that held it in place.

I gave one last glance at the empty hallway before I quietly stepped back inside to rip open the pretty envelope. Inside was an eggshell brochure with beautiful handwriting staining the paper in black ink. Black ink that said the time of the event for induction of The Order of the Scarlet Quill had changed from seven to eight pm.

But the letter was addressed to no one.

And yet somehow, they knew Heather and I were rooming together.

Because Heather still had no idea.

Which meant us being placed together was no coincidence.

My head was hurting, and it wasn't even midnight yet.

I had already ripped the envelope open, so I couldn't pretend to Heather I didn't read it, but I could recreate it and just put her name on the front.

Well, now I *had* to find out.

Was my invitation still under my desk near the trash can?

A few minutes passed, and I luckily found a new envelope—unfortunately, not the color of blood, but she wouldn't know the difference—and tried to mimic the elegant writing, somewhat successfully. I grabbed my purse and phone and taped the letter back on the door before skirting out of there as fast as possible before anyone saw me.

Born and raised in New York City, I refused to take the subway at night by myself. The horror stories I heard over the years of young girls like me getting kidnapped or, worse, sexually assaulted, instantly made up my mind never to ride it alone.

Besides, our family hired a personal driver, so I'd never need to, but the odds of him coming to get me were slim to none, mainly since my parents use him constantly. And if they found out I left campus, that was another load of unwanted questions I didn't intend to answer at this hour. *Or ever.*

A cab was the next best thing.

It took only fifteen minutes from campus to reach Electric Haze in record time, considering it was a Friday night in New York City. Nickie and Jeremy were waiting outside in line as the car pulled up to the curb. Their outfits were coordinated, and I wondered if they got ready together.

Then it got me thinking, how often had they done that without me?

Securing my crossbody purse, I gave the cab driver a generous tip for risking his life in the heavy traffic to drive my ass out on a Friday night and met them in line.

Nickie hugged me so tight I thought she would pop my head off like a bobblehead. Jeremy kissed me on each cheek and spun me around like a ballet dancer.

"Did lover boy slay you yet?" he asked, handing Nickie our signature silver flask.

I smacked him hard on the arm. "No!"

"He better lay the pipe soon. You're getting rigid," Jeremy stated.

Nickie smacked him upside the head. "She knows; don't remind her."

"Wow, thanks for that," I said to both of them.

"We love you and want what's best," she reminded me,

and then gave me a weird look after her eyes scanned my outfit. "Excuse my French, but what the fuck are you wearing?"

"What?" I gazed down at my attire. Sure, it wasn't my typical tight black dress, but I'd had a long day, and she was lucky I put in the effort with my makeup. Eight a.m. classes tended to catch up to someone if they were used to staying out past midnight on weekdays, and I refused to nap.

"You look like you just got off a shift at Old Navy," said Jeremy. His facial expression of horror matched Nickie's.

"It's one outfit, not a whole personality change," I grumbled. We hadn't even entered the club yet, and they were already getting on my nerves. The feeling of jealousy subsided with each snide remark, and I was in no mood to deal with any of it.

"But that's just it, soon you'll change your hair, the music you like, and the next thing you know, you're a part of some tacky sorority where girls pose drinking from a wine bag, thinking it's trendy," Jeremy explained while he fiddled with his collar.

Little did they know, I was already drinking by myself, almost succumbing to my anxieties.

The line moved, and they followed suit, but I stepped aside. "I think I'm gonna go."

"What?" they shouted together.

But it wasn't their comments toward my outfit, it was the lack of excitement I usually experienced with them. Something was off, and whether I figured it out now or later, I couldn't stand here any longer.

The place where I once belonged was turning into a shitty memory.

"I think I need to be alone tonight," I announced.

"No, girl, come on! We were just kidding!" panicked Nickie.

"We only half meant the Old Navy comment," confessed Jeremy.

"I'm going to walk back to my place. I'll text you guys later," I said over my shoulder, escaping before it got ugly.

I could hear them both in the distance yelling at one another for whose fault it was for making me leave early. Hearing them hash it out on the busiest street in New York City was priceless. All eyes were on them, and at one point, someone yelled at them to shut up.

I let my feet carry me to a familiar location in my neighborhood, only two blocks from Electric Haze. The summer heat refused to let up, once again drenching my clothes that proceeded to cling to my already hot skin. The only parts of the city that didn't have excessive amounts of trash and random druggies in back alleys, the only time I felt somewhat safe walking home, were these two blocks.

I could go back, apologize for... honestly, nothing. It was only a few days into the college experience, I hadn't changed that drastically. They overreacted to the dumbest shit sometimes. I wondered why I stayed so long being friends with them. Well, Jeremy, yes... Nickie...

For now, I just needed the space to think.

I took extra time getting back home, wanting to bask in the crazy buzz of the city. All the smells of overly fried food, the occasional hot dog stand, and I could never forget the city performers that appeared randomly to put on a show until they harassed you for money.

I had no idea how to approach this society's bullshit. Heather still didn't know I had been invited, and part of me wanted to tell her the other night, but how did I come out and say it? It wasn't something to have a normal conversation about, let alone one I wanted to have, but it might help me understand why we were chosen, if she knew anything at all. And how would I go about telling her I found it under her bed, potentially snooping in her personal belongings?

My options were slim, just like my patience with Nickie and Jeremy.

A couple more blocks until I got home, and the idea sent a warm tingle through my body. Just the thought of being back in my bed, even for a couple of hours, the softness that would engulf me the minute I curled under the covers, was all I wanted and more.

A familiar scarlet fabric caught my attention.

From my home at the end of 77th Street, no taller than my five-foot-five stature, was a person cloaked with that same scarlet fabric. Striking against the hues of the city lights, I watched them hide in a nearby alleyway, unsuccessfully since I could see them clear as day. Or maybe I was utterly observant and nobody else gave a crap. Why would you try to be secretive but wear one of the most obvious colors?

A mystery I might never solve.

They kept turning their head as if they were watching out for someone or something, but I couldn't quite make it out from where I stood. Trying to get a better view, I dipped around a few cars that lined the city streets and inched closer. *If I could just see the person's figure, I might get a better glimpse of their actions.* The further I got, the harder it seemed this person was frantically checking down the alleyway. Then a soft whistle blew across the street, and the hooded figure's head snapped up, revealing Chloe.

The same girl who caught Kal and me in the janitor's closet.

Stay away from the elite. You have no business with us.

Her words began to bounce inside my head, and my heart hammered in my chest like a hummingbird.

What the hell is she doing out here? Is this what she meant about the 'elite?'

Suddenly, a tall figure walked across the street; a black hood covering their head, and they somehow avoided eye contact and strange stares from people. They wore dark, fitted, long-sleeved shirts with matching pants and black shoes. It looked like this person had a bow and arrow strapped across their chest. I was baffled how nobody thought it was strange that a random person walked around with a bow and arrow strapped to his chest, but then again, this was New York, and nothing seemed crazy in a city like this. Without warning, they gave a quick look back, stunning me as recognition dawned.

Josh.

A beautiful, chiseled face was cast from a nearby street lamp, eyes flashed stone-cold. He whispered something into Chloe's ear, lips urgent with each word leaving his mouth. Chloe shook her head vigorously, while Josh's hands gripped the strap around his chest, anger plastered to his face. More whispers were exchanged, almost like they were in a heated argument.

I needed to get closer.

Just as they reached each other in the comfort of the dark alley, I dashed through the traffic, hiding between cars and avoiding angry grunts from people trying to sneak through. Only a few more strides and I would be in perfect earshot of their conversation.

But I was too late.

Josh put a hand on her back and hurried her along in the dark alley, shifting his body in view to where I got a look at the front of his shirt. A large scarlet S was embroidered on the breast, standing against his dark attire. I'd seen it before, though I couldn't pinpoint where, but the design struck a familiar chord. Thankfully, he didn't see me and disappeared into the alley, letting the darkness swallow him.

I realized my breathing had become erratic, and I had to hold onto the side of the building to catch my breath. After the encounter with Nickie earlier, there was no way she'd believe what I saw.

Unfortunately, I couldn't follow them now, especially since I didn't know what they were doing or where they were going. *Do I even want to know?* I needed to get the heck out of there before they caught me. Oddly, they hadn't seen me, but I wouldn't stick around to change that. Chloe already made it clear I wasn't allowed to be around them, but that only fueled my curiosity after tonight.

Especially since this was clearly more than just a silly college society.

Dashing across the street, I ran as fast as possible to my house, hitting the button in the elevator to my floor repeatedly, getting more impatient by the second. Once it took me up, I quickly squeezed through the opening of the elevator doors and swiped the key card on our front door. The place seemed quiet, which meant my parents were out at some dinner function, and since Aiden was back in Hicksville for school, and Rose, our housekeeper, went home for the night, I had the whole place to myself.

Not taking any chances, I found my dad's stash of his most expensive whiskey. Thank heavens it wasn't a fresh bottle, and I grabbed the flask inside my purse. Careful not to spill, I filled it until it almost touched the top. Somehow, I needed to convince my dad to buy more stock so I could snag a whole bottle. Easier to refill, less likely to get caught.

Getting a bottle of water from the fridge, I trekked up to my bedroom, my feet dragging from exhaustion. From eight a.m. classes to useless social gatherings, my body was beaten. But my mind was far from tired.

My body collapsed on my neat bed. Everything seemed the same since I left it last week. Then again, why wouldn't it be? It had only been a week, yet it felt like a month.

I chugged the water, letting it slide down my throat, cooling me down from the adrenaline burst earlier.

What were Josh and Chloe doing, and why were they dressed like they were going on a secret ops mission? Not only did it come across as suspicious, but it made me question a few things about the school. Or was it part of the school? They both went, but could it be some outside activity? Some secret club? Or were they mentally insane and had made this into some weird kink? Shit, did that mean Josh was cheating on Nickie? But why wear a scarlet cape?

As those last words filled my head, my eyes wandered over to my desk, where a scarlet card still leaned against the trash can underneath.

Rose missed a piece of trash.

A vital piece of trash.

Placing the half-empty water bottle on my bedside table, I got down on all fours and crawled across my bedroom floor, reaching for the thick card. Turning it over in my shaky hands, that large scarlet S carved in the front sparked the familiarity of what I saw not five minutes ago.

My decision was made when I tucked the invitation into my back pocket.

CHAPTER 14

Before I entered Carman Hall, I moved the invitation inside my purse, making sure it stayed hidden. There was no going back now. I had made the decision on my way back to the dorms, and if shit hit the fan, at least I tried to save Heather and Nickie from whatever catastrophic damage was heading their way. If this society was dangerous and I succeeded in shutting it down, well, then maybe getting involved was the right thing to do after all.

Next time something like this happened, I needed to ignore all the signs and act oblivious. That way, it untied my hands.

I came back to find Heather and two other girls in our dorm room drinking cheap wine coolers—minus Heather— laughing about some lame math problem their professor assigned to them for the weekend. None of it made sense to me, and I had no intention of trying to understand; I was just happy she had a distraction.

I only wanted to get to bed.

All three had thick textbooks open to some complicated scribbles, and with the heaviest-looking calculators I'd ever come across, they typed away aggressively, trying to solve the equation.

"Remi, this is Colleen and Meghan," Heather introduced, interrupting my need to escape.

The girl in the pink shirt stretched her hand to me. "Colleen."

I took it gingerly. "Nice to meet you." Colleen's wrists were coated with silver bangles from Tiffany's. Her hands were well-manicured, and her palms were soft as silk. The gold-plated bracelets were a dead giveaway of her economic status, and she wasn't ashamed to flaunt whatever tax bracket her parents belonged to.

I prayed she wasn't stuck up, for Heather's sake.

"Meghan," the other girl said, her back leaning against the wall, sipping on a blue wine cooler. Her calm demeanor gave me the sense that she would rather be drunk at a party than sitting in a dorm room figuring out the square root of some outrageous number.

I waved sheepishly at her and returned to my side of the room. Rummaging through my desk drawer, I finally found some makeup wipes and erased tonight's pathetic attempt at a social hour from my face.

"Professor Toke has a crush on you, Heather," said Colleen.

"No, he doesn't!" she squeaked. My back turned to them; I could only imagine her face turning tomato red.

"Please, he can barely keep his eyes off you," Meghan added. "Is he young?" I chimed in, peeking over my shoulder.

"Very, and delicious," purred Meghan.

"No!" She covered her face with her hands, trying to hide her embarrassment.

"First week of school and you're already creating a scandal," I joked, tossing the used makeup wipe in the wastebasket under my desk.

"It's not like that," Heather mumbled into her hands.

"The man asks you every class to help him. It's definitely like that," snickered Meghan.

"Yeah, and when you do, my God, he makes it obvious," added Colleen.

"How so?" I asked, genuinely curious and surprisingly thankful for this odd distraction. I watched Heather's face sink when I interrogated her friends more.

"You're going to have to sneak in and see for yourself," said Meghan, downing the rest of her drink.

But Heather refused to meet anyone's eyes as tears welled in her own.

Shit. "Alright, well, I hate to ruin this little party but I have to be up early, so, out you both go," I announced.

Both girls apologized, afraid of me, and gathered their belongings, saying a goodnight to us on their way out.

"Thanks," she said sheepishly, pulling back her covers and fluffing her pillow.

"I didn't mean to put you on the spot like that," I said, doing the same.

"No, it's okay. Maybe they're right." Her voice sounded so fragile it bothered me.

Heather slipped off her socks and got under the covers, flicking her lamp off.

"Are they? Or are they making fun of the fact he just likes you as a student and they don't get the same attention?"

She sighed like my questions were annoying her. "I'd prefer we move on from this topic, if that's okay?"

"I'm sorry, Heather," I said sheepishly. *Shit.*

"Besides, the idea of someone of his caliber even giving me that kind of attention is laughable," she grumbled.

Usually, at that point, I would shut the hell up, but Heather pushed my nosiness to its peak. "Do you want him to?"

Silence stretched between us for several minutes. More than several minutes, because I could hear a light snore from her side of the room.

I guess I'll never know her answer.

CHAPTER 15

I had no desire to move from my bed. Not one ounce of strength seemed to be with me anyway, and I was okay with that. Heather had already showered, dressed, and was out the door before the first alarm went off. I was unsure if she wanted to avoid any embarrassment for being the teachers' pet or if she was one hundred percent mad at me for feeding into her friends' antics, but by the complete lack of communication that morning, I'd have guessed she wanted nothing more than to forget last night. I would have loved to, because I could move past it and toss it in the trash like it never happened. But other events continued their stay in my head.

The image of Josh and Chloe hiding within the shadows of the alleyway had me staring at the ceiling in deep thought. *If*, and that was one big *if*, they could potentially and clinically be insane and were running around the streets of New York City like they were part of some anime convention, I'd been looking at this all wrong.

I may be looking at this all wrong and wandering into forbidden territory.

After the freshmen breakfast, I knew they were a part of something. The negative energy had rolled off them as they all stood glaring me down like I was a nuisance to society.

I knew what I needed to do. The invitation was tucked inside one of my desk drawers, screaming at me to go. Stalling had been one of my talents since birth, and I did that often when it came to the inevitable.

Because the idea that something sinister could lurk in the shadows scared me the most.

If I went tonight and everything checked out, I could just slip out, and nobody would know of my absence. But how would I explain myself to Heather if she saw me? She was already pissed at me for last night; I didn't need another nail to my coffin.

I groaned and covered my face with one of the many designer pillows my mother had bought. Telling Heather now would be another blow, especially since I embarrassed her. Keeping this lie for so long only to reveal it before the big night, how could she ever trust me?

I could sneak in. Just peek inside, ensure everything seemed okay, and bounce before anyone noticed me. That way, my conscience was clear, and it would leave her none the wiser.

The real question that nagged at me was how the heck would I pull it off?

I couldn't waltz in there; I needed a well-thought-out plan to disguise myself and not get caught. Thankfully, the attire was all black, and I had a few pieces that would mesh well to match my incognito status.

I finally made the effort to get out of bed and trekked to

the little closet in the corner on my side of the room. Successfully finding black jeans and a shirt, the only thing I lacked was a hoodie to cover my striking blond hair. My mom seemed pretty good at packing the essentials, so I wondered if she'd packed a black hooded sweatshirt. Just as I found what I'd been looking for, it dawned on me that we weren't even close to winter yet and I pictured myself sweating profusely with it on. Scratching that idea, I came across a bag of old baseball caps toward the back of the closet. It was odd that my mother would move these for me here, let alone pack them, but I was thankful that she had. Grabbing the darkest shade of the bunch, I laid the outfit on my bed, viewing it from above.

This will have to do.

Folding the clothes and tucking them under my covers to hide my special ops attire, I gathered my bag of toiletries for a quick shower and decided to get ready to scope the church's layout.

Doing it in the daytime would be less suspicious, and it would be easy to see the access points of the building. Snapping some pictures might be a challenge, but playing off enjoying the scenery would most likely work in my favor. Besides, nobody was going to care about some random chick taking pictures of a church.

I braided my hair away from my face, thinking there was a possibility that Heather could've been in danger. But what kind of danger would there be on a college campus? Josh was adamant about breaking curfew, but how convenient he'd arrived while I chased after the mystery scarlet-cloaked figure. Stupid, good-looking son of a bitch he was. Why did Nickie have to pick him?

So much for relaxing my mind with the shower.

Brushing aside the negative thoughts, I went outside into the warm, sticky air. Students were enjoying the weekend, some sprawled out on the lawn soaking in the sun, others retreating under trees for shade.

With a sports water bottle in one hand and my phone in the other, I traveled down the college walk, heading toward the cathedral, nodding and giving small hellos to my classmates.

It seemed awfully quiet on 114th St. as I pressed the button for the crosswalk while resisting the urge to jaywalk and bolt across. Eventually, the lights turned red, and I was signaled to make way across the street, deciding to play up my facade and run across like I was training to join the track team. Pretending to check my pulse, I leaned on one of the lampposts and stretched out my legs while staring up at the behemoth of a building.

The Cathedral of St. John the Divine sat in all its glory, holy and preserved for only the lovers of the Lord himself. Its structure was intimidating, its peaks higher than the trees surrounding its perimeter. Gray stone made up the entire building, only stunning stained glass occupying the center. Rotating my shoulders and neck like I just ran miles to get here, I stepped forward until I reached the stairs. Hands on my hips, I pretended to breathe heavily as a couple walked past me, giving a small smile.

Nothing compared to the giant rose on the stained glass window in the center. I could imagine the colors cascading through the building once the sun hit, filling the church with a multitude of reds that any artist would envy. Now that I had a simple front layout, I observed the building up close to determine if any other doors were behind the main one, while nonchalantly taking photos, making it seem I was merely interested in the structure rather than possible hidden passageways. Thankful for not finding a no trespassing sign, I was about to go investigate the grounds when I found the front door slightly ajar. I took it as a sign to enter. Maybe being inside would serve better than just walking around aimlessly, hoping to find a crack somewhere.

A blast of frigid air chilled my arms, the AC circulating the Cathedral, keeping the heat at bay. Pews on either side were empty, and my footsteps creaked under the carpeted aisle.

The smell of incense lingered as I made my way to the front, only my footsteps echoing in the open space. The ceiling, higher than any tree inside Central Park, gave the space an eerie atmosphere. It felt too quiet. Making my way to the front, I stopped just before the dais, where a dark wooden podium stood. Behind the podium sat a long marble table adorned with gold cups and a pitcher, with a cross the size of my head in the center.

Because I couldn't help myself, I made my way over, about to touch the gold, intricate design, when a throat cleared behind me.

I jumped, shrieking in fright.

"I'm sorry, Miss. I wasn't expecting company this early in the morning."

Placing a hand over my pounding heart, I turned to find a man, probably in his late fifties, dressed in a cream robe, holding a brown, leather-bound book. "No, it's okay. I just wasn't expecting there to be anyone here either."

He smiled, the wrinkles around his eyes expanding, his

gray hair styled to one side. "I'm Father Benedict. Are you here for something?"

I looked around, noting it was just the two of us. "Uh..."

"Perhaps, maybe, a seat in one of the pews for alone time is all you needed?" He gestured to the many behind us.

Did he believe I was here to pray in silence? His genuine offer took me by surprise. "No, I just saw the door open and was always curious about what it looked like inside. Thank you, I'll be going now."

Walking past him, he gave me a simple pleasantry. "Have a wonderful day."

"You as well," I called back.

"Let the Lord guide you on your travels."

HEATHER WAS NOWHERE to be found when I returned. I waited, and even searched for her, but not a single ounce of evidence led me to where she could be. Her 'posse' of math nerds was clueless about her whereabouts, and she hadn't answered one of my texts. Notifying campus police was an option, but upon arrival at their office, they were dealing with a group of girls bitching about one of the seniors breaking their floor's vending machine. I didn't have the patience to stick around.

The only thing I could do was hope she would show up tonight at the induction.

Anxiety crept in like an unbearable chill as I dressed; even the summer breeze rolling through the window wasn't enough to dampen the feeling. The more I reviewed the plan, the more anxious I became. Induction started at eight; I would arrive after it began while everyone involved was distracted. Get in the side entrance, make sure nothing appeared fishy, and get Heather—if she was there—out, then leave through the rear before anyone caught on. Simple, really, yet I found myself second-guessing every step. Maybe because I knew the whole idea seemed like utter garbage. But I'd spent hours studying all the photos I'd taken, drawing lines of where I could go and escape— marking x's over dead ends and false exits. Saturday night and zero church service.

It should be easy.

One last look in the cloudy dorm mirror, and I double-checked the time, swallowing the anxiety back down where it came from.

Now or never.

Shutting the lights off and locking the door, every step toward the cathedral felt heavy, as if the weight of what I was about to do would consume me before I could get the chance. I wouldn't be in this predicament if I had just told Heather the truth. Instead, I'd lied and avoided the conversation altogether, and now there I was, sneaking into the goddamn church, making sure no sacrifices were being made. To ensure she was safe, regardless of how mad she was at me. *Here's to hoping she skipped out.*

What a pathetic way to spend a Saturday night.

It was a surprise to find fewer students than average walking around campus, and even more of a surprise to find nobody near the cathedral. All the windows were black, indicating the main floor was closed. Wouldn't there be a welcome party? Was I too late? Was it canceled? Not a speck of light illuminated the gorgeous building. The very peaks of its structure looked down upon the campus as if it were judging everyone who dared to walk by. In the morning light, it appeared less intimidating, welcoming almost. But the night sky gave it a haunted mood, blackening the land around it like an eerie graveyard.

I never wanted to turn and run so badly in my life.

But I had to keep going. I had to know the truth.

The light at 114th street took longer than usual to turn, and with every passing second, I grew more unsure of going inside. I pulled at my dark shirt, trying to air out my already sweaty body. Black was such a bad idea.

A deep, shaky breath later, I slid right through the entrance, tiptoeing down a carpeted hall. The silence was deafening, and one wrong move could set off more than just the alarm. The cathedral was exactly how it had been this morning. Empty. If a pin dropped, it would not have gone unnoticed.

Another set of doors was at the end, but they were wide open this time. Inside, the cathedral's center was pitch black; I had to be extra careful about where I stepped.

I inched my way down the center aisle, brushing my hand against the pews as I trekked by, guiding me through the darkness. The path before me, uncertain as it would seem, stayed the same as I continued along. I knew eventually I would hit the dais and then the wooden podium, but it was the marble table I was worried about. Trying not to collide with it was another challenge, when a thick cloth covered my mouth and nose, muffling my screams. Strong hands circled my waist, forcing my body to remain still. I tried to fight against their hold, but I became unsteady on my feet. More hands gripped me, dragging me backward as my body became limp. I could feel my mind slipping as they began to drag my body. Whatever chemical they used on the cloth was enough to snuff out all my senses.

That was when everything went black.

CHAPTER 16

I awoke sitting in a chair, a piece of cloth obstructing my vision. The smell of sage filled the air, and the shuffling of shoes echoed not too far from where I sat. I tugged one of my arms, testing the tightness of the rope and found it barely budged from the force. Panic rose in my throat as I tried to free the restraints. The more I fought against the bonds, the more my skin burned from the rope. *Shit, shit, shit.* This was it. I was going to die, and all of this was for nothing. I pulled until I began to rock back and forth, praying I could at least snap one of the stupid legs..

"We will release the rope once you calm down," someone said.

"Fuck you," I spat, pulling harder on the rope. My wrist rubbed against the material, hissing with each tug.

"She's more resilient than we thought," another voice chimed in.

A small hand rested on my shoulder. "We are not here to harm you."

"Then why did you drug me and tie me up?"

Someone sighed heavily to my right. "Forgive us if we thought you were trying to break in."

"Or steal."

"So, your first thought was to drug me? How the hell is that okay?" I snapped.

"She has a point," A deep tenor spoke up. *So... familiar.*

So many voices sounded like they were coming from every direction. "Can I at least get this stupid thing off my face?"

"I see no harm in that."

Hands untied the knot from the blindfold, and my eyes landed on three figures watching me blink several times, until I recognized a familiar man in the corner. "I knew it."

"Shit. Get the rope off her now," he commanded.

Two girls in scarlet capes untied my hands and feet from their binds. Massaging my wrists, I observed the small room they crammed themselves inside. Josh wore that familiar S on his right breast, the same bow and arrow strapped to his back. I looked down at my arms to find red patches of irritation forming.

"Why am I not surprised you're behind this?" I sneered.

Josh knelt before me, forcing me to look at him. Eyes of the bluest water stared right into my soul.

"If I knew it was you breaking in, I would've escorted you out myself," Josh said.

I swallowed hard, the invitation burning in my back pocket. I reached for it, feeling its edges on my fingertips. "The door was open. Am I not allowed to be here?"

"Not without an invitation, and since you snuck in, I assume you don't have one," said one of the girls in a scarlet cape.

A smug look on her face made it much more entertaining when I revealed the invitation. "You mean this one?" I held up the pretty card, flashing it in her face.

She snatched it before I had a second to register what had happened. "Impossible."

Josh uncrossed his arms and peeked over the girl's shoulder, his eyes following the words on the back. "What do you know, Zo. An invitation."

Annoyance crossed her face. "Well, Ms. Remi Watson. What were you doing sneaking in like that?"

"I wasn't sure if it was still happening," I fibbed.

"Did you not get the time change?" the other one asked.

"No," I lied.

"She's here now. Let's join the others." Another male appeared from the shadows. My heart stopped at the sight of his face.

Kal.

He wore the same outfit as Josh, with a matching bow and arrow strapped to his back. That stupid scarlet S was stitched in the same spot.

My fists curled, shaking at my sides. It had to be him, the one person I couldn't trust.

"You," I whispered, my voice laced with rage. The last time we spoke was when he basically said I should finish trying to fuck him because *I* started it.

All eyes were on Kal. He seemed unaffected by the fury I projected at him.

"The introduction is about to begin. Come, let's join the others." He held his hand out for me to take.

Everyone else left the room but Josh, who lingered by the door.

"Why? So, you can make *me* finish what *I* started?" I hissed.

Kal's face fell. "I didn't mean for it to come out like that."

Josh stood straight, his eyes darting back and forth between us. "What's going on?"

Kal ignored him and took another step toward me, a hand outstretched. "Please, Remi."

"No. I'm not leaving with you," I snapped, stepping back.

Josh pivoted so he was now blocking me from Kal. "What did you say to her?"

Kal's jaw flexed, his nostrils expanding. "For once, Josh, this doesn't concern you."

"Actually, it does," he sniped. His arm extended to secure me behind his back.

"Remi and I..." Kal rolled his neck as if he were trying to hold back from getting physical. I wouldn't lie and say that didn't scare the absolute shit out of me. "We had a moment outside Electric Haze after our gig, alright?"

Josh peered down at me. "With him?" Disbelief coated his words like he couldn't believe I let him touch.

As much chagrin as that one look gave me, now was not the time to revisit my past mistakes. And I'd be damned if these two clowns distracted me from the true reason I came here in the first place.

"Where's Heather?"

Kal leaned to the left so his eyes caught mine. "At the ceremony, which we should be going to now."

Josh crossed his arms, once again obstructing my view of Kal. "Only you, Kal, would find an excuse not to face your terrible actions."

"Assuming makes an ass out of you and me," Kal retorted.

I don't have time for this right now. "As much as I enjoy

this banter between you two fools, I need to find my room-mate, so if you'll excuse me—"

Josh stopped me mid-step. "You have no idea where you're going. Let *me* guide you." The emphasis on 'me' made it pretty clear that Kal wasn't allowed to come anywhere near us on our little adventure through the cathedral.

Without taking his eyes off me, Josh signaled for Kal to move along. I'd never seen Kal so furious when he breathed a rough sigh and slammed the door behind him, shaking the hinges in his wake. Relief from the absence of him released the tension from my shoulders.

"Remi, promise me something." My eyes wandered up to those baby blues, dazzling under the ceiling lights. He was too close; way too fucking close. His breath, a delicious peppermint, caused my mouth to water for such forbidden feelings. I desperately wanted something to hold on to, just to keep my wits about me. "Yes?"

"Don't ever find yourself alone with that man again. I don't give a shit if he's a part of the society. I don't trust him alone with anyone, especially you."

"I think after what I just witnessed, the likelihood of that happening again is slim to none."

His eyes lingered a little too long on my lips as he wet his own with that fucking tongue. "Good, because I don't think I can hold back from crushing his fucking skull."

I cocked an eyebrow. "Violent, aren't we?"

"For you, *yes*."

CHAPTER 17

I blinked a few times, trying to register the words that just came from that glorious mouth. "For me?"

"Nickie would kill me herself if I let anything bad happen to you." His words were a giant slap in the face, enough for me to regain common sense. How stupid was I to entertain the idea of him feeling anything toward me?

I nodded, internally embarrassed by his false declaration. "Right." Then another thought occurred. "Speaking of Nickie—"

"Not now, we have to get to the ceremony." *Not now? Or not ever? She must know, right?*

Josh didn't waste another second as he led the way. I stepped past the threshold to find myself in a well-lit hallway with a deep, rich-blue carpet and walls made of beige marble.

Josh had me follow him out the door at the end of the hall to reveal a spiral staircase descending to God knows where. I hesitated at the top step, looking over the railing to see others dressed in scarlet capes, some in white. A few males escorted a white-caped lady at the bottom, the identical bows and arrows strapped to their backs.

We eventually followed the small group, and we ended up in front of a wide, open room with intricate designs of stained glass covering one whole wall. Swirls of blues and greens sparkled under the fluorescent lights, the colors dancing on every surface. Its design had been replicated to match the cathedral's main floor, minus the high ceiling. Shorter pews sat along the aisle, one side dedicated to those dressed in scarlet, the other were the males in all black.

I immediately recognized Chloe and Anna from past encounters. The two men dressed like Josh and Kal sat to the right, and then there was the group sporting long, white capes behind the dais. From what I could see, six sat directly behind a man dressed in a black robe with scarlet swirls of gems starting from the arms until it spread like twisted vines on the front. It was the priest from earlier, Father Benedict.

"Glad you finally decided to join us, Remi," he said.

"Forgive us, Father," murmured Josh, bowing to the man before taking his seat with the rest of them.

Father Benedict gave a nod of acknowledgment. "It is now time for the induction. Collin, please let the others in."

Collin, who wore an identical robe to him, appeared with a group of six girls, leading them to the center of the room. One of them was Heather, but nothing surprised me more than her friends, Colleen and Meghan. They lined up next to Father Benedict, looking out into the crowd as if they were all proud to be there.

That flipped my stomach several times.

"Come here, Remi," adjured Father Benedict.

Heather locked eyes with me, waiting to see if I would

join them. I had never seen her so stone cold. She had become someone I barely recognized.

"I'll pass," I managed to say.

Josh stifled a laugh, while others simultaneously turned to gawk.

"Forgive me for having you here; I assumed you accepted our invitation," Father said.

"She is here and will participate," said one of the white capes. Her long silver hair peeked through the hood.

I crossed my arms in protest. "Excuse me?"

"The Lord has let you enter; you shall participate. It is the will of his doing."

Another situation I wasn't prepared for, and with Josh nearby, who could easily carry my ass up the steps to the altar, I had no choice but to continue with their little charade.

I forced a smile as I awkwardly made my way to the line of the other females. Everyone stood proudly, facing the rest of the room.

Father Benedict smiled like he had just won the lottery, walking gracefully as he spoke. "Tonight, only the purest will be chosen to follow our lead in the Lord's path of redemption. Tonight, we will witness the Lord's work once again."

Everyone bowed their heads, including the inductees, minus myself, as I glanced around the room, trying to discover hidden exits or possible weapons to use in self-defense in case things got ugly.

"But first, we must purify our souls to fulfill our duty."

The men in the front disappeared, only to return with buckets, placing them at our feet, filled to the brim with water. Next, they positioned chairs behind each of us, instructing us to sit down.

"We walk this earth leaving a carbon print. To begin the purification, one must place their feet in the blessed water. If the water turns black, the Lord has decided to release you from your duty," explained Father Benedict.

Right on cue, the others removed their shoes and socks, placing their feet in the water as it splashed over the floor. I sat there, unsure if they had filled it with poison.

"It would be in your best interest, Ms. Watson, to follow the steps for the purification," said one female in a white cape.

I gritted my teeth and followed the others, surprised to find the water warm. Everyone continued to observe as we soaked our feet, waiting to see what might happen.

Father Benedict leaned over one of the girls, eyeing the bucket where her feet were submerged. "Your water has turned black, Amelia. I am afraid the Lord has chosen to relieve you."

Sadness swept across her face as one of the men removed the bucket, her feet dripping with black water. She gathered her belongings and exited the room.

My stomach twisted in the tightest knot. *What the fuck is going on here?*

Father Benedict continued down the line, peeking over each shoulder to examine the water, stopping once again at the pretty brunette two seats away from me. "Unfortunately for you, Colleen, the Lord has chosen the same fate."

Like the girl before, a look of disappointment twisted her delicate features, and she exited the room with her belongings.

I gazed down at my own feet in the water. Not a single

trace of black could be found when Father Benedict approached.

Was that a good or bad thing for me?

"The first trial is complete," he announced.

So far, Heather and I, her meek friend Meghan, and a couple of the other girls had made it through. The rest of the room watched with such intensity—especially Josh. Anxiety hit my nervous system, my hands shook, my legs unsteady.

Father Benedict placed a hand on my shoulder. "Our hands symbolize strength and power. It is with our hands that the Lord guides us to salvation."

Our buckets of water were replaced with a long table rising from the floor, holding silver bowls with more water. I could only guess what he was looking for.

"Just like our feet, we must purify our hands. Ladies, please proceed."

I watched the others dip their hands delicately into the silver bowls. My slight hesitation was enough for one of the members dressed in white to grunt a warning, pushing me to take part in the next act of the purification ceremony.

Grinding my teeth to hold back a snarky remark, I took a deep breath and proceeded. The water was cool as I submerged both my hands, watching for any sign of the water of black swirls. Mine never did.

"My dear, sweet, Meghan. Unfortunately, the Lord has relieved you of your duty," announced Father Benedict, patting her back with sympathy.

A quick drying of her hands, and she was escorted from the room without looking back. Three girls remained, including Heather and me. I began to sweat, my anxiety coming out from the shadows to destroy me, cursing myself for not stashing my flask somewhere on my person.

"But the rest of you have clear water. It is now time for the third and final cleanse."

Once again, the men had removed the silver bowls and long table, only to place them behind our chairs instead. A new set of silver bowls was added—more significant than the hand bowls—to then have us stand to turn our chairs around so the back was to the front.

Father Benedict took one long stride to stand behind us, observing the table. "The mind can be swayed if tainted by those of a negative nature. The Lord has granted us one final chance to cleanse our senses from the doings of others. Ladies, please lean back into the water."

Heather and the other remaining two gently leaned back, their hair soaking in the blessed water while I sat, a baseball cap hiding my blonde locks. If my water turned black and Heather's remained clear, I would have no issue dragging her out. And I wouldn't hesitate to kick and scream in the process.

"Remi," called Father Benedict.

"Right," I said, taking off my cap and tossing it aside. With one last look at the crowd before me, I leaned back into the water, my scalp embracing the warmth.

"Kennedy, my dear." Without another word, she sprang back in her seat and left the room, the sound of water dripping from her hair on the marble floors.

"Tiffany." A sad sigh echoed through the quiet space, then a door slammed.

So, Heather and I had been chosen.

"Excellent, ladies! You have completed all three steps of purification!" declared Father Benedict.

The crowd clapped in unison; no smiles touched their mouths.

"Now, we shall have you both dry off and enjoy the supper we have prepared for everyone."

I felt a small hand touch my own. "Remi?"

Heather. Water dripped down from her forehead, and pure happiness radiated from her body.

"Heather." It occurred to me then; Heather's participation was willing from the start. I'd never seen her so happy and at peace with what just transpired, and that had me thinking, what the fuck was I still doing here?

She pulled me to my feet, our hair dripping on the marble floor. Finding my baseball cap, I laced up my shoes after drying off my feet with one of the softest towels I'd ever felt in my life.

Josh nodded in my direction before guiding us to another room. What surprised me was the number of rooms the basement of the cathedral held. With doors left and right, I was unsure where any of them led, yet the mystery left me a little curious to find out.

Inside, a long white table covered in a variety of fruits and meats made my stomach rumble in hunger. Glasses of red wine glistened under the lights, while a violinist sat in the corner, playing a beautiful tune. The white capes—some female, some male—sat at a separate table, eating silently. Father Benedict was seated at the head of the long table, motioning for us to join. Heather and I chose chairs next to the scarlet capes, while the men in their prestige uniforms shuffled to the opposite side.

Heather began to pile her plate with fruit, roasted vegetables, and a piece of steak. The food looked more delicious than what they served at the school, and that was saying a lot because they didn't skimp on anything.

But it was her sheer ease that made my stomach upset.

How easily she dismissed what happened, like how do you explain water turning black? Magic? There was no way, yet she was unharmed beside me, feasting as if it were her last supper.

"Remi?" Josh said. I hadn't realized he sat across from my place at the table.

"Yeah, sorry. Just a little... surprised," I confessed.

Kal had finally joined the supper, only to sit as far away from our little group as possible. Thank God.

I looked back over at Josh to find him handing me a plate filled with different meats and sides.

Heather topped it off with a garnish before pouring a hearty glass of red wine. "Eat, please."

"The food is excellent and you're missing out just sitting there with a frown on your face." Josh scooped up a spoonful of veggie mix and devoured it in one mouthful.

I aggressively stabbed some baby carrots. "Happy?"

He raised an eyebrow and took a sip of the wine. "Ecstatic."

"If I knew sooner of your acceptance, Remi, I wouldn't have been so secretive around you," said Heather, drawing my attention away from Mr. Pain in the Ass.

Nibbling on the baby carrot, I eyed her from the side. "Yeah, I didn't realize it was a secret."

The entire table fell silent. A clear sign they were all eavesdropping.

I caught Chloe's stare, her words floating back to me for a second time. *Stay away from the elite. You have no business with us.*

I guess I'm one of them now.

"There is a lot to discuss after tonight, but for now,

ladies, we will feast in honor of your successful cleansing," said Father Benedict, raising a wine glass.

Others followed suit, but Chloe remained fixated on me. I squirmed under her stare and turned my attention back to Heather and Josh, thankful for their distraction. We chatted as if what had happened before was a distant memory, which made swallowing the food a bit easier. The white capes never looked up from their meal, and after finishing before us, they exited the room without glancing in our direction.

Josh must've been following my gaze and said, "Those are the Aces. The head of this Order."

"The Aces?" I asked.

"Only a select few from the Scarlets and the Tutelary Saints are chosen to guide the others after they've served a certain number of years in the Order," explained Josh.

I dropped my utensils and leaned forward. "What and what?"

A light chuckle came from Heather's left. "Josh thinks he's the master of everything in the Order."

"Fuck off, Baron." Josh threw a dinner roll at him, but he caught it with ease. Baron had a familiarity about him; I couldn't quite put my finger on it.

"Sensitive, are we?" he teased. His dark hair fanned his brows, those bright hazel eyes filled with humor, right down to his dark, flawless complexion. He was quite mesmerizing to look at. Jeremy would find him delectable. Which reminded me...

"Does Nickie know?" I asked Josh, ignoring Baron.

His hand was frozen mid-air with a piece of steak stuck to the fork. "No."

"Who's Nickie?" asked Heather.

"His lover," snickered Baron.

Josh's eyes turned into dangerous slits. "Mind your business." His words were filled with venom.

"Well?" I edged.

"Well, what? Our relationship isn't up for discussion."

So, it's a relationship now. "She's my best friend," I stated. Irritation trickled in. If what I'd become a part of was dangerous, there was no way in hell Nickie would be involved, regardless of us not speaking. I still cared for her safety.

"I'm well aware of the status you share, but unfortunately, that does not extend to *us.*" He took another sip of wine, glaring at me over the glass.

"I don't want my best friend involved."

"She won't be."

"I don't trust you."

Baron whistled. "Jeesh, you could cut the tension with a knife over here."

Heather went back and forth, waiting for one of us to speak. "I would be careful of Remi. She looks like she's ready to cut Josh instead."

"My money is on Josh. He's not afraid to get his hands dirty," commented Baron.

Heather shook her head, laughing. "Remi has claws. I would be extra careful."

The tapping of glass caught our attention, a relieved look on Josh's face at the interruption. But if he thought I would forget this little conversation, he was sadly mistaken.

"It is time for Heather and Remi to be inducted. The Blessing awaits," announced Father Benedict.

Confused, I looked over at Heather. "I thought the purification ceremony was it?"

She shook her head. "No, there's one more step. Didn't your family prepare you for this?"

Before I could respond, Chloe came to where we sat. "Follow me so you can change."

"Into what?" She ignored my question and started to walk in the opposite direction. *All right.*

Heather shrugged and rose from her chair. The others watched as I remained seated, unsure if this part of the induction was safe. I'd made it this far without bumps or bruises, and although the purification ceremony still didn't make sense to me, what did I really have to lose? Besides a more open social schedule.

"Let's go, you two. We don't have all night," called Chloe.

Not waiting for our response, she motioned for us to follow to a side bathroom off the dining room. Stainless steel stalls and white porcelain sinks occupied the space, with gray paint on the walls—zilch décor but a few mirrors to force you to look at your crappy reflection. I saw two girls with soaked hair about to be inducted into a society nobody knew about, and one of them looked terrified.

CHAPTER 18

To the right of the sinks were folded white gowns, along with white flats. I handed Heather a pair and chose the last stall, stripping off my half-soaked shirt and pants and kicking them to the side of the bathroom stall. The white pants and shirt hugged my body nicely; kudos to them for guessing my size right.

"Heather? You're first."

I poked my head out of the stall and saw Heather do the same. It had been Chloe calling out to her.

"Really?" she asked, looking over at me in confusion.

"Yes. Remi, you will wait back in the dining hall," she instructed with an attitude.

"We're not going together? Why?" I questioned.

"Would you like to go first?" she snapped, clearly annoyed with my constant questions.

I stepped forward, a plan already forming in my head. "Yeah, I just need a few minutes."

Chloe's eyes squinted in suspicion. "For what?"

142

I shrugged. "Oh, I don't know, to breathe? Maybe take a piss?"

She rolled her eyes then. "You get two, that's it. Otherwise, I'm dragging you both out by your hair," she warned before shutting the bathroom door.

I rushed over and locked it. I didn't know how long we had until she realized what I'd done, but it would have to be enough. "Heather, what the fuck is going on?"

She adjusted her long sleeves, confusion on her face as she said, "What do you mean? This is exactly how it's supposed to go."

I shook my head in disbelief. "Okay, did you not witness the same shit I did during the purification ceremony? The water turning black? That's not normal."

She balanced on one foot while slipping on one of the white flats. "Yeah, and thank God ours didn't."

"Do you hear yourself?" Was I the only one thinking rationally here?

"You're acting like you had no idea this was coming. Remi, it's clear we were placed together in the dorms for a reason. Our families' lineage is the reason we are here *right now*."

I backpedaled. "Wait, what does my family have to do with any of this?"

Heather turned to fix her hair in the mirror. "The lineage of the Scarlets. It belongs to certain bloodlines." She finished taming the frizz in her hair before circling back to me. "Are you sure your family didn't tell you?"

I leaned against the counter, trying to recall anything of my family history. Besides Grams' side originating from Scotland and my dad's side from Canada, nothing came up about Scarlets. Hell, Grams barely acknowledged her family history, stated that they all became nomads and hid in the mountains. My mother refused to even have the subject brought up because of her own shitty relationship with Grams. For as long as I'd been alive, they never saw eye to eye on anything, especially my upbringing.

"Heather, I swear, I have no idea—"

The doorknob jiggled, and then it shook. "Open the door, now!" Chloe commanded from the other side.

Shit. I unlocked the door, and a pissed-off Chloe appeared, tapping her foot impatiently. "You're holding everyone up."

I elbowed past her piss-poor attitude. "Sorry if I just need some time for myself."

Chloe sidestepped me until we were nose to nose. "You should be grateful the Lord has chosen you to proceed. If you continue to act like a spoiled brat, I won't hesitate to throw you on your ass. Got it? Now, let's go."

About to swing at her face, Heather held me back by the arm. "The Blessing is the final step. After this, there is no going back."

Looking over my shoulder, I shook out of her hold. "What are you saying?"

"I'm saying, you won't be the same once you begin. Everything will change after this." Her eyes almost looked sad, as if she were telling me a silent goodbye.

Chloe huffed in frustration. "Well, are we going or not?"

I gave her a light squeeze on her shoulder, not totally prepared for the unknown. "I'll see you on the other side."

"See you," she said, returning the gesture.

I followed Chloe past the dining hall, back into the vacant hallway and up the winding staircase again. Then I realized I was returning to the same room I had awoken from.

Only, they added a stainless steel table in the dead center of a half-empty room, where a spotlight hung from the ceiling, swaying softly. My heart began to pound heavily when I noticed the steel handcuffs, two at the top, two at the bottom.

All around, they stood, masked by their white capes, circling the table, watching and waiting for something to happen. I stood on the outskirts, Kal a few steps to my right, watching the table as well. Chloe walked to her spot within the circle, right next to Josh. His jaw flexed, but he never looked my way.

Father Benedict stepped forward, away from the crowd, and caressed the steel table, mumbling a prayer before turning to me, beckoning me to come to him. My feet remained glued to the floor, my fight or flight ready to kick in.

Something didn't feel right.

Back and forth, from Father Benedict to the empty table, I knew this was a terrible idea, and I needed a way out, fast.

"Come, Remi. Your blessing awaits," announced Father Benedict.

"I'm good, thank you," I said. The sweat from my pores dripped down my back with each passing second where I stood by the door. If I could just create the right distraction—

One of the white capes stepped forward. "The Lord has chosen you to proceed with the Blessing, Remi. Consider this a gift."

I scuffled back, only to be barricaded by the others, and one pushed me forward, where I stumbled back to where I originally stood. "I thought it was finished. I passed all the purifications. What is this?"

"Do not question. Just accept."

Every pair of eyes observed my awaiting decision. If I ran now, would I make it? Would anyone try to stop me? My hesitation was enough for a couple of solid hands to drag me out from the back, my feet skidding along the floors in protest.

"Please, no, this isn't necessary," I interjected, trying with all my might to break free.

A glimpse of Josh's stone-cold demeanor while the others surrounded the table scared me for what unknown awaited.

I now understood what Heather's silent goodbye meant.

I might not make it out alive.

The harder I fought, the harder they tugged, until I was mere inches from the table and Father Benedict. His smile was bright and inviting, never touching his eyes as he patted the steel table, instructing me to lie down.

"No! NO! PLEASE!" I screamed.

Hands all over hoisted me onto the table as I continued to scream in terror. Steel cuffs held down every limb I tried to thrash around. For a split second, I caught a glimpse of Josh, emotion vacant in his eyes. I screamed even louder, trying to break free from the binds.

"PLEASE LET ME GO!" I pleaded, trying my best to break free from their rough hands.

Father Benedict approached the table, a needle in hand. "Let the Lord guide you through this trial, Remi." He gave a couple of flicks to the syringe as he reached for my arm. A soft chant began to form around the table I was strapped to.

"NO! STOP! PLEASE! GET AWAY FROM ME!" Tears

escaped my eyes, falling down my cheeks as I struggled to escape this nightmare.

The chants grew louder when the needle penetrated my skin. I shouted in fear, certain that he had injected me with some toxin and would use my body for some twisted sacrifice.

Whatever had been in that syringe ran through my bloodstream in record time. My skin burned until my insides ignited that same flame, licking every part until it consumed my entire being. Eyelids painted with sleep, I tried to fight against the comfort of it, knowing if I shut off the world too soon, I might never escape.

"She's fighting the dose," someone said.

"It won't be long until she succumbs," Father Benedict said.

"And if she doesn't?"

I wanted to move, to find who was speaking, but my head felt heavy. My arms and legs had become phantom limbs. Drifting like a boat out at sea, a giant wave came, casting me overboard. I let the current take me under, washing the fear with it.

"It will be the Lord's plan."

CHAPTER 19

I was floating like a feather, cascading down from the sky into a pool of diamond light. Warm air hugged the Earth, comforting its craters, mountains, and vast lands, blanketing the world with protection, saving whatever was left from evil. An evil that had ripped through every inch and surface of remaining peace that now rested in the hands of someone who took refuge in the clouds—time looped in endless circles, waiting for the circuit to break. To break free from the leather cuffs and the fire suffocating the lands. Until there was nothing left but smoke and ash.

My body rose from the debris, followed by buds of flowers growing with me. They began to bloom, from red tulips, daisies, and lilacs to morning glories of vibrant shades of reds, yellows, and oranges. The sky above was the bluest I'd ever seen; no cloud disrupted its beauty. The heat from the sun's rays warmed my skin as I walked barefoot through the soft, green grass. Each blade tickled my toes and kept my balance steady. I wore a white sundress; it clung to my skin protectively like a suit of armor. My hair fell in loose curls on my back, a delicate breeze escaping a few strands from behind my ear, dancing in the wind. I continued to walk through the open field, with no real destination but to wallow in the senses of what was around me.

Closing my eyes to feel the warmth on my eyelids, I trekked in silence, breathing in the scents of freshly cut grass and newly bloomed flowers. The air never smelled so clean and calming. I was afraid to open my eyes to find all of it gone. For just a few moments of bliss without the chaotic life waiting for me whenever this place decided to kick me out.

I wandered ahead with my eyes closed for a long time, using my other senses to bask in the peaceful sounds and floral smells. Paradise. That was precisely what the place reminded me of.

An endless trip of eternal bliss, sun, beautiful flowers, and the bluest sky. Then my feet began to touch the pavement, a surprise that had me open my eyes to a giant white oak looming over where I stood. The leaves barely made a sound from the timid wind. A white bench made from a birch tree was perfectly stationed just underneath, on which sat a woman so otherworldly, any model would envy her looks. Her skin glowed in the sunlight, almost luminescent. Her hair, a brilliant shade of red, tumbled down and around her shoulders. She wore a similar white dress and a pair of light brown sandals as she rested casually on the bench.

At first, I didn't think she was aware of my presence, as she continued to look ahead as I approached, but a smile slowly crept upon her full lips, indicating she very well knew.

"Remi, please come sit," she instructed kindly. Her voice sounded like a thousand angels singing in a choir at Sunday service. A sound I hadn't heard since my grams brought me as a little girl. It took my breath away.

I followed her instructions silently, afraid to shatter the moment with my average voice. Her hands rested on her knees as we stared straight ahead, watching the flowers sway in the breeze. The absence of fear resonated deep within my bones while sharing a bench with this stranger.

"I've been waiting for you," she finally said.

I peered slightly to my left, watching her intently, and said, "You have?"

She nodded once, the smile never faltering. "Yes, my child. Your path had been chosen before your birth. Regardless of how far you strayed, I ensured certain obstacles put you back."

"I don't understand. Am I dead?" If it were true, I wished Grams had greeted me at the pearly gates.

"Not dead, but reborn." Her smile never faltered.

Looking around once more, I noticed a marble structure in the distance.

"Remi?"

"It's just... I thought I would see my grams here."

"I'm sorry, my child. She is not allowed to be here."

A strange wave of emotion came over me, prickling my skin with tiny goosebumps. If Grams were exiled from whatever this place was, could it mean she ended up in... hell?

She touched my cheek, her palm feeling the finest silk as she looked into my eyes. "I've shown you the beginning."

Her unexpected change in subject brought more questions than answers. "I'm sorry... I don't understand."

It was the first time since arriving at the beautifully carved bench that she truly looked at me, wearing the brightest smile. Lush green eyes swirled in the sunlight, her complexion flawless, like her presence. Freckles kissed her nose and cheeks. She was the epitome of holy, a rare purity that became somewhat blinding, but her hair, the color of fire, was familiar to me, yet I could not recall why.

"Let me show you," she said.

"Wait—"

A bright light obscured my vision, and I felt like I was being pulled through a vortex, spinning uncontrollably until my mind suddenly became clear in a memory that wasn't my own but one I'd had many times before.

Once again, a beautiful redheaded female approached the two-story building made of gray stone with wide wooden doors. Snow fell sporadically, coating the ground and dead trees. Her hand was about to reach the handle when that familiar voice called out to her.

"You made it."

But I couldn't see him; I was too busy staring at *her*. My breath hitched in my throat as she turned, her hair moving across her back, and the same lush green eyes pierced through me.

Realization hit as I returned to the beautiful meadow, her hand still pressed against my cheek. Her smile was warm like the sun, but her eyes seemed sad, as if she, too, were watching the same memory she showed me.

"It's you," I breathed.

Her hand finally left my face. "Yes, it's me."

I shook my head, disbelief coating my tongue. "This can't be real. None of this can be real." The woman I often saw when I dreamed sat mere inches from me on the bench, the essence of beauty.

"It is very real, Remi. It was real the first time you saw that Magidoz demon outside that night."

An intense wave of shock rocked my body. The gruesome memory of the sludge-like beast in the alleyway, claws scraping against the brick walls, stalking in a stance that only made sense to a lion about to kill its prey. Her knowing something I never spoke of to anyone...

I inhaled a shaky breath, tears threatening to escape. "I don't want this. Please. I can't." The floodgates opened wide as tears escaped my eyes, and my chest tightened with fear. I never told anyone about the creature, and her knowing what I saw made everything all too real.

"What we fear often makes us stronger," she said softly.

I wiped my eyes aggressively, taking deep breaths to calm my emotions. "What I fear shouldn't exist."

"They exist because one could not simply let the world be." She rose from the bench, extending a hand to me. "Come, we must go now."

I hesitated, looking at her open hand. "What if I don't want this anymore?"

She shocked me by lifting my chin, her bright green eyes fierce with emotion. "You have the strength of thousands of Scarlets within you. Harness their power and embrace yours."

Wide-eyed and unsure, nonetheless, I clutched her hand as she led me further into the meadow. Cobblestone pathways jutted in different directions, but she kept us on the path in the middle, the forest thickening the further we explored. Light started to fade, the temperature decreased, and my arms were raised with goosebumps. Colors were less vibrant, fading into grays and blacks; even the sky's blue lost its intensity, and an uneasy feeling formed in my gut.

"Where are you taking me?" I questioned. The once beautiful meadow I arrived at did not compare to the gloomy, almost death-like atmosphere now.

"Autumndare Lake. The Blessing isn't complete," she clarified.

All at once, the tree's leaves fell from the now-dead branches, coating the cobblestone path in blood red. Soon, the way widened into an oval-shaped lake, the water lapping against jutted rocks along the shoreline. The path ended with a set of stone stairs, where we stopped, her hand still clasped with mine.

A cold breeze sent loose strands of my hair dancing in the wind. I wanted to run the other way, but my body was cemented in place. "How is it not completed?"

I never got my answer, as the water lapped aggressively against the rocky shoreline, spilling on the dead grass, spraying my feet. The wind picked up, nipping at my cheeks, making the dead leaves fly around, creating an almost mini tornado. A once peaceful oasis veered in the opposite direction, representing the very pits of the underworld.

"The final purification is in Autumndare Lake." She let go of my hand then, waiting for me to enter the water.

But I hesitated, not on board with the plan. "And if I say no?"

Her hand squeezed my shoulder, just enough to indicate she understood my fear, but instead of comforting words, she guided me herself into the ice-cold water.

The water lapped on my thighs, and my breath hitched from the freezing temperature, goosebumps coating my skin. We walked until it touched just below my breasts, my teeth chattering.

She turned away from me abruptly then, gazing off into

the distance, and said, "She who wields, the rest shall follow."

Puzzled, I watched her attention come back to me. I had no time to respond, as the water began to swirl around my body, pulling me into the current.

Without warning, she put two fingers in the middle of my forehead. "Remember when you need to, not when you have to."

My vision started to become hazy. "Wait! Please!"

"Remember when you need to."

Blackness began to creep in, clouding every sense, the water coming in bigger waves, submerging my head. When I broke the surface, I gulped a lungful of air, shouting, "Stop! Please!"

She barely moved an inch, the waves avoiding her altogether. "Not when you have to."

I got sucked under, my air supply cut off, the memory of her stone face engraved inside my head. I tried to swim to the surface, my arms thrashing along with my legs, but the water was too strong no matter how hard I fought against it. All at once, my strength withered, the last of my oxygen dissipated, and I started to sink, water entering my mouth. The outer edges of my vision turned black, closing in, ready to face the unknown, or most likely death, but before I succumbed to the comfort of nothingness, beyond the veil of haze, a soft, golden glow illuminated before me.

I sank deeper, my hand outstretched, as my eyelids closed with the final memory of the golden glow coming from my fingertips.

CHAPTER 20

I jolted awake, throwing up water all over myself, coughing until air passed through my lungs. Hard intakes of breath left my throat raw and dry, while I regained my sense of awareness. Leaning my head back, I stared at the ceiling, counting backward from ten. The front of my long, white night grown was soaked, the water dripping lazily down my legs. What the fuck just happened? My nerves were shot, and my body shook in a way it never had before. I needed to get a grip, otherwise I might pass out. Counting backward one more time, trying to steady my heart, I was able to lift my head enough to get a sense of where I was.

The room was furnished with multiple beds lined neatly in a row, with machines ready to be used. White bedspreads identical to one another covered every twin-sized bed I could see. I wiggled my toes and fingers, ensuring mobility and that my limbs were intact. Yet I couldn't shake the feeling that something was different about me. Soft light entered the room from a nearby window, dust dancing in the sunshine. Where the fuck was Heather? Was she in a different room? I hoped everything was okay, and maybe her reaction to the Blessing was less intense than mine.

My mind felt murky, almost like a thin sheet covered something important I couldn't grasp right away, or at all, and that left an uneasy feeling in the pit of my stomach.

Sitting up, a slight sting came from my left arm where I noticed an IV drip was inserted. I tugged, feeling where the needle was embedded. Breathing through my nose, I counted backward from three and ripped it from my flesh, a pool of blood spilling from the small wound down my forearm. Swinging my legs over, I planted my feet on the cold tiles, the chill running up my spine. Adjusting the nightgown, I braced myself, standing, surprised to find solidarity within.

Not a second thought crossed my mind as I made my way across the room, heading to the first door I saw, the taste of freedom on my tongue. If I could locate Heather, then I could get us the hell out of here and find a safe place to hide. Victory sprang forward when I reached for the golden doorknob, only to open it to find Josh standing just outside the threshold, a water bottle in hand.

He was wearing jeans and a casual shirt, his hair in disarray. He had sun-kissed skin and flushed cheeks from the heat of mid-September. Brown locks of loose curls dangled on his forehead, his eyes as blue as the sea squinting in suspicion.

"You're awake and wet," he said. It didn't go unnoticed how his eyes traveled down my body, especially to the exposed wound where the IV was previously stationed, a dried line of blood down to my wrist. "And bleeding."

My eyes darted from the small space beyond the door to

Josh, contemplating kicking him straight in the balls to flee. If I aimed it just right, I'd have enough time to slip right by before he could catch up.

Between where I stood and the tiny escape route was enough to take the leap of faith. I lifted my leg without remorse, heading straight for his manhood.

He caught my ankle before it reached its target. "Easy, killer." Josh's reflexes were quicker than I expected.

I hopped backward, his grip tight around my ankle in midair. "Let go of me!" I used the door for leverage, trying not to lose my balance, unsuccessful in trying to shake him off.

"Why? So you can escape?" A sly smile crept on his stupid face, a set of beautiful teeth mocking me. Under the fluorescent light, every detail, from his perfect nose to his strong jaw, forced my mind to wander a bit. His thumb absentmindedly caressed a patch of skin, shooting a zap of electricity up my body, accompanying a familiar sensation in my lower region.

Embarrassment flamed my cheeks, along with shame.

When I didn't answer, Josh released his hold, catching me off guard, and spun me around, one of his arms wrapping around my waist, his lips barely an inch from my ear. "I'm putting you back to bed."

I jabbed my elbow in his ribs, and a grunt tickled my neck. "Ow, that hurt."

With a strong hold around my waist, he guided us toward the messy, vacant bed. "Lie back down and drink this." Josh tossed the bottle of water at the foot, crossing his arms, standing to block any attempted escapes.

"This is ludicrous," I muttered, accepting defeat and

crawling back under the covers, leaving the water bottle where it lay. A silent protest for his rudeness.

When it became obvious that I would behave, Josh sat across from me on the other bed. "Are you sore?"

"No," I grumbled.

"Hungry?"

"No."

"Tired?"

I cocked an eyebrow. "What are you, a doctor? Because the last time I checked, your dumb ass was getting a degree in music."

"Are you always this vicious when you wake up?" The mocking tone in his words sent a pillow flying to his face. Josh dodged it, letting it zoom past his head. "Or physical?"

"You're insufferable," I commented. One minute I wanted my hands around his neck, cutting off all air supply, the other, well, I wouldn't entertain those thoughts now.

He winked. "I've been told before."

Groaning with frustration, I tilted my head back toward the ceiling. Although his questioning did annoy the living shit out of me, I mentally said no to all, but I refused to give him the satisfaction.

"Is there a bug up there?" Josh asked.

Dirty looks were exchanged, and I would be lying to myself if I said his eyes didn't stir something in my insides. *No, Remi. Stop thinking of him in that way.* "Why are you here? To harass me to death?"

His laugh was something to behold, light and easy to join in, and there went my rational thinking, out the fucking window. He needed to leave. I wanted air and space to think without these sinful distractions.

"Well?" I edged angrily, crossing my arms.

"The Aces usually go over the logistics, but long story short, I am your guardian." He spoke in such a matter-of-fact tone that I almost threw the water bottle at his head.

"My guardian?" I repeated.

He nodded. "Yes. The correct term is Tutelary Saint. Saints are chosen at birth to train and prepare for the Scarlet that will be assigned to them. Some are not chosen right away. I'm to help you train in combat and—"

"Sounds like you're my little bitch." I snickered. If his goal was to be a cocky bastard, then I had no problem being a bitch back.

Josh glared, the muscles in his jaw tensing. "I get you're angry, but these are dire circumstances."

I rolled my eyes and said, "I highly doubt that."

"My God, do you ever stop being so argumentative? It must be tiring."

White hot rage burst through my core. "Do you ever stop lying?"

Josh looked taken aback by my accusation. "Why would I be lying about this?" He leaned forward with a serious expression. "What do I have to gain? Remi, we're all fighting the same battle. Surely somebody from your family told you—"

"No," I interrupted. "Nobody told me. Nobody even hinted at it. I've been living in the goddamn dark since my invitation. So, excuse me for having a hard time trying to wrap my head around this."

"Your grandmother?"

"My grandmother? What does—" Suddenly, a woman in all white entered the infirmary, pushing a cart with medical supplies. She first took notice of Josh lounging casually on the bed and then me, where her eyes bulged from their sockets, most likely because of the absent IV and dried blood down my arm.

"Did you get into a bar fight since the last time I saw you?" she asked, coming to my side, examining the wound with her cold hands.

I flinched from the contact. "I move a lot in my sleep. I must've ripped it out by accident." Better to lie than admit to my half-assed escape.

Josh coughed back a laugh, clearly amused by my feeble attempt.

A stethoscope hung around her neck, her nape exposed by the tight bun, crow's feet at the corners of her light brown eyes. She then put the rubber pieces in her ears and positioned the round part to my chest. "Breathe in and out deeply for me."

I did it awkwardly a few times, Josh watching, peeking around the nurse to get a better look, which irritated me. Nosy bastard.

"You sound great," she commented.

"As opposed to?"

She didn't answer, just moved on to extract the portable blood pressure machine from the cart. Taking my right arm, she cuffed it securely in place and pressed start. "Having fun?" joked Josh over the sound of the cuff expanding.

"Can I stab him?" I asked the nurse.

She smirked. "Only if you clean up after."

Josh found it hysterical by the sound of his chuckle, but I had every intention of kicking his ass after my check-up.

The cuff slowed, finally releasing the pressure and relieving my arm. She wrote something down on a clipboard, checking the time on her watch. Next was the eye and ear check, asking if I felt weak or sore, moving my limbs, and testing my reflexes. All were normal, according to her. Unbeknownst to me, a table was attached to the side of the bed, and she set it up, gave me a closed takeout container, a set of utensils, and snagged the water at the end of my bed.

"I want you to eat and drink all of this before you leave," she instructed, handing me the water bottle. I took it without protest, getting a smug look from Josh, and flipped him off in response. He pretended to grab it and stuff it in his pocket for later, adding a sassy wink to top it off.

"I'll come back in a little while to give you the okay to leave and some fresh clothes. It seems you were sweating a lot during your recovery." The nurse strutted along with the cart, exiting as calmly as she'd entered.

"You can go now too," I sniped, avoiding the steamy takeout container on the table. I wouldn't lie, whatever she gave me smelt incredible, but I was too stubborn to find out.

Josh sighed, running his hands through his hair. "Please eat and drink something."

I pursed my lips, holding in a nasty comment, and opened the white takeout container, discovering white rice, steamed broccoli, and two seasoned chicken breasts inside. The steam rose out and into the air as I took the fork out of the plastic and stabbed a piece of broccoli, eating it without acknowledging Josh and forgoing any snide remarks in my attempt to follow directions.

"I expected hostility. It's not easy being chosen and going through the Blessing. I'm sorry, truly," he said.

I halted mid-bite, the broccoli hanging on for dear life on the fork. The sincerity in his words struck a chord because not only did I get an apology for what had been happening, but I got it from somebody who belonged to the Order. I knew in my gut I most likely would never hear it from any other member. "You are?"

Josh nodded once and said, "Yes, Remi. I never got a choice either."

Well, I'd had a choice, but my dumb ass decided to show up anyway to save my roommate.

And in the end, I was wrong to assume she needed saving.

I continued to eat my meal in silence, observing Josh. He kept his eyes averted, while I mesmerized his features. He really was attractive, but that didn't excuse his actions from before. The more I stared at him, the more I felt something was off. Like a weird invisible string tied us together, or maybe it was just me because he was now involved in my extracurricular activities. Then again, there were a few times he was not so nice to me, and that all revolved around the Order. It finally made sense.

Maybe if I played nice, Josh might be more forthcoming regarding my questions. He hadn't tried to murder and hide my body yet, so that seemed like an okay sign to me. Even though warning bells went off in my head about pretty much everything else. "I'm sorry too. For being so hostile."

Josh looked relieved and a little taken aback by my apology, but instead of a sarcastic comment, he smiled and said, "The Aces, who you saw in the white cloaks during the purification ceremony, run this sector of the Order. They will meet with you after you get the okay from Nurse Amelia to leave."

I chugged the water Josh brought almost all in one go, surprised to find myself beyond parched. "They seemed... nice." A blurry memory of the others in stark white cloaks came to mind, but I couldn't recall much of their faces.

Having no recollection of anything prior to last night didn't sit well with me either.

He chuckled. "They can be."

Picking up a knife, I began to cut off pieces from the seasoned chicken breast. "Is it normal to not remember the Blessing?"

Josh cocked his head to the side. "You don't remember?" I watched as his face revealed the gears turning inside that pretty little head. "So, you don't know why you woke up all wet?"

"Doesn't everyone wake up puking water?"

He scratched his head, not quite sure how to answer. "Not really. Are you sure you don't remember anything?"

Taking a bite of the chicken—which was delicious—I shook my head.

"I've never met a Scarlet who didn't. They usually tell us they were in paradise, greeting the Lord himself, baptizing them in Hundrath Lake," explained Josh.

I talked around the food I chewed. "Not me." The more I ate, the better I felt. "It's like I have a thin layer of film over my memories, and I can't wipe it away."

Josh contemplated what I said, leaning forward with his hands underneath his chin. "Maybe with time, it'll come back to you. Either way, you're here, and not many can say that."

Closing the container, satisfied with a full stomach, I leaned back against the comfort of the soft pillows. "I was under the impression that all go through it."

"Yes, but you could've died during the Blessing. Not everyone survives."

I blinked a few times, trying to understand the words coming out of his mouth. If I made it... did that mean...?

Heather's face came to mind as I shot forward, ready to race out the door, when Josh caged me in his thick arms.

"No, no, Heather!" I thrashed against him, his feet staggering back with every push I gave. I kicked the table, the closed container tumbling to the floor, the contents of my half-eaten food scattering in different directions. We ended up on the other bed, him underneath, my legs kicking in the air. The food I devoured sloshed around in my stomach.

"Remi, please stop!" shouted Josh.

"No! Where is she!?" I screeched. I put all my weight on his stomach, the sound of struggling grunts coming from Josh's throat. If I continued to push all my weight on him, it might loosen his hold enough to slip through and run.

"Remi..." A whoosh of air escaped from him, "Heather..." he choked, "...is."

He didn't have enough air to finish that sentence, when my elbow slammed down on his stomach one more time, knocking the breath completely out of him. I rolled off the bed, slipping to the floor, then regained my balance, sliding on lukewarm rice, and dashed toward the exit.

Before I made it to the door, I slid on a wet spot, only to end up back in the arms of Josh. "Now, let's behave."

"Bite me," I snarled.

"And there goes that apology out the window," muttered Josh.

"You can shove that apology right up your ass," I snapped.

"Easy, ya little porcupine," Josh growled, getting to his feet, keeping me locked tight in his embrace.

"I want to see Heather *now*," I demanded, twisting, and shoving against him.

"Would you just hold on a second?"

"I said *now*."

"Oh, good, you're awake."

We turned our heads to Father Benedict's voice under the threshold, observing us. His long, flowy white robe touched the floor; his hands clasped securely behind his back. Gold trim lined the bottom and around his sleeves, while intricate art swirled in patterns across his chest. His salt and pepper hair was slicked back neatly, his brown eyes sparkling under the lights.

"Nurse Amelia said your vitals are good," he mentioned, speaking directly to me.

"So?" I snapped.

The corners of his mouth twitched as if he were suppressing a smile. "So, it would seem the Blessing was a success."

"Yeah, about that..." I paused. Josh's eyes were wide with fear, waiting for my response.

"Yes?"

"Does the dean of the school know you're running a cult?"

Father Benedict laughed as if I'd told the funniest joke in the world. "He is one of the Aces."

My back stiffened in response to his answer. No way in hell was the dean of one of the most prestigious schools involved. "You're lying."

"Please, come with me, and I will explain everything," he offered.

"Not until I know Heather is okay," I said.

"She is in recovery in another wing."

"Why another wing? Why isn't she in this one with me?"

"Her process through the Blessing wasn't as quick as yours. She needed extra care."

Josh's silence behind me had the hairs on my arms standing.

"Come. They wait for us back in the dining room." He motioned with his hand toward the door.

Stepping on Josh's foot, I heard a hissed curse before he released me. Flipping him off behind my back so Father Benedict was unaware, I stomped out of the room, ready to find my friend and to get the fuck out of that place.

CHAPTER 21

Through the familiar hallways of the beige marble walls and carpeted floors, we returned to the dining hall, only to find the same six white-capped figures sitting around the long table. Three females and three males, all stone-faced, were engrossed in whatever they were doing. None of the others were present, but I was thankful that Josh had accompanied us, even though I still wanted to bash his head in.

Not a single head turned to greet us as we made our way over, each taking a seat. Father Benedict insisted I take the head of the table since the meeting would be about me, and I attempted to keep a level head about the whole thing. Because Josh had been assigned as my guardian, he was allowed to stay for the meeting, and he stationed himself beside me, one hand on the back of my chair. Strange how just moments ago, I was threatening his life, now I felt comforted by his protection.

I clearly needed to seek intense therapy after this.

As they sat ignoring me, each Ace had a scroll unfurled

before them, scribbling nonsense with white feather quills. Did they not live in a world full of computers? Pens and pencils? For fuck's sake, we had lined paper, and they were acting as if technology didn't exist.

But I was done waiting. "Excuse me?" I called.

My words echoed off the marble walls of the hushed dining hall. Not one shifted in their seats at my disruption.

"I said ex—"

"Father Benedict. Please remind the newly Blessed of her manners," said one of the females, not looking up from her scroll.

The same female had advised me to continue with the purification ceremony.

I bit the inside of my cheek, holding back my rage.

Josh lightly squeezed my shoulder for support, as if he could sense my irritation.

"My apologies for her outburst, Nora. She is eager to discuss what has happened," said Father Benedict, who bowed his head in respect.

She gave a silent nod in his direction before closing the scroll, placing the quill in an ink jar, and adjusting herself before turning to the others, motioning for them to do the same.

Simultaneously, they obeyed the one called Nora. Scrolls rolled up, quills returned to ink jars, and then they shifted their attention to me. At the other end of the long table, one of the males stood from his seat, pulling down the white hood to the cape. Tall and lean, with short, dark hair, worry lines on his forehead, and crow's feet around the softest brown eyes I'd ever seen, he bowed to me, while the other Aces followed suit.

Holy shit, the fucking dean of students *was* in on this.

"Ms. Remi Watson," he announced.

The voice of a man with great power had me almost soiling my pants. Josh kept his hold on my shoulder, unaware he was keeping me from passing out.

"The Lord has chosen wisely," Dean Poverly continued, addressing me and his fellow Aces. "Today begins your destiny that the Lord has chosen you for. Like your fellow Scarlets, each one of you holds a purpose within this order to keep the world safe from unholy creatures."

I blinked several times, trying to comprehend what he spewed. "Unholy creatures?"

"Demons," he clarified, then added, "Demons that can only be seen by the Blessed."

"There's no way stuff like that exists," I scoffed.

"You would do well to hold your tongue," advised Nora. The harshness in her tone set me on edge.

Dean Poverly waited until the room was quiet again. "Now that you have gone through the purification ceremony and been Blessed, you have been given the sight and strength to fight these—"

"But demons? Surely this is some sick joke."

Ignoring my second outburst, he walked graciously around the room, the white cape trailing behind. From left to right, every Ace lowered their hoods. "We have days set aside for your history lessons of our Order, but for now, I will explain your role. The females are gifted from birth, passed down from generations of warriors' dormant powers until they're Blessed. The Tutelary Saints, known as the guardians to our Scarlets, have their separate gene that allows them to be Blessed as well." He halted and monitored the room, making sure he had my undivided attention before continuing. "We must make sure we give all potentials an opportunity."

"The others from the purification ceremony?" I asked, trying to wrap my head around what he was saying. It was all just too much. Demons? But my gut had been clenched since he uttered the word, something in me whispering caution, and the memory of the nightmarish creature that night at the club flitted through my mind.

"They retained the gene but were not chosen to continue. The Lord is very specific on which bloodlines are strongest to defend against the demonic."

The idea of either parent of mine possessing such a gene left me with more questions. Could they have known before sending me here?

"Why did the water turn black?" I questioned. I realized this was my opportunity to get answers, to make some sense of all this.

"To fight demonic entities, one must be pure."

My head spun around like a carousel, slow and tortuous. Not only did I apparently have the gene, but I passed every step through the purification process. And again, the image of the beast, dripping black ichor, stalking me through the night flashed through my mind. The inevitable sank in, and I realized I was now on a path I wished never to take but had no choice in. At least Heather and I were in this chaotic mess together.

"So, I carry the gene, pass the purification ceremony and the Blessing, as you call it. What now? I'm supposed to ignore my studies and slay demons?" I guessed. Though I tossed it out like a joke, there was something in me that responded to the notion... a part of me that I hadn't met before.

He toyed with the cuff on his sleeve. "Your studies will cease to exist from here on out. A false schedule will be made to help disguise your actions from outside peers. You will, however, live on campus for your training to commence."

Dean Poverly gestured with his hand at the others in their white capes, stone faces to match their stiff personalities. "Professor Nora Thatcher." Her nod was cold like her, that familiar silver hair flowing out from under the hood. Nora Thatcher, the woman who demanded I follow the Lord's plan. Poverly then moved on to a man of darker complexion, skin smooth as silk and eyes as black as the night sky. "Professor Callum Adler." His smile was welcoming, the first since my arrival from anyone in the Order. Poverly laid a hand on another female's shoulder and said, "Professor Ophelia Levine." She gave a slight nod, her eyes green as the leaves of spring. "Professor Raven Stoll," he introduced next. A petite woman with crimson lips. "And Professor Archer Toke." Poverly motioned dramatically to the last gentleman on the left. Professor Toke nodded once, a serious expression plastered to his face. A scar was nearly invisible over his bottom lip.

Toke. Why did that name sound so familiar? I must've heard it before, but I couldn't quite place where. And Professor Levine, were they the same Levine as my best friend, Jeremy? Didn't he say one of his aunts was a professor at a local college?

Dean Poverly found his seat again, observing me with his beady little eyes.

"That's it?" I asked.

"There's more to explain," he answered. "Father Benedict will begin your history studies of the Order on Monday. Training with your guardian will begin on Tuesday."

"And I'm supposed to go on as normal? How do I know you're telling the truth?" I exclaimed, though I knew it was. I did, as my gut was clenched, and my bones told me all he said was true. But I resisted. For that too was in my bones.

Poverly's expression turned dark, a cloud of doom circling his stature. "Those who have not been Blessed cannot see the wicked. From here on out, you will encounter many demons of all shapes and sizes. It is up to us to train and prepare you for what will come."

Unaware that Josh had left, he returned to where I sat, a scroll and red quill in hand. Gently unfolding the scroll and laying it down before me, Josh placed the red quill on top, hiding the text underneath. I lifted the quill and gasped at what I read. Names upon names written in scarlet ink were signed, along with dates, as far back as the 1800s. Names of people who belonged to the Order.

Like Elizabeth Jones. My grandmother. Her familiar scrawl glistened in scarlet ink, and my heart hammered behind my ribcage as the reality of the situation set in.

"All the women who have served the Lord in our Order have signed this scroll. He has chosen you, Remi, to help us undo all the wrongs in this world," explained Poverly.

With clammy hands, I hovered the scarlet quill over the line at the bottom of the names, the ink creating tiny droplets on the scroll-like blood-spatter. Grams' name stood out among the rest, and I couldn't tear my eyes from it as my mind raced. Even before passing, she never mentioned her extracurricular activities when attending Columbia University. Never cared to give me a heads-up about what my future would entail.

Not even my own mother shared what was behind closed doors.

"It's okay to be afraid. I just want you to know I'm here for you," Josh whispered.

His breath tickled my neck, the hairs standing on end. "What if this was a mistake?" I whispered back, the quill mere inches from the line.

"I refuse to let you believe that. You will succeed, Remi."

Josh's confidence in me gave me the push I needed, and as I pulled my gaze from Grams' signature, I understood now why she had written her will as she had. And why my mother had been so strongly against me coming here. There was so much I wanted to ask her now... though I also didn't. And in defiance of her, of both of them for keeping me in the dark, resulting in this mess, confusion, and fear, I picked up the quill to sign the scroll.

With a shaky hand, a half-decent signature appeared on the line following the year.

I took a good hard look at the company around the table. All eyes hyper-focused on me, then I got up and turned to Josh. "I would like to go back to my room now." I'd had enough of their intense stares, their proclamations, their expectations and orders, and my brain shifted into over-drive. Sleep was all I wanted.

Father Benedict cleared his throat and said, "I agree. Some rest and space are a good idea." He eyed the others, waiting to see if they would protest, but silence indicated they wouldn't object to my request. Relieved and exhausted, I followed Josh as he led the way out of the dining room, my feet dragging.

The amount of information they'd presented began to swirl in a never-ending loop in my mind, and a headache began to form in the center. We kept to ourselves, Josh guiding us through the maze of the cathedral's basement. The Scarlets and Tutelary Saints had been MIA since I'd awoken from the Blessing, except for Josh, who refused to leave my side.

Mindlessly following him, I became unaware of how far we traveled until the summer heat blasted us in the face. The sun beating down began to create sweat above my brows and then at the nape of my neck, and it seemed as though I stepped into a new, unfamiliar world as students walked in small groups, preoccupied with their own simple lives. My clothes, the ones Anna gave me for the Blessing, stuck to my skin like Velcro, and my inner thighs began to chafe. A cold shower called to me like a lover lost at sea, and I desperately needed to sort out my thoughts before my mind exploded, or, better yet, contact the authorities.

Picking up some speed, I took the lead, avoiding Josh's confused look as he tried to keep up with my steps.

"Why are you in such a hurry?" he asked, matching my pace.

"Just need a shower, that's all," I mumbled.

"A shower? You look ridiculous. Slow down," Josh said.

"No," I snapped.

"You're acting crazy right now."

"Crazy?" I started, getting right in his face. "This whole goddamn school is crazy! Who in their right mind has a secret society for killing demons?"

"Keep your voice down!" Josh hissed.

His command pissed me the hell off, and my obstinate nature took over. "Look at me, everyone; I'm part of a weird cult that kills—"

Josh put a hand over my mouth and pressed my back

against one of the buildings' brick walls. "Stop. You can't go shouting this information around like a crazy person. Do you want to be sent away to get a psych evaluation?"

My voice was muffled by his hand, so I kicked him in the shin.

He stepped back, releasing his hold on me. "Ouch! Seriously?"

"Do you honestly expect me to go along with this? You all need to check yourselves into some mental hospital if you truly believe demons are walking among us." I said the words, though I shivered at the memory of dreams with clawed hands and alleys with moving shadows... demon-like in form.

"I was under the impression you understood everything before we left. Did you not see the water turn black? Your Blessing?"

I shuddered. The images that returned were unpleasant and gave me more reason to report them to the authorities. "I was drugged."

Josh ran a hand through his hair in a frustrated manner. "Remi, what happened from being inside the cathedral to now?"

"I have no idea what you're talking about," I said nonchalantly. But it was the fight in me that had come alive. I'd woken up, stepped outside, took a giant sniff of the fresh air, and realized they were all off their rocker. They had to be. For a while beneath the holy building, in the dim rooms, with robes and candles and quills that set the tone, they had me swaying to their will. But here in the sun? With frisbees being tossed across campus and tests to study for? Yeah, no. Crazy. It was all just too crazy.

Josh took a step closer. "Are you sure?"

"Positive."

Josh moved until he was mere inches from my face, my back again up against the wall. The proximity of his body, his breath fanning my face... something stirred, something forbidden.

"Tell me. Did you see your grandmother's name on the scroll?"

I swallowed, my throat dry from the sudden intensity of our conversation. "Yes." I saw her name as it burned a permanent reminder inside my brain. Grams' life had also been mysterious in ways I never thought of until last night. She never opened up about her younger years, only that she met my grandfather at some club, and they wed right after graduation, before his untimely death. I was starting to think that 'club' was the Order of the Scarlet Quill.

"Then you and I both know you were not drugged." Josh then held up a familiar cell phone. My phone. "I took the liberty of adding my name and number to your contacts. Go back to your room and rest. I'll text you soon." He then took my limp hand and shoved the phone into my palm before walking away from our heated bubble.

After several minutes of trying to regain control of my labored breathing, I raced back to my room, shut the door, and prayed for the first time in my life that it would shut out the monsters too.

CHAPTER 22

I barely slept. My mind kept wandering back to the steel table, the syringe piercing my skin before the substance claimed my body, letting the fog of sleep hide me in the dark. Grams' elegant handwriting was forever stained on the scroll of previous members, and now my name was added to the never-ending list.

Dean Poverly's stern face hovered in my mind as he explained a small portion of what the Order represented for him and the others.

Heather.

I rolled over to gaze at her empty bed, her belongings untouched. Her bed had been made on Friday morning, with not a single imprint of a body part to be found to disrupt its perfection. Heather had become more than just a roommate in the first week, she'd become someone I could easily see myself having a lasting friendship with. The unknown outcome of her health as she slept scared me the most. Whatever happened during her Blessing had harmed her. More than me. And I had volunteered to make sure it was safe... but it took her anyway.

How can any of this be real?

I'd never been religious. In fact, my mother forbade us from attending mass whenever Grams suggested we go. Not a single cross or rosary bead was allowed inside our house, as my mother always thought Grams was crazy religious and believed in false history claims from the Bible. But what if she wasn't crazy after all? What if these were all signs of her trying to prepare us for our future with the Order? Another thought crept in; why me and not my brother? Aiden could've easily been the one chosen to suffer through this nonsense, but instead, he'd bypassed the horror, and it had landed directly in my lap.

Then I remembered the gene discussion Dean Poverly mentioned, and he'd also said the Tutelary Saints had their genes. Did Aiden not have it? Or did he know and choose to run from it? Did Grams mention it to Aiden before her passing? And why didn't she ever say it to me? Then again, if my mother knew something and chose to avoid anything religious, why would she send me to the same school her own mother attended but give Aiden the freedom to do what he wanted?

It wasn't even eight yet and my head was already starting to pound. Nothing added up, and I wanted to crawl into a cave and never come out.

I decided while staring aimlessly at the ceiling, waiting for the pain in my temples to subside, that I would ditch all my classes. My energy level was nonexistent, and I needed to figure out where or who was assigned as my new professor. Yes, Dean Poverly had mentioned in passing that the

Aces would become my new professors but failed to give me a new schedule to follow.

So, here I shall lay until I decide to find a way to rescue Heather.

I had half a mind to get the cops involved, but once Josh mentioned a psych evaluation, there would be a good chance they would send the white coats after me if I started talking nonsense about demon-slaying. Asking Grams was out of the question, given she'd passed four months ago, and my mother had tossed out her belongings, calling them junk. My instinct believed she hid them from us, but I refused to open that can of worms.

A couple of rough knocks interrupted my inner rant. "Remi, open up." Josh's voice carried underneath the gap of the door.

When I didn't answer, he knocked again, only this time louder. "I know you're in there."

I groaned and hid under the covers, praying he would disappear. How long would I need to ignore him for him to go away?

It seemed that wasn't an option, as the knob jiggled and the door swung open, hitting the wall.

"Are you seriously hiding under the covers?" Josh asked while trying to stifle a laugh.

"Go away," I said. Space, that was all I wanted, to figure everything out.

"Nah, I think I'll stay right here."

"How did you get in here? The door was locked."

From under the covers, I heard a jingle of something. "I have my ways."

Stealing a peek from underneath the blanket, I spotted him sitting on Heather's bed, dangling a set of keys mockingly. Josh caught my not-so-stealthy move and flashed a devilish smile in my direction.

But what irritated me the most was Heather's once perfectly made bed ruined by Josh and his cockiness.

I jumped out from hiding and dragged him by the arm off her bed. "Stay off her bed!"

Josh shrugged out of my touch and took a step back. "What is your issue?"

"Why are you here?" I ignored his question and posed one of my own.

"Are you going to answer me?"

I stood my ground, not wanting to explain myself for protecting Heather's belongings. Because the truth was, it had become the only reminder of her being alive while death gripped her by the neck, waiting to pull her under.

Then I remembered the long T-shirt I wore to bed, my bare legs exposed to his lingering eyes, which I caught looking me over.

Josh adjusted his posture. "All right, then." He flashed a white folded piece of paper before my eyes, waving it around like a flag. "First, your new class schedule," he paused and then removed a small black device from his front pocket on his jeans, "and a pager." He plopped it in the palm of my hand.

"Why not use our phones?" I questioned, examining the device further.

"We want easy two-way communication with no apps involved. It's a direct line to the Order; if other outside members come in to assist, they're already connected. If a demon is spotted, we can send out a warning and our location," Josh explained.

"And we can't do the same stuff with our phones?"

He sighed and shook his head. "It's hard to control drunk members, especially if they attend frat parties. You may think you're sending out a signal, but you just texted your best friend the details of a Magidoz demon."

"A what?"

Josh began to laugh and said, "How about we save the history lesson for Professor Toke?"

The idea of demons existing on the same planet as humans baffled me. How could we live in a world where true evil was able to walk among us? Part of me clung to the thought that our world was just toxic from ordinary people, but the other...

"I still don't believe you," I argued. Because after what I "saw," a part of me could not grasp the reality of the situation. The other part, though, I knew. My hackles rose at the mention of demons, tickling my spine even as I fought Josh on his claim.

"You will in time." The determination in his words left me silent.

We stared at one another for a couple of minutes, unsure where the conversation might take a turn.

I crossed my arms, refusing to break eye contact first.

Josh smirked, clearly amused by our little game. "I can do this all day."

I snorted back a laugh. "So can I."

The air around us shifted as I gazed into his eyes, and his hard exterior softened. Josh reached forward unexpectedly to tuck a loose strand of hair behind my ear. "Why are you so defiant?"

I swallowed hard. The sensation of his fingertips against my ear left me exposed to a new feeling. A feeling that curled my toes and left the pit of my stomach fluttering like I'd swallowed a jar of butterflies.

But in this case, it would be a jar of wasps, and it left a sour taste in my mouth as Nickie's face appeared in my mind.

Josh must have had the same thought, as we both abruptly stepped away from each other.

"Right. Well," he cleared his throat, trying to regain control of the situation, "I expect you to start attending your classes tomorrow. I also added the time of your lessons with Father Benedict and myself." Josh started to back up toward the door but halted with his hand on the threshold. "Um... Sunday will be your cape ceremony."

My eyes bulged out of their sockets. "What?"

"Don't worry about it right now. I'll go over everything on Tuesday night when we begin our training—"

"You can't just spring that on me before you leave." I tried to get him to stay to explain further, but he stepped out into the hallway, the hallway light shining down on him like an angel.

"Oh, but I just did." He gave me a farewell salute and left.

Too stunned to speak, I slammed the door and tossed the folded schedule on my desk, diving back under the covers to hide from the world. Maybe if I hid long enough, the others would forget me.

CHAPTER 23

I had every intention of going to my classes, truly, but the idea of facing any of the professors who were a part of the Order made the urge to disappear after Josh left irresistible. If anything, hiding in my room sounded much better, until I heard Chloe bust through the door. She stood with a scowl and tapped her foot impatiently, waiting for me to do something.

"I thought I locked that," I said.

Chloe sighed heavily and stomped over to me like a child who was told to get off the playground. "The fact that I have to babysit you is pathetic."

"You can easily leave how you came in," I muttered.

"I'm under strict orders to haul your ass to class," she stated.

"Go ahead and try," I challenged as I scrolled through one of my phone's many social media apps. If I continued to come off unbothered, maybe she'd give up and go away.

"Honey, you graduated from high school. It's time to stop acting like a spoiled brat," snapped Chloe.

I snorted a laugh and gave her my sweetest smile. "As I said, you can easily leave how you came in."

She caught my ankles and started to drag me off the bed until my ass hit the floor. "What the hell is wrong with you!?"

"First, don't say the h-word, and second, I warned you to get up," Chloe reminded me coolly.

"Yeah, I'm fully aware of that now."

"Now, get dressed. We have ten minutes before Professor Thatcher murders us."

I rummaged through my closet, then stopped and said over my shoulder, "Are you a freshman too?"

"No."

Okay, so I wasn't getting anything more from her than that. Clearly, Chloe had no interest in being quizzed about her personal life. Fair enough.

Changing quickly, I gathered my materials—a couple notebooks and some pens—and shoved them hastily in a backpack, following Chloe out the door. Because what the hell do you bring to your first demon class? A cross and some rosary beads?

My stomach growled in protest as we exited the building. Chloe retrieved a granola bar from her bag and tossed it at me. "Wake up when you're supposed to."

I ripped open the silver packaging and chewed in disdain. Letting her lead the way, navigating through the sea of other students, she kept her pace even, avoiding interaction with anyone who crossed her path. "I like my sleep."

She rolled her eyes and continued through the halls until we were out the door. Chloe had an intimidating demeanor, which I took notice of as we walked through the crowds of students to the academic buildings, while others made it a mission to dodge her.

I wondered how she got her reputation.

We arrived right on time to find Professor Nora Thatcher at the front of the room, setting up the day's work. Her pin-straight, silver hair was sleek and shiny. A matching plum suit perfectly fit her figure, while her heels clacked on the wooden floors as she stepped away from the podium.

But I wasn't expecting the others to be there.

Josh, the one named Baron, and Kal sat huddled on one side, while the others were scattered throughout the room. So, all would be taking this class together. Fantastic.

Kal spotted us over by the corner, but I rushed down in front, taking the first seat I could. Chloe finally caught up and sat to my right.

Josh leaned over and smiled. "Nice of you to finally join us."

Before I could say anything, Chloe flipped him off and said, "Next time, get your own Scarlet out of bed."

He rolled his eyes. "Sorry, I was busy."

She seethed next to me. "Busy being a lazy fuck."

He nudged Baron. "Tell your sister to take a chill pill."

Baron shook his head. "Does it look like I want an early grave? Hell no."

I leaned close to Chloe and asked, "Are you guys—"

"Fraternal twins? Unfortunately," she hissed back.

A look of utter annoyance crossed Chloe's face as Professor Thatcher called the class to attention. "Now that our annual Blessing has commenced, it is time we discuss the updated map of the city." She pulled out a small remote from her breast pocket and aimed it behind her. The lights dimmed as someone locked the door, closing the little blind to block out any light. A projector screen descended from the top of the blackboard, turning on to an image of Manhattan.

Red dots covered most of where she pointed with a ruler. "From where our Bose Detectors have been placed, it seems that more demonic activity has appeared in the past three days. Especially here." She tapped one section of the map, the Upper East Side, just a few blocks from where my parents resided.

Worry settled in my bones. What if my parents...

"Do you think a nest is nearby?" asked Baron.

She massaged her neck. "My guess is, judging by the rapid increase of signals, a Magidoz nest is festering underground."

"Have we alerted the other outposts?" queried Josh.

I sat up straighter. There were more of us?

"The others were notified last night when the report came in. Dean Poverly believes a nest hatched, larger than normal, explaining the influx. Which means—"

"Out of control newborns," interrupted Chloe.

"Precisely."

My eyes darted back and forth from the map covered in red dots to Thatcher and the rest of the Scarlets and Saints. It all sounded like utter nonsense. From the demon names to the terms like fleet and Bose Detectors... how did Grams keep this all under wraps for so long? Better yet, how did she keep this from *me?*

"When are we allowed to engage?" The man sitting beside Baron leaned forward at his desk. He was a little stocky, with a buzz cut, and he smiled from ear to ear.

Thatcher tsked a laugh. "Once the more experienced

troops intervene, I promise, Asher, you will have your moment with them."

He fist-pumped with all the men around him.

"But why do we have to wait until the others go after them?" I blurted.

Every head turned in my direction.

"Because we're in training, you moron."

"Shut up, Anna," warned Josh.

Thatcher smirked as she stopped directly in front of my desk. "It would seem your grandmother lacked the skills to teach her protégé anything about our cause, Ms. Waston."

I clenched my fists underneath my desk. "She taught me a lot of *useful* things."

She leaned forward, placing both manicured hands on my desk, her eyes burning with fury. "Not enough. The reason, as Anna kindly stated, is because you're all in training. Whether you become an Ace or join the elite troops on the battlefield, this is where you'll be."

"Besides missions selected by the Aces themselves," added Kal.

She raised a perfectly sculpted, silver brow. "Any questions?"

I answered with a forced smile, digging my nails into my palm. Thatcher removed herself from my desk and walked leisurely around the room. Clicking behind her once more, a zoomed in map of Upstate New York appeared on the screen. A cluster of deep red dots surrounded one specific area. "Here, we have another nest, but reports came in that both a Magidoz and Olemak demon were spotted."

"Together?" questioned Anna.

Thatcher nodded once. "It is not unheard of for other

breeds of demonic entities to nest in the same area; however, it is extremely rare.

Josh sat straight, eyes scanning all areas of the map as he said, "I'm assuming a fleet was sent not too long ago to handle that?"

"Wave one was sent at five this morning. If most of the horde is eliminated, then a few of you are allowed to go to clean up any scraps. Of course, it will be supervised."

I had zero knowledge or experience of this world. I kept pinching myself underneath my desk, hoping I'd wake up from this godawful nightmare.

"Yes! Finally!" hollered Asher.

Ignoring his excitement, Thatcher shut off the projector and flicked on the lights. "For now, we will monitor the area closely. No word is good when it comes to the special ops missions, but once we get the okay, I'll speak to the others and form a four-unit squad."

Class was dismissed as she returned to her desk.

"Miss Watson, a word please?" called Thatcher.

Chloe gave me a warning look before I trekked to the front of the class. Thatcher sat at her desk, typing away on her slim, black laptop. I waited with both hands clenched on my backpack straps over my shoulders as she clicked a few times on the mouse before slamming it shut.

Clasping her hands under her narrow chin, Thatcher's silver hair fell over one of her shoulders, striking against her plum blazer. "Care to explain why you have zero comprehension of what we discussed today?" When I didn't answer right away, she proceeded. "Do you know who the first Scarlet is?"

Silence was my only response. She rubbed her temples and sighed. "I informed Father Benedict of your *special situa-*

tion, and he has agreed to teach you the history from the very beginning."

"Is that all?" I muttered, finding my voice again.

"Is that all?" she repeated. "My girl, do you have any idea what an honor it is to be a part of such a blessed duty?"

"I didn't ask to be a part of some cult," I said.

Her expression darkened. "Some *cult*?"

Waves of her wrath crashed over an imaginary shore-line, threatening to flood and damage anyone or anything in its path. And I was in it.

My lack of response did not sit well with her because she stood, almost knocking her chair back, and leaned in until I had no choice but to look at her.

"I have never met someone so ungrateful in my life. You're just like your grandmother. A smart mouth, spoiled brat who was born with a silver spoon in her mouth." She paused to judge my reaction to her harsh remark, but I kept my mouth shut, waiting for her to continue her rant. "I'm going to give you only one warning. Do not defy me and do not underestimate the power of our Lord. He may have chosen you to fight with us, but you'll never be one of us. Now get out of my room."

It became apparent as I left her sour expression that she truly despised me, but not because of my 'ungrateful' atti-tude. No, this came down to my bloodline.

Apparently, Professor Nora Thatcher knew Grams and hated her guts, and I wanted to know why.

CHAPTER 24

Josh casually leaned outside the room against one of the vending machines, a look of pure amusement on his face. "You have a death wish, don't you?"

I ignored his childish remark and walked toward the exit, trying to calm myself before I punched something. Although, punching Josh wouldn't have been a half-bad idea.

He grabbed me by the waist and spun me around. "Wait."

I pushed him hard against his toned chest. "Let me go."

"No, Remi, not until we talk about what happened in there."

"There's nothing to talk about. I know nothing, end of discussion."

His grip tightened, the sensation making me a bit breathless. *He really needs to keep his hands off me, or I'm going to do something reckless.* "Why didn't your family, especially your grandmother, who is, by the way, a legend in the Order, teach you about it?"

I huffed in annoyance. "If I knew the answer, don't you think I would've told you by now?"

"Have you ever asked?" His hold loosened, giving me the chance to escape.

Brushing him off, I readjusted my backpack. "Hard to ask when I had no hint prior."

"I find that hard to believe. Why don't you ask her?"

"Who?"

"Your grandmother?"

I froze, swallowing back a wave of sadness. "Kind of hard when she's dead."

Josh's eyes widened in surprise. "Remi, I... when?"

"Four months ago."

"I had no idea."

"Now, I find that hard to believe if she was so *legendary*."

"Maybe your mom?"

I laughed a true belly laugh at his comment. "Please, that woman hates anything to do with the name God. I'd rather stick pins in my eyes than ask her for help with anything. She might put me in a psych ward herself."

He rubbed the back of his neck. The way his hair curled, right down to his defined jawline... he made empathy too sexy. *I need to get the hell out of here.*

His shoulders slumped. "I just... I don't understand."

"What I don't understand is why I keep entertaining all of this when we both know none of this shit exists."

The way his eyes shifted from sympathy to pure rage made my breath catch. "The faster you accept *what is*, the less likely you'll get your ass chewed out by Thatcher, or anyone, for that matter."

If I didn't calm my breathing, he was going to catch on that I was hyperventilating. I cleared my throat and said,

"But you will still be a thorn in my side. Excuse me, but I have somewhere I *have* to be." I didn't give him a chance for a rebuttal and stormed out, trying to shake away the effect he had on me.

THE AMOUNT of pacing I did before my first lesson with Father Benedict gave me an intense headache. Giant gears rotated inside my brain and kept my thoughts circling in endless loops of unanswered questions that I tried desperately to make sense of. Thatcher's reasoning for her strong dislike toward me stemmed from Grams, and although Grams was having her final comeback beyond the grave, not knowing why was killing me more.

Then there was the whole lineage bullshit and how she kept it a secret. Did my mother know? Could that explain her distaste for anything religious? But wouldn't she have gone to Columbia too? Instead of Brown University where she met my father? I didn't have the energy to bring it up in conversation, especially since she was already hellbent on Grams' will and going behind her back. I needed to bide my time, and Heather's when she was fully healed, call the authorities, and get all these crazy people arrested. I changed into lighter clothing and threw my hair up in a ponytail. After a glance at Heather's belongings to hold me steady, I took a deep breath and made my way outside.

Summer daylight lingered in the sky, though the air hinted at colder days to come. Days when hot chocolate and cozy sweaters made the darkest of days a little brighter.

Days when snow fell like little cotton balls, and bright colorful lights were strung across tree branches and ice rinks. Days when you watched your favorite people open presents while the TV played *A Christmas Story* for twenty-four hours in the background.

Instead, I walked up the steps to the cathedral, ready to hear more nonsense and possibly false information.

Entering in the daytime had a lighter atmosphere, which didn't include the sunlight casting through the many stained-glass windows. I discovered Father Benedict and recognized the young man named Collin at the altar. Father had advised me to come by after dinner, when students tended to stay clear of its perimeter. This gave us uninterrupted time to begin my first history lesson.

Collin greeted me with a kind smile, halting just before placing a thick book on the long table covered in white and gold material.

"Remi! Welcome!" he greeted me cheerfully. At least Collin enjoyed my company.

I couldn't help but smile at his warm welcome. "Are you joining us?"

Father Benedict finally noticed my presence and smiled —not as warm as Collin's, but kind enough. "He is. Collin is my apprentice. From here on out, he will be assisting me in our lessons."

"Cool." I shrugged. Unsure where to stand, I decided to shimmy my way into the first pew and sat.

They continued to adjust objects on a long table, shuffling them around to find the perfect spot and cleaning them with an old linen cloth to give them a polished look.

It was the silver cup in Collin's hands that caught my eye. The bowl had the reddest of gems embedded at the center, each a different shape of a swirl, thick and hypnotizing. The stem seemed to match the design, from the bowl to the flat base of the cup. There must have been over a hundred gems, all different sizes, with that striking red glistening from the lights. I'd never seen such a beautiful object in my life.

Father Benedict caught me eyeing it and said, "Chalice of Divinity."

"I'm sorry? What?" I stammered.

"The cup is called the Chalice of Divinity. It has been with our society for centuries. It is said to hold powerful properties once the water is Blessed," Father Benedict explained.

"We also use it for Sunday service. We drink from it after you receive the body of Christ," added Collin.

"How did it end up in your possession?" I asked.

"And that exact question will begin our lesson for today." Father Benedict walked behind the podium and unwrapped an item from the table. A thick leather-bound book with a red ribbon for a bookmark peeked through the off-white pages, marking the last place someone read. I watched him cradle it in his hands, caressing the worn spine with the tip of his fingers. "This is the Book of Allegiance. Pages of history written from past priests, Scarlets, and Tutelary Saints. This is the beginning of our story."

He carefully opened the marked page, traced a finger on a sentence, and walked back to the podium to lay it flat. "Fear not, for I am with you; be not dismayed, for I am your God; I will strengthen you, I will help you, I will uphold you with my righteous right hand. Isaiah 41:10." He then turned the page just as Collin walked over, handing over a delicate set of Rosary beads. Father Benedict clenched them to his chest and continued, "It is our birthright, duty, and mission from above to protect the children of our Lord."

He whispered a few words to himself, the Rosary beads dangling from his aged fingers, and I realized at that moment he spoke a prayer just as he performed the sign of the cross. "Centuries of faded documents were compiled and transcribed to convey *our* history. The history of the very first Scarlet. A young woman who had been given a second chance after her courageous sacrifice. Eighteen-year-old Juniper Findlay of Edinburgh, Sco—"

"How do you know this is accurate?" I questioned, not caring that I interrupted his profound lesson.

Collin looked back and forth between Father and me, possibly waiting for him to scold my ass for rudely interrupting such a severe topic.

But a smile stretched across his face, the wrinkles around his eyes creasing deeper as he said, "You're not the first Scarlet to question history. But because of Juniper's vigorous beginning, her story was written for us and us alone."

"Did she write it herself?"

"No, but I will get to that if you let me."

I kept my mouth shut and let him continue the lesson.

Father Benedict gazed back down at the old book and began again. "Eighteen-year-old Juniper Findlay of Scotland was the first but would not be the last. Living on the outskirts of Edinburgh, she was one of ten siblings. All of her sisters before her were either spinners, parchment makers, or stayed with their husbands to tend to their family farm. Her brothers were either weavers, masons, or farmers. Juniper would be the first to enter St. Maria's Convent—"

"How come?" Father Benedict silenced me with a finger

to his lips, freezing my words as my mouth hung open. Collin snickered behind him, clearly amused by our interaction.

How could he expect me to remain silent when every word from his mouth seemed so farfetched? It felt like he was reading directly from a script.

The only thing that kept me hanging on that rocky boat was sleeping five feet below. And if sitting here and enduring the most obscure bullshit that had ever graced my ears meant saving Heather, then so be it.

"On her eighteenth birthday, she left for the convent. The journey would be rough, considering her parents could not afford proper transportation. Her mother packed her food, warm clothes, and a handmade scarlet cape to battle cold nights. Her father gave her only a small dagger to protect her on the journey." Father turned the page, the sound somewhat comforting in the quiet cathedral, "Each of her siblings said their goodbyes, wishing her safe travels to her new life."

He turned the page once more, licking his lips. "Juniper used her scarlet cape against the frigid wind as she trekked up the most prominent hill in the village..." Time seemed to slow down, and Father Benedict's words faded into the background as an image of a woman in scarlet came to the forefront of my mind, traveling up a winding path to an old building with giant double wood doors. Sconces burned in the night, casting a soft glow at the front door. The familiarity played out like a time reel, and I felt stuck in its endless replay. But I somehow *knew her*. Almost like a roadblock was placed inside my brain, unable to pass and see what lay beyond. Ever since the night of the Blessing, my memory of what transpired had been hazy.

All at once, the image dispersed, leaving a voice in its wake. *"Remember when you need to."*

I shook my head and scratched the inside of my ears, looking from left to right, trying to find out where it came from.

Father Benedict's voice came back in place of the memory and whispered command. "The convent was welcoming, and Juniper knew her life would be fulfilled as she had always wanted it." Marking the page, he closed the thick, leatherbound book, looking at me over the podium.

I shifted nervously in the pew. "That's it?" Did I miss something when I faded out?

He smiled. "For now. There is much to learn, and we have plenty of time to listen and discuss, but first, I want to take you to the study room downstairs."

Collin took the book from Father and wrapped it back up with the cloth, setting it on the table along with the stunning chalice.

Gesturing for me to follow, Father in front with Collin not too far behind, we entered a side door behind the dais, where a set of stairs led to ground level.

Soft lights illuminated the way, until we reached the bottom, where the space opened to a decent-sized room holding a few long, solid wood tables and dark-blue cushioned chairs. Rows of shelves loaded with books and odd objects lined either side of the room. The smell of basement and stale air clung to the furniture and shelves. Walking by one of the many shelves, I brushed my fingers over thick, leather bindings, surprised to find it completely free of dust particles.

At one table sat Baron, head bent as he scribbled with a

quill on some paper. Didn't anyone use normal writing material here?

He spotted us from where we stood and greeted, "Good evening, everyone." Baron had such a contagious smile I couldn't help but return the gesture.

"Baron, what text are you studying today?" asked Father, leaning over his shoulder to observe his work.

"Going over notes from today's report on the giant nest in Upstate New York. Olemak demons are a little trickier than Magidoz." He held the piece of paper to Father to look over.

His eyes roamed over the text. "Yes, quite tricky to fight."

I looked between the two of them, somewhat intrigued. If I were to play along, I should at least ask the right questions. "What is an Ole... mark?"

"*O-le-MACK*, and that is what brings us to our next lesson. The two demons you discussed with Thatcher today that have been nesting in the city; you're going to learn their strengths and weaknesses." Father disappeared behind the shelves, only to return with two small, black books. Plopping them down next to Baron, he patted the cushioned seat. "Shall we begin?"

Baron barked a laugh and got up from his place at the table, materials in hand. "And that is my cue to leave. Good luck, Remi."

"Thanks," I muttered, sauntering over with a scowl on my face.

"Magidoz and Olemak demons are the most common. Magidoz blind their victims, while Olemak's venom paralyzes them before they feast." Father pointed at the first page, a drawing of a Magidoz in black and white.

I shuddered, taking my seat as I looked down at the

drawing. Its body of gangly limbs, with a head of three horns and rows of needle-shaped teeth, covered the off-white page completely. Some weird substance coated its flesh, its body half turned, with a hand of long talons ready to swipe out from the page.

The same grotesque creature I saw while tripping out on Mitch Lester's fucking drugs.

My gut swirled again, an instinctual response building in my core.

Father turned the page to show the Olemak demon. A face with no eyes and a giant mouth, smiling in a creepy manner. Its form was built like a human male who took weightlifting classes. My insides turned again to the images of the two creatures.

"Olemak leaves behind a powdery residue, and a Magidoz's sludge-like residue is hard to remove. Imagine a wad of gum under your shoe."

Collin slid over a stack of books, a piece of paper, and quill. "Ever heard of a pen? Computer?" I looked up at Father, who only shook his head and laughed.

"Yes, but it is tradition for Scarlets and Saints while in their holy sanctuary to write with a quill. It's how the first Scarlet, Juniper, signed the Order."

"Do I have to step outside to use my cellphone?"

Collin chuckled, placing a fresh ink pot down. "No, as long as you write with a quill while in the building, then anything else is fair game."

"Noted." I dipped the quill in the black ink, to then watch it drip on the piece of paper. I'd never written with one before, and I'd always figured you needed to be skilled in the arts to master such calligraphy. Stroking the smooth feather against my fingertips, I tested the point, getting comfortable with holding it, and slowly scribbled my name at the top.

Somewhat legible, but not half bad. "All right, so, quill only."

"I had Collin select some texts about the Magidoz and Olemaks. It's mostly the history and journal entries of other Scarlets' first encounters with them. Later this week, we can move on to another entry of Juniper's story." Motioning for Collin to follow, they turned to exit, Father saying, "I'll leave you to it."

CHAPTER 25

Underneath the cathedral, you would never suspect a well-built library with long tables carved from oak with matching chairs scattered around. The space was packed with rows and rows of hardback copies of religious texts, the binding worn down from excessive use.

Before I dove into my studies, I took a mini tour around, checking through the aisles of the bookshelves. Alphabetical order of every author known to have written about the history of The Order of the Scarlet Quill sat comfortably in its spot on the shelves. Some of the artifacts that occupied a few spaces were old daggers and arrows, even photos of ancient convents from around the world.

From the stack Collin provided, I picked a soft brown leather hardback titled *Demonist of the New World* by Cynthia Waters, written in elegant gold front. The blurb indicated past Scarlets fighting certain demons of great power with a handmade dagger of brimstone and iron. Both pieces must be Blessed by an anointed High Priest before they're forged.

I dove deep into the world of Magidoz demons and how they blinded their prey in order to gain the upper hand in battle. It took two centuries for the Order to discover how it happened and win a war. One Tutelary Saint named Jacobson Baird captured the Magidoz using only a candlestick and a piece of rope. Apparently, it didn't take a liking to fire. But only a Scarlet could slay the creature. Regardless of both being Blessed, a Scarlet had to destroy what evil had been created in order to return to its place of birth. If others attempted to, it would revive and continue to kill.

Because Juniper was the first to do so, her bloodline must follow with the slaying.

Sitting back in the cushioned chair, I rubbed my eyes, taking deep, calming breaths through my nose. I had so many questions; so many stupid questions. My goal had been to bide my time until Heather's recovery, get us out, and get this shit shut down, but instead, I continued to fall further into the rabbit hole of all this utter nonsense and became somewhat interested in their crazy stories.

But what didn't make sense, and I tried desperately to rack my brain to understand why, was Grams' involvement. How did she have the time? Especially with creating her own family. How did she manage this double life when Aiden and I were born? My Papa died when I was five, but was it from something medical... or supernatural? And now the real question, the one that had bothered me for the last hour, sitting here going through text after text...

Was my mother's anger warranted because she knew the whole time and wanted to protect me? Did she have to choose between my brother and me? Did she choose my brother to protect thinking she wasn't going to have a second child? Did my father know as well?

Behind my eyes, a pounding headache began to form. This was too much in just one day. My world as I knew it might very well be something else entirely, and I had been living oblivious to it all since my birth.

I stared at the pile of notes I'd compiled in the last hour, rubbing my hands together. Writing with the quill wasn't as hard as I thought it would be, it was just trying to remember when to dip for more ink. A couple of ink splotches were scattered around the area, but I found it quite enjoyable to write with.

Sealing the ink pot and gathering my belongings, I decided that was enough for the night and proceeded to make my way to the exit, when Kal stood at the bottom step.

I halted just before touching the railing, our eyes locked. He wore the familiar all-black fighting gear, the scarlet S embroidered over his heart, a bow strapped securely over his chest, and a quiver equipped with Blessed arrows the same color as the scarlet cape.

His eyes scanned my face as he rubbed his neck. "I was told you would be down here."

"Here I am." Honestly, I would rather run into Thatcher than deal with Kal right now. After our last encounter, it took every ounce of my willpower not to pummel him to the ground.

Kal hesitated on the last step. "It's Heather."

A warning bell went off inside my head. "Is she all right?"

"She's fine now, but her levels kept dropping. The Aces are unsure why the Blessing wasn't as successful as yours." Kal looked just as confused as I felt. Heather passed the purification ceremony with flying colors, and yet she was the one who failed.

Nothing else mattered but Heather in that moment, and I gripped Kal's arm, desperation in my eyes. "I want to see her."

He covered my hand with his and nodded. "I'll take you to her now."

No argument, no favor, only a simple request that he gave to me willingly. Josh's warning rang in my ear, but right then, all I wanted was to see Heather. To see for myself that what they said was true.

Without another word exchanged, I followed Kal to the opposite end of the library, where a door was hidden behind one of the bookshelves. We walked in silence, only our footsteps ricocheting off the empty walls, until we came to one of the doors labeled 'infirmary' and pushed our way inside. Not a single bed was occupied except one, where a curtain shrouded the only patient, Heather.

Bright lights illuminated the space before us, and the smell of sterilized products and loud machine noises filtered through the small room, which held a couple of twin-sized beds with matching white sheets like the infirmary I had awoken in. The bed, blocked by a white curtain, made my heart crack.

"She's behind here," he murmured.

Kal pulled aside the white fabric, and that's when my heart split in two.

Heather's face showed no sign of color; her lips held no pigment, as if I were staring at a corpse. Breathing tubes funneled through her nose. The machines buzzed on, keeping her stable, and when I reached for her hand, I found her temperature slightly chilled.

"Why does she look so..." I stopped, my throat constricting with emotion. This shouldn't have happened.

"It's rare. Only one other Scarlet has gone through stasis," said Kal.

I squeezed her limp hand, praying some of my warmth could spark something, anything to jolt her awake. Tears welled in my eyes, a few escaping down my cheeks, staining the bed sheet that covered her comatose body.

I felt useless, only able to hold her hand for comfort she might not even feel. None of this was right. "It should've been me."

Kal gasped. "Remi, that's not true."

I squeezed her hand one last time before placing it gently on the bed. "I had no desire to become a Scarlet. That night, Heather was so proud to go through the ceremony."

Kal's hand touched my shoulder. "Don't blame your—"

I turned, tears falling freely now, cutting him off. "I do blame myself," I shake off his touch, "for not telling her sooner about my invitation. For not talking to her about it. For not... *saving* her from this nightmare."

His face fell. "Remi..."

"I'm ready to leave."

Without another word, Kal moved the curtain for me to leave, but not until I looked back at Heather one more time, wishing there was some way to wake her up.

CHAPTER 26

Kal guided us up to the main floor, my eyes sore and red from the tears that had flowed down my face. The night air was surprisingly calm, despite the constant heatwave the city seemed to be held prisoner by. And that, for some reason, put Kal on edge. His hand tightened around my fingers before he pulled me to the side of the entrance, watching nervously over his shoulder.

The wind began to pick up, the temperature dropping with each passing second as we stood pressed against the stone wall. The thought of summer faded into the chilling air, stealing the warmth away and raising goosebumps on my arms. My heart pounded, and the sound pulsated in my eardrums, blocking out the noise from the outside world.

"This can't be right," he whispered, panic twisting his beautiful face.

"What? What can't be—" Kal covered my mouth with his big hand, hushing my panicked voice.

Then the smell hit. It smelt nothing like the typical trash

on New York City streets or the stale aroma of cigarette smoke and fried food from food carts. It was a rotting corpse smell, traveling with the way of the wind, suffocating whatever air lingered in the small space I shared with Kal. The familiarity of the aroma had my mind reeling from one previous encounter, one where lucid drugs had obstructed my senses. A giant knot began to twist and tighten in my stomach, a wave of nausea threatening to escape from my mouth. Kal held me tight against the side entrance, a trickle of sweat dripping down his temple.

He moved his mouth close to my ear, breathing heavily and shakily against my skin. "Don't move. Okay?"

A nervous bubble in my stomach tightened as he released me, disappearing before I could stop him. Silence replaced his absence, hanging over me like a dark cloud, ready to cause catastrophic damage. Every part of me wanted to go after Kal, but would going against his order cause more harm than good? Would I just get in the way when I didn't even know what was out there? After all, I'd become a part of his world now, I had every right to step in and help. But my type of 'help' required me to watch from the sidelines to witness what everyone kept trying to convince me existed.

My chance arrived unexpectedly, and it would steal a peek before Kal noticed anything out of order.

Bracing myself for what lurked around the corner, I breathed in and out for a couple of seconds to calm myself and stepped around, facing whatever danger lay head-on.

The contrast from the front of the building, where the shrubs and trees were a vivid green, did not compare to the dead, charcoal branches hanging limp in the backyard. But that wasn't what brought me to my knees. It was Kal jumping, bow and arrow drawn toward a grueling creature, swiping furiously at his head. Long claws swiped back and forth, missing his head by an inch while he drew his bow with one swift motion, firing directly at his long, twisted body. The gruesome creature dodged the pointed arrow and soared through the air, landing on top of the cathedral.

It was a fucking Magidoz demon.

I shrieked from its proximity, which made Kal flip in the air, landing on the perfect spot to fire another arrow. It zoomed past, and instead of focusing back on Kal, the creature turned to me, its crooked teeth bared in anger, with a black substance dripping down its mouth.

"Remi! Use the pager!" Kal called from the opposite side of where I stood in the small courtyard. His movements were so quick I didn't realize another arrow was shot from his bow.

It hit the bullseye.

The creature screamed in a demonic tone, piercing my ears. Then it fell to the ground, creating a loud thud, shaking the earth.

I slid down the brick wall, overwhelmed by the sound, the smell, everything. How could I be the only one seeing this? Why hadn't other students come to witness the obscenity?

I can't do this. I can't.

"REMI! NOW!" shouted Kal, tossing the small device at my feet.

His voice disrupted the self-doubt replaying in my head. Kal was now pinned to the ground, fighting off the thick claws of the creature swiping aggressively at his face.

I scrambled toward the pager, trying as fast as I could to signal for help, all while hearing Kal grunt in despair.

"REMI!"

I slammed my thumb down on the alert button just as his scream vanished with the wind. I counted down the minutes, which seemed to drag, not prepared to fight the creature alone, when another arrow went flying through the air, piercing the creature's side. A black substance sprayed all over the ground, tainting the already dead shrubs and brown grass. It screamed in agony, swiping left and right in anger as a flash of scarlet cape soared past, landing on the back of the creature.

Just then, Anna's face came into view as she stabbed it directly in the heart with a short dagger, jumping off just in time for it to melt on the ground, bubbling until it evaporated completely. The smell began to turn my stomach, and I clenched it as I slowly collapsed to the ground, trying to breathe.

Josh suddenly came into view, gripping my shoulders. "Remi, are you okay?"

My throat was dry, my voice nonexistent. I could only stare past his head, watching Anna help Kal up from the ground, assessing him to make sure he wasn't hurt.

"Remi, I need you to answer me," Josh said as he waved a frantic hand in front of my face.

I shook my head in disbelief, afraid to even utter a word.

The night of the club replayed in my mind. The dark alley, the slick sludge dripping off the buildings from the gruesome creature that haunted just beyond 85th street, the same type of creature that had entered campus grounds.

My body shook; I couldn't control my emotions any longer.

"Remi, please," begged Josh. He got down to eye level, but I just kept shaking my head.

"What the fuck is wrong with her?"

"Shut up, Anna. Go back to Kal."

She joined Josh, kneeling next to him. "Snap the fuck out of it." Her hand connected with my cheek, creating a sharp sting.

I yelped and pushed them away, stumbling backward. "Stay the fuck away from me!" Not caring about making a scene, I ran as hard as I could, dashing through traffic, where loud, angry shouts and aggressive honking were directed at me.

I didn't care. Pumping my legs to go faster, the burning sensation of trying to breathe through my erratic sprint across campus was enough to push harder to feel something, anything rather than death. The night air clung to my skin the further I got from the stench of death.

Realizing I must have dropped my bag back at the cathedral, I was lucky to slip right inside Carman Hall as one of the students clicked the door open. Shouts of protest came from the guy at the front desk but were forgotten when I climbed the stairs two at a time.

Pushing other students aside, I barreled down the hall, skidding to a halt and shouldering my dorm door, breaking one of the hinges off along with the lock.

There was no way to process what I just did, not while I searched for my flask. I tossed my pillows and blankets aside, realizing then that I never put it back under the pillow.

"Ugh! Where the fuck is it?" I shouted, stomping over all my belongings.

"Remi!" Josh's voice could be heard down the hall, but nothing mattered until I found my flask, until that alcohol touched my tongue and coated my bloodstream.

"Remi, stop!" he demanded at the doorway, or what was left of it. He stepped inside, trying to move the half-assembled door aside.

I whipped around, ready to tell him off, when I noticed something off on Heather's side. All her belongings, even the weird art on the walls, were absent. Her desk, which had showcased her variety of perfumes, was gone.

My breathing became ragged as I took inventory of everything missing, right down to her closet, where her impressive shoe collection had been emptied out.

"No... no," I whispered.

Josh stepped closer; his hands raised. "Remi."

"No..." I kept shaking my head, backing up until my ass hit my desk, rattling whatever contents were inside the drawers. And it sounded like my flask resided inside one of them.

Throwing shit left and right out of the drawers, the flask appeared under some notebooks. I snatched it, untwisting the cap in haste, when strong hands grabbed me by the arms, stopping my attempt to get a sip.

"Let me go!" I screamed, throwing my head back, hitting a very chiseled chin.

"Ow! Remi, what the fuck are you doing?" We struggled against one another, fighting for the flask in my hands.

"I need it. Please, I need it!" I cried, trying to twist out of his hold, which only resulted in the flask being knocked from my hand, crashing to the floor, staining the cream-colored rug.

I collapsed to my knees, trying to scoop whatever alcohol I could with the palm of my hands, sipping it.

"Rem—" Josh knelt in front of me, sniffing what was in my hands. "Oh."

I drank what I could, which were little droplets of my father's whiskey, then I licked my hands clean like the fucking addict that I was, begging for any of it to run through my bloodstream, hoping to soothe the pain that made it hard to breathe.

Josh put his hands on my shoulders. "How long, Remi? How long have you been like this?"

Shaking my head, I fell into his arms, letting my emotions boil over, sobbing until tears could no longer form and fall. "All her stuff is gone."

He stroked my hair, a tender touch I wasn't expecting. "I'm so sorry."

"Please, get it back," I choked through my tired sobs, shaking in his arms. "Please, it's all she had left."

He continued to stroke my hair, rocking us back and forth. Whatever spat we had prior didn't matter as he tried to soothe my sorrow.

I welcomed the sudden silence. I welcomed the emotions that were sure to drown me. There was nothing left of her stuff, nothing left of her and how she lived and breathed, right down to the shitty color scheme of her bedspread. The smell of whiskey in the air, along with the sounds of my cries against Josh's chest, couldn't snuff out the agony that began to build within my heart. Breathing became harder with each passing second, my chest rising and falling as I sobbed without restraint. The Magidoz demon stood at the corners of my mind, the smell of decaying flesh invading my senses. Everything became too real too fast.

I was going to be sick.

I turned, breaking free from Josh, and found my waste

basket, dumping all the contents of my stomach inside the small bucket, choking back gasps.

He held my hair, rubbing my back, whispering calming words, but it wasn't enough. It would never be enough.

Because all that was left was her body, stone-cold and immobile. And I could do nothing about it.

CHAPTER 27

J osh called for maintenance after stashing his bow and quiver inside my closet. Chloe arrived moments ago to help me to my feet, fixing my bed and pillows, even went as far as emptying my waste basket. She sat me down, only to put everything back I threw from my drawers, but not the flask. She handed it straight to Josh, who took it upon himself to hide it on his person. Chloe gave me a water bottle and a black shirt for Josh before saying her goodbyes. Anna only stopped by for a brief second to dump my backpack on the floor, avoiding acknowledging either of us.

Josh then stripped off his long-sleeve shirt, putting it with the rest of his stuff. His body, sculpted to perfection, didn't have the effect I wanted. I blamed the numbness settling into my bones, because on any other day, I would have been drooling.

Instead, I stared aimlessly at the ceiling, swaying on my bed, letting everything consume me.

Maintenance arrived, speaking to Josh about what

happened. I chose to block it out, not wanting to hear the excuses he was making for me. I wasn't sure how I broke the door in the first place. Maybe from adrenaline? Fear? Regardless, he fixed it within thirty minutes, stating he might have to request a new door in the next month if it started to break from excessive use.

Josh eventually joined me on the bed but kept silent. I sensed him watching me, his eyes traveling all over my body, possibly to check if I had any hidden injuries.

What seemed like hours were merely minutes, and he cleared his throat, trying to get my attention. "Remi, we have to talk about what happened."

Did we? Could I just stay frozen there forever? Never having to face demons or knowing Heather might never wake up?

"Did anyone explain to you what happens after you are Blessed?"

That caught my attention. Our eyes locked, and he searched my face, probably trying to decipher how I was feeling, which was absolutely nothing.

When I didn't say anything, he proceeded, clearly remembering the lack of communication my family presented. "You're blessed with strength, agility, and rapid healing. We're not immortal, but we are blessed with those gifts to withstand the evil that plagues this world."

"But not to survive the Blessing itself?" I retorted. My voice sounded rough, almost like I smoked too many cigarettes.

"No, that final test is up to the Lord himself."

"Too bad I don't remember shit. Too bad I'm here and she's..." Swallowing back my pain, my hands began to shake. I wanted my flask back.

Josh took notice of my body reacting to the conversation. "Why do you drink, Remi?"

His question shouldn't have come as a surprise, but it made me uneasy. Because he was the first to see me drink, privately, or attempted to before it dropped on the floor, spilling the delicious liquid everywhere. I cringed at how I'd acted, but desperation took over and I'd only wanted a taste, enough to keep the crippling thoughts at bay.

But lying, when he saw it all, would do me no good. "We all have things that comfort us. Mine is alcohol."

"How long?" he asked, watching my face.

"Since Grams passed. One night, I couldn't take the pain anymore. That empty feeling of losing someone you love, it became unbearable. My dad has a special cabinet of expensive liquor. I took one, not caring, and ever since then..."

Ever since it touched my lips, silencing all the noise my head couldn't take anymore, I became addicted. I drank when anything caused a stir of anxiety, afraid to submerge under the dark water of despair. It was what kept me afloat.

I masked it so well, especially since Jeremy and Nickie already drank underage. Nobody knew. My parents believed I was the smart one, responsible, and went out late because I enjoyed being out in a city that never slept.

It would turn into another Aiden situation if anyone did, and my parents were not equipped to go through that again.

"We're going to have to control that," he said.

"*We* are not going to control anything," I scoffed.

He stood then, gathering his weapons from my closet. "As *your guardian*, I refuse to let you succumb to your demons." Securing the bow to the quiver, he slung it over his shoulder.

"Funny coming from you."

"It's not. Not only are we facing them in reality, but it also looks like we have to face them mentally."

I stopped my mind from wandering back to Kal fighting for his life, the sounds coming from such a grotesque *thing*...

"You're a Scarlet now—"

"No! No. Don't call me that ever again. I'm not a *Scarlet*. I'm not fighting those *things*. You can't make me."

He started to laugh, actually fucking laughed at me. "Stop acting so heedless. It's getting you nowhere."

"Fuck you! And fuck the Order! You're all bat shit crazy!"

Josh grabbed me by the arms, pinning them to my sides, his whole body invading my personal space. "Denying it, pretending what you saw, what we all did, isn't real will do nothing to stop what is coming. It's always been around you; you're only seeing it for the first time because of who you are. You're Remi Marie Watson, a Scarlet, a Blessed child of the Lord, born to carry out a duty to protect mankind. I don't take lightly to childish antics, and if you continue to behave—"

"And do what? Huh? Are you going to threaten me, Josh?"

The room became too hot, our words slicing through the air to see which one would back down first.

His jaw ticked, those baby blue eyes scorching. "Hold that tongue, or I'll do it for you."

I had to be royally fucked up to almost fold at his threat. It sounded too sweet coming from that goddamn glorious mouth. I hated myself entirely.

Because I couldn't help myself, I just had to get the last word in. Wanting the final blow was in my DNA. "I'd like to see you try."

Smirking, he took a step back. But I knew, right down in

my core, he would always one-up me. "Try to get some sleep. Your ceremony is tomorrow."

"And if I don't show?" I threatened.

Running his hands through his hair in a frustrated manner, he paused at the door. "Oh, you will."

CHAPTER 28

S he stepped up to the altar as the eyes of her peers watched, proud and mesmerized by her graceful beauty and strength. She never expected to be chosen, never in her wildest dreams to have the Lord himself call on her to lead the line of warriors. But she stood, sure and ready, as Father Alpheus draped a new scarlet cape over her shoulders with the proudest smile on his face. Applause erupted in the cathedral as the stained glass glistened from the sun upon her stature, marking a new beginning. The warmth radiated throughout her body, glowing from the inside out, feeling the Lord's invisible hand touch her shoulder, reminding her of her purpose in life.

"For she is the Lord's descendant; she shall save us all from the evil that walks among us. Juniper, our Scarlet warrior, the first blessed and the first to lead!" praised Father Alpheus.

Juniper smiled and beamed like a lighthouse on a cliff as her fellow sisters returned the same feeling. The whole room exploded with pure light, leaving nothing but happiness radiating through the convent.

As time seemed to slow down, Juniper descended from the

dais, moving through a sea of her sisters. The others were unaware, but Juniper could sense his *presence, watching, waiting, biding his time until nothing stood between them. Until the stars aligned, when the veil was at its thinnest,* he *would return, only for ultimate destruction to follow.*

CHAPTER 29

Jolting awake, I untangled myself immediately from my bedsheets, only to hurl my guts up in the wastebasket, on my knees again. Dry heaving until there was nothing left, I pushed the basket aside, sweat dripping down my forehead and back. Every inch of my body shook, my teeth chattering like I stepped out of a walk-in freezer. Anxiety coursed through my nervous system, making it difficult to calm myself down now that my flask was confiscated.

Fucking Josh.

I managed to crawl back into bed, my stomach empty. The idea of consuming food gave me a queasy feeling in the pit of my stomach.

No breakfast today.

Bits and pieces of my dream came back, but not enough to decipher whatever message was hidden beneath. A scarlet cape, a brilliant white light, cheers of excitement from whoever stood before them, all were masked in shadow. I had no problems before remembering my dreams.

Now, it had become a struggle, and that didn't sit well with me.

Rolling over to face the windows, the early morning sky, a cloudless blue, reminded me of summers in the Hamptons. Grams would bring her tote of yarn and tried every year to teach me to knit some type of article of clothing, and every time it would come out like a big blob, but she never stopped encouraging me to keep going.

But how could I keep going now, when Heather's life hung in the balance? When monsters were...

To even say the word inside my head and acknowledge its existence... I reached for the wastebasket again, wanting to die.

SOMEHOW, I must've fallen asleep after that second round of vomiting, only to awake to my phone blaring in my ear. Swiping it from the little bedside table, I checked the caller ID. Josh's name flashed on the screen.

Groaning in annoyance, I pressed reject and tossed my phone at the end of the bed, throwing the covers over my head. My feet started to vibrate from it going off again, but I ignored it. Because the plan was to hide forever, hoping he give up and leave me the fuck alone. Maybe my body would camouflage against the comforter so I...

Barely able to finish the thought, the covers were ripped away, Josh standing over the bed. "Hiding will do you no good."

"But pretending none of this exists sounds like paradise," I sneered.

Josh scowled. "Do yourself a favor? Keep your comments to yourself for the next hour. We have a meeting with Toke in five minutes."

I rolled my eyes and ignored his suggestion. "A meeting for what?"

"You have two minutes to change. I'll meet you downstairs."

Asshole.

Once he left, I had half a mind to roll back over, but Professor Toke called the meeting, and the last time I saw him was during my signing. Of course, he had to know about Heather's condition, but that didn't mean he had the power to change her outcome.

Cursing under my breath while gathering a fresh set of clothes, I dressed hastily, remembering I only had two minutes.

Locking the door behind me, I bolted down the hall, only to run into Colleen and Meghan. Staring at one another, an awkward silence stretched with each passing second.

I was going to get yelled at if I didn't hurry up, but I couldn't help myself, I had to ask them. "Have you gone to see Heather?"

They gave each other a look before Meghan took the initiative to speak first. "We're not allowed to. In fact, we're not allowed to speak with you anymore."

"Once our path has been decided, we cannot converse with anyone from ..." Colleen paused, looking around before continuing, "The Order. It is considered a sin."

Dumbfounded, I took a step closer. "I don't understand. You participated."

"But we were not *chosen*. Our lineage may be qualified, but not all pass what the Lord needs for warriors," Meghan whispered.

Colleen grabbed her by the hand. "We must be going." Then both girls darted down the hall out of sight.

I eventually made it downstairs to a pissed-off Josh, but I couldn't shake what Colleen and Meghan shared. Now they were outcasts, not allowed to speak with anyone who belonged to The Order, regardless of their bloodline. The purification ceremony gave them the easiest way out, yet they lost all contact and had to remain hushed in the shadows.

Heather would never get them as visitors.

Josh, surprisingly, opened the door for me to exit. "Thanks."

"We're late, keep up."

Prick.

The heat decided to take a little break and give us a breather. Cooler air touched my cheeks, with the sun hidden behind clouds. It was a relief in some ways; in others, it reminded me of the night before and how drastic the temperature had dropped, only to bring a demon on campus.

I kept up with his brisk walk, glaring at his back. He wore a white shirt that clung way too well to his body and dark jeans. His hair, a disheveled mess, worked well with the mop of dark brown curls he sported. I had an urge to trip him just to watch him fall on his face, then had to choke back a laugh, only to receive a dirty look from prissy pants himself.

We cut across South Field, heading in the direction of Hamilton Hall. Baron appeared out of thin air beside us, walking with his twin, Chloe. She gave me a tight nod, keeping pace, a black bag slung over her shoulder.

Baron, however, fist pumped Josh, easing into conversation. "Do you know what this meeting is about?"

"Besides the obvious?" joked Josh.

Baron peeked over his shoulder, his eyes catching mine before turning back around. "She seems to be doing better."

"Thank god she stopped throwing up."

My foot purposefully stepped on the back of Josh's heel, getting a hard huff of air out of him. Chloe only shook her head, while Baron stifled a laugh.

Good, I hope that hurts.

Entering Hamilton, we took a staircase down to the lower floor and into one of the lecture halls. I was taken aback by not only the Scarlets and Saints in attendance but every one of the Aces, including Dean Poverly. Standing next to him was a well-built man in Saint's attire, only the "s" embroidered on his right breast was silver.

He had a crossbow strapped to his back, the feather on his arrows the same shade of silver.

I wondered if the color difference showed rank.

Chloe motioned for me to sit next to her, behind Josh and Baron, in the first few rows in the front. Anna sat in between Kal and Asher, with Zoey to the right. All the Aces stood to the left, watching Dean Poverly's interaction with the Saint.

Minutes passed until both parties ended their rather tightlipped conversation, then Dean Poverly walked over to the podium.

The lights dimmed just as he cleared his throat. "It is no surprise that Captain Harrison has joined us for this meeting. I am aware of what breached our campus grounds yesterday, and as not only your Ace in rank, I am still dean of this school, and I must assist Father Benedict in damage control. Professor Toke will lead the rest of the meeting during my absence." He said his goodbyes to the other Aces and exited through one of the emergency doors. Toke then approached the podium, adjusting his collar on his dark polo. "Captain Harrison, Dean Poverly, and I had discussed at length the possibilities that could've caused the breach. It would seem upon further inspection that the prayer Father Benedict performed to secure the perimeter has become faulty."

Audible gasps were heard around the room.

I gave Chloe a quizzical look, not too sure what it all meant.

Thatcher was the first to speak up. "How? Security has been in place for years. The prayers performed are fool proof."

Captain Harrison advanced toward the podium, moving Toke aside with just a sweep of his arm. His shiny bald head gleamed in the light, and he sported a gray goatee. "Our *well-trained* Saints and Scarlets took the liberty of scouting the area and found small nests on the outskirts of the campus. It seems they were overlooked."

Thatcher glowered, her hands flexing at her sides. "That doesn't explain the breach."

"Actually, it does." Coming down the stairs to the lecture room, a woman of dark hair and fair skin reached Captain Harrison, with another male in toe. Dressed in black leather fighting gear, she came face to face with Thatcher.

"Emilia. It's been a while," she commented, looking her up and down.

Her smile did not reach her eyes. "It has."

I leaned over to Chloe. "Is there something I'm missing?"

"Emilia is one of the top Scarlets in the region. That tall, scary-looking man behind her? That's *the* top Tutelary Saint, and her guardian, Cillian. Together, they're one deadly duo and have killed thousands of demons." Cillian's dark eyes scanned the room, his reddish hair half shaved on one side. Some type of symbol was tattooed on his scalp there. The man had to be over six and a half feet, with a broad stature that could shoulder someone to death.

"So, why are she and Thatcher beefing?"

Chloe snorted. "Because Thatcher was training her to become an Ace. Emilia called that position weak and incompetent."

Stunned, I continued to watch their exchange unfold.

Thatcher crossed her arms, fists tucked underneath. "So, how does any of what Captain Harrison said explain a security breach?"

"Because the security prayer was never placed." Emilia took notice of us in the crowd. "And with that came the nests, festering for months. That Magidoz demon was a female."

"That's impossible," whispered Thatcher, her eyes wide, her mouth somewhat agape.

Toke dabbed some sweat from his forehead with a handkerchief. The man, good-looking as he was, seemed a nervous wreck after Emilia's claims. "You tested the area with holy water?"

"Doused every inch," confirmed Cillian. The way he spoke, his words were laced with a cautionary tone that dared anyone to challenge not only him but Emilia herself with what they claimed.

Emilia leaned casually against the podium, twirling a

piece of her midnight hair. "Like I said, the prayer was never placed. It seems like an oversight from *your* Priest."

"She acts like she's never worked with Father Benedict before," whispered Chloe.

Then it all clicked together. "That's why Dean Poverly left to assist Father Benedict." Josh stole a glance in my direction, a curt nod to confirm my train of thought.

"The real question is, how long has it been broken? Because that would mean—" Chloe never finished her sentence. Emilia must've been paying attention to us because she strolled over, Cillian not too far behind.

"Oh, please, finish your thought," she purred. Never in my life had I been scared of another person, but Emilia oozed power from her poreless face.

I watched Chloe's throat bob, her eyes slightly wide. I'd never seen her so nervous. Usually, people avoided her because she gave off an I-don't-care attitude, but her body language said otherwise. "Because that would mean..." she took in a deep breath, "that would mean it's been open season for the demons to prowl right through. It also means whoever 'placed' the protection prayer on the perimeter did it wrong... on purpose."

Thatcher clutched her blue blazer, worry crossing her face. Toke stopped dabbing his sweaty face, eyes wide as saucers. Professors Levine, Stoll, and Adler exchanged hushed words, panic rising in the room.

"Glad to see *someone* has been paying attention," remarked Emilia.

She started to retreat toward the front when a thought struck.

"But that doesn't explain how only one Magidoz came through," I said.

She froze. Her eyes traveled over to my face, and a smile appeared on her lips. "And you are?"

I squared my shoulders, aware that all eyes were on me now. "Remi Watson."

Recognition crossed her face, and her smile turned genuine. "Ah, the famous Remi. Lizzie's granddaughter."

"You knew her?"

"She was a fine lady. One of the best in her rank during her time. I'm sorry she passed."

It dawned on me that Emilia knew of her passing, but Josh didn't. Something didn't add up.

"You were saying?" she pushed.

Clearing my throat, I proceeded. "If the security was never placed for a period of time, wouldn't there be more breaches of other demons? I don't think it was ever placed, I think it was recently broken."

A pin could have dropped in the long stretch of silence in the room. Thatcher looked back and forth between Emilia and me, waiting for some type of explosion to occur, but all she did was nod, accepting my opinion.

"I like the way you think, Remi. It seems we have a Scarlet who's not afraid to question all sides."

I swallowed a nervous lump in my throat, shocked to find Chloe clenching my arm for dear life.

Captain Harrison called attention to the front, a stack of papers now in his hands. "I have the reports here. This way, everyone's map can be updated. Let's hope Father Benedict can rectify the situation before things get worse. In the meantime, our fleet will be hidden, keeping an eye out until no other activity is spotted."

Captain Harrison led both Emilia and Cillian toward the

exit, but not before she looked at me, giving me a small smile before she exited the room.

Everyone seemed to release the breath they were holding, as chatter began to rise in the lecture hall. Josh gestured for me to follow him to the back, wanting to speak privately.

"I'm glad you caught that," he said. There was a gleam in his eyes. Was he proud of me?

"Did you know too?" I questioned.

He nodded. "Yes. But it also means there could be someone working in-house."

"Are you saying... are you saying someone might have double crossed us?"

Josh rubbed the back of his neck, a nervous habit he seemed to have whenever we spoke of a possible demise. "Not double crossed us... yet, but they're on their way to."

Panic rose in my blood. "What can be done?" Heather lay vulnerable just a couple blocks away with only a ventilator keeping her stable.

"Nothing yet. I was going to wait until after your ceremony to start your training, but I think after today's meeting, now would be a good time."

"And this training entails?"

"Get dressed and meet me at the cathedral in an hour."

CHAPTER 30

It took me a solid twenty minutes to realize the training room was behind a red curtain in the main room where the purification ceremony took place. Pulling it back revealed a wide, spacious room with black floor mats scattered about. Workout machines such as treadmills, rowing machines, and ellipticals occupied a small portion of one area. Across from that, a mirror stretched on one of the walls, with weights of different pounds and styles sitting on shelves.

The warmth of the training room slapped me in the face, and I immediately hoped this part had air conditioning.

Josh was nowhere in sight, so I began a simple warm-up, getting my muscles ready for whatever tortuous routine he had in store. I started with a simple standing shoulder stretch, along with my triceps and biceps, then I worked on my torso. As I sat in the middle of the matted floor, about to stretch out my legs, the sound of a man awkwardly clearing his throat interrupted my flow. I twisted just enough to see Josh standing with a bag slung over his shoulder, and he wore an unreadable expression. Dressed from head to toe in workout gear, it took every ounce of mental strength not to let my mind wander to inappropriate thoughts of him.

Because wearing a tank top, exposing those well-toned arms, was enough to send me into cardiac arrest.

"What's in the bag?" I asked, trying to break the one-sided sexual tension.

"Wooden daggers." He dropped the bag, creating a loud thud on the mat. Josh then untied the giant knot on top, letting it flop open to expose different sizes and colors inside. "Pick your poison." He seemed off, slightly guarded as he stepped back, giving me more than enough space to pick from the sack.

I let my hand graze over a few different ones, feeling the rough edges to the soft tips and selecting a black dagger with a crooked tip. Pieces were chipped off from excessive use, threatening to give splinters if not careful.

"Excellent. Now, show me how you would hold it in combat," he requested.

Was he serious? I fiddled around with the dagger, trying to hold it properly in my hand, unsure whether to point it toward my enemies or away. "You do know I have zero experience with this, right?"

"I'm well aware of your lack of experience. I just needed a good laugh before we began." Josh smirked with amusement. His change in demeanor gave me whiplash.

I scowled. "Ha. Are you going to teach me something, or should I ask a *well-experienced* Saint? Perhaps Cillian?

He nearly choked. "You don't want him for company."

"Why? I bet he's fun to be around. Why don't you spar with him?" I teased.

"Cillian could break my neck using only two fingers. No thanks."

I shrugged, repositioning myself on the mat, but my balance was off. I guess that wasn't on the list of Blessed perks. "Is there really a point to all this?" I waved the dagger around like a baton.

He frowned, clearly not amused, and said, "Here, let me show you." Josh grabbed a dagger from the bag, a skinny, brown, wooden one with a crooked tip. "You can hold it the natural way." He kept the dagger pointing up, his hand grasped firmly on the handle. "Or this way." Josh effortlessly twirled the handle, facing the blade toward him. "I prefer the tip to the back. You're more comfortable and faster at striking and don't want to stab yourself. It's like carrying a pair of scissors around."

"What if I stabbed someone behind me?"

"Don't swing your arm back; keep it firmly at your side. It's about control."

I mimicked the movement, the dagger fumbling as I tried to adjust it until it matched Josh's. "Like this?"

"Yes. Raise your arm so the handle is near your chin."

Simultaneously, we lifted our daggers so the handles leveled with our chins, ready for battle.

"At all times, you should have this prepared. In this fighting stance," Josh advised.

"Why the dagger?" I asked.

"The dagger is the signature weapon for a Scarlet. It's sleek and lightweight. It's also the weapon that was designed for the first."

Juniper. I remembered her name from my first lesson with Father Benedict. She was the first to be blessed by the Lord and the first to slay a demon fallen from heaven to protect the vulnerable ones. She had become the anchor to our Order and the foundation of our powers. But none of the lessons had indicated that a dagger was the first. Then again, the records before could have been documented better after her journey to the convent, so I was interested to find out how he knew such valuable information.

"How do you know it was a dagger?" I questioned.

"Didn't Father Benedict teach you the history yet?"

"We're not that far."

"Oh, that's right. Thatcher made you start from scratch."

I flipped the wooden dagger in my hand. "Yeah, before her tyrant of words about Grams."

"Jealousy is the best form of flattery."

"Except I have no idea why she loathed her so much."

"A mystery not even I can help you solve."

He grabbed a few more daggers from the bag and then went to the other end of the room and tapped his foot on the concrete. The floor separated, and up rose four dummies with bullseyes painted on their rubber chests. "You're going to throw the dagger. You cannot leave until it hits the center." For demonstration, Josh rejoined me on the other end, only to roll full body on the floor, throwing the dagger the minute he cleared his move. It soared through the air, landing perfectly dead center, the dummy swaying from being impaled.

My eyes bulged. *Holy shit.*

"Your turn," he announced, moving off the mat.

Rolling my shoulders, I practiced the stance, not risking an injury by copying his maneuver. I cocked my arm back, about to release, when he tsked loudly with disapproval behind me.

"You're doing it wrong," said Josh.

I dug a shoe in the mat, frustrated. "Sorry, I don't have *years* of experience like some people."

"I cannot fault you for that, but I can fault you for not paying attention the first time," he commented.

I gave him a dirty look. "You're a shitty trainer."

"Is that your defense? It takes some time to master your skills, regardless of the strength you were blessed with." Josh trekked off the mat, wholly annoyed with my bratty attitude.

I stood there with my arms crossed, the wooden dagger draped over one, watching him take out another weapon, only this time the dagger was real.

"This," he held it in front of my face, the shiny metal reflecting from the lights above, "will be given to you to train with once I see improvement."

I rolled my eyes. "That could take months."

Josh laughed and said, "Chop, chop!" clapping his hands for dramatic effect.

I shoved him playfully back off the mat, returned to the center, and waited for my next round of instructions.

"Do it again," he ordered.

"The stance?" I asked.

Josh nodded once, pointing with the real dagger to proceed as he leaned against the marble pillar. Awkwardly, I tried my best to get the fighting stance in a quick and steady motion, failing each time because the dagger would fall or I'd somehow manage to scuff the mat with my sneakers too hard and trip over myself. I thought being Blessed gave me the advantage of fighting better, and my mind went to Grams, wondering if she had just as hard a time as I did. I bet she had early training. I bet *her* parents didn't lie to her and prepared her for what was to come. I got the shitty end of the stick. Literally.

After some time, and Josh's loud remarks of how I moved, I prepared once more, arm cocked, and sent the wooden dagger straight to the bullseye, stunned that it landed just a few spaces over from the center.

Pride swelled in my chest for myself. "Not half bad, right?"

He smiled, and it touched his eyes, the first genuine smile he'd given me since move-in day. "Not bad, indeed."

I made my way over to remove the dagger, pulling it out of the rubber dummy. Touching the hole where the dagger pierced it, I thought of Emilia and her scary guardian, Cillian. "Can I ask you a question?"

He gestured for me to continue.

"Why didn't anyone tell me there were more Scarlets and Saints?"

Josh took a sip from a black sports water bottle. "As you stated, you knew nothing of this world, especially its history. Once our training is complete here, we are allowed to join the fleet or become an Ace."

"Where would you go?"

"Where my Scarlet goes."

The word *my* shouldn't have given me a weird stomach flip, but of course, how it sounded coming from him did just that, and more.

"That doesn't sound fair to you. We didn't sign a contract where you're my personal bodyguard for life." I cracked my knuckles, lining up my shot.

"Guardians are bonded to their Scarlets for life."

For life? Shaking my head, I positioned myself toward the dummy, cocked my arm back, and threw, just an inch off from where I needed to land. "How were they able to come on school grounds, dressed like—"

"Like warriors of the night? After your ceremony, you'll receive a blessed stone, which is able to hide you from nonmembers when trying to sneak around." Josh removed a silver chain from his neck, dangling an amethyst stone from his fingers. It shimmered in the light as it swayed.

God, I truly knew *nothing* about this world.

Clasping it back around his neck, he threw a few more wooden daggers at my feet, some sharper than others. "Again."

For about an hour, and that hour felt like eternity, I perfected my stance, only to miss the bullseye by a fraction. Frustration rumbled in my chest every time I threw the stupid, fake weapon, groaning. "I can't do this."

"Yes, you can."

I threw my hands in the air. "Clearly, I can't. Are you not paying attention?"

Josh joined me on the mat, but only to turn my body by my waist, his hands gentle with the movement. "Pick a dagger." Releasing his hold, Josh gave me two to choose from. I picked the weird brownish one with the crooked tip, stroking the smooth pommel.

"Get your stance ready," he commanded, the light in his eyes darkening.

Readying myself for the hundredth time, Josh slid his hands down my arms, cocking the dagger back with me. His breath tickled my neck, his body flush against my back. "Breathe in as you aim and release that breath when you throw. On the count of three?"

Our movements mirrored one another as I inhaled deeply, feeling his chest rise against my back. Completely in sync, we exhaled as the dagger soared through the air, landing perfectly on the bullseye.

We stood, pressed against one another for what seemed like a while, his hands closing over mine. Breathing heavily, I looked over my shoulder, his lips only inches from my own. Our breaths mingled, his eyes downcast, heating my body from the inside out. Those curls fanned his forehead, and I resisted the urge to run my fingers through them. But when my eyes landed on that little silver hoop in his ear, I risked such an action and tapped it gently with my finger, watching it move back and forth.

"Better?" he breathed; his eyes dilated on the last syllable.

"Much," I responded breathlessly.

Voices could be heard over our stare, breaking its intensity. We pulled apart, readjusting ourselves as Baron and Chloe strolled in, dressed in similar attire. Soon after, Kal, Anna, Zoey, and Asher joined. The girls hopped on the treadmill, while Asher and Baron spotted one another over by the weights. Kal hesitated by the dummies, his eyes searching between Josh and me. I wasn't quite sure what he was looking for, but he trailed off, preparing himself in front of a rowing machine.

Josh's lips were inches from my ear, the sensation sending waves of chills throughout my body. "Tonight, wear black."

Understanding what he meant, I watched him gather the wooden daggers we'd used, his back to me. The way his muscles moved, veins protruding as he gripped each dagger, made my toes curl.

After cleaning our spot, a loud ring went off, coming from inside Josh's pocket.

He answered on the second ring. "Hey, Nickie."

With my heart in my throat, he waved goodbye, sauntering off past the red curtains, speaking animatedly to Nickie on the other end.

Chloe nudged my shoulder. "It won't last."

"I don't know what you're talking about." But even as I denied it, it sounded fake, leaving an awful taste on my tongue. Because I'd be damned to openly admit how he'd curled his irresistible vine around my heart.

CHAPTER 31

From the window to the door, I paced, shocked to find that the cream-colored rug did not catch fire from the friction of my goddamn feet.

My ceremony started in thirty minutes, and I threw most of my clothes out of the closet onto my bed, hating everything I owned. Having zero idea of what was appropriate to wear and almost giving up, I took one last look in my half-empty closet and found a gray garment bag shoved all the way to the left, hiding behind two heavy winter jackets. Inside, a black cocktail dress with a plunging neckline and sheer shoulder straps screamed my mother.

She would stash something this form-fitting in my closet.

I had just slipped on the black dress when a rough knock came on the door.

"Come in," I replied, attempting to zip the back of my dress.

"You look ridiculous," said Josh.

I rolled my eyes, trying to grasp the stupid zipper at the

bottom. "Shut up." So far, I'd tried to hold back my anger and unrelenting inappropriate thoughts about him.

He swatted my hands away and glided the zipper up my back while the tips of his fingers brushed against my too hot skin from the summer heat. Goosebumps rose from his touch, but thankfully, he wasn't paying attention.

"Thanks," I mumbled, trying to create some distance between us. Josh wore his black fighting leathers and a black jacket zipped up to his neck. At first, I wondered what kind of lunatic would wear sleeves in this heat, but it dawned on me that he had his Saints uniform on underneath, and the jacket concealed it from the world.

"Don't you have that nifty stone to hide yourself? You look crazy all zipped up like a snowstorm is about to hit."

"You won't be able to see me until you get your own, so I will have to make do."

"How miserable."

He shrugged in response. "Judging by your tone, you sound utterly excited to attend tonight's events."

"Is a cape ceremony necessary?" Opening the closet door, I gave myself a once-over in the full-length mirror, smoothing out any wrinkles, adjusting the sheer sleeves, and ensuring the girls were secured.

The goofiest smirk erupted on his face just as I peeked at him through the mirror. "It's not that bad."

"My roommate is in a coma," I reminded him, snagging my heels at the bottom of the closet and balancing on each foot as I strapped them in place.

His lips were set in a hard line. "I'm aware of how bad it is."

"Really? Because the others are walking around as if her life means nothing to them." A whole week had passed, and no news on Heather's frozen condition came. It left me up most nights, tossing and turning, uncertain of her future, and left an ache in my chest because I felt hopeless. I wouldn't know where to begin to help her. This was all new to me too, and that tore me up inside.

Josh took it upon himself to sit at the edge of my bed, pushing a pile of discarded clothes aside. "No news is good news, but I won't lie and say I haven't been worried about her too."

I looked him up and down. "Since when do you care about Heather?"

Josh rolled his eyes. "Remi, when will you stop painting me like some villain?"

"I'm not."

"You're a terrible liar."

I slammed the closet door shut, the mirror rattling from the impact. "Excuse me for having a hard time believing anything that comes out of your mouth."

Josh shrugged nonchalantly. "Fair enough, but I only lied once."

I took a deep breath through my nose, taming the anger within. "If you care, then why haven't you done anything to help?"

"This has never happened before. Nobody knows what to do. The Aces have been researching—"

"It's still not good enough." Fixing my curls, I applied one more coat of red lipstick and clasped a simple silver necklace around my neck.

Without warning, Josh grasped my arm until we faced each other. The sincerity he projected left a doubtful cloud hanging over my head. Josh's eyes searched mine, a silent plea to understand the truth, but what was the truth anymore? Between my family and Josh, who could I even trust? Nickie was out of the question. I thought about talking to Jeremy, but how much could I say to him? When all I had now was serious doubt about him too.

"I'm sorry. I know my apology seems empty, but I am sorry for your friend." Honesty reflected in his eyes, but he was right, his apology wasn't enough to ease the anger I felt simmering under my skin.

I slipped my arm out of his hold. "I'm ready."

He flexed his empty hand and nodded, leading the way without another word.

Our walk to the church was quiet, other than the other students on campus walking past us, laughing or chatting excitedly about the party at one of the junior dorm rooms tonight. For the first time, I envied how simple their life was. To only worry about what outfit I wanted to wear and how drunk I wanted to get rather than officiating and sealing the deal with my future that involved demons and possible death.

Funny, the one thing I fought against was something I craved the most.

How *fucking* ironic.

Instead of going through the front doors, Josh had us enter through one of the side exits, a faint light illuminating the small hallway just before the main room. The chapel, or what everyone else liked to call it, the nave, was blasted with cool air from the AC, leaving an unrelenting chill on my body. I shivered, not used to the arctic air compared to my dorm room, which felt muggy most days.

We walked silently the entire way to the bottom floor, which was probably for the best. I could hear chatter just outside the double doors to the dining hall, my nerves twisting deep in my stomach, swallowing back overproduced saliva. The doors opened independently, Josh strolling ahead, utterly at ease, while I spiraled internally.

All the Aces stood on the dais, talking to Father Benedict and Collin. None of them paid attention to me or the other Scarlets and Saints.

Josh left me to fend for myself, and thankfully, I spotted the refreshment table, beelining it toward the punch bowl and pouring myself a cup, surprised to not find any wine bottles displayed; they wanted their members sober tonight. Then again, Josh probably took it upon himself to have any trace of alcohol removed from the room.

I quickly walked around, debating on a finger sandwich stuffed with meat and lettuce.

Chloe also wore a simple black dress, only she'd added a ruby necklace and bracelet to her ensemble. Her usual dark, tight curls hung loose around her shoulders; her wide brown eyes dazzled with sharp, winged eyeliner.

"Are you ready for tonight?" she asked.

My nerves zigzagged inside my stomach. "Is it anything like the Blessing?"

Chloe's face softened. "No, but all eyes will be on you... again." She then surprised me by pulling out a tiny flask between her cleavage. "He will kill me if I give you some, and I would be a shitty person in allowing you to partake in my alcoholic stupor, but, girl, you're shaking."

Taking my cup without my consent, she poured a decent amount of golden brown liquid almost to the brim. "Cheers."

She left me with the overflowing cup, my eyes watching some of the liquid dripping down the side, onto my hands. It would be so easy to dive back into old, bad habits, to let the alcohol calm my never-ending episodes of intense panic attacks.

Before I moved or even had the chance to decide, Josh grabbed my elbow and then the cup, tossing the whole drink in the trash. "She's already drunk, so I'll yell at her later for her stupidity."

"I don't think I can do this," I confessed.

His lips barely an inch from my ear, he encouraged, "The hardest part of the ceremony is choosing your dagger. Do not choose because of its look; choose because your heart calls to it."

"What if nothing sings to me?" I asked worriedly. Would they cast me out if a dagger didn't call to me? My biggest fear wasn't receiving a weapon but facing gruesome demons on the streets of New York City.

"You'll know." He stepped back and offered me his arm. Taking it for support, I let him guide us to the second row of seats. All the Aces occupied the first row, dressed in their standard white robes.

Smoothing down my dress again, I made my way over to the middle seat, the only one left, between Josh and Chloe, I shimmied past Josh, who stood to let me by. His hands brushed against mine, sending a sizzle of heat through my body, and we briefly locked eyes. Whirlpools of the ocean swirled in the depths of his, and I had to refrain from reaching toward his face just to hold him still a little longer to get lost in them.

"You have to sit," he reminded me. His voice was somewhat husky, breathless even. Did he feel the pull too? I was too lost in the idea of what could've been instead of accepting what never would be.

I pulled myself together just in time for Father Benedict

to arrive at the altar, with Collin at his heels and a few Saints carrying a long, oak table. The Aces came out next, each carrying a dagger, to then place them strategically on the table. Anxiety crept in like an unwanted guest, making my palms sweaty and my stomach uneasy. Even though Josh verified that it would be nothing like the Blessing, my mind couldn't help but wonder in fear.

Father Benedict lifted his hands in the air, drawing the attention of everyone in the room. His golden robe, bedecked with red roses and intricate swirls, made him look elegant, powerful even, while the Aces remained in their stark white attire. Collin matched Father, except his robe lacked the stunning red roses.

Taking his place up on the dais, a brown leather book tucked securely under his arm, he saw my anxious expression and smiled in encouragement.

The lights dimmed when everyone took their places around the room.

All of us waited, ready for the ceremony to begin.

CHAPTER 32

"Tonight is about celebrating another of the Lord's children who have joined us in our battle against the evil that walks among us," Father called out. His voice boomed throughout the dining hall, commanding attention. "Tonight, we welcome Remi Marie Watson to The Order of the Scarlet Quill. Just like her ancestors before her, she has shown immense purity that only the Lord himself could have granted." Father then motioned for Collin to retrieve a brand new scarlet cape from the chest at the bottom step of the dais.

Josh stood abruptly, making his way over, where Collin lay the cape gently in his open arms. I swallowed a nervous lump in my throat, realizing at that very moment that Josh would be the one to cover my body with it.

"Rise, Remi, and let your body receive the armor from your ancestors," Father Benedict called.

All eyes were zeroed in on me as I rose from my seat, meeting Josh at the altar, his expression bleak, unsure why he seemed so stoned faced during such a life-changing moment.

Father Benedict had me turn toward the audience, dipping his fingers in a gold bowl Collin brought over, coating his fingers in ash, then marking the sign of the cross on my forehead. "Remi, from this moment on, you are a Scarlet. Protector of mankind, servant of the Lord, and sister of The Order."

The soft fabric of the cloak draped over my shoulders, and Josh walked around to secure the clasp around my neck. Reaching forward, his mouth mere inches from my own, he raised the hood to sit perfectly on my head.

I could've sworn he said the word beautiful under his breath, but I barely had time to register it before he stepped aside for Father Benedict to gesture toward the table of seven silver daggers. Each one twinkled under the lights, some boasting large rubies on the pommel and others smaller and more intricate. The handles were molded the same, easy to carry and to thrust, but the blades were either pin straight, wavy, crooked, or even curved.

Father laid a hand on my shoulder, trying to incite a feeling of excitement in me. "Let the guidance of your purity help you designate the weapon your ancestors have fought with and will continue to protect and serve with today."

I stood before the display, each dagger placed pristine for my choosing. Josh said one would call to me, but so far, it'd been radio silence. I inched closer to the table, leaning over to examine the crooked blade, but nothing tugged at me to pick it up; it was just a simple dagger with shiny rubies. I moved on to the next, the edge curved to the right, and the rubies were small and designed in swirls on the pommel. Hoping it would strike a chord of recognition, I reached for the handle, the cool, slick steel smooth to the touch, the rubies delicate but striking, and yet, it didn't call to me.

Frustration coated my feelings while everyone watched to see what I would do next.

Sighing to release some of the anxiety, I moved on to the next. Before I could even consider the wavy dagger with the engraved pommel, someone's presence shadowed over the table, their body a centimeter from my back.

"Block them all out," Josh whispered. His words traveled like a soft breeze, helping to rid me of any doubt that took over.

I stole a glance, his eyes piercing, silently communicating. At that moment, he knew the fear I hid, and for once, I saw him as more than just a pretty face. I saw him as my guardian.

A deep breath escaped my lips as I closed my eyes, disassociating myself from everyone and everything that overshadowed my clouded thoughts.

To get my mind completely blank and open my senses took a little time, and I was beginning to think some were becoming impatient, but I was desperate to try anything at that point. I didn't know how long I stood there, facing the others, trying my hardest to center myself and letting everything go just to answer a call that would never come, but a strange feeling crept inside at some point in the midst of it, starting from my toes. It tingles through my legs, reaching higher, until every inch of my body was coated with the sensation of pins and needles.

Nobody uttered a word when my feet began moving of their own accord, guiding my body along the table. My fingers barely brushed against the smooth oak surface; the hum of an unknown song vibrating inside my head. The more I walked, the louder the hum grew, pulling me along like an invisible string. Opening my eyes, my hand hovered over one dagger, the humming now a voice, singing in a language I couldn't understand. Heat warmed my fingers, flexing them to feel the sensation spread to my palm and then up my arm until my whole body tingled with warmth. A dagger of the finest point glowed in a shimmery gold hue; the pommel had a single garnet stone in the center with small swirls of diamonds branching off the stone. I reached for it, and the cold steel handle clashed against the heat emanating from my palm. Lifting it to eye level, I examined the blade of the dagger that reflected from the lights above, turning it at different angles, and engraved words flashed on the edge. As instantaneously as it appeared, the words faded, ceasing to exist.

What was that?

I looked over at Father Benedict, befuddled, but he took it as a sign of choosing my dagger. Because even though it sang to me, it reached deep within my body and soul. Why did it take Josh to clear the chaos?

"From this day forward, a Scarlet is born. Swear to protect and serve, to guide and follow, but most importantly to create a sanctuary for the fallen," spoke Father Benedict.

The room erupted in applause, accepting my position in the Order. It took me by surprise, mainly because they all seemed so rough around the edges with their hospitality, or maybe because I wasn't used to being a part of something so tight-knit.

Josh firmly squeezed my shoulder, nodding his head in approval.

The crowd suddenly halted as Father Benedict raised his

hands again. "And now, for the bonding of the Scarlet and the Tutelary Saint."

"The bonding? You never said anything about that," I whispered to Josh.

"I thought I told you," he whispered back.

My nostrils flared. "No!"

Father coaxed us forward, and Collin scurried over to take my dagger so my hands would be free. Baron came forward to remove the remaining daggers, then Asher and Kal started to set up for the next part of the ceremony. The table, once covered in decorative weapons, was replaced with a thin, white table runner, a silver knife, and two white towels. We stood before the display, and my hands shook with anxiety. Whatever the bond meant, it clearly gave the impression of some type of blood oath, and that made my stomach flip upside down.

Father Benedict picked up the silver knife, examining it in his palm before handing it over to Josh first. "The bond of a Scarlet and the Tutelary Saint is sacred." Josh sliced a thin line on his palm before giving it to me. I took it without protest, but my anxiety never faltered. I held the knife. Josh's blood lingered, dripping down until it touched my hand.

Father Benedict then gave us his attention, waiting for me to slice my hand as well. Breathing through my nose, I did a quick cut down the center of my palm, hissing from the sting. Blood began to ooze from the wound, coating my palm.

I didn't have time to react as Father Benedict grasped my and Josh's arms, forcing our palms to connect. "Bonded by blood, chosen by fate."

Our joined hands began to glow with a gold aura.

How in the world?

"In the eyes of our Lord and savior and fellow members of The Order, bear witness to a holy binding." The light became blinding, to the point where everything disappeared, but I could still feel the connection of our hands pulsating. Josh's fingers intertwined with mine, and the sense of security from his hold sent a wave of sudden relief through my body. Suddenly, I was flooded with a vision of us connected, fighting back to back, protecting one another, and I never thought I would feel such a sense of gratitude and security by viewing our future selves fighting alongside one another. Our weapons, his bow and arrow, and my— long sword? The dagger I'd chosen moments ago was absent from the vision. The sword's pommel was designed similarly to the dagger's, only the stone in the center glistened a honey yellow in the light whenever I swung. We fought until every gruesome creature perished, our clothes caked in black tar and blood. I'd never seen so much carnage in my life.

Eventually, the scene changed, our hands joined on a cliffside, with luscious green valleys as far as the eye could see, surrounded by others alike, basking in the realization that we'd survived a war. I went to turn to Josh but instead found a man with shoulder-length, raven hair, violet eyes, and a sense of death coating his presence. The valley's green grass suddenly browned at our feet, trees lost leaves, and the sky twisted in an eerie gray. Bodies of once healthy warriors dropped dead, some rolled down the hills, blood staining everything in its path.

I tried to rip my hand from his, but he held tight, pulling me close to his chest, his breath of sugary sweetness fanning my face. "My Juniper." He lifted my hand to his lips, the cold kiss sending an unwanted chill throughout my body.

"That's not my name!"

I tried to escape, but his grip only tightened, to the point where his fingers dug into my skin, the feeling of bruises already taking form. His eyes swirled with dark shadows, making the violet color fade, his lips inches from my own until he leaned off to the side, his cool breath against my ear. "You can't win."

The golden light faded, bringing our sight back and everything and everyone around us into view. Father Benedict separated our clasped hands, and I gazed upon my palm to find the wound healed, not a single trace of blood in sight.

But that wasn't what had me taking a step back from them; it was the catastrophic nightmare I bore witness to during our bonding.

My heart pounded erratically against my ribcage, the pressure so intense that an ache began to form. Josh cocked his head to the side, unsure why a look of fear plastered my face. Did he not have the same experience? Was I the only one to see such tragedy? And who was the man calling me Juniper? My eyes darted toward the crowd as they patiently waited for something to happen. Father Benedict looked over at my labored breathing while I clutched my healed hand against my chest. Without a word, he nodded to the others, a signal for them to leave. I needed to get a grip on myself, just enough to get out of there and try to make sense of what just happened.

Collin took the bloodied knife from my other hand and cleaned it with one of the white towels on the table. Baron cleared the remaining weapons before carrying them out of the room. I continued to stare at my healed palm, waiting for something to happen, but there was no trace of the golden light from moments ago.

The members began to leave the room, but Josh remained, standing just inches from me, watching my reaction, a look of concern on his face.

"Remi?" he called. My name echoed in the empty room, and a taste of anxiety coated my tongue.

I swallowed back the bile that threatened to ruin the nice carpeting. "What?"

"You're as pale as a ghost. Are you okay?" Josh asked, moving forward, trying to bridge the gap I'd created between us.

I wanted to say something, but I couldn't find the words. It all just seemed so real, regardless of my encounter with an actual demon not too long ago. How could my life go from harmless drunken nights and annoying fancy parties to blood, death, and chaos?

Life has always been that way. The words traveled to me in a whisper, caressing the walls of my mind, a lingering itch I couldn't scratch.

I frantically looked around, not sure if I was hearing things, when Josh smirked. "It's the bond."

"Excuse me?" I said, taking a step back. "Get out of my head. That's creepy." Panic swept in like a tidal wave, taking control of my nerves. Because if he could hear my thoughts now, that would mean...

I slammed the images of what I'd witnessed during the bonding down, locking them away until I could separate myself from him.

"Kind of impossible when we are bonded and your thoughts are so goddamn loud," he retorted.

"You have got to be kidding me! Now I have to hear you

inside my head? It's bad enough I have to listen to you now," I groaned, ripping the hood off my head.

Josh dramatically grabbed his heart, looking wounded. "Oh, that hurt."

"I don't know how you can joke at a time like this."

"At a time like what? I'm your guardian. It's not like we're some part of an arranged marriage," he scoffed.

I gritted my teeth. "I can barely grasp the concept of demons roaming around, now you have to be planted in my head?"

"And you're not in mine?" He crossed his arms, annoyance on his face.

He had the audacity to act so irritated by my dislike for our situation that I wanted to stab his eyes out.

"We have only *one* common goal, and that is to fight and protect the citizens of this city," Josh stated.

"Glad that's all *we* have in common," I muttered. Arrogant son of a bit—

"Heard that."

"Good."

We stood, glaring at one another. "If you're going to insult me all night—" Josh turned to leave.

I surprised not only him but myself. Although I wanted to, that wouldn't get me anywhere with navigating my new lifestyle, and as much as I wanted to kick him in the teeth, he was my guardian, and I couldn't do this without him. I had to rein in my anger to ask the next question. "How does it even work?" I let my hand drop off his arm.

His eyebrows rose in confusion. "How does what work?"

I gestured my hands between us. "Reading each other's thoughts. Communicating?"

Josh massaged his jawline, his fingers playing with the

stubble as he sighed deeply and rolled his eyes, clearly experiencing whiplash from my ever-changing mood. "It only works if we're close to one another. It's quite useful in battle. Our psyche is connected because our bond finally received its own blessing from a holy figure."

Father Benedict's weird declaration suddenly made sense. "Is that what Father was spewing earlier?"

"Yes."

I pondered over this new information. "So, you can talk to me telepathically... I'm assuming it works the same for you?"

He nodded. "Give it a try."

"You make it sound so easy."

"Because it is."

Hi. I thought. God, this was awkward.

Hey, and it's perfectly normal. I watched the smirk appear on his lips.

My eyes bulged. "I didn't even think about the last part."

"Like I said, your thoughts are very loud," he said in a matter-of-fact tone.

"All because we're connected..." I trailed off, because from here on out, Josh was going to know all my inner thoughts, unless...

He started to laugh. "Unless you learn how to shield."

"Ugh! Teach me then, I'm already about to lose my goddamn mind!"

Josh pushed his hair away from his forehead. "We'll do that tomorrow. "

"Where did Collin take my dagger?"

"It's getting doused in holy water, and then Father Benedict prays over it in a separate room. That is where the power of our Lord grants them to be used in battle," Josh explained.

"So, my dagger is only useful until after it is prayed upon?" I questioned.

"It's not written anywhere in our handbook, but it was passed down from priest to priest. Once the dagger chooses you, it gets a final prayer to activate because it's tethered to your soul."

"Should I be with my dagger for that to happen?"

"You already touched it after it recognized your soul." Josh adjusted himself and stepped off the dais. "Anyways, there's a party tonight at our frat house to celebrate your... achievement."

"You? At a frat house?"

"I'll text you the details." Without looking back, he exited the room, leaving me standing in a brand new scarlet cape and with a quiet mind.

CHAPTER 33

W alking up the steps to one of the many frats off campus was something I'd never thought I would do, especially after this week's events, but there I was, dressed and ready to kick someone's teeth in if they so much as looked at me the wrong way. All I really wanted to do was go back to my dorm and sleep. The Ceremony had already given me a headache, and any more social interaction would send me over the edge.

Josh texted me the details like he said he would, advising me to dress casually and be prepared for a knock at my door.

Of course, he failed to mention the person who did the knocking was Chloe. She barreled in, assessing my clothing only to make a disgusted sound, then raided my closet and shouted at me to change.

Now, I stood in a line outside a two-story house, where music thumped and rattled the windows along with flashing strobe lights from the bottom floor. Screams of students chanting some weird pledge inside were like nails on a chalkboard, and if I weren't so deep in this line or Chloe wasn't my unassigned bodyguard, I would've bounced.

"I thought this was an Order party? Why are there so many people here?" I asked Chloe.

She sighed heavily and rolled her eyes. "Because Baron, Josh, Kal, and Asher own this house. They are known to be the party kings of this school. Plus, I like the drama."

Approaching the front doors, I plastered on a tight smile as I was greeted by Asher, one of the Saints from the Order, at the front door. He ushered the hostess at the door away so he could reach us. His hair was disheveled, much like his attire, and he already reeked of some type of vodka. Asher blundered down the front steps, barely making it safely on two feet toward us.

"Remi, my girl! Come on in!" Asher threw his arm over my shoulder and guided me out of the line and inside the crowded house. Chloe snorted and passed us quickly, leaving me attached to the drunken idiot.

An hour ago, Asher stood among the other Saints, poised and mute, watching the scarlet cape drape my shoulders; now he was long gone and stumbling over his feet, wholly sloshed.

I slipped under his hold and escaped, only to look behind and see him lean against the banister, trying to flirt with a group of girls, completely forgetting about little old me.

Chloe returned to my side with two red solo cups. "Josh already yelled at me earlier when I was trying to sober up. It's soda."

Taking a sip and enjoying an ice-cold Coke, I looked around the kitchen. Bodies were stuffed in every corner, with a couple of girls on the countertop, either making out with someone or throwing empty beer cans into the sea of people.

"Some party," I commented dryly.

"Yeah, well, they needed an excuse to throw one."

Following her through the crowd, we shouldered past a group of guys at a keg stand, hollering like animals.

Music thumped, rattling the chandelier in the hallway; even the photos of the frat boys on the wall shook. Whatever trap beat they played reminded me of my club days with Nickie and Jeremy.

We hadn't spoken since the night they both trashed my outfit, and I was debating on texting her later when a familiar laugh was heard over the music change. A laugh I knew anywhere, no matter how many people occupied the house.

Nickie.

Her laugh grew louder as I left Chloe behind, following the sound to the center of the living room, where she was perched comfortably on Josh's lap. Hands intertwined, he nuzzled against her neck like a cat in heat.

Accompanying them were Anna and Baron, sharing a couch on the opposite side. A few other students were scattered in little groups, smoking pot or throwing back shots.

"Remi!" squealed Nickie. She rushed off her spot from Josh and collided with me, my drink hitting the floor before I could register what happened and soaking my shoes.

"Oops!" She giggled, clinging to my neck.

I tried to untangle myself from her, only to step in a giant puddle of beer, almost slipping on my ass.

"Nickie, give her some air," said Josh, coming up from behind her. She giggled again before stepping back into his arms, curling against his chest. She began to play with the collar of his white shirt, swirling her finger along his collar-bone. It was hard seeing them this way, cozied up and oblivious to the crowd. He bit her ear, enticing a moan from her lips, and I hadn't realized I bent the cup, soda flowing through the slit in the red plastic.

Chloe came up beside me. "Girl, you just hulk-smashed your cup."

Josh glanced at me as I fought an internal battle with my emotions. I should not be feeling this way. *Why am I feeling this way?*

His voice filtered through my head. *Feeling what way?*

Panicked, I turned to Chloe, desperation in my eyes. "How do I block him out?"

Catching on, Chloe leaned in so only I could hear. "*Block him out.*"

"I don't know how, that's why I'm asking you."

She shook her head, taking the damaged cup from my hand. "No, I mean, block him out. Build a wall inside your mind."

Was it that easy? Keeping my eyes averted from where they embraced, I imagined bricks stacking on top of one another, shutting out his voice and face entirely. Relief flooded my body, tension easing from my shoulders.

"Nickie, what are you doing here?" I finally asked, ignoring the intense way Josh was studying me. If he was trying to gain access, I couldn't tell.

"Well, that's a stupid question," laughed Nickie.

Snickers from Anna on the couch had me grinding my teeth in frustration. "You know what I mean." Nickie hated frat parties just as much as I hated attending the college that threw them.

"My *boyfriend* is hosting it, silly. Of course I'm going to be here," she slurred. I wondered how much she had already drunk. Judging by the empty solo cups on the table where she sat, I assumed more than her typical amount at a club.

Josh had a firm grip on her waist, ensuring she didn't topple over.

"Woah, someone's half in the bag," Chloe said behind me.

Clenching my fist, I stepped forward, ready to take her out of his hands and bring her home, when the words out of Anna's mouth had me seething. "She told us some fascinating stories about you, Remi."

"Oh, yeah, how she peed herself in the fourth grade because—" Nickie slipped on her heels, dragging Josh halfway down with her.

"I think it's time you sober up, hun," suggested Josh. Nickie ended up on the couch courtesy of him and Baron. She was sprawled out, laughing hysterically over something, and it only boiled my blood more.

"You think?" I scoffed.

Josh pivoted, glaring at me. "What the hell is your problem?"

"My problem? My problem is you!"

Anna laughed hysterically on the couch. "Oh, this is great. A Scarlet fighting with her Saint."

"Shut up, Anna," warned Baron.

"Why? Remi is nothing but a loose cannon. She's going to get us all killed," Anna stated.

"That's rich coming from the girl who almost got half the squad killed," sniped Chloe.

"Will you all keep your voices down? We're not alone," Baron advised through gritted teeth. I'd never seen him so furious.

"Give us a minute." Josh unexpectedly grasped my arm and led the way out of the living room. He turned a sharp right up a set of stairs and opened the first door on the left, showcasing a room with a big queen-sized bed in the middle. Posters of heavy metal bands covered the walls, with an acoustic guitar displayed in the corner by a desk to the far left. Stacks of notebooks were piled on the floor, and a laptop lay open, playing a slide show of family photos and soft music.

Nothing could have prepared me for the words out of his mouth. "Now that we don't have an audience for you to get attention—"

"What the hell is that supposed to mean?" I snapped.

"All during the ceremony, you were fine. Now, you have a problem with me. Why?"

"Why is she here?" I questioned angrily.

A puzzled expression tainted his face. "I'm not allowed to invite my girlfriend?"

"I didn't mean it like that."

"Then how did you mean it?" Josh crossed his arms over his chest, muscles flexing, every vein pulsating. His brown hair fanned his forehead, and those dark lashes fluttered every time he blinked. The jeans he wore hugged him perfectly, never leaving anything to the imagination.

I swallowed hard, trying to refocus on the conversation. "It's not safe."

He cocked an eyebrow and snorted back a laugh. "But with you, she is? We're on the same mission here, Remi. What's the difference between you and me?"

"She doesn't know—"

"She won't. I would never put her in danger like that.

You honestly think that little of me?" His words sounded like a wounded puppy, and that left me embarrassed.

Did I? He knew more about this life than me, and that wasn't by choice, but was I judging too quickly? He was my guardian, after all...

"Not answering makes it worse, you know."

"You didn't give me a chance."

Tension increased in my shoulders as I tried my best not to lose my goddamn cool with him.

"Then please." He gestured for me to continue, clearly amused by the conversation or lack thereof.

"This isn't funny, so stop being an ass about this," I retorted.

"Would you like me to repeat?" he asked condescendingly.

I clenched my fist, digging my nails into my palms, trying not to hit the smug look off his face. "No, Josh, but she's my best friend. If anything happened to her, I wouldn't be able to live with myself." The mere thought of something happening to Nickie, even Jeremy. A shudder went through my whole body. I didn't care if our friendship was on the rocks. If she ever got hurt...

Josh's eyes reflected an emotion I couldn't detect as he pushed himself off the doorframe until we were inches apart. "Remi, I promise nothing will happen." Unexpectedly, he brushed a loose strand from my face, tucking it neatly behind my ear.

"Don't do that," I whispered. One second, he was brutally cold, the next, his words and eyes lit me on fire from the inside out.

Realization crossed his face as he snapped his hand back. "I give you my word."

"What if your word isn't good enough?"

The room became too hot.

The sound of the doorknob turning had us jumping back from one another. Nickie's head poked around, smiling like the Cheshire Cat. "There you both are!"

Suddenly, the door was kicked fully open by Chloe. "Come on, we're playing beer pong, and you're my partner, Watson."

Josh gave me a curt nod, clearly not done with this conversation but done enough to drop it. Without a second thought, I pushed past him, feeling the brush of his fingers against my clenched fist, an electric tingle sparking a fire.

Only when I saw them together did my heart hammer, my pulse quicken, and the feeling of envy clouded my better judgment. I went feral with jealousy; I almost didn't recognize myself. The more time I spent with Josh, the more those emotions heightened, and I started to not like this version of myself. What led me to have these feelings? I honestly couldn't understand myself. When distance separated us, it was easier to feel normal, but every time Josh entered a room or simply glanced at me, it was as if every rational thought I had went out the window. From the moment we bumped into each other at the club, all my logical thinking had crumpled. I tried my hardest to push it six feet under, but I would gladly suffocate myself to death only to feel the high of what he gave me.

At that moment, I knew I'd become the worst possible friend to Nickie; regardless of her safety, she had no idea I'd already created our path of destruction by letting my feelings for Josh get in the way, and I needed to stop it now. I couldn't let years of friendship go down the drain over some guy who didn't feel the same way.

Touching the last step, I felt an eerie sense of someone watching me. The hairs on my arms stood up with an unsettling chill creeping along my back as I scanned my surroundings. Everyone appeared to be enjoying themselves; nobody paid attention to the girl who monitored the crowd, trying to find something or *someone* who most likely wasn't there. Chloe had already headed toward the kitchen when I eventually found the nerve to move again, but the uneasiness following me never left.

Entering the kitchen, Chloe somehow had a new partner, Baron, on one side of the table, and then there was Kal on the opposite end, using his pointer finger to signal to me to come over.

Great.

"What happened to Chloe being my partner?" I asked, taking the spot next to him.

"I convinced Chloe to trade," he said with a smile.

"He paid me a hundred bucks," she deadpanned.

Baron began to laugh just as Kal's face turned a striking shade of red. "In my defense—"

"Oh, please," interrupted Chloe. "Your defense is as weak as your ability to stay away from her. Now, shut up and play."

Ignoring her remarks, he handed me an orange ping pong ball. "Would you like to take some practice shots? It'll help you warm up."

Snorting a laugh, I lined up my shot and extended my arm with just enough force, flicking my wrist in a downward motion, landing it directly in the center cup. A low whistle came from Baron and a loud curse from Chloe.

Kal stood awestruck, rubbing his neck, and said, "I take back what I said."

"Underestimating me was your first mistake."

I stepped aside, watching Kal line up his shot, sinking it perfectly in the cup in front.

"We're so screwed," commented Baron, looking at the ceiling.

Baron carried his team, while Kal and I took turns sinking every shot, winning three solid games in a row. Chloe shouted at us for a rematch, determined to win at least one or get close.

We were at the very end of game four, and each team had one cup left, we kept missing our shot since Baron decided to add in tricks to show off. It was funny to watch Kal try and fail, throwing it behind his back, and hitting Chloe dead center in the forehead.

"Nice going, Kal," she sneered, rubbing the spot.

Stifling my laugh with my hand, I tried my left, watching it sink effortlessly into the final cup. High fives were exchanged and jokes told, making us laugh. Kal slung his arm around my shoulder, a goofy smile on his face. "Does anyone else want to try and take our throne?"

Baron gave him the middle finger. "Nobody wants to play with you anymore."

Kal released his arm around my shoulder and strolled over to Baron. "You're a sore loser." They both began to bicker playfully, giving me a chance to make the slip and find a bathroom.

Ascending to the second floor, I found a line of females to the bathroom, extending just before the top of the staircase, most of the girls hanging over the banister, talking to a few others below. I stood behind a short girl with long black hair, swaying her hips to the music playing throughout the house, a red solo cup clenched in a perfect set of nails.

I tapped her lightly on the shoulder. "How long of a wait?"

She half turned in my direction and said, "I don't know, girl. Whoever is in there is leaving a nasty smell."

One of the girls up front protested for the wait and left, muttering curses to herself. A few more started to leave, trying to find another bathroom someplace else. Only me and the short girl I spoke to stood in line, the smell wafting from underneath the crack. I had no desire to find another bathroom, not when my bladder was about to explode.

Eventually, the girl before me left, not wanting to stick around and wait any longer. The smell intensified by the minute, and an uneasy sense of something bad crept under my skin. Nausea snuck up, twisting my stomach as the smell of rotting flesh invaded my space. I twisted the golden doorknob, the smell making my eyes water. When I entered, blood and black sludge coated the white tiles on the floor. My heart thumped erratically against my ribcage when my eyes landed on the distorted body of a female in the tub. A scream got caught in my throat, the wind completely knocked from my lungs. I wanted to fall on my knees, but my hand remained glued to the doorknob.

"Remi?" Oh, no. Why was he here? I knew that voice.

Petrified to move an inch in case the corpse came to life, Josh's presence appeared over my shoulder, and he saw the same grotesque image.

"Fuck!" he hissed. Before I had time to process, he ushered us inside with the rotting body. I clung to the porcelain sink, slipping on sludge and blood.

"Try to keep yourself still. We can't disrupt the evidence."

"But you're allowed to?" I remarked.

He ignored my comment as he knelt just before the tub, assessing the situation, a shaking hand running through his tousled, curly brown hair. "At a fucking party too."

The walls were coated with the same bodily fluids and substance, staining the shower curtain and matching rug. Her eyes hung outside the sockets, her shirt ripped open, a giant hole protruding from her chest. Someone or something must've turned on the water, because the tub was half filled, with her organs floating to the top. I didn't think I'd ever get used to this type of carnage, especially if it was once a living, breathing human.

"I don't understand how this slipped past us," Josh muttered.

I kept my mouth shut so I didn't vomit, taking quick breaths through my nose.

The victim's lower jaw was snapped down, teeth were missing, and her tongue hung loose. But what frightened me the most was the weird symbol drawn on her forehead, possibly with her own blood.

Josh must've noticed it too, because he risked almost falling in the sludge and walked closer, taking a picture with his phone.

"What does it mean?" I whispered. I never signed up for this. I never wanted any of this. I only went to the stupid induction to save Heather, but instead, she's lying in an underground infirmary asleep, while I try to navigate being a Scarlet, fighting off demonic forces and trying my best not to get myself killed.

Josh hesitated to stand, and I watched his shoulders tense from where he knelt.

After what felt like an eternity, he finally rose from his position, a look of concern fixing his features when he finally looked at me. "It's an omen of death."

CHAPTER 34

Asher sobered up real quick when Josh reported the body, emptying the house for the Aces to arrive without questions arising from civilians. He was able to get Nickie a ride home, stating he was feeling under the weather. After she kissed him, leaving a hickey on his neck, she left somewhat coherently in a taxi. I did my best to keep that mental wall up, trying not to let my personal feelings slip through the cracks.

Although we didn't expect Father Benedict to come sporting a silk pajama set, we did prepare ourselves for Captain Harrison, flagged by Emilia and Cillian.

Captain Harrison called in a clean-up crew to remove the body for examination and sludge from the bathroom, while we all gathered in the living room, watching Saints and Scarlets from the experienced fleet come and go out the front door, monitoring the house or removing buckets of demon residue.

Some Saints carried down the black body bag, while

Josh and I exchanged a nervous look. We couldn't identify the female, but he informed Father of the strange symbol on the deceased's chest. I wondered if they'd located her heart and shuddered, holding back my vomit, becoming numb to the butchery of innocent humans.

Emilia wore the signature scarlet cape, cleaning her blade with a white cloth. "Dare I ask how this happened when we were told security was put back into place?"

Father Benedict cleared his throat. "Security only extends so far."

"I find that hard to believe," she challenged, polishing the pommel of her dagger. The design showed three rubies in the center, with swirls and loops creating an intricate pattern.

Father Benedict didn't respond. Instead, he whispered something to Dean Poverly.

Captain Harrison returned from upstairs, stroking his white goatee in thought. "A house full of college students, and only one pronounced dead."

Thatcher wore a casual outfit, crossing her arms. "I think this attack was a message."

"But to whom? The kids? Wouldn't they make it clear for us, the Aces?" chimed in Levine.

"Why not threaten the next generation? Deter them from continuing their training?" commented Toke. I swear that man always looked like he was on the verge of a mental breakdown.

Josh pulled up the strange symbol from his phone, showing Captain Harrison. "Definitely was a Magidoz. No other demon leaves behind that amount of residue, but this? Only someone with human hands could draw a symbol like this."

Cillian asked to see the picture, zooming in with his fingers. "An omen of death." The symbol in question, a circle with a line slashed down the middle, two perfectly formed dots on either side of the line, made no sense to me when I first saw it.

"We've been cleaning nests left and right, but I've never seen the city so infested in all my years," said Captain Harrison.

Stoll spoke then, worry lines forming in between his dark brows. "Have the other Orders been informed?"

"Yes. Different fleets have been taking turns patrolling the city, all the way upstate. I got word from Orders across the country that their numbers are down, barely any demonic activity."

Enjoying the silence from the mental wall I built was necessary, but Josh had knowledge I needed to access. Sighing internally, I smashed the mental wall apart, crumbling it into rubble at my feet. The floodgates opened once again, gaining direct access to his mind.

I tugged on that invisible string, and his eyes darted in my direction.

Are there other Orders across the state? I bit my lip, gauging his reaction, only to receive a cold shoulder, my question returned with silence. I guess I deserved that for blocking him out.

Dean Poverly finished his private conversation with Father Benedict. "There's a way to strengthen security. After speaking with Benedict, another Priest must participate."

"Strength in numbers," muttered Emilia, sheathing her dagger at her waist. "But that should've been dealt with prior, especially if *you knew* that was the case from the beginning."

Dean Poverly frowned. "With all due respect—"

"I would rethink what you're about to say," warned Cillian, stepping closer to Emilia.

Watching Cillian protect Emilia, not just physically but verbally in front of members of the Order, pulled at something deep within.

Putting my pride aside, I tried again. *I'm sorry.*

Josh's eyebrows rose, and then he cleared his throat, stealing a quick glance in my direction. *Forgiven. But don't ever lock me out again.*

Relief coursed through my body. *Noted. So, about the other Orders?*

His laugh echoed inside my head. *We'll do a crash course soon. Right now, pay attention, especially to Emilia.*

Confused, I hadn't realized she'd moved to the center of the room. She used the space to circle inside, staring at every single one of us. "We can't pretend anymore that the streets are any safer than they were a few years ago. Something has shifted, something we've never dealt with before. I think it would be wise to have stronger patrols, and requesting help from other—"

Dean Poverly stood, interrupting her suggestion. "Calling other Orders to assist is unnecessary."

"Then what do you suggest? We leave the younger generation of The Order, along with every innocent human on campus, open for slaughter?" growled Cillian.

Fear spiked my heart. *You were right. He could break our necks using only two fingers.*

I told you so. Josh then added, *Cillian has a point.*

Then why doesn't Dean Poverly let more patrols have access?

Because he has too much pride. It'll show everyone that he doesn't have control over New York City. They could replace him.

Captain Harrison pulled a piece of paper from inside his collar. "We have the authority from the Spades to overtake this jurisdiction."

All the professors' eyes widened in shock. Dean Poverly snatched the paper from Captain Harrison, reading vigorously several times before letting the paper fall to the floor. "It's true."

Thatcher snagged it before anyone could get their hands on it and read it herself. I watched her mouth whisper the words she read until her fingers crinkled the paper. "They move in tomorrow. We must provide housing for the patrols."

Chloe gasped quietly beside me, then whispered to mostly herself. "This is serious if the Spades are involved."

Before I could even ask Josh, he'd already infiltrated my mind. *The Spades are* the *highest council to exist in our world. Only a select few make it to that status. If they got word of what's happening over here, that would mean everyone across the board knows.*

Emilia looked taken aback. "I didn't hear of this. Were you holding back for shock factor, Captain?"

He smirked, gesturing to Thatcher to return the note. "I always have a surprise hand up my sleeve."

Cillian didn't look amused.

Looks like Cillian isn't happy being left out of the loop. In fact, Emilia's face said it all—pure rage.

I'm surprised he didn't tell them. They're the highest-ranking members in their fleet.

How many fleets are there?

Seven.

Captain Harrison made his way over to the front door, tossing out his final words. "The Spades know what's coming. Be prepared to send your trainees into battle." He left the command hanging in the air, with Emilia and Cillian not too far behind, anger rolling off their backs.

Chills ran up my spine, and nobody spoke for several minutes. Nobody could even look at one another. If what Captain Harrison said was true, the idea of joining those well-trained fleets in an all-out blood bath, my mind began to spiral. I built a tiny wall in my mind just to hide behind in order to figure out what this all meant without having my fears displayed front and center.

Regardless of my chosen fate, I couldn't, *wouldn't* participate. Being responsible not only for myself but other lives too, even strangers', was too much to think about. I knew what I saw that day outside the cathedral, there was no denying the presence of demons any longer.

But I wasn't strong enough to fight them, even mentally.

I could use a stiff drink right about now.

"We'll start fresh on Monday," announced Thatcher before storming out of the house.

Soon after, all the Aces trickled out, even Dean Poverly, but Father Benedict remained, his hands clasped behind his back. "Times are changing. A collapse in the balance of what we know could very well crumble before it's too late to change what is already set in motion."

Not a word was uttered when he left. Only the sound of a muffled trap beat playing in the background filled the emptiness of the room.

My phone buzzed inside my pocket, a text message from my wonderful mother reminding me of tomorrow night's dinner plans. Her condescending tone telling me how to dress never failed to seep through our text conversations, or any for that matter.

She had no idea her daughter had witnessed her first dead body.

CHAPTER 35

My mother *could* have picked a less conspicuous location to eat dinner as a family, but her attitude and aesthetic said otherwise. And for the first time, my desire to attend these family gatherings in such a setting made me want to crawl under a bridge and never resurface. I wouldn't lie; what Thatcher said kind of deterred me from certain aspects of my parents' lifestyle. Was she right about the silver spoon concept? Yes. But she was dead wrong about my Grams. That woman would have given the shirt off her back if it were her last one.

I didn't think Thatcher would do the same.

She could go fuck herself for all I cared.

I sat in somewhat sophisticated clothing, with my parents and Aiden in a private dining area at The Heron on the Upper East Side. A dimly lit restaurant with portraits of castles and vast countryside occupying the wall space, along with red velvet curtains sectioning off from the main dining area to keep the privacy of the rich secured, it was top tier, especially since we had our wait staff. My parents, particularly my mother, knew people in high places, and The Heron was tough to get a reservation at; I wondered which client she'd sucked up to get it.

Aiden was eating a dinner roll when my mother asked the waiter for one of their expensive champagnes.

My dad peeked over the menu, his reading glasses at the brim of his nose, watching my mother quizzically. "Do we have something to celebrate, Linda?"

She gave her best coy smile and clasped her hands under her chin, leaning on the table, her plum suit barely wrinkled from the action. "I can't have a nice family dinner at one of my favorite restaurants?"

I rolled my eyes. "There's always an ulterior motive."

My mother's eyes darted over to where I sat, her lips in a fine line until she sighed as if *she* were the one annoyed. "Honestly, Remi, your attitude is unnecessary."

At this point, Aiden was on his fourth dinner roll, buttering the shit out of the inside. "I hate to agree with little sis, but... why are we all gathered for dinner?"

I cocked an eyebrow, surprised that Aiden for once sided with me, especially against our mother.

However, she did not find that amusing. "Wow, both my children are conspiring against me."

Dad chuckled across the table. "Linda, please, you're keeping us in suspense."

Before she could utter a word, the waiter returned with the bottle of champagne and a bucket of ice, pouring both my parents a hearty glass as my mother sniffed and sipped appreciatively like a wine fucking connoisseur. The waiter then took our orders, and Aiden requested another bread-basket. I chugged my ice water, anxious to get this night over with.

I could really use my flask with Dad's whiskey right about now.

When she'd had enough of her obnoxious antics with her wine, I leaned back against the velvet chair, crossing my arms with impatience. I would rather deal with Josh and his nagging than sit here another second with my mother smacking her lips like a toddler with a juice box.

"Are you ever going to get to the point, *Mother*," I sneered. Irritation came off my body in waves, overtaking the rational part of my brain to keep my temper at bay.

That similar blonde brow rose. "Excuse me?"

"Why are we here?"

"We're here because I—"

Remi.

Whatever my mother was trying to convey faded like background noise. My name being called by an all too familiar voice had me searching the private space of the restaurant, but only faceless strangers occupied the tables.

Why couldn't I see him?

Better yet, how the hell did he know I was here?

"Remi, are you even listening to me?" my mother snapped.

I glanced at her. "Yeah, I just thought I saw someone." If he were here, that could only mean one thing...

After last night's briefing at the frat house, I shoved all my Order attire and dagger at the bottom of my closet, hoping that if I didn't look at it, I could pretend this was all a dream.

She followed my line of sight, searching with me, and said, "A friend from school?"

I ignored her much too excited tone. "No." I picked at my nails underneath the table.

"Like I was saying, I have taken an offer to buy—"

Remi.

My heart stopped. Just beyond the table near ours sat Josh, dressed in his hunter gear, the bow and quiver strapped securely to his back. He twirled a stone that hung from his neck; the pearlescent color reflected off the dining room lights. I abruptly stood, the chair hitting the table, causing some glasses of water to spill on the white tablecloth. Could they see him like I did?

"Remi!"

Go to the bathroom. Now.

I flinched from his harsh demand. "Fuck no."

"Remi! What did you just say to me?" Mom snapped. I didn't realize I'd said it out loud.

I tore my eyes away from Josh's stern expression to see my father dab at the damp cloth with his napkin. Aiden was unaffected by the chaos I sparked, while the look Mom gave me would've burned through my clothes if she could produce fire from her eyes. If I didn't move fast, Josh might make his presence known, and I wasn't ready to deal with that encounter with my family. Ever.

Josh sat, watching, waiting; not a single crack in the hard exterior of his face told me he wasn't going to leave until I followed his order. There wasn't any other way to escape without him finding me either.

There needed to be a way out of this without exposing Josh, who sat unbothered two tables down. Mom waited for me to respond, but instead, at the last second, I slapped my hand to my mouth, pretending to be sick, and rushed to the nearest women's bathroom, hoping it was the right one.

"Remi!" I prayed she didn't follow me.

Thank heavens the bathroom had a lock. I double-checked under the stalls, finding every one empty, and secured the door.

I pushed my back against it, giving myself a few seconds to chill out before noticing a sticky note taped to one of the stall doors. The words 'change here' in black letters were written in the center. Confused, I opened the stall to find a black garment bag tacked to the wall behind the toilet. I unzipped the bag, finding the color scarlet spilling out inside.

"How the hell…" How he got this inside without one of the staff catching him, I couldn't imagine. Hidden inside was my pager, beeping. How the f—

"Are you just going to stare at it all night or change? We're on a tight schedule."

I swung my arm around, only to have it blocked by Josh and his rough hand. "Easy there."

"What the hell are you doing in here?" Still holding onto my arm, Josh leaned forward, his lips inches from mine.

"You did one hell of a job hiding all day, only for me to locate your belongings at the bottom of your closet? Did you think trying to hide them under a pile of shoes would mask it?"

"And your point?" It wasn't like I trashed them… the thought was there, though.

"Stop trying to run from this. I am well aware of the little wall you built between our connection, but know this, *I will always find you.*" That last sentence sent waves of desire in the lower region of my body. I clearly needed therapy.

"I'm not running from this, I'm just going to pretend it doesn't exist, that's all." Out of sight, out of mind."

"I never met such a pain in the ass before. Your grandmother would be disappointed."

Fury flamed inside me. "Don't you dare talk about my grams. Ever."

"Then get your act together. I will fight with you all day, and I'll even enjoy it, but I won't ever stop pushing you. This is where you belong."

Those baby blues pierced through my soul, leaving me trembling. "Why are you even here, dressed like that?" My voice, breathless from his words and proximity, was enough to send anyone overboard, begging for the cool tide to snuff out the fire.

"Since you shut your phone off, I had to track you. We were chosen along with Baron and Chloe to check out the nest upstate."

I didn't even want to know how he tracked me; the idea would send my thoughts into unwanted territory. "Don't you think it's a little risky to send an untrained, unprepared *Scarlet* on this mission?"

"Four members of Captain Harrison's fleet will be in attendance. What better way to improve your training than to be there front and center."

I gulped. "Fantastic."

"You have two minutes to change." He released his grip, turning his back to give me privacy.

Stepping inside the stall, I unhooked the garment bag from the tack, stripped down to my underwear and bra, shimmied a pair of thick black leather-type pants over the thickness of my thighs, and pulled a skin-tight matching shirt over my head that somehow had a unique type of padding in the chest area. I found a matching belt and looped it through the waist of the pants. Patting my chest, trying to understand the mechanics of how they got the hard padding inside, I was shocked to find black ankle boots at the bottom and slipped them on, clasping the buckles one at a time. I tucked my phone in one of the boots, hoping it was secure enough and didn't come flying out and smash onto the concrete.

I hesitated with the cape, the soft fabric clutched in my small hands. Grams wore this at one point, fighting evils I couldn't even understand, and now there I stood, about to wear the symbolic clothing and follow in her path. Tears stung my eyes as I clasped them around my neck just as the bathroom door swung open.

I looked back in the stall. "What about my clothes?"

"Leave them; I'll have someone grab them later." Josh pulled out a black holster from his pocket, got down on his knees, and grabbed my right leg, extending it.

"What are you doing?" I panicked, trying to balance on my other leg.

"Stay still." He began to buckle the holster around my thigh. His strong hands gripped my outer leg, creating inappropriate thoughts I had to squish before he picked up on it. A space was attached to the holster where a weapon, most likely my dagger, could fit. He then removed the quiver and dug around until he retrieved an object wrapped in a black cloth.

Unwrapping the material, my dagger showed in the palm of his hand. "May I?"

All my thoughts jumbled into one. Josh and the way he knelt before me. How he held the dagger in his big palm, asking permission, how his blue eyes traveled up my body. It took a few seconds for my heart to catch up, and I could only nod approval.

There is something seriously wrong with me.

He gently placed the dagger inside the sheath, slowly

pulling his hands away from my leg. The sensation of his touch sent thrills of pleasure along my spine, and I had to hold my tongue to keep from exposing myself. Josh gazed up at me under those dark lashes, and his blue eyes swirled. "Next time, don't forget your pager." He got to his feet, readjusted his weapons to his back, and strode to one of the windows by the line of sinks. All sexual thoughts were deflated the minute he opened his mouth.

"What are you doing?" I questioned, watching him unlatch the window and climb onto the heating vent.

Josh looked over his shoulder. "We can't go through the front; I only have one amethyst stone to conceal myself."

Josh twisted his body out the window and stood outside the restaurant, then peeked his head back in and offered his hand. "Ready?"

I sighed deeply and hoisted myself onto the heater, reaching for his calloused hand. I gripped the windowsill and jumped up, Josh using his other hand to grip underneath my arm and tugging lightly to get me through. I twisted my body as he did until I came out on the other side, standing upright, his hands lingering a little too long on my waist.

Barely an inch separated our bodies, the heat creating something sensual, the lingering of his stare pulling me in.

CHAPTER 36

Until his pocket beeped, shattering the moment.

I stepped back from his touch and pretended to smooth down my attire.

He pulled out the pager, watching the screen with concentration. "The van is picking us up in two minutes."

I surveyed my surroundings and found us standing just at the beginning of the alley, two big dumpsters to our right, where staff from the restaurant disposed of the old food. One of the lids was open, the smell wafting toward me, and I had to hold my breath to keep from gagging. No matter how long I lived in the city, the smell of rotten or spoiled food never got easier to process.

A sleek, black van owned by the Order pulled up, barely missing the curb, screeching as it halted just as the doors slid open, revealing a disheveled Baron in the back. "Hurry, Emilia and Cillian are already there."

"Why am I not surprised those two were chosen," Josh hissed as he got into the back of the van. I followed suit, finding no seating but instead black crates taking up most of the space. "This is really bad timing."

"Yeah, well, we weren't expecting the pit stop," commented Baron, giving me a quick look.

"Nobody was."

"What are those?" I asked, ignoring their obvious conversation about me.

Josh grabbed my hand and placed it on one of the handles. "Before you go through the windshield."

"As for the boxes, those are spare bows and makeshift bombs," answered Baron. He took his position in front of me, grabbing his handle.

Why would they need makeshift bombs? While my mind tried to keep up with everything going on, I peeked at Josh, who held on tight to his handle, looking straight ahead.

Chloe looked over her shoulder from the driver's side. "Hold on!"

She put the van in drive and peeled away from the curb, skirting hard into oncoming traffic and barely missing the minivan behind us. I lost some of my footing and almost collided with Josh's back, but Baron gripped my arm and held me in place.

"I'm not used to standing in a moving vehicle," I admitted.

Baron smiled, and when he did, so did his eyes. "I can see that." Then he winked like he wasn't just bitching about the inconvenience of picking me up, but I couldn't help but giggle, because he had a charm about him.

I peeked back over to Josh, his eyes catching mine out of his peripherals.

Josh, I said.

I watched him stretch his neck, massaging it at the same time. The action was somewhat attractive, and I caught a glimpse of black ink just under his shirt when he stretched forward, but I wasn't getting his attention to pant like a dog in heat. He deliberately chose to ignore me.

Josh, I hissed.

What? he hissed back. The tension was inevitable in his shoulders, as he rolled them back. What the fuck was his deal?

Are you going to ignore me all night? I snapped.

No, I'm trying to clear my head. I don't have time for petty conversations, and neither should you. Your focus should be on the mission, he chastised.

Anger sizzled under my skin. *Are you serious?*

Hundred percent.

How did you find me, Josh?

Not an appropriate time to ask me, Remi.

Fuck you, it is.

I saw his jaw clench as if he were holding himself back from shouting at me. Good. I hoped the restraint hurt.

Please don't make me ask again, I muttered.

Please don't, your voice is grating, Josh deadpanned.

I gripped my dagger in the sheath, not missing the glance from Josh, his eyes wandering down my thigh.

Are you going to use that on me? He chuckled.

Do you want to find out? I threatened. The sudden urge to pierce him in between the eyes had me grasping the pommel until my knuckles turned white.

The van continued to swerve through traffic as we rocked back and forth, never letting go of the handle no matter how bad it began to hurt my fingers.

I heard his audible sigh. *Father Benedict assisted me with your whereabouts.*

How?

You're not going to like it.

Something told me to press further. *Tell me, now.*

Chloe bolted through a red light, jerking our bodies around as we entered the highway.

It requires my blood and your hair.

Excuse me?

Now's not the time to have this conversation. Next time, don't go through drastic measures and maybe keep your phone on too, he reprimanded.

What the hell? His blood? My hair? What kind of sick freak collects someone's hair to locate their Scarlet?

Who builds a mental wall up and hides from the world? he muttered.

"We're taking the tunnel. It'll get us there faster," announced Chloe from the front.

Baron groaned. "I hate the tunnel."

"It helps to skip all the traffic," mentioned Josh.

Not quite sure what they meant, I looked at Baron. "What's the tunnel?"

"The tunnel was built about twenty years ago. It's a way for us to travel throughout the states without getting caught in traffic."

Chloe veered the van onto a random exit, still somewhat in the city, and swerved between cars, dodging every possible side swipe, or almost collision. I was thankful I only drank water back at the restaurant.

It was only a matter of time before my family realized my disappearance, but I let that concern sit in the back of my mind as I focused on the present.

Taking a sharp right, we ended up in a narrow alleyway, the van barely skimming by between brick buildings on either side. Chloe slammed her foot down on the gas pedal, picking up speed, heading straight at a closed garage door. My heart ended up in my stomach, clutching the handle with both hands for dear life. Why hasn't she slowed down?

I closed my eyes, waiting for impact, or hoping Chloe would come to her senses, when the van suddenly came to an abrupt halt. I felt like the air was knocked out of me, struggling to control my labored breaths, like I ran a marathon.

Open your eyes, Rem. Josh's voice, a soothing tone, coaxed me out of my panic state.

"You missed the best part," deadpanned Baron. He breathed hard through his nose, sporting an ashen face.

Taking notice of his shaky appearance, I wasn't even going to attempt to ask how we managed to bypass all that heavy traffic.

Chloe put the van in park and exited the vehicle only to slide open the back door, gesturing for us quickly to exit. Parked a few spots down sat an identical van but no sign of Emilia or Cillian.

Josh followed my line of sight and scowled. "Impatient pricks."

Chloe yanked me aside and clasped the same amethyst pendant Josh had worn underneath his shirt around my neck, whispering a few words while she clenched it in her fist.

After she released it, I touched the smooth stone as it hung from my neck. It was cool to the touch; even under the lampposts, it glittered.

Chloe handed me a folded piece of paper. "Two words.

One to conceal, one to reveal. Right now, you're concealed. Nobody can see us but each other."

Tucking the paper in one of the many pockets on my pants, I surveyed the landscape. About seven three-decker apartments sat untouched for what seemed like years. With boarded-up doors and half-shattered glass windows, only a small overgrown patch of grass was left behind. It even had a junkyard of beat-up cars.

The street we parked on was empty. Not a single pedestrian in sight. Some of the lampposts flickered the muggy summer heat hanging in the air. Whatever material they used to make our fighting gear prevented any chance of sweating to death.

"Where are the others?" Josh questioned, adjusting his quiver and bow.

"Probably ran ahead because we were late," commented Baron.

Chloe pulled out her pager and flipped the screen up, revealing a wider view. "I guess they shot a tracker on one. That could explain their disappearance."

"Leaving four trainees out in the wide open is a rookie mistake." Josh got his bow ready, pulling a sleek arrow from the quiver.

I was either going to die or get seriously hurt if I didn't get my shit together.

"Any casualties?" Baron queried as he dragged one of the black crates from the back out onto the pavement.

"Just one." Chloe pointed to a dead man by the steps, slouched over; his skin had a powdery complexion. Most of his clothes were ripped to shreds, showing wounds in all different angles, blood gushing from the one on his stomach. "He looks fresh, which could also explain why they're not out here waiting for us."

My anxiety made my stomach turn. The poor guy never had a chance. "I thought the original fleet cleaned out the nests?"

Baron tucked a makeshift bomb in his quiver, handing a second to Josh. "Looks like more showed up."

"More victims, more Magidoz. Who knows? That's why we have the bombs," affirmed Chloe.

I gulped. "What if there's more victims?"

"If there's more, we will cross that bridge when we get there."

That wasn't reassuring, and the longer we debated this, the more civilians could be suffering or dead. Was I about to shit my pants from fear? Yeah, but knowing innocent civilians were getting killed awakened something inside me.

I took a step closer to the apartment, but the cape snagged on something. "What the hell?"

I twisted, struggling against the hold that appeared bunched up in the back to find Josh grasping the material, shaking his head in disapproval.

"Chloe and Baron are taking the front; we're going out back. Let's pray the other four are already underground."

He dropped his hold on my cape to then line the arrow up with his bow. "I want you to lead the way."

"Is that wise considering I'm new to all this?" I asked nervously. There was a solid chance my stupid ass would walk us right into the claws of a Magidoz demon.

Apprehension must have been obvious on my face because Josh lowered his bow, using his free hand to cup my cheek. "I'm sorry I'm making this difficult for you. I don't mean to come off like an ass, but I know you can do it, Remi. You were born to be a Scarlet."

His words caught me off guard. I tried to scramble my brain after his apology, one I didn't expect nor think he would need to give.

I swallowed a hard lump in my throat and stepped back from his hand, watching it drop to his side. There was a good chance he spoke those words to get my ass into gear, and I got it, but in some twisted way, I wanted it to mean *more,* and it was wrong. I knew that.

Even now, as we stood inches apart, my body called to his touch, begging for it to come back to caress my skin.

Josh's face dropped back into that serious expression. How quickly that sincere speech disappeared into thin air.

I rolled my shoulders and unsheathed my dagger from the holster, nodding once to both Chloe and Baron as we made our separate ways to the vacant apartments.

CHAPTER 37

I tried to keep my cool by breathing steadily through my nose, the pommel slick from my clammy hands, Josh right on my tail as we inched our way toward the back.

The smell of rotting flesh hit us just as we rounded the corner, discovering four bodies were scattered throughout the small parking lot, or what was left of them. Black sludge coated most of the ground, and some cars were painted in the aftermath. From the street, you couldn't tell what carnage lay just beyond the property line, and that scared the absolute shit out of me. How many places had I passed by, not aware of what was beyond?

The sight of the slaughter of innocent individuals had me hesitating just before the steps that led down to the basement of the building.

I wanted to vomit so bad from the smell alone.

How many more were victims of such gruesome creatures?

"Fucking Magidoz residue," Josh muttered.

The back of my neck tingled with unease. The last time I saw that demon was behind the church on school grounds while Kal fought for his life, and I cowered in a corner.

"Keep going," Josh said, nudging me lightly. "I know this is hard, but we have to keep going, and remember, Olemaks are also around."

It took a couple of minutes to make my legs move, but eventually, we stood in front of the steel door, slightly ajar, with human blood smeared on the rusted knob. Using my foot to open it wider, a blast of cold air was something of a relief from the wretched heat as we prowled inside. But that signified death, ruining the reprieve, even if it were only for a few seconds.

A flickering lightbulb hung from a wire in the ceiling, swaying softly, illuminating small parts of the damp basement. A trail of blood continued from where we entered, leading around crumbling drywall. Water dripped off one of the many pipes that lined the ceiling into a puddle on the cement floor. The smell of decaying human flesh became stronger, to the point where I had to swallow the vomit that was forming in the back of my throat. A body was nailed to the drywall to our right, and not a single drop of blood oozed out.

"Looks like a Drarkoth has joined the party," he muttered.

That was news to me. "I'm guessing we'll discuss that later?"

"Yup."

Just as I was about to peek around the damaged wall, Josh's voice filtered into my mind, halting me in place. *Don't move,* he warned, stepping around to examine the body more closely. He opened the half-torn button shirt, revealing a symbol on the sunken chest. The same symbol as the girl we found in the bathtub had.

Fuck, he hissed.

What does it mean?

Another sacrifice was made.

Pulling back the hood of my cape to cool down, sweat had dripped down my neck and drenched my hairline. Josh's forehead creased with worry, his own sweat leaving a trail down his temple as he typed something into his phone. Between the intensity of the heat and the stench of decaying bodies, I was seconds away from passing out.

Were they capable of working with other demons? Like the Magidoz and Olemak?

Remember what Thatcher said? It is not uncommon for them to nest near one another, Josh explained, interrupting my internal questioning.

"Josh—"

He covered my mouth with his rough hand. *It's best if we continue to communicate mentally.*

I removed his hand. *There could be a good chance they already know.*

He rolled his eyes and nudged me forward, following the trail of blood ahead. *They're too busy feasting on their victims to care about us right now.*

Thanks for that mental image.

Just trying to keep you on your toes.

If I die, it's your fault.

At the very end of the trail was a wide, open hole in the basement floor. The sides slanted in, causing crumbles of dirt to roll down along with pieces of cement at the bottom, hitting what sounded like an empty echo. It also happened to be the designated spot where Chloe and Baron met us unintentionally, covered in what seemed to be Magidoz sludge. It would seem they faced more peril upstairs than what we countered out back.

Chloe and Baron exchanged looks before nodding to us, then jumped one after another inside the gaping hole.

I stood frozen over the edge, waiting to hear a scream or shout, but nothing happened.

You can do it too, you know, encouraged Josh.

I turned to him; a small smile displayed on those full lips. The way his eyes looked over at me, blue and crystal-like, mesmerizing with long, dark eyelashes. His hair was tousled and damp with sweat, just like his face, and his lips parted slightly the more I stared deeply at him. Josh reached forward and brushed a loose strand of hair behind my ear. Moments like these, where he seemed to genuinely care, were few and far between, and—

Suddenly a rock flew out of the hole, landing in between us, almost knocking one of us on the head. It was clear that either Chloe or Baron—and my money was on Chloe—were not happy with our delay, and I was grateful for the wake-up call.

Clearing my throat, I took a step back from Josh and edged myself around the opening. A cool draft along with the smell of fresh dirt greeted me, but not enough to shake the fear of dropping down some odd feet that could potentially break my legs. What if the hole was deeper than we expected and that's why I didn't hear their shouts of pain?

A tender hand touched my shoulder. *Close your eyes and let your gifts guide you.* Josh's soothing voice became the diving board of my actions and my physical strength as I jumped straight down into the unknown.

CHAPTER 38

I landed with a soft thud on more dirt, the rush from the drop sent a thrill through my nervous system. A flashlight blinded me in the face, and someone pulled me aside so Josh could land where I stood just a few seconds ago. The flashlight was then angled to the ground, revealing Baron behind the bright light and Chloe's tight grip still on my arm. I patted her off and readjusted myself, relieved to have made the drop, surprised that the impact didn't break my kneecaps.

Baron dimmed the light just enough to where we could recognize our silhouettes and motioned for us to follow him through the underground tunnel.

Are Drarkoth's known to make tunnels? I asked Josh, trying my best not to trip and blow our cover.

They don't. This was done by a Magidoz, Josh responded. *A fucking big one.*

We continued in silence, only our soft steps heard in the vastness of the tunnel. To imagine anything else lurking within the shadows down here seemed tamed compared to what I'd witnessed outside the cathedral.

I wished I could hear the others. Maybe it would be easier to prepare when we reached the end.

No, you don't, laughed Josh.

I wasn't talking to you, I sneered.

Loud thoughts, remember?

You're insufferable.

Likewise.

I huffed loudly and thought, *Why wouldn't we want to hear the others?*

It could get overwhelming and could distract you in battle. Being bonded to one is better than none.

I prefer not, period.

Josh stifled a laugh from behind me. *You're lucky it's me. If you got paired with anyone else, they would've already requested a transfer.*

I rolled my eyes, inching my way through the tunnels. *Is that what happened to your last one?*

I only had you.

Why the hell did his comment warm my skin? Even the cooling material of the fighting gear I wore wasn't enough to sizzle out the flame along my skin. Then a thought occurred, already filtering through our connection. *Wait, I'm your first—?*

Just then, a slight rumble vibrated our feet. We froze, Baron shutting off the light as we waited, unsure if it would happen again. Time seemed to tick on, until another rumble sounded, and then another, until it became constant, a nagging vibration like one of a cell phone when someone was calling.

We're close to the nest. Looks like someone didn't do a thor-

ough job cleaning it out. The hairs on my neck stood up at Josh's warning, neither of us sure whether to continue down the darkened tunnel.

Baron dimmed the flashlight once more, barely a glow illuminating from the bulb, and whispered, "We have to keep going."

I barely heard him over the rumble. *What if there is more than just Magidoz?* If Josh's claim was true about the size of the demon, then another one of that size could also be lurking down here.

Be prepared to fight, Josh warned.

Because I have been for my whole life?

As we trekked further in, the rumbling got louder, causing a ringing in my ears.

With one foot in front of the other, I kept my balance and wits about me as best as I could, but it was Josh's voice inside my head that made me halt.

Remi, your hilt is glowing red.

I stalled, Josh's hand stopping himself at my shoulder from colliding with my back as I gazed down to where I clutched the pommel. A soft glow shined through my hand where the garnet stone was forged.

Is this normal? I asked.

"Baron!" Josh whispered.

The faded light from the flashlight was directed at us. "What—"

His sudden silence made Chloe swear in disbelief.

That's when the rumbling stopped.

I stood, gripping the pommel as it glowed brighter, my hand vibrating from the intensity as if some other force was behind it. *Is this normal?*

Not that I'm aware of. He grabbed my dagger, inspecting

the stone, the glow illuminating his features. Josh's fingers traced the pommel, only to look up into my eyes, a curious expression to match my own.

"I read somewhere that Juniper's original weapon glowed when danger was near, but..." Baron took it from Josh, lowering the flashlight, his eyes scanning every part, trying to see if there was something hidden within the depths of its forgery. "...her dagger is lost. Not even The Order knows what happened to it."

"Lost?" I said in disbelief.

Baron handed me back the dagger. "It's been missing for months."

"How did you find this out?" questioned Chloe.

"Acting oblivious around the Aces comes in handy," he informed us.

A deep growl shook the tunnel, a warm breeze whipping through us as if someone huffed their hot breath in our direction.

Forgetting about my shiny weapon, we bolted down the tunnel, running blindly in the dark.

I pumped my legs, Josh only a couple steps behind, Baron leading the sprint. My dagger glowed brighter the further we traveled, snapping teeth coming from behind us.

Praying we didn't hit a wall, Baron shouted over the rumbling. "Left!"

My sense of awareness when pumped with adrenaline was enough to determine when Chloe made a turn. Following closely behind, Baron continued to shout directions, until the tunnel opened to a wide space revealing one Saint and Scarlet battling in the center against the biggest Magidoz I'd ever seen. Its arms were enormous, with pulsating veins and a head sporting four horns instead of three.

Anxiety pounded in my bloodstream.

The Magidoz snarled, showing all three rows of needle-shaped teeth, snapping at the air, hissing with each attack. Black sludge coated its entire form, making a protective circle where it stood.

Cillian fired arrows left and right from a sleek black crossbow, dodging every counter move effortlessly. A deep gash oozed from his left cheek, dirt was caked on his fore-head, but he showed no signs of debilitation.

Emilia climbed its back, shouting in rage, aiming her dagger directly at its head, only to get tossed off into a heap of broken metal pipes, Cillian screaming as he fired an arrow.

Baron got his bow ready. "We have to help!"

Shit.

There was no way I could do this.

Petrified, my bones locked in place while everything played out before me.

Josh's positive affirmation filtered into my head. *You're a Scarlet by blood. You have the power to fight this.*

Do you not remember a couple nights ago? I was completely freaked out when a smaller one was behind the cathedral! I reminded him. And how I ran away like a coward, almost drowning in whiskey to ease the *very real* nightmare.

Remi, you have the strength of past Scarlets burning inside you. The Blessing gave you what you need to overcome the terrors of what plagues this world. Grasp that fear and destroy it.

What if I fail and get everyone killed?

Josh grasped my chin, forcing me to look directly into his eyes. "Failure only happens when you don't *try*. So, try,

Remi. Try and win." His eyes blazed with each word he spoke.

"I won't fail," I whispered, repeating the mantra until Josh let me go.

Swallowing any sense of terror I had moments ago, I began to circle the Magidoz with Chloe until we reached Cillian, who kept knocking back arrows to distract it from his Scarlet.

"Get her up!" he ordered, an arrow whizzing in the air, striking the Magidoz in the shoulder. Sludge spewed from the wound, spraying down like a broken faucet. It cried an ear-piercing scream, causing me to cover my ears.

Chloe ran in the opposite direction, then rolled until she landed near Emilia's unconscious body, shielding her as much as possible.

Josh and Baron started releasing their own arrows, some barely grazing it while it swung with its long claws. Baron climbed up a makeshift shelf of metal piping, getting a better view before knocking back an arrow. Josh took it upon himself to move to the other side, almost slipping in a puddle of sludge. It turned as Josh made it around the beast, sniffing the air.

I suddenly realized its eyes were missing, and its nostrils flared with rage.

Holy shit, it was blind!

Josh! He's blind!

Remi, get as close as you can.

Its sludge left a trail leading up to where it stood, swiping vigorously, screeching. If it was blind, then the odds were, it was using its sense of smell to track our movements. Sight robbed, but the demon wasn't stupid. How to get across was another issue.

But what if...

Tossing my cape to the side, I sheathed my dagger. If this didn't work, then I might as well expect an early visit to the afterlife. I got down on all fours, making sure from the neck up didn't touch the residue, and rolled through the stench, masking my scent with its own.

When I finished, zigzagging through flying arrows and dangerous swipes, I found leverage on a busted pipe and jumped, to then push myself off the wall, gliding through the air. In just seconds, removing the dagger, I aimed, hands overhead, ready to strike.

Before, there was no way my body could perform such acrobatic moves. Now, it felt like second nature, a rush of strength and power guiding my every move. Any sense of doubt went away, giving me the courage to take on such a grotesque task.

I landed directly on its back, stabbing right between its shoulder blades and dragged the dagger down, going with it and creating a deep gash, more sludge spraying, hitting me in the face.

Its cry shook the tunnel, and its contorted body swayed. Making it to the bottom, I ripped the blade free, backing up against a wall, my hands slick with demon sludge. It began to stumble, and the men shouted to get back, halting their assault. Dozens of arrows covered the ground, some broken, others stuck to old crates and barrels. Chloe had Emilia leaning on her body, supporting her weight, eyes half closed and blood oozing from her scalp. Her shoulders bore deep gashes, part of her leather pants torn at the knees.

Time slowed to an agonizing speed as Josh shoved Baron and Cillian, getting them out of the way. He barely missed the Magidoz, crying for the last time, falling forward and hitting the ground with force, steam escaping from the wound on its exposed back. From the impact of the fall, some sludge hit the men, and Baron cursed loudly.

Ready to go to them, I stopped short, noticing what the Magidoz's strong build blocked from view. I found the other Scarlet and Saint ripped to shreds, their heads barely hanging onto their spines.

Covering my mouth, I dropped to my knees, a cry forming in my throat. We were too late. *I* was too late.

Josh knelt beside me, cradling my head against his chest. "It's okay. You're okay. You saved them."

But I didn't save them all.

Cillian walked over to their lifeless bodies, lowering his crossbow. "And God shall wipe away all tears from their eyes; and there shall be no more death, neither sorrow, nor crying, nor shall there be any more pain for the former things are passed away."

Josh bowed his head along with Baron and Chloe. But I couldn't look away from what was lost, never to come back, gone to wherever their resting place may be.

Tears welled in my eyes. "How is this okay?" My voice was barely above a whisper.

Josh stroked my hair. "What we sacrifice is what we gain in the afterlife."

Looking up from my tear-soaked lashes, Josh stopped stroking my hair. "It still doesn't make it okay. How can we continue, knowing every day could be someone's last?"

"If you let the fear of death control your actions, then you might as well dig yourself an early grave." Cillian took Emilia from Chloe, carrying her like a rag doll. "Thank you for showing up in time."

"How did this even happen?" asked Chloe.

Cillian replied, "We were ambushed. The first fleet failed to do a thorough search."

"Are you sure?" Josh seemed unconvinced.

"Bold of you to question your superiors, West."

That was the first time I'd heard his last name. Come to think of it, I knew nothing of any of them. Trusting a bunch of strangers, running around in dirty tunnels was not on my bucket list.

"Just trying to cover all the bases here. Ironic that we were chosen for this mission." He stood then, taking me with him.

I wiped my cheeks with the back of my hand, finding sludge residue lingering.

"Whatever you *think,* you're wrong."

"Sorry, just find it hard to believe that one of the top Saints and Scarlets were almost taken down by a somewhat large Magidoz." Of course, he wasn't going to let this go.

No, you should be questioning this as well, he added.

We don't know what happened before our arrival, I challenged. All I wanted was to get the hell out of there, strip the sticky clothes off, and take a long, hot shower... or two. Instead, he chose to pick a fight against the deadliest Saint in the northeast.

I have every right to question his actions. As someone of his caliber, why did we find two other members dead and his own Scarlet flying headfirst into a pile of junk?

Right now, our best bet is to get out of here and regroup later. Because if another one of those freakish, large beasts come again, I don't think I have it in me to go another round. I was quite astonished to have even fought, let alone still be standing after what I'd done.

306

"Glad to keep you in suspense." Cillian stepped over a small puddle of goo, exiting the way we originally came in.

"Prick," muttered Josh, securing his bow once again on his back. Half his arrows were depleted, and some of the ends looked broken.

"Great idea, masking your scent, Remi," praised Baron, leading the way out.

I smiled, kind of proud of my quick thinking. "Thanks."

Josh handed me my cape, our eyes meeting once again. He searched my face, checking every inch, probably to see if I got hurt. When he couldn't find a scratch on me, something shifted. His eyes became softer and his body language changed, enticing a feeling only I would get from a serious situation, like a moron.

I'm so proud of you, Remi.

CHAPTER 39

After our debriefing with the Aces, Thatcher continued to cuss about how terrible Captain Harrison was. We left the part of my glowing dagger out, saving it for when we had alone time with Father Benedict.

I managed to drag my ass through campus, thankful the stone concealed my disgusting presence.

Unfolding the semi-damaged paper Chloe gave me, I tried to pronounce the two words she wrote that controlled the stone's abilities, *Nochd* and *Falach*.

A quick search on the internet helped me out, finding that it derived from Scotland. More specifically, Scottish Gaelic.

It would make sense. Juniper was from the area, but nobody here spoke it that I was aware of, so I found it odd they used certain words in the language. I wondered if past generations became less accustomed to the old ways, only keeping what was necessary. Either way, it worked, and after an hour in the showers, scrubbing my body until it turned red and watching the black water finally turn clear, a girl smiled before heading into her stall as I stepped out.

My feet ached a little. A pedicure would sure have eased some of the tension in my heels.

Collapsing on my bed with the towel wrapped around my body, I stared at Heather's empty side, promising to visit her as soon as I got some rest. I brushed through the wet tangles and got into a freshly washed silk pajama set, then curled under the covers, exhaustion sweeping me away into oblivion.

STANDING on the precipice of battle, readying myself to draw my sword, Josh stood beside me, sporting an identical weapon. His smile was reassuring, moving the scar on his left cheek. Touching where the wound had healed, I kissed his cheek gently, returning to the battle before us.

"Are you ready?" he asked, taking my hand in his.

"I'm ready to finish this," I declared. It was time to end the evil.

Josh shouted for our fleet to commence as we barreled down the hill, weapons raised, joining the others on the battlefield.

The first swing I took sliced an unfamiliar demon, almost humanlike, its head rolling away. Josh and I stood back to back, swinging every blow, hitting our target every time. Blood flew, bodies collapsed, some human, some demon, as demons of every species plagued the field we fought on, working together to take all of us down.

My sword glowed, power emanating from the blade. I grunted, finding myself in a standoff between two more, not sure what they were called, but I kept fighting.

Josh shouted another command, only to give me a private one in my head. *Back up a bit. Use me as leverage.*

Knowing exactly what he meant, I put all my weight on his back, rolling off to switch sides with him. *How are more showing up?!*

They had time to build their armies. I wouldn't be surprised if the numbers were—

I heard his grunt. The sound of metal on metal colliding caught my attention.

Finishing off a demon of my own, I tried to help Josh, only to be caught by several more invading my space. Chloe stood on the outer edges with Baron, trying to stop any more from coming through.

Josh cursed, metal clashing. "You're a fucking coward!"

"And you're dead." That voice iced my skin, threatening to end someone I cared deeply for.

Josh struggled, then the noises stopped, and I turned at the last second to see a sword stab him directly in the heart.

I dropped to my knees, screaming, "JOSH!"

Standing over his body was an all too familiar man, hair black as night, clothes of the same color. A smile, one of deceit and destruction, mocking me from afar. I lost my will to move, to continue, feeling the connection of our souls fizzle out, fading into the abyss.

My chest throbbed, the absence of his voice, his soul, weighing a heavy burden inside. Leaning forward on my hands and knees, I tried to catch my breath.

A dark shadow blocked out the sun, and the dark man

bent down until his rough hand gripped the back of my neck.

"Now you're mine."

GASPING, I awoke to the sight of Josh shaking my shoulders. Without thinking, I pulled him into a tight embrace, making sure it felt real.

"Rem... you... you're... crush... ing... my... wind... pipe!" he choked.

I didn't care, because he was there, alive, in my room, the smell of his musk easing the terror away, never to scare me again. "Give me a minute. Please." Easing the pressure off his lungs, I continued to hug his strong build.

Tears escaped, hitting his shoulder. "Are you crying?"

Yes. "No." Soon, they flowed, and I tried my hardest to muffle my sobs.

He circled his arms around me, and we sat, holding onto one another. He let me cry for what seemed like forever until nothing else came out, but he never once let go. I focused on my breathing, my stomach hurting from the intensity of my sobs. Josh, warm and sturdy, rubbed my back in circles, waiting it out in silence.

My throat was parched and sore, and breaking away, I looked into his eyes, blue as the ocean, a sea I happily got lost in.

Pushing my hair back behind my ears, our bond sizzled underneath the surface. What to say when a dream that realistic plagued my mind? "I'm sorry."

"Remi, it was only a dream," he soothed.

Was it? When all of it, right down to his death, might follow into reality. "How did you get in here, anyway?"

His eyes searched my face, and he brushed more of my hair aside. "I have a key, since I'm your guardian. It was wise to obtain a spare."

"That's kind of creepy."

He cocked an eyebrow. "I guess from your perspective."

I snorted. "From all perspectives, Josh."

He rolled his eyes. "Alright, time for bed."

"Wha—"

Josh scooped me up in his arms, only to gently lay me back down. Gathering a fistful of my designer comforter, he tucked me in.

"Was that necessary?" I asked.

He doesn't say a word but lightly touches my cheek. "Sleep, Remi."

"Where are you going?" But he didn't bother to turn around, and softly closed the door behind him.

Why was he here? Why must he... show me he cares?

Josh gave me a heads up to prepare for our second training session. I stomached what food I could in the cafe, but whatever appetite I had faded as the day went on.

Before going, I stopped to visit Heather. The machines beeped away like nothing had changed, keeping her stable. According to Nurse Amelia, her body temperature never reached the standard but dipped a few times during my absence. I gave her my personal number and firm instructions to call me if that ever happened again.

Making my way to the main dining room underground, the curtains behind the dais were wide open, showing a very shirtless, very sweaty Josh running on the treadmill.

Sweat dripped down his pecs, right into the waistband of his shorts. His body, of godly perfection, glistened, tempting me to lick every inch—I never built a mental wall so fast in my life, heat spreading to my cheeks.

Wireless headphones blasted some heavy beat inside his ears, and he picked up the pace, matching the tempo. He ran his fingers through his hair, drenched in sweat, finally looking up to see me gawking on the side.

He waved, taking one earbud out. "Hop on, killer."

Dropping my bag, I used the other machine to his right, setting up my incline, when he handed me his other earbud. "Thanks." He must've lowered the volume, but the beat was catchy, getting me into a groove rather quickly.

I peeked over at his time, watching the clock tick up to forty minutes. *Was he here the whole time while I checked on Heather?*

We ran in silence, only the sound of our shoes hitting the tread, his music accompanying our workout. It was no shock that his tastes were like what he played, and I wondered when the last time was. Between the infamous party and our little escape upstate, when did he have the time to gig out with his fellow bandmates?

My muscles groaned in protest, not used to working so hard since freshman year track; the only time I took part in anything in all my high school career.

I picked up speed to match him, and he took notice of our pace and smiled, his face covered in perspiration. For someone to be that sweaty running and look hot while doing it was enough to put any runway model to shame.

Double-checking my mental walls, I smiled in return, my heart pumping overtime with the physical activity and his sensual lips perking up at the corners of that goddamn mouth.

Thirty minutes came and went, and calling it quits, I leaned forward, hands on knees, trying to control my breathing.

The music stopped, and Josh hopped off the treadmill, grabbing two dark blue towels off one of the benches and handing one over. "I think we should do cardio at least three times a week."

I groaned, taking the towel and wiping the sweat off. "Great. What's next? Hike a mountain?"

He laughed, rubbing the towel over his abdomen. I swear if I had zero self-control, there was no doubt in my mind I would have been on my knees.

"Nah, although, never say never." Chugging back water from a black bottle, he wiped his mouth on the back of his hand. "Time to lift weights."

Smirking, I got an idea. "Lift weights, but you answer any question I have?"

Patting the empty seat by the mirror, he grabbed two five-pound weights. "Sit, do a few reps, then we talk?"

"Deal."

Josh stood behind my head, arms crossed, instructing the workout I would perform. He had me start with a chest press, correcting my form several times until he approved of my movement. Little did he know the reason for my shit formation was his choice of continuing to instruct shirtless, right above me.

After finishing another rep, I took a little break, my arms like noodles. "I want you to explain how you found me the other night."

He groaned, looking at the ceiling. "Right." Taking one sixty-pound dumbbell, he sat at the end of the bench, curling. "A strand of your hair dipped in my blood was given to Father Benedict, who then placed it on a map. A prayer is performed, and then he drags the strand over the map. The blood only stains where that person is."

Flabbergasted, I half-chuckled. "Wait, what? That's—"

"Impossible?" He switched the dumbbell to his left. "Yet we just battled one of the biggest Magidoz I'd ever seen."

Sitting back, hugging my knees, I watched his muscles expand with each rep. even his shoulder blades moved, the sight delectable. But I had to focus. "Yes, demons are real. I have a sense ghosts are as well, but what you're claiming is... magic."

"Magic, prayers, it's all the same. Father Benedict is a gifted priest, equipped to help us survive another day." He moved to stand, lifting a brow at me. Taking the hint, I carried my weights over, creating some space between us. "Reverse fly."

I watched him first, bending halfway and lifting his arms at a ninety-degree angle, feet spread evenly apart. Sighing, I mimicked his stance, right down to the lift, my back screaming in agony.

Damn, I was out of shape. "What is a Drarkoth demon?" Speaking in between reps was a workout on its own.

"The most human-looking abomination to walk the planet. Think of a vampire. They can drain someone dry but are short on beauty."

I thought of my sick obsession with vampire romance

books at the ripe age of thirteen. "Damn, and here I thought my dream man, Edward Cullen, lived."

Josh howled, almost losing his balance. "Nowhere near that disco ball."

"Oh, so you've seen it?" I teased.

"I got a sister, so yeah, I've seen it, one too many times," he replied, returning the dumbbell.

I followed suit, lying on the mat. "Funny, I pictured you as an only child."

Josh joined, only to kick me in the shins to start a round of sit-ups. "Our age gap is nine years." He counted backward from thirty.

Getting to twenty-five, I paused to rest. "Wow, uh, that's wild."

He kept going with the sit-ups. "Not really. Some in the Order have bigger ones."

"Aiden and I are exactly one year apart."

Josh stopped mid-sit-up. "You have a brother? How is he not in the Order?"

I shrugged. "Honestly, nothing surprises me anymore."

"But there's no record—"

Glass shattered from the dining room, a loud groan coming soon after. "Father!"

Josh bolted upright, running at full speed, jumping off the dais. It took me a couple of seconds to catch up. Collin knelt on the floor, Father Benedict shaking, foam spewing from his mouth. Panic clenched my stomach, but Josh kept his cool, arms spread, blocking any attempt to approach the scene.

"He's seizing! He needs help!" I tried to get past Josh, only to get knocked back by his arm.

He shook his head. "No! Don't touch him. Let him finish."

"What the fuck?" I gasped, pushing against his back. "Josh, he could die!"

Collin stayed mute, watching in horror from the floor less than a few feet from where Father lost control.

"He's a Seer. It's a vision," explained Josh.

What the...?

Eventually, Father stopped shaking. The foam from his mouth dried, and he lay face up, eyes bloodshot red, soiled from head to toe.

Josh leveled Father's head on his lap. "Someone get a towel."

Collin, finally coming to, rushed out of the way, only to return moments later with several clean towels. I watched, dismayed by what had taken place.

Josh dabbed his face gently, soaking most of the wetness up from the towel, Father Benedict's stark complexion began to return with color. "M—"

Josh hushed him. "Not yet. Wait until everything passes."

Judging by how Josh handled the situation, it seemed to be a recurring event. "Is he okay?"

"Yeah, he's going to be all right." Relief washed away my worry, giving me the courage to join them on the floor, helping cradle Father's head.

"What's a Seer?" I asked, brushing back some of his gray hair.

"They receive visions of future events. It's an intuitive power." Father opened his eyes again, staring at the both of us. "Not all visions are bad. Some, like the one you just witnessed, happen rarely, and unfortunately, it was one of those times."

Father Benedict's color had fully returned, the bloodshot appearance barely noticeable. "Hello, Remi."

Taken aback by his nonchalant response, he waved us away, sitting up, his robes clean and wrinkle-free. "I'm sorry you had to see that. Sometimes they come on without warning."

"Father, I tried to catch you, but—"

"Collin, it's okay." Father smiled, making sure Collin understood he did nothing wrong.

Josh started. "The vision..."

"More like a prophecy." Father Benedict requested aid to help lift him to his feet. Testing his balance, he shooed us off, fixing the sleeves of his white robe, then he cleared his throat and quoted the prophecy verbatim.

A dying light, forever in the night

He comes, bearing sorrows

The Shepherd and the lamb

Lost in the shadows

She who wields, the rest shall follow

"What does it mean?" questioned Josh.

Father moved around the room, time ticking by until he stepped up to the dais. "It's time we pay a visit to Father Abraham."

CHAPTER 40

The mission was simple. Meet with the former priest named Abraham and have him help decipher the prophecy. So why did we need a backup plan? According to Father Benedict, we were exiting blessed lands placed on the school grounds to protect staff and the students. Anything beyond the perimeter became dangerous and unpredictable, especially demon activity. Since we were still in training and leaving without supervision, it all came down to the skills Josh provided from his years of experience and my measly four days.

Baron and Chloe were on standby, the only other two allowed to know about the mission. Josh fought with Father about it, stating he trusted them more than any other member, but Father wanted it contained, especially from Captain Harrison, so I understood his hesitation.

We did receive word that Emilia made a full recovery but no other information on how the two other members died.

Josh voiced his suspicion with Father while getting

ready. "I don't care how well he's trained or the years of experience he's given the Order. Having two others die with him as leader doesn't sit right with me."

"I advise you to pay close attention to Cillian," said Father.

Collin returned with my polished dagger. "Thanks," I said. "I had a hard time removing the Magidoz residue."

"A little pure acetone does the trick," he stated.

Who would've thought?

Father wrote the prophecy on a piece of paper, giving Josh the job of keeping it safe. "I will pray for safe travels, and keep close to one another."

Leaving the comfort of campus grounds, all we had was a prophecy and a hunch as Josh and I concealed ourselves, walking through a sea of people who had no clue we walked among them.

116th Street had the closest MTA, so the walk gave us some time to prepare and ease my stupid nerves. "Is he expecting us?"

"I assume so. I'm sure Father Benedict gave him the heads up," said Josh.

"If not?"

"Then we'll find out, won't we?"

FROM THE OUTSIDE, it looked rather quaint, but upon entering, we noticed rather quickly that wasn't the case.

A few lights were dim, flickering, trying to stay on for

dear life. Josh took the lead, weaving through dusty furniture and debris from the ceiling. The living room was eerie, creating goosebumps underneath my cape and sending shivers down my spine. Dust covered every piece of furniture, right down to the silverware in the kitchen. Judging by the amount built up, nobody had lived there in months.

"I don't get it. Father said he would be here," I said, swiping a finger over the coffee table, a lump of dust on the tip of my finger.

"And yet," Josh paused, blowing a heap of dust off the top shelf of a bookcase, a cloud of it filling the air, "nobody's home."

Patting the couch cushions, more dust puffed in the air, filling my lungs and making me cough. "You don't say."

Rolling his eyes, Josh motioned for me to follow, bow raised, arrow in position. I unsheathed my dagger, keeping a firm grip on the pommel, tagging closely behind his tall stature.

The further we moved through the house, the darker it became. Dust floated in the air from our steps on the carpet, tickling the back of my throat. "I don't think Father Benedict told him we were coming."

"Yes, I'm beginning to think that as well." His tone dipped in sarcasm, almost making me step on the back of his shoe.

Circling back to the front, we decided to ascend the stairs, taking our time and making sure no ounce of noise was made in the process. The walls were empty, just ugly wallpaper covering every inch of the second floor. Reaching the top, Josh leaned against the railing, lowering his bow, his brows furrowed in confusion. "I don't get it. Everything is here. The furniture... even the dishes are stacked neatly, but the person who lives here is missing."

From where we stood, the hall extended further down, showing a single window at the end, fading sunlight trickling in.

My dagger began to glow that same golden hue around the blade.

That was when the glass shattered, a body tumbling inside.

Weapons at the ready, before us stood something of human form, only its skin sagged, yellow eyes wild with rage, and blood dripping from its revolting set of teeth.

Drarkoth muttered Josh.

Patches of hair were missing on its scalp, bruises tatted spots along the cheeks, and its clothes were shredded and muddy from wherever it came from, bare feet stepping on glass from the window.

But nothing sent the hairs on my arms rising faster than the noise that came out of its mouth. A screech so terrorizing that my stomach turned inside out.

Remember what I said about them? quizzed Josh.

I nodded, reciting his words. *The most human-looking abomination to walk the planet.*

Yes. A ritual creates them, stripping them of their humanity until all they have left is an empty void inside their minds. They become mad and starve for blood, he informed. *And he looks hungry.*

Right on cue, the Drarkoth stalked forward, its pace picking up until it sprinted down the hall full-on, emitting a sound so horrific it could have curdled milk.

The fueled nightmare jumped, about to land mouth first, when Josh and I rolled in opposite directions. Josh fired an arrow, piercing its shoulder, and dark blood seeped from the wound. I watched it rip the arrow out, throwing it at my head.

I dodged just in time, and it barely missed my ear as it pierced the ugly wallpaper. "Well, that was rude."

"Please, don't have a conversation with that *thing*," complained Josh, knocking another arrow back.

It hissed, catching me by the cape, the sound of it tearing down my back. Driving my elbow back, the crunch of bone to its chin was enough to stun the foul thing. Dipping low, I kicked a leg out, knocking the Drarkoth on its ass.

Seconds from ending the fucker's life, the same ear-piercing screech came from the first floor.

Don't hesitate! Kill it now! ordered Josh.

Just as the tip of my blade pierced skin, the second Drarkoth came into view, and two more appeared seconds after. The others were just as homely. One even had a missing eye, both wearing the same battered clothes, blood staining their faces.

Three against two.

Finishing the job, I worked in the limited space, catching the eye of a second Drarkoth at the top of the stairs. Josh had already removed himself, firing arrows left and right, hitting different limbs.

I got the last two. Don't keep your eyes off the one in front, instructed Josh.

Got it.

My dagger glowed triumphantly, and wielding the blade in close combat, I battled the next Drarkoth, slitting its throat two seconds into our fight. Blood oozed from the wound, and it began choking dramatically. I kicked the ugly son of a bitch over the railing, its head smacking on the floor.

But when one fell, two more took its place.

I kicked another in the chest, my boot creating a dusty imprint. *We're going to get overrun.*

Josh grunted with each arrow that was fired. *Well aware. We need to find Father Abraham's prayer room.*

I stabbed another Drarkoth, this time in between those ghastly yellow eyes. *I didn't know priests had them in their homes.*

Do you trust me? An arrow flew into its eye, blood squirting everywhere.

Do I have a choice?

His answer never came because he was too busy retrieving one of the makeshift bombs in his quiver. Fighting back as much as I could, Josh turned it on, lights flashing, beeping noises coming from the contraption.

Duck!

In a matter of seconds, Josh tossed the bomb right into the mob of Drarkoths, hitting one directly in the head. He dragged me with him until our backs hit the window at the far end of the hallway.

That was when the bomb went off.

Covering our heads, debris flew in every direction, body parts in pieces scattered throughout.

That was our chance to move.

Josh searched vigorously, for what I had no idea, but I watched his hand glide against the wall, almost as if he were searching for some secret knob to get him out. I stood frozen, afraid to even try and help, figuring I'd distract him, when a light tap came from his knuckles, indicating a hollow surface just beyond the wallpaper.

"Yes," he whispered in triumph. He reached inside his pocket and pulled out a switchblade, cutting a perfectly neat square and revealing a small brass handle. Josh pulled with just enough force to unstick the door, where an even smaller room with a dirty window sat untouched.

"We'll hide until the coast is clear," he said, rushing inside.

I hesitated for just a second when another bang shook the walls. Not wanting to see what was coming, I dashed inside; Josh shut the door quietly and propped an old wooden chair against the doorknob.

"What kind of room is this?" I asked in a hushed voice.

"Monks would have secret rooms to pray in if they lived away from the church. Although, this room seems pretty empty and unusual," he explained.

"Why is that?" I asked.

"Because no one is allowed in but them, not even family."

"But the rest of the house...?"

"Yeah, I can't make sense of it either."

The space was a lot smaller than I'd anticipated. Josh and I were almost chest to chest, with just enough room to move to the window and just enough late afternoon light to illuminate the space, and that didn't include the tiny desk pushed up against the wall by the window.

"The window is sealed shut," he whispered. His minty breath fanned my face.

"Great," I replied a little too loud. Josh covered my mouth again, smiling.

I stifled a laugh under his palm, my body shaking from my muffled giggles. He rolled his eyes at my attempt to stay quiet, removed his hand, and hissed.

"Shit." A deep gash oozed on his left arm, and some of the fabric of his shirt was missing.

Not thinking twice about it, knowing my cape was already damaged, I tore a piece off with my teeth, wrapping the wound. "Better?"

He smiled, dust on his cheeks. "Much." Then he took a piece of debris from my hair. "I'm so proud of you."

Hearing him say those words, out in the open, not in my head, made my heart swell. "For not getting us killed?" I joked.

Josh tapped the tip of my nose. "No, silly. I'm proud of you because you're becoming someone I knew you would be."

"And that is?"

He tucked my hair back behind an ear. "Someone of strength and courage. All those doubts and fears of the unknown that plagued your mind, I barely hear them anymore."

"Might be because I'm good at shutting you out now. I almost shit myself when the Drarkoth screamed."

Josh chuckled, leaning his forehead against mine. "So brave, so *fierce*."

His words caressed my heart, filling it with pride, matching the tempo of our rhythmical breaths. My focus wasn't on the dangers outside the room. Instead, it was on his eyes. Blue as the ocean, swirls of darker hues burned into me like a white-hot branding iron. Josh's hands slowly descended from my shoulders down my arms, giving me a sensation like no other. All this time, training, studying, and our time together seemed so insignificant, yet at that moment, for the first time, he was all I wanted. At that moment, I felt something much more powerful than the Lord himself.

Because even at the height of danger, I wanted *only him* to protect me.

"Fuck this," he breathed.

As if the stars finally aligned, his mouth crashed on mine. His hands left my arms to grip my waist, pulling me closer to him as if the small space between us tortured the need for one another. Reaching for his face, our lips matched, perfectly in sync, and the explosion of my emotions overwhelmed me in the best way. Breathy moans filled the air, and the heat of our bodies plastered together. Josh held me tight against him; not getting enough of my touch seemed to intensify our kissing. Pulling my hood back, he intertwined his hands through my hair, fully controlling my mouth. I found myself gripping his shirt, and if that chair wasn't propped against the doorknob, we would already have been on it. Every ounce of me knew how wrong it was, but my heart screamed something else.

Josh's calloused hands made their way down my waist, where he took it upon himself to hoist me up on the small desk. Our kisses became frantic, and his tongue invaded my mouth, the sensation curling my toes and engulfing my already heated core.

"Josh," I moaned, only for him to snuff it out with more kissing.

He devoured me until my head spun. "I can't stop, Remi." His words were breathless as if strained from holding back.

I needed him like the goddamn desert needed the rain.

And *more*.

More?

I nearly lost my shit when his voice filled my head. When I didn't answer right away, he continued, his tongue claiming mine. *Tell me what you want.*

But how could I when he was seconds away from swallowing me whole?

Catching on, he slowed down, giving us a second to get some air. "Tell me what you want more of. Tell me..." he paused, his throat bobbing from a hard swallow.

I guided his hand to the front of my belt, making sure he knew exactly how I wanted more. "I want you to touch me."

With half-closed eyes and swollen lips, he undid the buckle, pulling it free from the loops and tossing it aside. Kneeling before me, he reached for the waistband of my pants. "Lift that perfect ass."

I did as he said, using my hands to keep balance on the table while he tugged down my pants and underwear to my ankles.

Josh inhaled sharply. *"Remi."*

Breathing heavily, I spread my legs a little wider, his pupils were blown out, mouth hanging slightly open. In that moment, nothing else mattered. Not the prophecy, not the Order, not even the demons possibly lurking outside the tiny room.

All that mattered was us.

Still on his knees, Josh began to trail kisses up my right inner thigh. Rolling my eyes, I gripped the edge of the table for support, breathing erratically and moans escaping my swollen lips.

Slow and torturous, he moved to the left, stopping, a sensual smile almost sending me over the edge. "Josh, *please.*"

"So needy," he purred, blowing cool air where I *wanted*

his mouth, making me squirm with need. Fisting his hair, I tried to push his mouth closer, but he only laughed, fighting against me.

Panting, Josh slipped one finger in between my folds, trailing down my entrance until that one finger slipped inside, and then another, until three were inside me. "That's my girl, already so wet."

I nearly folded then, my wetness soaking his hand as he pumped in and out. I rocked against his palm with each thrust of his fingers, that intense coiling sensation beginning to form in my core, tightening by the second.

Using his thumb, he circled my clit, heightening the sensation, electrifying my nerves, my skin aflame with desire. That was when his mouth took over.

His tongue swirled while his fingers worked, the combination so deadly that I rocked faster, the desk slamming hard against the wall behind me. Leaning my head back against the windowsill, I moaned, never letting go of his hair, getting lost in the way he took control.

He growled from my whimpers. "You taste exquisite."

"Don't you dare stop," I warned breathlessly.

He chuckled, swirling his tongue once more, my clit throbbing, begging for release. Pressure built faster this time, bracing for that tight coil to snap.

As I ground against his mouth, he removed his hands from inside, only to lift me by my ass until I perched on his strong jaw. Squeezing and kneading my ass, along with that fucking tongue, my control snapped, the coil springing free into an intense orgasm, my shouts of pleasure filling the small space we shared.

I most likely blew our cover, but I didn't care, not after what we had done. What *he did*.

Coming down from the high, Josh gently put my under-wear and pants on; he even funneled the belt back through the loops and buckled it. His mouth was glossy from my wetness, and I brushed my thumb over his bottom lip, cleaning the leftovers, only for him to stare right into my soul, licking the fingers he used clean, my mouth slightly agape.

I could have come again after that.

I ran my fingers through his curls, his eyes closing, sighing deeply. He looked so peaceful. "You touching me is like—"

"Josh? Remi?" yelled Chloe.

Suddenly, the world seemed to shatter beneath our feet, causing a catastrophic disaster.

We pulled apart, realizing what we had done.

I tried to regain control of my breathing and smoothed down my clothes and hair, afraid of making it even more apparent.

Josh readjusted himself before peeking through the door crack, then slowly removed the chair.

"In here!" he called.

Baron entered first, hugging Josh. "Dude, you've been gone for two hours."

Chloe surveyed the small space, her eyes eventually landing on me, suspicion on her face. "Quite a mess you both made out there."

"Never leave the campus without a bomb," laughed Josh, avoiding where I stood.

"I'm guessing no sign of Father Abraham, then?" questioned Chloe, never taking her eyes off me.

"No," I managed to say, my voice somewhat hoarse. "Empty upon arrival."

"We should probably head out before any more show up," Baron advised.

Josh didn't look my way when he left with Baron, and my heart sank further into my stomach.

I couldn't take back what I'd done, but I also couldn't bask in the glory of how it felt, not when he still belonged to Nickie.

CHAPTER 41

Days went by, and Josh went MIA in the process. I asked where he was, but they all chose to keep a tight lid on his whereabouts.

I took a huge blow to my already damaged heart.

Father Benedict requested a full report after that night. Unfortunately, that task was left to me. I explained in detail, leading up to the ambush of Drarkoth's, and Father praised me for my courage and fighting abilities, but even then, nothing soothed the ache Josh left behind.

His theory of Abraham's disappearance was that he sought refuge somewhere, knowing what was coming for him. I found out all priests in the Order are Seers, a gift bestowed upon the chosen. Collin, according to Father, was already showing signs of one.

It was only a matter of time before he was transferred to a new location, becoming a priest at another cathedral to help train.

We then discussed more of Juniper's history, but I got sidetracked. My mind kept wandering back to that night, the way Josh's hands touched my skin, right down to his mouth claiming mine.

Father Benedict wasn't oblivious, so he sent me on my way, advising me to take some time for myself and maybe see old friends.

Instead, I finished a load of laundry, ready to fold, when a knock came at my door.

I didn't have time to open it; Josh entered at his own risk.

He stood under the entrance to my dorm room, arms crossed, and a scowl on his face. We hadn't spoken in three days, since our intimate moment, the one I hadn't stopped thinking about, and judging by the look he gave me, he wasn't pleased with what happened.

"Remi..." He paused, blowing a gust of air out in frustration.

"Nice to see you too," I muttered and returned to folding my laundry.

Mental wall up, Josh out.

The floor creaked from the pressure of his walk, but I didn't dare turn around to see where he stopped. Suddenly, the door shut, making the air thicker and harder to breathe.

"I had a family matter," he stated.

I aggressively folded a shirt. "Riveting."

"So, I dip for a couple of days and you're *mad*?"

I started to laugh because it was better than feeling pathetic. "Whatever helps you sleep at night."

Josh spun me around, his eyes blazed with fury. "You don't think I haven't lay awake every night since, trying to understand what we did?"

"Are you here to tell me what I feel is wrong?" I asked, shaking from my anxiety.

"No. I can't control how you feel. That wouldn't be right."

"Do you... regret what we did?" It was stupid to ask such an obvious question.

He ignored it, and my heart began to rip down the middle, making it harder to breathe. "It was reckless to even have done what we did in such a dangerous area, let alone act on it."

"Because of Nickie, right?"

He hesitated.

"That's what I thought."

"I can't feel the same," he confessed. Josh averted his eyes, knuckles flexing from our anger toward each other when it was something more.

"Can't or won't?"

"I CAN'T!"

"I don't believe you," I breathed, defeated. My legs felt like Jell-O, losing strength with each passing minute. It was all wrong. My feelings, our argument, hurting Nickie, all of it, and yet there I stood, desperate to hear what he truly felt.

"I'm sorry, Remi." It sounded empty coming from his lips.

What else could I say? Nothing. So, I returned to folding my laundry, my back facing him.

He took it as my final acceptance and left the room, leaving me alone to remind myself that I'd been a shit person from the very start.

How DID I find myself back at the cathedral when I wanted to run far away from it? I knew the answer, and to be frank, I never wanted to knock Josh out as badly as I did right then, but to calm the short fuse I had, visiting Heather seemed the better choice. Even in a coma, she always listened, regardless of whether she desired it.

I quickly nodded hello to Collin at the front altar before disappearing by the side door behind the thick red curtain. After a fast stride to Heather's private healing room, I sat by her side, stroking her limp hand. Nickie and I, yeah, the friendship needed some mending, but Heather felt like a long-lost sister—a young one—and the need to protect her never stopped, even now as she lay like a statue in her coma. It didn't matter who went first when it came to the Blessing; Heather's fate was already sealed when she accepted the invitation. So, there we were, me alive and her—sleeping beauty.

"Heather," I whispered sadly. The likelihood of her understanding anything or even hearing me left a sadness in my heart.

"Demons, Heather. Fucking demons. I wish I had told you sooner about my invitation. I wish I could turn back the clock and tell you everything. I'm confused about my feelings for Josh and my role as a Scarlet. And don't even get me started on this prophecy Father Benedict received. I don't know anymore. I just want to run away," I rambled, breathing deeply to calm my jumbled nerves.

The silence was expected from her, but her presence was enough to help me relax and release the tension that had been building for a couple of weeks. At least she lent an ear to my insignificant problems.

I continued. "Are they genuine feelings? Lust? His very

essence invades my mind. It's like a sickness with no cure. How fucking pathetic of me."

Tears spilled silently down my cheeks, falling on my jeans and creating dark spots. I gripped her hand tighter, trying my best not to ugly cry. "Please, tell me what to do." I choked on my sob, bowing my head on her hand, letting it all come out.

I wished she had woken up and helped me navigate the good, the bad, and the ugly. Instead, I cried because I had no way of saving her, saving the world, saving myself. The weight should have crushed me and ended the misery inside me. I was a pathetic excuse for a Scarlet, one of the chosen ones to help defend evil.

A soft vibration in my jeans pocket gave me a heads-up that someone might be trying to reach me. I pulled it from the tight space, getting two texts from Jeremy asking where I was and that I should call him. Wiping the snot from my nose and taking a deep breath, I hit his number and waited until he picked up on the second ring.

A cheery voice on the other end sliced through my dark veil of sadness. "Hey, chica. What are you doing right now?"

"Uh, nothing at the moment. Why?" We hadn't spoken since girls' night at Electric Haze went sour.

"I'm hungry, and I miss you. I wanted to apologize about the other night too. Dinner is on me if you wanna come?"

Ah, yes, there it was, the apology mixed with a nice gesture. Typical Jeremy. I'd have been concerned if he failed that tactic.

I kept a strong hold on Heather's hand, dry sockets from the tears I'd spilled on myself. "Where for food?" Maybe just talking to Jeremy with Nickie absent gave me a sense of relief. I loved her, I genuinely did, but Jeremy became the anchor if I ever needed a second to stay in the moment, to feel my emotions before they swallowed me whole.

"Peg's Diner! Where else?" Jeremy enthused.

The best breakfast in downtown Manhattan. I smiled at the phone. "Right now?"

"You got it!" Jeremy laughed, the speaker cracking from the sound.

"All right, I'll see you in a few." With that, I hung up the phone, a little less tense than before. I guessed Father Benedict's advice to follow was a good call.

I brushed Heather's beautiful red hair from her forehead, the curls perfectly coiled to her scalp. "I'll find a way to save you, Heather. I promise."

CHAPTER 42

The taxi ride to Peg's Diner took a little longer than usual, mainly because I procrastinated on my outfit and then tried to find a good hiding spot for my dagger. That part took some time, especially finding a place to keep it without Jeremy becoming suspicious. I had to run back to the dorm because I had almost forgotten my pager.

I didn't leave until nearly five, the worst New York City time to travel. But Jeremy didn't care; he greeted me like we hadn't seen each other in years with a hug so tight I almost lost the air in my lungs.

"I'm so sorry for the other night. I should've called you right away." He apologized again, kissing my head.

"It's okay. I just want you to know I'm still me," I said. Well, me physically. My occupation was questionable.

Jeremy linked his arm through mine and led us toward the entrance of Peg's Diner. A small line began to form, but luckily, we chose a Wednesday night, with fewer crowds and wait time to get a seat.

Jeremy and I were discussing the latest drama of our old classmates when I heard my name being called from behind. "Remi?"

I turned and never wanted to melt into the nearest drainage so severely in my life. Nickie's well-manicured hand draped over Josh's arm seductively, sending a pang of jealousy rippling through my core. Nickie smiled brightly, releasing her hold on him to hug Jeremy and me together. Josh lingered in the back, looking anywhere but at me, which hurt. It hurt because the last conversation between us left me broken and lost. And I had no right to feel the way I did, not when my best friend belonged to him.

"Are you eating here too?" she asked excitedly.

"Yes! Want to join us?" Jeremy offered.

She glanced at Josh, a small smile in her questioning eyes. "We would love to!" Nickie turned back to us, smiling from ear to ear.

"Awesome!" Jeremy said.

I smiled at my best friend, trying desperately to avoid the beautiful man beside her.

"Oh, Josh! By the way, this is my other best friend, Jeremy. Jeremy Levine," she introduced.

He held out his hand for Jeremy to shake. "Levine? Are you by any chance related to Ophelia Levine?"

Jeremy clasped Josh's in return with a firm shake. "Yes! She is my aunt."

"I didn't know she was your aunt," I said, keeping my attention on Jeremy after I spoke.

Their hands disconnected as Jeremy peeked over at me. "Yeah, I thought I mentioned it before."

I shook my head, about to say something else, when Josh interrupted. "I'm surprised you're not attending."

There was something weird about the tone that finally caught my attention. Sensing my stare, Josh ran his hand through his dark hair, biting his lip, trying so hard not to look at me.

"Table for four?" the hostess said at the front door.

"Yes, please," replied Jeremy.

She grabbed four menus and led us to a cozy corner booth in the back of the diner. Josh slid into one corner as I slid into the other. Jeremy to my left, Nickie to his right. We faced each other, but Josh instantly grabbed the menu to dodge conversation with me. I snatched the menu the hostess left on the table, gripping it in anger. If he wanted to play this game, then so be it.

"So, Remi, how are classes?" Nickie asked over her menu.

I bit my lip behind my menu. "Oh, you know, boring."

Jeremy snickered beside me. "Columbia *is* a dry campus."

"We know how to party," mentioned Josh with a smirk.

Nickie's eyes sparkled in delight. "When's the next frat party?"

Josh casually put an arm behind her, leaning into her ear. "Soon."

I ground my teeth, trying my best to keep my cool. The waitress, Liz, finally came over and asked what kind of drinks we wanted.

We ordered our meals, and with the menus taken by our waitress, it left no barriers between us. Josh leaned comfortably into Nickie, arm draped over her shoulder. He wouldn't look directly at me but I know he sensed the intensity of my stare. I had no business acting this way. No business to lust after my guardian, who was currently dating my best friend.

Liz returned with a tray of drinks, some straws, and a

basket of bread and butter before attending to another table. Jeremy grabbed the first slice, buttering the crap out of his piece. "God, this bread is my favorite."

"That's why your ass is so big," joked Nickie, grabbing a slice for herself.

I took a long sip of my Coke, keeping a composed face.

"So, Josh, have you slept with Nickie yet?" asked Jeremy in between bites of bread.

I choked, spewing my Coke all over the table, barely missing the breadbasket. Jeremy's habit, or lack of table manners, never failed to appear at the wrong time.

Everyone began to wipe up the mess with brown napkins, including myself. "Sorry, guys."

"It's okay, girl. We can't control Jeremy's potty mouth," said Nickie.

"You're very direct, I must say," Josh chuckled, dabbing the table with some napkins.

"I like to know my girls are happy," Jeremy mused.

Nickie rolled her eyes. "And you're super nosy."

Jeremy gave her the middle finger with a sweet smile. "Only love, baby."

Liz came at the right time to take the soaked napkins away, promising to return with more. "Your food is almost done," she added before leaving again.

"Thank God. I'm starving," said Jeremy, rubbing his stomach.

Josh perched his arm behind Nickie, only this time around her shoulders. "It's been a while since I've been here."

"Really? Why'd you stop?" asked Nickie.

"My extracurricular activities have been getting in the way," he said.

"Oh, yeah, your band," mentioned Jeremy.

"Yes, my band. We have a gig this Saturday night if you guys want to come. It's at that new club, Arctic Sin."

"I highly doubt your band is playing," I blurted.

The table fell silent, and Josh finally turned to me, those fucking baby blues killing me softly.

"And how would you know," Nickie inquired, and a perfectly sculpted eyebrow rose.

"Heard the place was shut down for maintenance," I lied, downing the rest of my Coke.

Nickie waved my face away like it was nothing but nonsense. "I'm sure by Saturday it'll be fine."

Liz popped out from the employee-only door of the kitchen with another tray, baskets of our food steaming as she maneuvered through the restaurant to get to our table. We thanked her profusely and dug right into our meals, grateful for the silence as I chewed my food, or tried to. Nickie and Josh's arms rubbed against each other, smiling whenever they bumped a little too hard into one another. Oblivious, Jeremy got on to the topic of music, quizzing Josh on his taste, fishing to see if it passed Jeremy's test of a decent guy.

What I needed was space and a place to clear my head. "Excuse me, Jeremy. I need the bathroom."

"Sure thing, chica," he said, moving out of his seat to let me by.

Not daring to glance back, I found the bathroom, rushing over to the sink to splash my face with cold water. I let it trickle down my cheeks, on my neck, seeping into my shirt, praying it would ease the tension. My reflection, the girl who seemed unrecognizable yet familiar at the same time, never looked so lost. I touched the mirror, unsure what she wanted, what I wanted. Yet I knew, deep within, underneath the layers of being a shit person, fighting evil, and trying my best not to relapse with drinking, I had a choice to make, and it wouldn't be easy.

The beep of my pager made me jump back from the mirror, wiping my upper half clean. I checked the message, and the symbol shaped like a scarlet quill flashed on the screen, then the address underneath where demon activity occurred.

Nobody would suspect my absence if I left now without bothering to return to the table. Well, Josh would. But to leave them both at the table, what excuse could he use? I had my chance, and I was going to take it.

No second-guessing, I went in and out undetected, running to 89th Avenue, my dagger strapped securely on my leg, hidden by my pants. My lungs burned with each long stride, but nothing mattered more than reaching that spot. Yes, Josh *should* have been with me, he was my guardian, and my inexperience would probably get me killed, but if the message went out to everyone, I was sure backup would follow. Heck, I was sure the fleet was already there.

I could smell the sour stench of demonic activity right near the alley between 88th and 89th. A light tap on my shoulder had me spinning around, ready to strike, when Chloe caught my arm.

"Where's Josh?" she asked, releasing my arm.

"Occupied," I said.

"Not likely." He came up behind Chloe, looking over me into the alley.

How? How did he escape the booth?

To my surprise, Kal appeared from the alley, his bow

strapped securely to his back. "A body is in there. Well, what's left."

"What do you mean?" asked Josh.

"Take a look. I also alerted Captain Harrison," Kal said, moving aside to let him through.

"Surprised they're not the ones who found it first. They've been slacking, too busy caring about Columbia."

I walked in front of him when Kal grabbed me by the arm. "Prepare yourself. It's brutal."

I gulped, nodded once, and then went further into the dark alley, Josh on my heels. There, sprawled out on the ground, blond hair knotted and pieces of it missing from being pulled out, was a woman, completely naked. Her body was half-submerged in black sludge... I froze mid-step. A human body, yes, but one where she had been sucked dry. One touch, and she would combust into dust. A life-sized prune in human form. Mummification in the flesh.

But the eyes, so kind, so lifeless, so...

The food from Peg's Diner began to rise in my esophagus. "I know," Josh whispered behind me. He took a step forward, bending down to examine the body, black goo staining his white shoes.

"Josh," I said.

"It seems this type of demon likes to strip their victims first. Why? I have no idea," he said, more to himself than me.

"Josh," I repeated.

"Granted, they have brains, but to be this precise in murdering their victim," he continued, unaware of my pleading.

Everything spilled over. "Goddamn it, Josh, look at me!" I shouted. My words bounced off the walls in the alley; I'd never been so furious in my life.

He stilled and remained kneeling in front of the body.

"Why won't you look at me?" I whispered, defeated. Hurt. I was hurt. Pathetic, because I thought we could at least communicate normally regardless of what happened between us.

"Don't, Remi," he breathed.

"Don't what?" I repeated in that same breathy tone. Did he feel the longing too? "I can't..."

"Maybe *I* can't."

"You guys good in there?" called Chloe, breaking our private bubble.

"Almost done," Josh replied. Whatever moment we tried to share evaporated into thin air. Josh retrieved something from his jacket, took a small sample of the demon's sludge-like matter, and stored it safely in the little vial. He stood, rolling his shoulders, and then without a single glance my way, stalked off to where Kal and Chloe stood waiting.

Tears threatened to escape, but I needed to pull myself together. After a few deep, calming breaths, I met the rest back on the sidewalk, hearing them discuss taking the sample to Father Benedict to test what kind of demon was lurking in the New York City streets.

"Strange, right? The body shriveled up like a prune," commented Chloe.

"It could be a Drarkoth," suggested Kal.

"Nah, the body would've been an odd gray. This looked like the demon stripped the victim's muscle right from her bones," Josh pointed out, scratching his head.

Chloe got a phone call, talking urgently and nodding a few times before hanging up. "Collin said Asher and Baron are coming with a body bag; we're going to transfer it to the cathedral at night. Father will still take the sample to begin the process," she explained.

I felt sick and clammy. "Kal?"

"Yeah?" He grabbed my hand.

"Can you take me back to the dorms? I don't feel so good," I said weakly.

"Go, Kal. Josh and I will wait for the others," said Chloe.

Kal brushed my cheek with his thumb. "Yes, of course. I'll call a cab."

Josh rested casually against a brick building, flipping the vial back and forth, watching the black substance move up and down. "It's similar to a Drarkoth but yet..."

"Yet what?" countered Chloe.

"Yet..." Josh never finished because Kal returned to say a cab pulled over for us, and I threw up by a half-empty trash can.

"It was only a matter of time before she spewed her guts," said Chloe.

"We've all been there," Kal reminded her in a cruel tone. He held my hair back for me as I emptied the contents from my stomach, Peg's Diner food in a pile on the sidewalk.

Kal helped my weak body over to the cab after I stopped dry heaving, and I rested my head against the cool window. Kal warned the driver to take it easy, otherwise he would need new seats if he went faster than thirty miles per hour.

He sat beside me in the back, giving directions. I could barely keep my eyes open, my throat raw and hoarse. I wanted it all to go away. Every memory, every touch, every inch of pain that plagued my mind.

Because how stupid was it for me to go behind my best friend's back, to let Josh touch me so intimately, only for him to act so closed off and cold in return.

I drifted into an unexpected sleep, cause at least when I slept, the ache of what I never had went away.

CHAPTER 43

T ime was fleeting, a thief of the good and the bad, and lately it had been taking more of the good than the downright tragic.

Training days were the hardest. Mostly because Josh only spoke to me when he gave instructions or yelled when my form was off. Other than that, it'd been radio silence, especially mentally.

I tried some days during training when he was distracted by our zealous workouts to peek inside, only to be met with a brick wall the height of a skyscraper.

I shouldn't have tried, not after how we left things, but it hurt knowing our connection would probably never be the same.

Then again, I tended to jump the gun sometimes.

At nine in the morning, I received a message from the Order to meet in fifteen minutes. Since the weather had finally let up against the pestering heat, I yanked on a simple blue shirt and some jeans before I made my way to the stunning cathedral.

Josh and I met up at the same time. He nodded to acknowledge my presence, but other than that, we kept to ourselves.

But what we didn't expect was Captain Harrison and the entire fleet occupying every pew.

Our Order stood in the back, while the Aces joined Captain Harrison on the dais, their faces stricken with worry. Father Benedict and Collin were nowhere to be found.

Never in my life would I witness an entire fleet inside the cathedral on school grounds. Each member, from Scarlet to Saint, wore a stoic expression, statues in fighting gear. There must've been over forty occupying the space.

None of it looked good.

"A horde of Olemaks was seen outside of 116th Street station last night around one in the morning. Luckily, we had a curfew in place and patrols stationed around to keep the demons at bay. However, it does not explain the horde being on campus grounds." He removed himself from the dais, wiping his face with a handkerchief.

A horde? On campus? I sent my thoughts straight to Josh, shocked to find the wall that kept me out wide open.

I can't fathom it either.

Emilia stepped up, looking fully recovered and ready to kill. "You're missing a valuable piece of information." All eyes were on Emilia; her dark eyes blazed with fury.

Captain Harrison cleared his throat, clearly uncomfortable at being called out. "Right, well, that information is still being discussed with the Spades—"

Dean Poverly appeared from the back. "If it's on *my* grounds, I have a right to know."

If Captain Harrison was intimidated, he didn't let it

show. Rather, he clasped his hands behind his back and stalked forward down the middle aisle, grabbing the attention of everyone in the pews. "The Olemak horde entered the school grounds, and we have footage showing their... odd behavior. Someone might be... controlling them."

Nobody uttered a word at this possible revelation.

Can that happen? I asked Josh, panicked.

If it's true, then we're looking at a whole new enemy.

Toke, for the first time in his life, looked somewhat okay compared to his usual sweaty appearance. "What you're suggesting can't happen."

Captain Harrison ignored Toke, continuing his speech. "It's time the trainees of this Order step out into the field with us without supervision. If hordes keep showing up, then we need all hands on deck to prepare for what could come."

"They're finally old enough to train properly and you want them out in the field to get slaughtered like cattle?" snapped Thatcher.

"They have one hour to gear up and report back here." He didn't give anyone a chance for a rebuttal, leaving down the aisle, each pew filled with his fleet single filed out.

Emilia was last, stopping in front of me. "Suit up, Watson. You're with me."

I CHANGED with the other Scarlets, listening to their conversation.

"I hope I'm in Owen's squad. The guy is deadly with the crossbow," said Zoey.

Anna rolled her eyes, shimmying her pants over her hips. "We're about to invade a horde of Olemaks, and you're horny over a dude with the same crossbow the rest of the fleet has."

Zoey braided her long brown hair. "He's on the market, so yeah, I'm gonna shoot my shot."

"Girl, you're insane," laughed Anna, throwing the scarlet hood over her head.

Chloe snorted beside me. "Anna may be a twat, but she has a point."

Lacing up my combat boots, I sheathed my freshly polished dagger. "I don't know. It's nice to hear some sense of normalcy before we head out to die."

"Wow, you're super optimistic tonight."

I shrugged, tucking the amethyst stone inside my shirt. "We're constantly trying to stay alive. I think a negative attitude deserves a pass."

Before she could respond, a soft knock came at the door, and Kal's voice was heard on the other side. "Are you ladies ready?"

Filing out of the changing room, Kal lingered by the threshold until I was the last to exit, taking an easy stride to match my pace. "How are you?"

Kal was kind enough to bring me home the other night, vomiting several times on the road, but Josh's warning always stayed with me whenever he was around. "Better. I'm sorry I never got to thank you for that night."

His sandy blonde hair was gelled back from his face, giving a clear view of the freckles dotting his nose and cheeks. "A thank you is not necessary. I should be the one apologizing for my actions at the beginning of the year. I never wanted to paint you as some—"

"Whore?"

Kal's dark, hazel eyes bulged. "No! I wasn't—"

"Relax," I said as we made our way upstairs to the main floor. "I just want you to know, what happened between us, it was a one-time thing."

"Probably should call it a two-time thing," he joked.

"Right, the night of Summerfest." That night felt so long ago. Less complicated, less *everything*.

When we arrived back on the main floor, some squads were already set and ready, and others were starting to call names to join the remainders. I'd never seen so many members in one room, dressed in all the same attire, right down to the shoes.

Josh stood with Emilia and Cillian and two other members of Captain Harrison's fleet.

Emilia caught sight of me before anyone else and smiled. "There you are, Remi. This is Silas and Jules. They'll be a part of our group."

Silas's dark skin and hair in contrast to those light green eyes were breathtaking. He stood no more than six feet tall, slightly shorter than Josh's towering build. He waved sheepishly, and a stunning set of teeth flashed my way.

Jules's white-blonde hair hidden underneath her cape came down in long waves, and eyes the color of mahogany brightened at my arrival. "Hello, Remi. Nice to finally meet you."

We shook hands, her grip tight and confident.

Josh's voice filtered inside my head. *Emilia boasted about you slaying that Magidoz.*

A sharp whistle blew, followed by Captain Harrison's

voice booming through the cathedral. "Each squad is labeled with a number. Everyone will acquire a Bluetooth earpiece, the frequency matching only the members of their squad."

Cillian handed us each an earpiece, and I secured mine in place, turned it on, and heard a soft buzzing of static.

Emilia tapped hers, testing it out. "Making sure everyone hears me. We're squad number seven." Her voice came in nice and clear, though a little echoey because of us being so close. Captain Harrison continued. "Your squad leaders were all given a map of the campus and surrounding areas of New York City. Coordinates are highlighted where you'll be stationed. You'll dispatch on arrival and wait for your next instructions. To infiltrate and eliminate successfully, we all must work together, and make sure to follow the instructions promptly."

Why do I get the vibe that he's trying to run a play with a high school football team? I asked.

Probably trying to prove to Dean Poverly what a shit job he's doing.

Speaking of Dean Poverly, none of the Aces were in attendance, not even Father Benedict, to watch us depart on our mission. *Where is everyone?*

I was just thinking the same thing. Something's off. Keep your guard up and your head on a swivel. I have a bad feeling.

That made two of us.

Squads began to whisper the word *falach*, preparing for their departure. Cillian recommended that we do the same, double-checking our attire and making sure weapons were secure one last time before opening the map.

Emilia pointed a finger at one of the coordinates highlighted in yellow. "It says we're stationed at Sunset Park... in

Brooklyn?" She looked around, searching for someone, probably Captain Harrison, but he'd gone MIA.

Cillian rubbed his chin. "I wonder if another horde was located here."

Josh, however, wasn't convinced. "If the horde was last seen here on campus, then why are we being stationed miles away?"

By now, all but us had left the cathedral, making it difficult to ask anyone if they were also stationed near us.

I guess we're about to find out, mumbled Josh.

Emilia folded the map and looked at us with a smile. "So, who wants to drive?"

CHAPTER 44

Silas as the designated driver was nothing compared to Chloe and her crazy, unhinged turns and race car speed.

For once, I didn't feel like my stomach ended up in my throat.

Clutching the handle in the back seat, we arrived at Sunset Park before midnight, the night sky somewhat clear, a few stars shining through the haze of city lights in the distance. Silas parked the van along the docks, the ocean water lapping lazily against the shoreline. A sea breeze kissed my cheeks, and the smell of smoke and stale fish tickled my nose.

Emilia pulled out her pager, most likely notifying Captain Harrison of our arrival. Josh polished an arrow on his shirt, surveying the grounds, sometimes catching my attention with a look of uncertainty.

Jules, Silas, and Cillian looked over the map, commenting on possible locations of other squads, but judging upon first sight, we were the only ones around.

"Anyone else having trouble with their pager? I can't seem to get a signal." Emilia held the device high in the air, trying to get through.

"Odds are, if yours is down, so are the rest of ours," commented Silas.

That's not good. How is anyone going to know we arrived? Anxiety prickled my skin.

Whatever happens, do not *leave my side.* Josh finished polishing the tip of his arrow, walking over to Emilia. "What's the plan?"

She gave up then, storing the pager back on her person. "We're here now. Might as well scope the area. Silas and Jules, you take the rear. Cillian and I will take the second building over. Can you handle the first one on your own?" She looked over at me, then back to Josh.

"Is it wise to split up?" he questioned.

"Considering we're not that far apart, we should be okay," noted Cillian, eyeing him like a pesky bug.

I was surprised Josh didn't fight harder on the matter, and he motioned for me to go first. "Lead the way, Rem."

Removing my dagger, I gripped the sleek pommel and took a deep breath, walking with my chin held high but anxiety not too far behind.

I slid the wide doors open to a three-story abandoned factory building, revealing old machines and empty boxes filled with shriveled peanut packing material scattered in every direction. Our steps were strategic, keeping close as we traveled further in, finding the first set of stairs.

Josh positioned his arrow while he looked up from the bottom step, judging how far it went. *I'll go first.*

He led the way up the winding staircase, bow and arrow

aimed. My heart raced with each step I took; the higher we got, the thinner the air became, dust kicking up at our feet.

Josh signaled to everyone through his earpiece that we had made it to the top floor. "Zero demon activity as of," he paused to check his pager, "nineteen hundred hours."

Olemaks leave a burnt smell, like rotting flesh, explained Josh.

That's concerning. How are we going to tell the difference between an Olemak and a victim burning alive?

We pray it's the former.

I was about to ask another question when the iron stairs began to rattle underneath our feet. We stood frozen in time, waiting for the rumbling to stop. In the distance came a laugh, making the hair on my arms stand, my neck prickling with fear. It sounded so human-like that I wondered if I misheard, mistaking it for our other squad members.

Josh grabbed my arm. "It's not an Olemak nest."

I gave him a confused look. "What do you mean?"

"We just walked right into the hive of an Azroneg." The fear in his eyes scared me.

Azroneg? "Dare I ask?" I kept my voice low, scanning the area, wondering when it'd make its presence known.

"A trickster demon."

Pressing his finger to his earpiece, the following words out of his mouth made my skin crawl.

"I don't know how long we have." Josh was talking as if we would fall into our graves any minute.

"Where is it coming from?" I asked, scanning the area around us. We had limited space on the second floor to fight if the Azroneg decided to attack. I gripped the handle of my dagger and kept it close, watching any unexpected movements from my peripherals.

Josh added a bow to his arrow, aiming over my head. "Whatever you do, don't look it in the eye."

"Eye?"

Silence filled the tight space as we waited for it to appear, but only dust swirled, the creaks of the iron stairs protesting as Cillian came into view. "Have you seen it yet?"

"Josh, it's Cillian," I said, lowering my weapon.

He shook his head, the arrow still aimed. "No, it's not. He would never leave Emilia by herself."

I stilled, every inch of my body paralyzed in fear at the realization that the Azroneg, the trickster, stood before us as Cillian. Suddenly, his face contorted, shifting into a skeleton-like demon with a mouth more extensive than a shark, hissing like a cat. One eye, red like the blood that ran through my veins, in the center of its forehead. I quickly averted my eyes to another spot on its hideous figure.

"Remi! Duck!"

I crouched just in time to see one of Josh's arrows fly past, striking the Azroneg in the shoulder. Black liquid sprayed from the wound as it pulled the arrow out, teeth grinding in anger as it charged for us. The power of the Blessing ran through my veins as I skidded across the limited space, gripping the railing to keep from falling over. Josh had already dodged its first attack, another arrow ready to be released. The Azroneg wasted no time with its next assault, throwing punches left and right at my head, my reflexes reacting on instinct to avoid damage.

It screamed in fury, its mouth widening, when another eerie laugh came from the floor above.

We got fucking company, announced Josh.

The Azroneg ran at me headfirst, mouth wide open,

trying to latch onto my arm, and I spun past, landing my attack straight into the back of its skull.

But I wasn't fast enough to catch the second Azroneg. It landed a blow in my side, tackling me to the ground.

Remi! cried Josh.

My head hit the stone floor, stars flashing behind my eyes. Bones crunched and I caught sight through my distorted vision of the beast collapsing in a heap beside me. Emilia helped me to my feet, her face covered in dust and blood.

The iron steps rattled as another set of feet rushed to the top, the real Cillian sweating and bruised.

Cillian saw me first, then quickly quipped his bow.

The sound of arrows whizzed by, hitting their target, and the Azroneg screeched in pain.

Then I heard the snap of a bow.

Emilia and I turned to Josh just as it seized him. My heart thumped erratically as it caught him by the throat. Cillian dove, firing an arrow from his crossbow, stopping it from choking Josh to death, its claws releasing him, and he stepped back. But more kept coming. No matter how hard we fought to keep them at bay, it wasn't enough.

Josh was surrounded, trying to fire as fast as he could.

I screamed in fear and ran forward, my dagger aimed directly at its chest as I pounced, putting all my force into the jump, about to drag the dagger down its back, when it reached around, striking me in the chest, and I slammed back against the iron railing. It shook from the force as I landed face first, pain shooting up my chest to my neck.

The dagger I once held skidded across the floor, and suddenly the space was filled with the sound of bones breaking and a rough scream.

Josh.

Emilia tackled it to the ground, using my dagger to fight it off. Josh lay broken on the floor, blood seeping through his clothes into a puddle by his feet, one of his eyes swollen shut. I held onto the railing for support, pulling myself up to reach him. Every step felt like an eternity, my eyes glued to his limp body, unchanging when I finally got him. I collapsed on top of his chest, cradling his face in my hands. While Kal swiped left and right, knocking the Azroneg to the floor, Josh remained still, pulse weak and blood coating his clothes and hair. Tears slid down my cheeks as I prayed to the Heavens he pulled through.

Then the iron stairs began to collapse.

Cillian had been tossed aside like a rag doll on the stairs, creating an earthquake from the force. Emilia screamed, trying to get to him.

The Azrodag laughed menacingly, its one eye socket oozing with black blood, craning its neck to peer over to where I lay on top of Josh.

"Come and get me," I taunted.

Another bone-chilling laugh came from its hideous mouth, and it launched forward. I extended my palms out, shielding Josh, screaming with rage at what it did to my guardian, when warm light shot from my hands, frying the Azroneg demon into dust. Every surface of the room illuminated from its brightness until it returned inside me. I gasped for air, stunned and spent from the energy that surged through me. Not a single Azroneg survived the blast.

Hunched over, I checked for Josh's pulse, relieved to find his heart continued to beat.

Suddenly, some of the dirty skylights shattered, shards

of glass crashing to the floor as four Tutelary Saints dropped from above, along with their Scarlets, surveying the room.

Baron spotted me where I sat, Josh's head in my lap.

Emilia sobbed where the stairs once were, leaning over, trying to find Cillian.

"Is he...?"

I pointed to the collapsed stairs, tears flowing freely down my cheeks.

Silas shouted from the bottom. "I found him!"

Three Saints jumped down, landing with a hard thud at the bottom. I choked on my tears, stroking Josh's face for comfort. His breathing was shallow, nearing death with every second that passed.

"Remi..." Baron touched my shoulder.

"I need him here. I need him," I cried.

Baron took my hands away from Josh and forced me to look at him. "We have to get up and move him. He's lost too much blood."

"How?"

"To the window. Asher has a stretcher attached to the ladder. We strap him in and slide him down," explained Baron.

When I didn't say anything, Baron forced me to look at him. "If we don't move now, he could die."

I nodded weakly as Baron and Kal lifted Josh in their arms, the sight of him broken nearly sending me back to my knees.

Baron instructed me to keep the window from shutting, and Asher from below hoisted the ladder right onto the windowsill. Another Saint I didn't recognize dragged the thin stretcher up the ladder, helping Baron and Kal place Josh slowly down, strapping him securely in place.

I watched them both inch down, keeping two hands on the stretcher, making sure it didn't tip.

Gazing down at my palms, I saw dirt and half-healed cuts, wounds to remember the battle we almost lost, but not a single trace of that golden light was left behind.

CHAPTER 45

B efore transportation arrived for the rest of us, Emilia got herself together and dragged me over to an area that concealed our private conversation.

"That light coming from your hands, was that the first time?" she inquired.

After everything that had happened tonight, all she cared about was the light from my hands? Was she not sobbing hysterically for Cillian possibly being dead moments ago? I had no desire for this conversation. All I wanted was to get the hell out of here and go see Josh in the infirmary. But judging by her stern expression, she wasn't going to let this go. "I've never done that before."

"Never?" she echoed.

I sighed, frustrated. "No, never. I'm assuming the others are aware since I blasted the light in front of them."

"Some are, but I already threatened them not to say anything."

I backpedaled. "Uh, why?"

"We may work for the Lord, but we don't trust everyone involved."

"Then what's the point? Why even bother fighting the same battle if you can't even trust the ones who are supposed to have your back?"

Emilia shook her head. "It wasn't always like that. Just recently, I've noticed a shift in the Order. Right now, try to lay low and don't tell anyone."

"Or what? They're going to shun me for having power?"

"For too much power. They will use you as a weapon. They will push aside your feelings and who you are as a person just to exhaust your power, even if it kills you."

THE LIGHTS in the infirmary were harsh, causing uncomfortable specks in my vision as I tried to adjust. Recovering from a concussion wasn't an easy feat.

Josh rested with tubes and needles that either penetrated his skin or were shoved up his nose, keeping him stable as he healed. I had no recollection of time. All that mattered from the moment I went to bed to the time I awoke the next day was monitoring Josh. A few times, I left to see Heather, explaining to deaf ears what happened, crying nearly to the point of making myself sick. Nurse Amelia had to escort me out, forcing me to drink water and eat saltine crackers. But I had no appetite when my guardian hadn't opened his eyes in days, anxiety stealing my sleep and hunger.

I could use a shot of my dad's whiskey right about now.

Sometimes, Baron and Chloe stopped by to keep me company, and even Collin visited, stating Father Benedict encouraged him to read me some of Juniper's history while we sat, but I couldn't process any of the words he spoke. Not when Josh slept, afraid I might miss a twinge or a jerk of a finger.

Cillian was transported to a special infirmary, his injuries much more complex. Emilia left shortly after and would remain wherever her guardian resided until he made a full recovery.

No word if he was awake yet.

Captain Harrison was updated on the events, stating he could've sworn our coordinates weren't his doing and wanted a full investigation. Thatcher nearly killed him. Dean Poverly had to come between them before her right hook connected to his face. Chloe gave me all the details, claiming at one point, Thatcher had Captain Harrison by the collar, almost choking him out.

Debriefings resumed, training commenced, but I didn't dare move from my spot, stroking Josh's hand, wishing for him to open his eyes.

October arrived shortly after, and autumn leaves started to show in Central Park. The air had become crisper, a relief I desperately needed.

My phone buzzed excessively in my pocket, Nickie couldn't take a hint, I wasn't picking up the phone. I'd already gotten an earful from Thatcher for ignoring my training. Right now, my mind could only focus on one thing; Josh and his recovery. I had barely slept, or eaten, afraid to miss any update.

Chloe popped her head through the door. "If you don't leave, I will force you to."

I rolled my eyes. "I'm almost done."

She opened the door wider, crossing her arms. "He's going to be okay. Nobody's pulled the plug yet."

"Oh, that's reassuring," I bit the inside of my cheek, nails digging into my thighs.

"You need a break, Remi. Nurse Amelia will take care of him."

Josh's sullen eyes, bruised lips, and pale skin were a horrific reminder of who could've been lost if I wasn't quick enough.

I pushed loose strands of Josh's hair away from his forehead and kissed his cheek, hoping my time away would speed up his recovery.

We arrived at the gym, and Chloe tapped the treadmill next to her. "Thirty minute warm up."

I ran as if my heart would collapse, images flashing with every hard step on the running deck, Josh falling, my hands glowing...

The urge to scream rose at the back of my throat.

If I could go back in time, I wouldn't hesitate, I would be right by his side.

The absence of Josh, even in my head... my heart ached, struggling to keep a steady beat.

I stopped the treadmill, wobbling off, and laid flat on the blue mat, inhaling and exhaling as if I had run a marathon.

Chloe peered above me. "Do I need to call Nurse Amelia?"

I shook my head.

"How about dumping a bucket of water on your head?"

I cocked an eyebrow.

"Maybe shock therapy?"

"Where the fuck are you going with this?"

She sat crossed-legged in front of me. "Your guardian can sense when you're weak in mind, body, and spirit, and in return, it affects them. It won't help his recovery if you're sulking around."

"So, I'm supposed to be all happy-go-lucky?" How the fuck was that logical?

"No, but you can at least *do* something to make sure he stays afloat when the process is over."

"You're acting as if I knew any of this. Are you forgetting I wasn't trained early like the rest of you?"

She sighed. "I'm sorry. Sometimes I forget."

I stared down at my hands, looking for any signs of gold in the creases. I had saved him. I saved all of us that night. "Maybe I'll take the time to study." I said it more to myself than Chloe while I traced each individual crease in my palm.

We parted ways, and I was about to head straight for the library, when I spotted Father Benedict at one end of the room, reading a book and whispering as he held his white rosary beads to his chest.

We hadn't spoken in a couple of weeks or even discussed the prophecy. Everything was put on the back burner, and I wondered if he was still searching for answers—better yet, for Father Abraham.

I approached, and he looked up and smiled. "Remi, how are you?"

"Okay, I guess. It's been a while since we crossed paths," I commented, noticing facial hair had begun to grow around his mouth.

"Yes, it's been a rough couple of weeks. I know Josh will recover."

His confidence was enough for both of us. "Have you gotten word from Father Abraham?"

He closed his book, returning it to the shelf. "No. It concerns me greatly, and I have reached out to other priests, hoping they spoke to him before his disappearance."

"I'm guessing no word on those either?"

He shook his head, pulling out another thick text. "I'm afraid his end was near, and it took him before anyone could know."

A heavy weight of sadness sank into my chest. "I'm sorry."

"The Lord takes when he knows it's time."

But he could also give...? Do I risk asking? Emilia made it clear to lay low, but what if Father knew of a Scarlet who had the same ability as me? It might help to understand better what ancestor's blood ran through my veins. "Father, were there any known Scarlets to have... powers?"

"Powers?"

"Specifically golden light shooting from their palms?"

Father Benedict looked at me like I'd sprouted a second head. "Records show no sign of such. Do you know of someone who has?"

I gazed down at my palms, wondering how much I should reveal, if anything at all. How could I explain that for just a couple of seconds, warm, golden light fired from my hands, killing everything in its path? I chose the latter. "I always wondered if Scarlets had more than what was Blessed to them."

He considered my words and lightly touched my shoulder. "I believe some are chosen to fight a greater evil, more so than what others constantly face."

"What a burden to carry," I mumbled.

"But what a blessing it can be."

CHAPTER 46

I promised myself to at least do an hour workout so I wouldn't slack while Josh recovered, and knowing him, he would reprimand my ass for not keeping up. When I arrived in the training room, I saw Baron leaning against one of the pillars, arms crossed, smirking as I approached. "Welcome. I thought you might show up here."

"Uh, hi?" I replied, dropping my backpack at my feet.

"Since Josh is out of commission for a bit, I will be training you," he declared.

"And here I thought I would get off scot-free."

Baron gave a hearty laugh and chucked a dagger at my head. Thankfully for his sake, I caught it without blinking.

"Nice. Your reflexes are quick. A good sign that you're catching up to the others."

"Should we test yours?" I asked, getting ready to throw it back at his head.

Baron held up his hands in defense. "Hey, I'm only trying to help."

"Where's Chloe, your *actual* Scarlet?"

"We finished training this morning. She's an early bird."

"How miserable." The idea of rolling out of bed that early was nauseating.

"Are you ready?" He held out his hand for the dagger.

"I guess so." Plopping it in his open palm, I joined him on the blue mats.

Putting the dagger away, he replaced it with a long sword. "We're going to try this today."

"Why? My signature weapon is a dagger. When will I ever wield a sword?" Was he losing it?

"Sometimes, using something other than your weapon makes you a better fighter. If you can master a dagger, a sword, and a bow, then anything can become a weapon in your time of need." He slashed the air, testing its weight.

"But a sword?"

Baron rolled his eyes. "Yes, a sword, now catch." He tossed it high in the air, directly over my head.

I watched the weapon come down, judging where the pommel would land, exactly in my hands.

"Let's begin."

Baron taught me how to wield a sword properly. Every pace, swing, and lunge became a mantra as I counted the steps in my head, swiping at the air, pretending to slay a demon. Next, he rolled out a few dummies, lining them up on the sidelines, and locked the wheels so they wouldn't roll away. He instructed me to try the different combat moves and to pay attention to my form as much as possible.

I swung the sword directly through a dummy's neck, the head slicing clean off and falling to the floor. I gave Baron a triumphant smile, who only sighed in response.

I deflated like a balloon. "What?"

"Great job." The dummy head made a loud thump,

rolling across the floor. "Only *some* demons grow back their heads," noted Baron, picking it up and tossing it out of the ring.

"Since when?" I scoffed.

"Since forever. The heart is their direct line to their life source." Baron rolled a second dummy from the line, replacing the old one. It occurred to me that the first time I slew a Magidoz, I got a lucky shot to its heart.

"Demons have hearts?"

"They all came from something; nothing is born sinister." He pushed another couple dummies my way.

"Again?"

"Yes. It seems Josh has slacked a bit in his training."

"In his defense, we only had two training sessions, and then they threw us to the wolves." I positioned my body back into a fighting stance, ready to strike.

Baron shook his head with laughter. "Excuses, excuses."

I re-positioned my body and pivoted several times, driving the sword through the dummy's chest, missing my mark by a fraction of an inch.

Baron wheeled another dummy over to the far right of the ring. "Again."

"We've been at this for at least an hour," I complained, a soreness beginning to form in my bicep.

"Any sign of weakness is a free trip to your grave."

"You're worse than Josh."

"I don't have feelings for my Scarlet."

His remark fueled the fire that started to sizzle in my body, and I steadied myself in the line of sight of the dummy, my feet clockwise. With perfect precision, I pierced the heart exactly where I swung the sword, stabbing through the fabric and removing the arm. "He doesn't have feelings for me."

Baron kicked two more my way. "What do you call it then?"

"It's his job to protect me." I got into position, sword at the ready.

"It's not a job, it's an honor and a privilege."

Spinning once, I threw everything into my hit, slicing the dummy clean in half. "Doesn't count as feelings."

"It seems my words have affected you, because that was another shit move. Again."

I groaned, getting more irritated by the second. What the fuck did he know? *Stab the heart. Just stab the goddamn heart.* Focusing on the last dummy, blocking out whatever negative comments or thoughts came my way, I jumped, sword raised above my head, landing the blow dead center.

"Nice. Next time we'll try the bow." Baron removed the last dummy and slipped on the punch mitts. "Grab the black boxing gloves and come stand before me."

I returned the sword to the table of weapons and followed his instructions.

Baron lifted both mitts and said, "I want you to punch. I'm not looking for proper technique. I just want to feel your strength."

"That's it?"

Baron barely moved an inch. He nodded once, signaling with the punch mitts to hit. I held up my gloves and gave them everything I had in one punch.

"Not bad. Now, keep going," he ordered.

I huffed in protest and wailed in more than just a punch, with each strike starting to yell, freeing the tension and frustration, tears falling down my face as I punched with all my strength.

"That's enough," Baron demanded.

I kept punching and sobbing with each blow.

"I said, that's enough, Remi." Baron stepped back, throwing me off balance.

I threw off the gloves and rested against the wall, breathing heavily. "Sorry."

Baron gathered the boxing equipment, organizing the gloves on the table. "No, I'm sorry about my comment from earlier. It was out of line."

I wiped my tears away with the back of my hands, and Baron handed me a bottle of water. "It wasn't that." He waited until I continued, knowing there was more bottled up inside. "It's everything, from my grams' death to Heather not passing the Blessing. I'm losing control."

"In what way?"

Tossing the water bottle aside, I threw my hands in the air. "Everything! Baron, how the fuck does someone go from having no idea any of this shit exists to being dead center, fighting for their life?"

"Your grand—?"

"Ugh! No! Okay? No. I had no idea. All I had was her will stating I must attend if accepted because it would be paid in full. That's where her money mostly went."

"But she kept this life a secret? Why?"

"I don't know, and right now, I have zero energy to find out. I just need time to stop for a few minutes."

Baron squeezed my shoulder in sympathy. "Nobody is perfect, not even the others. I'm sorry you're feeling this way, and I'm sorry about your grandmother."

I felt the weight of his words seep in, giving me a sense

of peace for a brief moment. His kindness was genuine, just like his smile.

"You remind me a lot of my friend Jeremy," I said.

A cocky grin spread across his face like a naughty little child. "Is he as good-looking as me?"

I punched his arm playfully. "Ass."

A hearty laugh rattled his chest. "Do you want to continue your training... or?"

"Is it okay if I go see Heather?" It was time to switch and check in on her.

Softness appeared in his eyes. "Of course. I'll go with you."

"Oh, you don't have to."

"I insist."

We cleaned the area before heading out to the infirmary, discussing future training sessions, when we noticed a smear of blood on the door to Heather's wing. My heart quickened with each step, my fingers trembling over the doorknob, Baron next to me on high alert. A silent understanding happened between us as I slipped out my dagger; Baron had one of his own, keeping quiet until I completed turning the knob. With a slight push, it creaked open to more blood trailing on the floor, a body battered and bruised on Heather's bed, except it wasn't Heather. All the air escaped my lungs as the realization hit Baron; his face contorted in worry.

Ready to run inside, he held up an arm, blocking my path, signaling with his finger to be quiet while he surveyed the area. When the coast was clear, he beckoned me to follow him in, rushing to the body on the bed. Asher lay with blood-curdling from his mouth, his eyes rolling as he gurgled up his blood.

"Dammit!" shouted Baron, trying to cover what wounds he could with his bare hands.

"Do...n...t," Asher choked, blood pouring down his chin.

"Remi, page the others! Quick!" he ordered in a rush.

I hit the panic button on my pager, which sent a signal to every member in the Order, pinpointing our exact location for help.

"Ul... ro..." Asher coughed some more, blood spewing out of his mouth like a sprinkler.

"Shhh, save your energy," soothed Baron, putting pressure on the wound in his chest.

Asher gripped Baron's collar, trying to get him to listen through his stuttering words. "Ulro... DAK." The last part came out in a harsh cough, spraying Baron in the face with his blood.

The light from his eyes dimmed, and his mouth drooped, blood trickling from his blueish lips.

I slid down the wall to the floor, unable to keep my body standing with my wobbly legs. My stomach twisted in the tightest knot from the scene displayed before me, nausea bubbling in my throat. Heather was missing, and Asher was dead.

Not soon enough, Kal, Anna, and Father Benedict rushed in, halting just before the bed covered in Asher's blood, then panned over to me hurling my guts onto the floor. Kal came to my aide, pulling my hair back as I emptied my stomach. Anna approached Baron and removed his hands from Asher's open wound.

"I'll call the morgue. Kal, check on Josh. Anna, find the Aces, have them check the perimeter, and get everyone into the dining hall. Make sure everyone is accounted for," instructed Father Benedict. I got my wits about me, wiping the back of my mouth as they left to follow Father's orders.

Dean Poverly and Thatcher arrived, their eyes bulging from their sockets. Father Benedict explained what they needed before moving to the bed, placing two fingers on Asher's forehead and whispering some type of prayer before shutting his eyelids.

Baron became a ghost, swaying as he stood, watching the interaction.

"Baron, did you see what happened?" Poverly interrogated.

He could only stare at Asher's lifeless body, the color completely drained from his face.

I held onto the wall with clammy palms and tried to stand up, my legs shaking with the effort to do so. "No," I managed to say, my voice hoarse from vomiting.

"Where's Heather?" asked Thatcher. Her attitude was thick with each syllable.

"I don't know," I admitted harshly, trying to breathe through my nose, nausea rising again.

"You don't know?" she snarled.

"Enough, Nora. Remi doesn't know," snapped Father.

Dean Poverly had taken it upon himself to help remove Baron from the room, hopefully to allow him to recuperate from the shock of losing a member of the Order and his friend.

"Nora, go to the dining hall," ordered Father.

"I will no—"

"NOW."

His command echoed off the walls. Thatcher stilled, shocked by the force in his voice. Without another word, she turned and stalked out of the room, her white cape trailing behind her.

Father Benedict turned to me, his expression eased, and said, "Remi, did Asher say anything to Baron before he departed?"

It took me a second to register what Father Benedict had asked, "What did he say?"

He nodded once, waiting for an answer.

"His words were jumbled, choking on his blood," I said.

"No mention of a demon?" The words Ulro and dak came to mind. Words that meant absolutely nothing to me, yet Asher was desperate for Baron to hear.

"Asher managed to say only two words. Ulro and dak. Does that mean anything?"

Father's face drained of color as he whispered, "That's impossible."

FATHER BENEDICT and I finally joined the others in the dining hall; hushed voices filled the room until we approached. My eyes landed on Josh.

He was awake, sitting next to Anna, with a sling over his left arm. He took notice of my presence, but there was a lack of emotion on his face.

Not the reunion I wanted.

My heart twisted, afraid to mind-speak, fearing a wall was back up.

Dean Poverly rose from his seat, his lips in a hard line

before he said, "One of our own has been welcomed back into the arms of the Lord."

The air was thick with sadness, heads bowed in response to Poverly's unfortunate news. Images of Asher's body flashed in my mind, his blood staining every corner until my nails dug into my palms.

Dean Poverly let the weight of his words seep in and said, "But another has been stolen."

Observing the looks of my fellow Scarlets and Saints, I took notice of Zoey's absence, remembering that he was her guardian.

"The whereabouts of Miss Heather Price are unknown at this time. I have called in an aide from other Orders who will assist us in finding her," informed Pover

Voices began to fill the room, their senses on high alert from the attack.

"We have an even greater threat, and I cannot fathom why it has returned," voiced Poverly.

He captured the room's attention again, but no one dared to breathe above a whisper this time.

"An Ulrodak demon has been spotted in our city."

Everyone began to panic, voices raised in pure terror, and some started to cry in fear. Father Benedict never explained what an Ulrodak demon was, and it never came up in our previous history lesson. But just by the crowd's reaction to its name, I could only guess the severity of the threat.

"Is it true?" asked Thatcher. Her eyes bulged out of her head in disbelief, waiting for Poverly to confirm. The rest of us sat at the edge of our seats, the atmosphere thick with anxiety.

"I'm afraid—"

"We don't know for sure," interrupted Father Benedict.

Poverly glared at him, his lips curling back in a snarl, and said, "What other evidence do we need?"

"The body doesn't match how an Ulrodak kills," Father said simply.

"TO HELL WITH THE WAY IT KILLS!" he shouted, slamming his fists on the table. Dean Poverly then rose from his seat to get into Father Benedict's face and continued his tirade. "One of my men is dead because of our lack of caring. That's on me. On all of us. We should have been better trained. Instead, we fussed over a goddamn prophecy!"

"How much more could we have prepared for them?" challenged Father.

We all sat in complete silence, watching the argument unfold. The other Aces remained neutral, refusing to intervene.

"It wasn't enough! I am ordering longer hours of training and more patrols throughout the city."

"So, Captain Harrison finally got to you."

"He's right, they need to be put out in the field more, actually fighting."

"THEY'RE JUST KIDS," roared Father.

Thatcher then stood along with Toke and Adler, stepping in between the alpha males, creating enough space to ease some of the tension. Not a single Scarlet or Saint dared to help, afraid of the consequences.

"Enough, please. Discussing patrols is one thing, but these kids are not immortal," Thatcher said. Her concern for our safety despite her lack of kindness surprised me.

"The Lord granted them powers to heal and fight. It is their duty," snapped Poverly.

It took every ounce of my strength not to walk right up

to Dean Poverly and tell him to shove it where the sun didn't shine. Were we just disposable chess pieces in this game of war?

"We need to reassess ourselves before we walk in blindly," Toke conveyed.

A loud bang from upstairs made us all jump, followed by someone falling down the stairs.

"Father Benedict!" called Kal, who had jumped from his seat to go to the base of the stairs.

I'd never seen Father run so fast, his robes whipping behind him. "Abraham!"

The man's face was grazed, blood dripping from his mouth onto the marble floor. Abraham's eyes began to flutter open; at least one did. The other was so bruised it kept shut.

"Ben," he croaked.

Kal took the nearest chair and helped him sit.

"Someone get Nurse Amelia," someone shouted, but I was too busy staring at the broken man, watching him breathe was a struggle.

Nurse Amelia came rushing inside with a medical bag, which she began to unzip on the floor in front of Abraham.

"We sent a Saint and Scarlet to come to find you but found your house was empty," said Father Benedict.

"You did what?" shouted Dean Poverly.

"Why didn't you just call him instead of almost killing two trainees?" Thatcher snapped.

Abraham coughed, the sound of his chest rattling with effort. "We always send a Scarlet and a Saint; it's always been done like that."

Father Benedict, watching Nurse Amelia attend to Abraham's wounds, started to dab his forehead with a small white cloth. "They told me you left everything behind."

Abraham squinted at him. "There wasn't time, not after the vision I had of—" He broke into another coughing fit, blood coating his palm, which prompted Nurse Amelia to take a small vial from her bag and encourage him to drink.

His voice was rough with fear and pain when he said, "Its presence was pure evil. The darkness that followed swallowed me whole."

"Ulrodak," breathed Father Benedict.

"I hid my wife and children, concealing us as long as I could before I made the trip to you. Little did I know it was following me. This one is different, Ben. Nothing like the books taught us." He winced as the nurse dabbed his face with a soaked cotton ball, cleaning the cut across his cheek.

My conversation with Father Benedict before we came to the dining hall filtered back into my mind.

"Father?" I had said. He'd just finished calling the morgue to retrieve Asher's body.

His eyes darkened, taking a seat on one of the empty beds. "An Ulrodak demon is lethal. Its power does not match the others."

"Why? Why is this happening?" I cried. All I could think about was the carnage it had left behind, and I wondered if it hadn't stopped at just Asher. What kind of chaos would we find?

"I don't know. I thought the prophecy would give us that answer, but it's just a dead end. This might be the end as we know it."

The wind escaped from my lungs at the possible inevitability of our future. "What is an Ulrodak demon?"

Father's eyes gazed upon mine; a look of pure terror sending unwanted chills down my arms. "A fallen angel of death."

"A fallen angel of——."

Abraham's attention flicked over to me, cutting me off. A single world left his cracked lips. "Yes."

The brush of a hand grazed my arm, and I pulled my attention away to find Josh standing inches from me. My heart fluttered at the sight of his closeness, surprised he'd wandered over to my side.

The other Aces stepped forward, Dean Poverly leading the group. "So, what do you suppose we do?" His question was directed only to Abraham.

The nurse had just wrapped a bandage around his hand when he finally looked into the eyes of the Dean. "We need the Accane Blade."

Poverly's face twisted with anxiety. "That weapon hasn't been seen in decades."

"Without it, we can't stop what is to come."

"Yes, the Ulrodak demon, we know," Adler repeated.

"No, something far worse than its presence," breathed Abraham.

"And that is?" asked Thatcher behind Poverly's shoulder.

"The end of the world."

CHAPTER 47

The early autumn night chilled my bones as I trekked through a sea of people on 87th Street. Nobody paid attention to the girl in scarlet, the cape wrapped securely around my frame, the hood covering the dark shadows under my eyes. My dagger was strapped tightly to my hip, hidden from any wandering eyes. Regardless, if they avoided my vacant stare, people tended to observe one's attire and judge. Fashion in New York City needed to make a statement, and if they noticed anything out of the ordinary, it would show up on a fashion blog the next day.

And that wouldn't fly with the Order.

I left the cathedral in haste after the death of Asher, making sure nobody saw my departure, slipping out the side exit, running for the hills, or in this case, the streets of New York City. The others mourned, while I remained on the hunt to find Heather.

Father Benedict found demon residue underneath

Asher's lifeless body, indicating that Heather was removed before his murder. By what, we didn't know.

But I needed answers, and the Order tended to pick and choose what they wanted us to know. And I refused to be in the dark any longer.

My home rose high in the city skyline, bright lights casting on me like a spotlight on Broadway. If I guessed correctly, and judging by when I left campus, my mother sat in the kitchen on a stool, reading one of her many interior design magazines with a glass of red wine.

And if luck were on my side, she would be the only one home.

Entering the building, surprised to find the lobby scarce, I took the elevator, watching the floors rise until I reached the level of the penthouse. The front door to my home mocked me as I approached, turning the knob ever so slightly so as not to alert my mother, and slipped inside undetected.

Silence came from every corner as I observed the few feet before me. I took a deep breath, calming my nerves and silencing the negative thoughts that tried to overtake my courage. Then I went through the rooms, trying my best not to make a sound and found my mother just where I knew she was. Hunched over, reading, a full glass of wine in hand. Her blonde hair flowed down her back in waves, and the smell of Dior rose from the oils of her skin, filling the room with familiarity and comfort. I bit my lip, watching her adjust on the stool, flipping through the glossy pages and tapping her foot against the island with her boat shoes. The wedding ring my father gave her glistened in the light on her freshly manicured nails.

Little did she know her only daughter stood under the

threshold in Scarlet gear, a dagger hung on her hip. I refused to hide what she kept to her goddamn self for so long.

I cleared my throat, not at all surprised to see her glued to her phone. Her head snapped up and her eyes narrowed when she spotted me. "Nice of you to show your face."

I pushed off the threshold. Apparently, we were taking a hostile approach to this conversation. "Mom, we need to talk."

"About you abruptly leaving dinner and ignoring every text and phone call from your father and me?" She typed away, not bothering to look at me as she went back to her phone screen. "Please, Remi, tell me you have a riveting excuse for your terrible behavior."

Reeling in my anger before I smashed her favorite expensive China set, I took another step toward her. "You want me to apologize? Sure, I'm sorry, but that's not why I'm here."

She laughed, typing once more. "I should fault myself for raising such an inconsiderate child."

Ignoring the sting of her words, I pressed on. "Mom, for once, please listen. This is important."

Her laugh returned, mocking me as she said, "I let you have your summer. I let you gallivant around with your friends in the city doing I don't know what, but somehow, it turns into me not listening."

"Mom," I said again.

"Never thought I would have such an ungrateful child. After everything I've done for you and continue—" I unstrapped the dagger from my hip and slammed the point of it right on her expensive marble counter, cracking it all the way through like a spider web. The light hit the blade, reflecting against my mother's pale complexion.

"Remi," she whispered.

I shook the hood off my head, letting her see the heavy bags under my eyes. "The truth, Mom."

With a trembling bottom lip, my mother held her hand close to her chest as if struggling to catch her breath and said, "I don't know what you're talking about."

"You and I both know what I mean." I rounded the island, making it clear I wouldn't back down. "Please."

Sadness clouded her vision, but she remained glued to the stool. "I never thought..." She trailed off, unable to form the right words.

Removing the dagger from the marble, I sheathed it back in place. "Grams' will."

Anger destroyed her features as if I had slapped her. "Your grandmother said it was over. I only sent you to the school because she'd already paid for it. You would've been halfway across the country if I'd known."

"Why me and not Aiden?" I questioned.

Her mouth was set in a hard line as her eyes flickered back and forth. "I don't know."

"But he never attended?" Something wasn't adding up.

"We hoped that your brother would fail, as he did. You will too. But your grandmother told me that the Order had fallen and was no more. I forbade her to tell you any of this."

"Were you ever tested?"

"Yes."

I guess she also failed, considering the lack of information she gave me. Dean Poverly's lecture on genes and bloodline filtered through my mind, but that didn't explain Grams' reasoning.

Why would she lie? The answer was hidden somewhere beneath the altered truth, and I wondered...

"Where are her things?"

"Remi, please don't let your grandmother's actions ruin your future."

I recoiled. "She may have had faults, but you lied to me."

"I had my reasons."

"And now I have mine. Where are her things?"

My mother's eyes darted from my face to the kitchen doorway.

"Goddammit, Mother. Where are her things?"

She sighed a shaky breath. "Remi." Her eyes looked behind me as if waiting for someone to rescue her.

"Mom, don't make me tear up the entire place to find it."

She held up her hands in defense. "Okay, okay. Come with me."

I couldn't wrap my head around her bizarre behavior. Why was she so reluctant to give me her mother's things? Was she scared of me? Of how easily I destroyed her beautiful countertop? I might have enticed some fear.

Not wasting another second, I followed my mother as she exited the kitchen and climbed to the second floor, stopping just before her master bedroom. Her shoulders slumped slightly forward in defeat, realizing now that she couldn't go back and save her daughter. I didn't need saving; I had already accepted my fate. It took a while, but I did, and now I had only one mission. To save the world.

Over her shoulder, she gave me one last look before unlocking the door. "Whatever you find, keep it to yourself." She stepped aside to let me pass and said, "Inside the walk-in closet, underneath the rack of my heels, you'll see a brass handle. Lift that, and you'll find everything you need."

I nodded once and left her standing in the hallway, her

eyes boring into my back. An invisible hand reached for me, but I continued, never looking back.

Flicking the closet light on, I found rows and rows of expensive designer clothes, ranging from Gucci to Prada and Burberry hanging on velvet hangers. My mother's closet was her shopping plaza, color-coordinated and organized by pant length and shirt style. One-of-a-kind Birkin bags were displayed neatly on top shelves, matching the color scheme below, and a center island boasted exotic perfumes in weirdly shaped bottles. On any other day, I would have browsed or tried things on, but my days of carefree activities were numbered. Now, I hid in the shadows to hunt demons.

Heading toward the back, I found the stationary shoe racks and rows of five-inch heels in various colors and patterns. I dragged some heavy frames aside, finding the brass handle as she said underneath. Carved in an intricate piece, I tugged, hearing a clicking sound as it opened. Deep inside, an expansive box covered in dust sat in the center. I expected more but had a sneaky suspicion my mother had discarded the rest.

Picking it up and blowing the dust off, I cut through the heavily taped top with my dagger. In an off-white envelope, my name had been written in an elegant script. My heart tightened, realizing my grandmother had meant to leave me her belongings.

Careful not to ruin the letter inside, I took my finger and gently tore through the fold.

My breath caught in my throat as the first few words hit me.

Dear sweet Remi,

I bet you're wondering right now how this could be true. How could a kind and powerful man let us live in a world with such evil? I wondered about that myself for a very long time. But we can't blame those trying to mend the world's wrongs. All we can do is take one day at a time and guide the lost ones home. We hope to make a difference, no matter how small, hoping that'll be enough to correct past mistakes.

But you, my sweet Remi, can make that difference.

Somewhere along the way, a path had been chosen just for you. Your purity has been blessed at birth because of the power you naturally possess.

That is why only you, Remi, can know what I've hidden.

Because she who wields, the rest shall follow.

All my love,

Grams.

At the bottom of the note were latitude and longitude coordinates marking a place on the map that Grams ensured only I would see.

But it was the last line that shook me to my core.

CHAPTER 48

I ran out of the closet with the box and letter clutched tightly against my torso. My mother stood just under the kitchen threshold as I rounded the corner, heading straight for the front door, when she abruptly stepped in front of my path, blocking the exit.

"Remi, just think about what you're doing," she whispered. A hint of hurt and panic laced her words, but nothing could stop me, not even her desperate pleas when all she'd done was lie to me for years.

"You don't get to tell me what to do anymore," I snapped. I gripped my grandmother's belongings like a shield, protecting me from my mother.

"I have every right to want to protect my daughter!"

"By lying to me? How is that any safer? For fuck's sake, Mom, I went in blind! I could've been killed."

She gripped my shoulder. "Don't you dare walk out that door. I refuse to have my daughter be a part of some cult!"

The irony of her words was not lost on me, but it fueled more coal to my already blazing fire. "Sucks knowing you

390

weren't chosen. It eats you alive, doesn't it? That your own daughter gets to live the life you always wanted."

Her face twisted in pure rage. "I bet your grandmother loved filling your head with that bullshit. She was such a spiteful woman."

"Keep her name out of your fucking mouth." I shouldered past her, pressing Grams' stuff tightly to my chest, my mother completely unaware of the small whiskey bottle I had stolen from my dad's stash hidden within.

I would rather chew on rusty nails than ever step foot in that fucking house again.

TAKING a hefty swig of whiskey to calm my nerves and then stashing it between a few books on one of the first shelves in the small library, I rushed toward Father Benedict, who stood over a stack of thick, leatherbound books at a nearby table. He twirled white rosary beads in his paper-thin hands, a worry line forming on his forehead as his eyes followed the text. After everything that had happened, I was surprised to find him alone and not surrounded by the Aces and their overbearing needs. For once, I got to talk to Father without an audience present.

"Father," I breathed, my hands shaking from escaping my mother's clutches.

He looked up with a somber expression, as if life was sucked from him, but when he saw the worry across my face, he stepped forward, placing a gentle hand on my shoulder. "Remi, what's wrong?"

With a shaky hand, I offered Grams' note to him. "I think you need to read this."

Father Benedict looked from me to the note, unsure whether to take it. I encouraged him with a simple nod to let him know he had permission to. He pocketed the rosary beads and took the letter, unfolding the creased spots.

I watched his expression change from confusion to shock, then—

"Elizabeth," he whispered more to himself.

"What?" Father placed a finger to his lips to keep quiet and then had me follow him through the line of shelves until we'd retreated safely inside his little office space in the back of the library. I shut the door behind me as he rummaged through his desk drawer, searching for something until he pulled out a long, gold pendant with a delicate cross for a charm. He caressed the cross with his pointer finger, then kissed it and whispered a prayer before meeting my eyes.

"Your grandmother was one special Scarlet. But she was very selective on who she trusted in the Order. It wasn't until you gave me her note that I remembered she'd entrusted me with this necklace to give to you," he stated. Father stepped around his desk and took my hand to place the delicate chain in my palm.

It was simple yet the prettiest piece of jewelry I'd ever owned, and she wanted me to have it. A silver cross hung from the chain, shining under the lights. Anything left in Grams' old room after her death had been stored in one of my parents' many storage units or thrown away. My mother claimed there wasn't much to sift through because Grams wasn't materialistic, but I'd always hoped something would turn up that I could keep. Little did I know that

Father Benedict held something so valuable this entire time.

I set the box of the rest of her belongings down on the desk and clasped the necklace securely around my neck, the chain cold against my already too-hot skin.

At that moment, for the first time, I finally felt like I belonged. "I don't think you realize how much this means to me."

A smile spread across Father Benedict's face. "I'm glad it's finally in your possession."

Then his smile faded into a severe frown, more wrinkles creasing his forehead. "Remi, your grandmother did something against the whole Order. I believe she did it intentionally." He gestured to me to take a seat.

I obliged and found myself unsure of what was going to happen next. "What did she do?"

He finally sat in his desk chair and took a long breath. "Did she tell you anything about the Accane Blade before her passing?"

"Father Benedict, my grandmother kept everything under wraps. When I received the invitation, I had no idea this world existed," I admitted, thinking of my mother, who knew and lied blatantly to my face.

He rubbed his chin and nodded, as I had told him this before. "The Accane Blade is a powerful weapon against a specific type of demonic presence. It is the only one in existence, and it has never been found since the mid-1800s. Some claim it was lost in battle, others believe it was stolen and buried somewhere deep, but it can never be truly destroyed."

"What does this have to do with my grandmother's note?"

"After reading it, I can fully confirm she found it and has it hidden."

I slumped back in the chair, unsure how everything had become so complicated. From the death of Asher to Heather's possible kidnapping, the urge to hide under my bed for the rest of my life seemed tempting.

"So, we need this Accane Blade?" I clarified.

"If what Abraham and Asher said is true, then yes, we need it." Father Benedict opened some type of black journal on his desk, skimming through the pages. "There is a meeting in November. All the Aces gather across the world to attend." He paused, finding the page. I watched him dog-ear it for future reference, "I'm assuming you looked up the coordinates your grandmother left you?"

I nodded. "Edinburgh, Scotland."

"I think your grandmother hid the Accane Blade there. I'm allowed to bring someone along, and Collin might have to sit this one out. I'm going to choose you." Father placed the dog-eared page in front of me, showing a long sword with yellow stones on the handle. And as I took it in, my essence seemed to reach out to it, recognizing the blade from the vision of Josh and me going to war. Of Josh dying in my arms. A nightmare that had felt too real and left me gutted.

"But why hide it in a place everyone gathers? Wouldn't that make it more obvious?" I questioned as I shoved the memory of the dream aside to focus on the here and now.

A rough knock came at the door, disrupting our conversation. "Father, I need to talk to you—" Josh froze just before breaching the threshold, a pain-stricken expression contorting his face as we locked eyes. His uniform looked ironed to perfection, the scarlet S glaring red upon his breast.

"I'm sorry, Josh, I'm currently in the middle of discussing—"

"This can't wait. A civilian was taken."

Father stood up, knocking his chair back from the force. "Who?"

I watched Josh swallow, avoiding eye contact with me altogether. Something stirred inside my gut, a feeling of dread taking over as I sat on the edge of my seat, waiting to hear the terrible news.

"Nickie—"

All I saw was red when I stood, swinging a perfect right hook to Josh's face. The satisfaction of connecting my knuckles to his cheek let out a primal reaction, a sound of agony and pain releasing in a mangled scream, all my anger, fear, and loss going into that blow before I collapsed to the floor, sobs wracking my body.

"Remi!"

I didn't care if I hurt Josh, and I didn't care who saw the assault, all that mattered in that moment was my best friend, who got caught in the crossfire, something that should have never happened. Strong arms circled me, holding my uncontrollable rocking back and forth, and by the familiar smell of sea salt and cedar that came over me like a cloud, almost suffocating me, I knew who held me in their grasp. I wanted to pull away. I even tried, but the whispers of okays and gentle strokes on my back rooted me in place, even though my mouth retaliated with unfiltered protests that sounded like gibberish. Every ounce of sorrow poured out of me until my eyes couldn't produce any more tears. My throat was raw from the screams of anguish, my joints stiff from being held in a crouched position for too long. When I finally hushed my whimpers and let the ache settle in my chest, I took notice of the absence of Father Benedict and broke from Josh's embrace, resting my back on the solid oak desk. Josh knelt in front of me, but I barely noticed the bruise forming on his right cheek, just below his eye.

"Remi?" Concern laced his words as he reached for my face in an attempt to comfort me.

Now that the loss had taken up residency, rage rippled like waves while I breathed aggressively through my nose. "Get away from me."

His hand froze in mid-air. "Remi, I'm so fucking sorry."

"You promised me," I uttered.

"Remi, —"

"YOU PROMISED ME!" I shrilled, and my voice bounced off the four walls, the sound mirroring my fury.

"I'M SORRY. You think I fucking wanted this?" He got to his feet, staring down at me, overtaking my personal space.

I found the strength to stand, and pushed him with all my might back, watching him stagger a bit before he got his footing. "It's because *you* work for this fucked up society."

"Newsflash, Remi, so do you. How do *you* know you're not being targeted?"

"Me? What have I done? I've only been here for a month. If anyone had enough time to make enemies, it's you and the rest of this fucked-up society."

Josh gripped my shoulders, desperate for me to listen. "Think about it, Heather was your roommate. Nickie is your best friend. Don't you find it suspicious that they were the ones taken? Don't you think the Aces should've spoken to you about this by now?"

I struggled against his hold, but he wouldn't budge. "I don't care what you think. You're the piece of shit who brought her into this world."

"Who's to say that you wouldn't either?" he sneered. I'd never seen him so pissed before, and truthfully, I didn't care. The bruise I gave him became more noticeable, spreading near his nose, and I had the sudden urge to strike him again, just to prove my goddamn point. Tired eyes and ruffled brown hair fanned his forehead, a look of possible defeat tainting his face.

I got close to his face, never breaking eye contact with those shameless blue eyes. No matter how I felt about him on the inside, my hatred grew tenfold, knowing he was the sole reason my best friend was kidnapped, and nothing would change my mind. "I hope you fucking rot."

Josh recoiled just as our pagers went off, his grip loosening from my shoulders. I shrugged off his touch, stepping back as much as I could in the limited space provided.

He reached into his pocket, checking the message. "We're ordered to gather in the church."

I never gave him a chance to follow as I stormed out of Father Benedict's office, leaving all Grams' belongings behind and ripping off my scarlet cape. Every step I took became heavier with sorrow, the dyspepsia settling in my stomach. Eventually, I heard him catch up, but I refused to give him any attention, and judging by the silence he projected, it would have been a wasted effort to interact anyway.

I HOPE YOU FUCKING ROT.

My cruel words ricocheted around in my head, but I refused to feel an ounce of guilt, not after the bullshit Josh spewed moments ago. The fact that he assumed I was the one targeted, as if this was all my fault, kept the fire inside burning bright, and if anyone crossed my path, it wouldn't end pretty. Did he not understand that he was her boyfriend? That he was just as much to blame for bringing her into this mess as anyone? Heather's situation shouldn't matter either. She was invited and went through the Blessing willingly, and she would have done it with or without me. If Josh wanted to play the blame game, then by all means, we could play it, but I'd be fucking damned if I would let him pin it all on me.

We continued in silence through the halls and winding staircase that led to the exit into the church. Most of the pews were filled with Scarlets and Saints from different sections of the city, along with our own. Luckily, there was an empty seat next to Chloe, and I snagged it before Josh could follow. He took a seat on the opposite side of us next to Baron, his head down, the bruise vibrant in the fluorescent lights.

Father Benedict stood at the altar with Collin, the other Aces gathered just off to the side in chairs, watching from their prestigious pedestal. I'd never heard silence quite this loud, and the eerie sense of doom looming over us didn't snuff the flame of my rage, rather it kept it lit, almost burning me from the inside out.

Because my best friend and roommate were gone, and if I had to burn everything in my path to get them back, I would.

Collin handed Father an off-white scroll and started to light some type of incense, cleansing the space around him. He began a prayer, reciting it with a voice so deep and commanding that not a single person turned away. He signed the cross to us and then to the Aces, who returned it without hesitation.

"I know these are hard times, and with the recent events of two kidnappings, one of our own and a civilian, it is best if we let the Lord guide us to salvation," he said.

"Bullshit," hissed Chloe.

A glance in her direction was enough to witness her jaw clench like she was holding in her fury. "You think?" I whispered back.

"The Lord himself, if he truly cared about his children, wouldn't have let two innocents get captured," muttered Chloe.

Father Benedict now moved to the center of the altar. "As you are all aware, my annual meeting with the Order is slated for Christmas break. I believe with my attendance, we will be able to find answers for the cruel outcomes and a possible breakthrough to our new enemy." Sweat glistened off his forehead while he adjusted the neck of his robe, almost as if he were struggling to get the next words out of his mouth. "I have chosen two from our Order to accompany me in my travels. The other sanctions outside were notified of my upcoming departure and will offer two of their own to assist with training and patrols."

I already knew Father had slated for me to attend, I just hoped he would choose someone I didn't want to murder.

More sweat dripped off his temples, I'd never seen Father so nervous before. "Remi and Josh will be accompanying me on the trip."

My teeth clenched, holding back the scream I so desperately wanted to let out. Chloe nudged my shoulder and said, "Dude, did you give Josh that bruise?"

"He fucking deserved it," I grumbled.

"I'm guessing he told you his theory?"

My eyes darted in her direction. "You knew?"

"He mentioned it briefly, but I brushed it off. I thought he was losing his goddamn mind."

As quickly as the meeting began, it ended. The others scattered, including the Aces, who showed no empathy for the stolen. Their blank expressions did nothing to help ease the tension of the others. Chloe claimed they had their private meetings downstairs to discuss the events and didn't want an audience.

I called it cowardice.

I said my goodbyes to Chloe and went straight to Father Benedict at the altar, where he started the clean-up process of the incense. "Why did you choose the vilest person to accompany us?"

"He is your guardian. It would be reckless to not have," he mused.

"He will only cause more problems," I retorted.

"Wow, Remi. Tell me how you feel." Josh's voice was like nails on a chalkboard. I couldn't believe how blinded I was by his sincerity, his good looks, his fucking everything.

It was time for me to grow up and face the reality of the situation.

"I believe I showed you with my right hook," I snapped, refusing to look at him.

"I haven't forgotten."

Father Benedict stopped just before the steps on the altar, completely soaked in perspiration. "We leave three days before Christmas break. Remi, you have a month and a half to train with your guardian and prepare for the trip. It would be in your best interest to refrain from killing one another."

Kind of hard when that was all I could think about.

"I'll prepare a list of things we need to bring. Any further discussion of what we talked about in my office, Remi, we'll continue when we get back. Josh, will you come with me please?"

They both left me standing alone in the church. A heavy weight of defeat and exhaustion crept in, and I couldn't find the strength to move. I watched the remaining light from the sun peek through the stained glass window above the altar, creating swirls of colors until fading altogether, until darkness engulfed everything I'd lost, including myself.

A sense of dread filled my bones, my chest throbbing from the loss of two important people, my anger and devastation colliding inside, making me drop to my knees because, under all the layers of hatred and despair, my stupid heart left a small fraction of love for Josh.

How fucking sick was that? How could I let myself keep a piece of what I felt tucked away when it should've perished within the fire of ferocity? How could he believe that my very existence spawned something so sinister that my friends became the victims? How was it that I knelt before a God who let such vicious actions commence?

I bowed my head, letting a few tears escape to release

some of the misery buried within, as if I hadn't cried enough in Father's office.

To grin and bear such wreckage only reminded me of what was to come, and I couldn't sit back and let incapable people take over. If I sat idly by, then what was the point? If Grams knew of such horrendous things to come, then she left it all to me for a reason. Because I would stop at nothing to save the ones I loved.

Lifting my head and wiping the last of my tears, I saw the silhouette of a female appear in the darkness of the chapel, her face barely visible but only recognizable in my dreams that plagued me for months, until the absence cut me right down to my core.

She smiled knowingly before fading into nothing.

My guardian angel.

Juniper.

EPILOGUE

JOSH

I hope you fucking rot.

The sting of the bruise began to fade, beginning the process of healing. Much like Remi's harsh words, but not enough to get them out of my head. Her anger toward me was warranted, and I couldn't blame her, not one bit, but how she said it; the look in her cold dead eyes ripped me to shreds.

For fuck's sake, the girl had a grip on my goddamn heart.

I ended up back in Father's office, sitting in the empty seat across from him, the sweat continuing to drip down his face. It could only mean one thing; a vision was coming.

Judging by the looks of his complexion and the nervous shake in his hands, it was going to be a big one, and that put me more on edge.

"Mateo," called Father Benedict. My birth name, and he was the only person allowed to call me such. A name I despised since I found the truth to it. The only other person who knew was Baron, and even he didn't dare to reveal it.

"Father, do you think it's wise for Remi to travel with us?" I questioned.

He smoothed down a spot on his robe, trying to remove a wrinkle. "You're her guardian. The Aces know what they're dealing with, and I have come to fear one among the pack plotting against you both."

"So, Remi is being targeted?"

"So are you. You remember the prophecy I gave you?"

"Yes, but—"

"The attraction will only build unless you can control it. I would rather her be angry at you than bring down the whole human race."

Father Benedict used a tissue to dab his forehead as I watched him breathe slowly, preparing himself for the blow.

After the Blessing, I'd found Father Benedict barely conscious in his office, covered in his sweat and vomit. I had called for help to the infirmary, unsure if this vision was the one to kill him. The same pain-stricken look and unsteady hands. A vision had come to him in the middle of the night of me and an unknown female with beautiful blonde hair, but chaos was pictured in the distance. Blood and sacrifice, the Earth tilting too far off its axis, trying to survive every known demon walking the Earth. All because my hands held *her*. All because the power we wielded together created a catastrophic disaster.

Father couldn't figure out why we were the deciding factors, and at first, I didn't believe it, but since meeting Remi, the magnetic pull of her very presence twisted all my morals and responsibilities to rubble. The night I met her at Electric Haze turned everything I built to protect upside down, and I tried so hard to be with someone else, to open my heart to a lesser evil.

Because Remi and I were forbidden, and if we let ourselves embrace the intensity of these feelings, then nobody would survive.

Father Benedict's head rolled back, a gurgling sound rumbling deep within his chest, and his body shook from the tremors of the vision. I bolted from my seat, keeping his body and head steady, avoiding any possible damage. Usually, his visions lasted for a few seconds, no more than a minute, but the longer he convulsed, the harder it would be to recover. Foam escaped his mouth, dripping down his neck into his already sweat-soaked robe.

"Father," I called. Usually, we were told not to disrupt the Seer's visions, it could alter or cut off too quickly and the message wouldn't make sense, but watching him convulse in a manner so violent left me no choice but to stop the pain.

"Father, it's Mateo. I'm here with you," I soothed.

The foam stopped just as he took a huge gulp of air, his breathing ragged, his eyes coming forward. The once white of his eyes was almost completely red, tears streaming down his face from the intensity of his vision.

"Father?" I called again.

He leaned forward, bowing his head as he tried to control his unsteady breaths, shaking and cold from his perspiration. "Water."

With one hand on his back to steady him, I reached for the handle on the bottom drawer of his desk and grabbed a small bottle of water he kept at hand, untwisted the lid, and fed him the warm liquid. Father drank every last drop, sighing with relief when I gently laid him back against the chair.

"You were out longer than usual," I murmured.

"Was I?"

Anxiety began to trickle down my neck and shoulders. "What did you see?"

"I didn't see anything, that's the problem."

I straightened my spine in response. "Nothing? So, you mean to tell me—"

Father cleared his throat and pushed the sleeves of his robe up to his forearms. "It means the world was covered in complete darkness."

When I didn't say anything, Father Benedict took out a set of white rosary beads and began to mumble a prayer until the words were barely a whisper. If the world was covered in darkness, and Father couldn't see any salvation, it only meant one thing.

We lost.

ACKNOWLEDGMENTS

Thank you Marni and Karen for taking such good care of this story. For my agent, Angie, thank you for believing in me and sticking by me. To my beta/alpha readers, Nicole, Holly, and Elena, for taking time out of their busy lives to help make Deck of Scarlets become even better than the original. Family, and friends, thank you for continuing for supporting my crazy dreams. It means everything to me. Thank you.

ABOUT ME

Amanda is a Netflix binge watcher, Buffy fanatic, and bagel enthusiast. Residing in the suburbs of Massachusetts, she lives with her black lab named Jack.

Visit www.amandasinatra.net for more information about her books and future events!

www.ingramcontent.com/pod-product-compliance
Lightning Source LLC
Chambersburg PA
CBHW030334120726
47901CB00007B/1789